The Secret House

GREGORY FROST

JOURNALSTONE
YOUR LINK TO ARTIST TALENT

ISBN: 978-1-68510-148-0 (trade paper)
ISBN: 978-1-68510-149-7 (ebook)
Library of Congress Catalog Number: 2025933057

First printing edition: June 13, 2025
Printed by JournalStone Publishing in the United States of America.
Cover Artwork: Mikio Murakami
Edited by Sean Leonard
Proofreading, Cover Layout, & Interior Layout by Scarlett R. Algee

JournalStone Publishing
1400 North Wood Rd.
Murphysboro, IL 62966

JournalStone books may be ordered through booksellers or by contacting:
JournalStone | www.journalstone.com

"Then is it sin to rush into the secret house of death
Ere death dare come to us?"
—William Shakespeare, *Antony and Cleopatra*, act 4, sc.16, l.82-4

For Joe

The Secret House

Part I:
I Will Have Such Revenges

One

The lamplighter stood in the back of his wagon, one foot on the sideboard, as he extended the brass-tipped pole up under the streetlamp beside him. The pole ended in a curled cap that he brought down upon the burning lampwick to snuff it out. Then, carefully, he drew the pole out through the open bottom and away, reeling it hand-over-hand back to himself.

As he bent to place the pole along the back of the wagon, his shoulders sagged and he gave out a low groan of exhaustion. He'd doused most of the lights along Pennsylvania Avenue, beginning at the foot of the Capitol and now nearly all the way to the Treasury Building. It was not an arduous job, but spindle-shanked Horace Felton did not have a particularly durable constitution. Tomorrow, he would bring his ladder and refill every receptacle along the way, as well as trim and replace the wicks. The thought of what was to come weighed upon him more than the efforts of this morning.

It was a cold and wet dawn following upon an unusually warm night, with the result that a disagreeable effluvium had rolled in off the downslope marshes and the Potomac. In that cloud, the nearer streetlamps, ahead and across the avenue, glowed like will-o'-the-wisps. Close as he was, even the final columns of the Treasury Building were lost in the murk.

He climbed onto the bench of the wagon, then flicked the reins; his mare was already heading diagonally across the wide macadam roadbed. She had tracked this course morning and night for three years and knew it by instinct.

A few lanterns hung off the sides of the wagon itself like the running lights of a ship, despite which, in the middle of the road, he nearly collided with a bent old man whose livelihood consisted of scouring the avenue each morning for coins and trinkets—valuables that had spilled out of the pockets of people as they boarded or exited carriages along the avenue. Most of the time he encountered the grubber closer to the Indian Queen or one of the other hotels, where far more people were picked up and let off and thus more treasure was likely to be gleaned; but this murky morning had significantly impeded the old man's progress. As Felton swerved around him, the grubber nodded up, but continued to creep spider-like down the avenue, shortly vanishing in the chilly fog.

Felton drew alongside the next streetlamp—or, more precisely, his mare came to a stop where she should. He let go the reins and climbed into the back of the wagon again to hoist his hooked pole up into the lamp. With only a half-dozen remaining, his thoughts now turned to home, a fire, and some bitter coffee before bed.

With such near-at-hand comfort in his thoughts, he laid his dousing pole down in the back of the wagon. It was then that a most unexpected figure stumbled out of the fog behind him.

It was a man, dressed as if returning from a party, in formal wear, a tailcoat, his tie undone, his collar half-sprung. The man's thinning hair spiked out every which way as if he'd been clutching at his head, and his long, large beak of a nose was red, from the cold if not from drink. Closer, Felton saw that he was barefoot as he stumbled and shuffled and muttered.

But then the man drew alongside the wagon; the light fell upon him, and Felton rose up in the alarm of full recognition. This surely could not be! Yet he knew his eyes did not deceive him, for he had encountered this man any number of mornings back in the early weeks of March, usually bundled against the cold as he strode with remarkable energy for his age along the avenue, taking his early constitutional in the days before the petitioners discovered his routine and began following him like the pack of rabid dogs they were. Felton had even given him a ride one snowy morning to escape the horde. They had discussed the price of lamp oil, and the coal furnace that had been installed to heat the public floor of "the President's Castle," as the general had joked that Mrs. Dolley Madison insisted it be called. There could be no question: This was that man.

Felton called out.

Confused eyes took him in, and a slow recognition widened them while the lamplighter climbed down from his bench.

"You," said the general, but immediately glanced around himself, clutching his tailcoat tighter across his belly. The pockets bulged strangely at his hips. He let go of the coat and pushed his hands through his hair as if to squeeze his skull together.

Gently, Horace Felton asked what he was doing out here like this.

"Their applications!" came the reply. "Don't let them give me more applications." Then he looked up and raised an arm overhead as if to protect himself from invisible birds, showing his sleeve to be tattered as if the talons of real birds had already raked it. Felton stared up into the empty fog.

The edge of the general's tailcoat pocket tore then, and stones spilled out. Some struck his bare feet and he jumped and howled. "No more petitions!" he cried. "No more!" Whimpering, he bent to pick up the stones.

Horrified, Felton helped him gather them. Then he took him by the arm and urged him to climb into the back of the wagon. "So that I might help you escape them petitioners a'gin, sir," he said. "Let me do that for ya."

"Petitioners, no...no more petitioners," the general muttered.

The horse looked around at them suspiciously. This was not part of her morning's routine at all.

The general folded up on his side, knees and elbows drawn in. The stones he'd clutched to his belly spilled onto the wagon bed and he reached for them slowly, like a dying crab.

Felton scurried around to the front and stepped up. With one foot balancing in the air, he glanced back to make sure that his passenger, General William Henry Harrison, President of the United States for barely a month, had not climbed out again; but the general lay insensible in the spill of stones.

Far behind them, an uncertain shadow stood motionless in the middle of the avenue, but even as Felton thought he saw it, the fog swirled like a curtain drawn across the road.

Disquieted, he sat up, morning comforts forgotten, snapped the reins, and set the wagon rumbling fast toward Lafayette Park and around the half-circle driveway of the President's Castle. He glanced out across the park. In the fog it seemed populated by dozens of shades and threatening shapes—trees and bushes and who knew what else among them.

The moment his mare drew up, he looped the reins around the bench rail, and then, with the aid of his dousing pole, climbed down. The general hadn't moved.

Quickly, Horace Felton went up the steps and across the front portico to the silent, unlit house. He raised his fist to hammer at the door.

Two

James Hambleton Christian

Somebody was pounding on the front door. The sound of it thundered through my sleep, a gavel of final judgment, parting me from Mel in my dream. I broke the surface, fully woke an' already sitting up. Mel's arm lay across my belly. We had been pressed tight and warm in my little bed, the fire in the hearth reduced to embers hours ago.

She muttered, "James, what you doin'?"

The judgment dream's echo hung like a sustained and fading piano note in the darkness. "Didn't you hear it?" I got out of bed and slapped at the shadows to locate my pants.

"I think you was dreamin'." Even half-asleep, her creole lilted like the sweetest music ever I did hear.

But before I could give answer, the pounding boomed a second time.

Mel come awake now, too, and got straight to her feet, a lithe blackness tall as me almost, like an extra-deep shadow in the room.

I got my shirt stuffed into my trousers, buttoned up my fly, and thumbed the braces over my shoulders. Mel had found her skirt but I caught her and spun her about, kissed her. The wet taste of her lips stripped the last cobwebs of that dream, whatever it had been. She pushed against me.

"Don't have time for that, you foolish man," she said, but she showed her teeth, and laid her palm against my cheek a moment before I sat to tug my stockings up, to put on my buckle shoes.

Dressing, she muttered, "Be careful. No good news comin' this time of night, James Christian."

Probably so, but I was expected to be presentable even if I was to open the door on a hooded lynching party. Anyway, weren't any runaways on the plantation of Mr. John Tyler, so that wouldn't be what awaited me. More likely it was somebody seeking Mel's help. That had happened a few times on account of what they called her *makaya* skill, her healing with plants and tinctures and salves; but then it meant someone was sick or dying, and somebody white at that—nobody would have been sent out this early over a slave what had taken ill.

I got my jacket on as I knelt before my tiny hearth, blew on the embers, got a punk lit, and pressed it to the wick of the oil lamp on the narrow mantel.

Mel was at the door. I reached for her shoulder. She caught my hand, kissed it, then slipped out into the hall, heading for the kitchen. "I love you, girl," I whispered, but she wasn't there to hear, only the ghost of her, disappearing.

I took the lamp and hurried out as the pounding came yet a third time, *thump-thump-thump*, like the house's heartbeat.

Rounding the parlor into the main hall, I lifted the lamp to see the face of the tall clock against the wall there. Right behind me, the stairs creaked and I almost jumped.

Mr. John Tyler himself was descending, a pale specter in his nightshirt, his hair all wild, his eyes wide and blinking.

"Not quite five in the morning, sir," I told him, and carried the light to illuminate his way down.

With one hand Tyler pushed flat his cowlicked hair. The other flicked toward the front door. "Yes, well, all right, open it up, James." Impatient like always.

I tugged my coat straighter and marched to the door. But when I gripped the handle, for a moment I hesitated. Mel's words returned like a premonition: Everything was gonna be different once I opened it.

"Well?" Tyler goaded. "It is *not* going to be the Devil."

I held my tongue for what was surely the five thousandth time and threw open the door.

The lamplight fell upon a bearded face with cheeks so darkly red and eyes so blurry that the man looked to be a drunk who'd lost his way. But it was cold and exhaustion that cast him. His hair was pressed in a greasy rut around the crown of his head from the flat-brimmed hat he now held to one side. The hat dripped, and I supposed it had rained someplace in the night. An indigo greatcoat wrapped him up. His head seemed to float upon it.

Tyler came up, squinting. "Fletcher Webster?" he said in some wonder. "Is that you?"

The bearded young man nodded heavily. Out in the dark behind him, a horse snorted. "Sir," he began, and the word weighed as heavy as a sack of hard-times tokens. "I've ridden the whole of the night."

Tyler's face went taut. "It's not your father then?" he asked.

"No, sir," replied Webster. "Though I am here *for* him."

"No, of course, 'course you are. Well, come in, sit down." Tyler spoke as if he knew already the import of this visitation.

Webster thanked him politely and stepped through the doorway. I smelled the horse lather on him as he passed, and turned, my lamp leading him into the hall, toward the two spoonback chairs against the wall. Once in, however, Webster paused and drew himself up stiffly. "Sir," he said again. "President Harrison is dead."

Discharging his message, he tottered quick to the chairs as if those words being held inside had been the only thing keeping him on his feet.

Tyler remained a few moments, back to us, staring out into the misty night as though expecting another arrival. Finally, he let out a long sigh, breath curling in a stream above his shoulder. His words seemed to ride to me on that smoke. "Go wake the household, James, and have Cyrus attend to Mr. Webster's horse. We must depart posthaste."

He came about and snatched the lamp from my hand, leaving me to close the door.

Standing over Webster and with a hand on his shoulder, Tyler glanced sidelong at me. "See that coffee is brought for Fletcher before you attend me." He walked away then, taking all the light with him. It rose up the stairs like life itself departing, wrapping me and the messenger in darkness again.

"Will you be all right here, sir?" I asked.

"I'll prob'ly doze. *Was* dozin' most a' the last ten miles." He folded up and lay upon the two chairs.

➤➤➤ ⬅⬅⬅

The glow from the kitchen guided me, and the warmth.

Mel stood near the hearth. She was flattening a ball of sourdough on the table. Other of the kitchen slaves were coming in through the mudroom door—Abigail and young Zenobia, then old Millburn, who used to be the cook before.

The women other than Mel glanced nervously at me as I came in. They knew something was up. I told Millburn we had an unexpected guest and to make coffee for him. She set straight to it, hauling out the cloth bag and scooping a handful of beans into the small grinder on the cupboard shelf. She started cranking the handle. I walked past her to where Mel continued rolling out dough for biscuits as if it was a usual morning.

She must have sensed me there but didn't look up. She took a tin cutter with crimped edges and began stamping out biscuit forms. Then, as if speaking to the dough, she said quietly, "Too late now. You goin' to Washington with Mr. Tyler."

"He won't take me," I insisted, wondering how she knew the situation. She stopped cutting, her body against the counter a furious spring that might fly off in any direction if I said or did anything more.

See, I had promised her that soon as I saw the opportunity, I would ask for my freedom. Mr. Tyler would never have agreed to it, but he didn't own me. I belonged to his wife, Miss Letitia, and hadn't she all but agreed to it before her infirmity, saying as how if I ever truly wanted to leave her service, I had but to ask? And now Tyler had to go off to Washington for a funeral, and I thought sure this would be the time to get Miss Letitia to agree, to sign papers making it so without him present to interfere. Maybe I could find out from her what I would need to do to buy Mel's freedom as well. *She* was his property. Still, if I could go north, make some money somewhere…

"You think that all you like," she answered and returned to pushing the cutter into the dough. "World changed on us already, James. That man's news is got inside this house, and you can't close the door on it no more."

"Why can't it be for our benefit?"

She gave me a look said I was talking crazy—the look she always gave when I told her how things were going to work out or called her *lambkin* or something else out of Shakespeare. I'd have stayed to argue, but I had already delayed too long. Infuriating Tyler now was the last thing I wanted to do.

$$\ggg\!\!-\!\lll$$

He stood before the dresser mirror in his room upstairs, the door open, and him only half-dressed.

Samuel, big as a puncheon, and with a scar down the left side of his face from a lashing when he was young, stood behind Mr. Tyler and held up his black coat. He shot me a belligerent and confused glance as if to say that whatever was going on in the house this morning, it surely must be my fault. He didn't know anything and I ignored him; but seeing him with Mr. Tyler's coat reassured me. I would be staying here.

Mr. Tyler was in such a froth that Samuel was likely to be stuck holding that coat out till noon. He give it a snap as if he had just brought it to bear and Tyler responded without realizing, putting out his arms till he stood martyred like Jesus hanging on the cross. Samuel began guiding a sleeve onto him.

Tyler glared. "I have no money," he said, as if he was expecting me to lend him some. "Not one cent for travel, for the train."

Well, I thought to say, why don't you just sell off one of us?

He had done that more'n once to raise money for his political campaigns in Virginia and with Harrison. But I kept quiet and nodded like always, my face as blank as if I was deaf and dumb. That was the way to survive in John Tyler's household.

Samuel finished working the coat onto him, straightened it, then began brushing his hair for him, forward toward his face at the sides in the fashion of Roman emperors.

In the dark hall behind me, the floorboards creaked as someone hurried past. I glanced around but they'd gone by. The whole house was waking up the way houses do, the signal like a breeze blowing down the halls and through the rooms.

Tyler considered himself in the dresser mirror. "I will have to ask Tucker for a loan," he seemed to tell his reflection, "that's what I'll do. 'Put money in thy purse.' Am I right, James?"

Mr. Beverly Tucker was a neighbor, a trusted friend of his. That about summed up the danger of being close to Mr. Tyler.

"You see the absurdity of it, naturally. I have to beg him for money because I have just become the president of these United States." He barked a laugh.

Yes, I saw it clear enough—him all formally attired with his hand out. They should carve his statues in that pose.

Samuel stepped up to fix his cravat, but Tyler waved him off. "James, you attend me," he said. "Samuel, go get yourself ready." He gestured me to come and tie the cravat.

Suppressing a smile, I stepped up and quickly measured, wound, and fixed the cravat for him.

"Such nimble fingers." He made the compliment sound like an accusation of thievery. He again looked at himself in the mirror, and I had to look too—two men side by side in black coats, him with his swept hair, thin face, and hawkish nose, and me with my auburn hair, darker skin, and hazel eyes. I looked more like his saturnine cousin than I did like blue-black Samuel.

I didn't much care for mirrors.

Mr. Tyler grabbed my lamp off the dresser then and with his other hand turned me about and propelled me ahead of him toward the door. "All right," he said, "let us go."

We strode along the dark hall. Many of the doorways glowed now from candlelight within: the breeze had blown through. We passed by them all, heading for Miss Letitia's room at the back by the servant stairs.

Her door was still closed. He hesitated a moment, but then knocked softly.

"Yes," a voice called. It was Devonee, Miss Letitia's constant companion, and after a moment the door opened and her big moon of a face filled the gap, her eyes sliding between us as if our identities surprised her. But the candle was lit within. They had been awakened, along with the rest. "Missuh Tyler, sir," she said as she stepped back and the door swung wide. She'd been chosen in part for her size, being strong enough to lift her mistress to and from the bed when the bedding was being changed or Miss Letitia needed the chamber pot or to be washed.

I followed him into the room. It was, for both of us and for different reasons, the most hallowed chamber in the house.

⸺ ⸺

Miss Letitia, wife of John Tyler, lay upon her bed beneath quilts and half-propped up by pillows. Even as a child, to me she had always seemed like a queen ready to hold court, and the more so after she'd been invalided. She was pale after a winter spent indoors, with a ruffled sleeping cap that looked like a doily laid on top of her black spilled hair. The lamplight glimmered in her eyes as her husband drew near. I stayed back beside Devonee.

Mr. Tyler perched beside Miss Letitia and slid the lamp onto the table next to the bed, atop the prayerbook and Bible stacked there. The curtains were still drawn on the windows, and it might have been the dead of night in here rather than early dawn. Quietly, he explained the reason for all the commotion in the house.

"I must go ahead immediately," he told her.

She reached and squeezed his hand, a show of her pride in him, then lopsidedly murmured something. Tyler leaned in close but shook his head that he didn't understand. She pawed the quilt, got hold of her schoolroom slate and the big piece of chalk that lay always beside her. Propping the slate up in the crook of her arm, she wrote on it, then slid it toward him. He took it and turned it about. She had written, *You'll meet the challenge.*

He nodded, smiling. "I will, but that is why I must go *now.* Congress will do all they can to try to make me the briefest of footnotes and elect their own man, who'll no doubt be Clay. I must act swiftly if I'm to seize the reins. Now, I'm going to take Samuel along and leave the household under Priscilla's direction, and James can run his folk." He squeezed her hands. "We'll have plenty of time after to figure out who will accompany you to Washington to join me. I'm sure there's staff there already and we'll quickly sort it out."

Hearing that, I let go a sigh of relief. But while he spoke, Miss Letitia had taken back her slate, smeared her hand over it, and written furiously.

He reached for it and turned it. His jaw clenched, and my heart fell.

She had written, *Take James.*

I stared hard and tried to make her see my consternation, even shook my head the tiniest bit, but she looked only at her husband.

Tyler turned and took stock of me as if reassessing my value. I shouted in my head, *Tell her you won't.* Tried even to make the words shoot from my eyes.

I could feel Devonee staring at me too, like to see which way I would bolt. She'd read the slate, same as me. Being able to read her mistress's handwriting was the other reason she was Miss Letitia's body slave.

Tyler leaned forward to hand the slate back to her. "You know, my dear," he said, being careful not to sound condescending, "I much *prefer* Samuel for my personal servant. He knows my routine to a fault, and I do believe your James...will be of far more use to you and Priscilla here. She needs him to keep the house running smoothly. And there are Alice and Tazewell's music lessons."

It was as if I wasn't even there. His daughter-in-law Priscilla and I got on well, it was true. I was happy to work for her. I was used to being dismissed by him; I expected his coolness toward me to carry the day. It didn't seem too much to hope for.

Miss Letitia wiped her hand across the slate and wrote some more. The chalk made a bloodcurdling squeal. She pushed the slate to her husband again. She was not the sort of woman who angered, but she could be as stubborn as anybody in her family. As stubborn as me. Stubbornness was keeping her alive after her strokes.

The slate read, *James presents best*. From the mass of pillows, she gave her husband an incontrovertible look. Moses had come down with the tablets.

I suspect I must have flushed with some pride that Miss Letitia defended me thus, but my stomach was scooped hollow with dread. Everything that I was seemed suddenly to work against me.

Before I became Miss Letitia's property, I'd served as her brother's body servant when he went off to attend William and Mary College. There, a bunch of students tutored me and gave me books to read. Mostly, it was a snub to their elders, who held that educating any colored one of us was a hanging offense. But they knew right well that they would not be hanged for it, ever. *I* might have been, but that was no concern of theirs either. They just wanted to see if I would prove uneducable, which is what their families maintained. It was all nothing but a jape, and maybe I would have failed outright, but my mother had long ago rescued a battered old New York Primer that Colonel Christian's children had finished with, and she'd taught me from it. She never said who'd taught her, never breathed a word of it, but she'd discovered that once I'd read something, I had the ability to remember it almost word-for-word. Those students fed me the writings of Shakespeare, Cervantes, and of course the Bible, and it became part of me, like a new limb that had grown out. I also read music, and so was tasked with teaching piano to the two youngest of Tyler's children. All that should have saved me from going with him if nothing else did. I was devoted to those sweet children as I was to their mother, and they to me. Instead of helping me as it should, my learning was working against me.

Tyler considered me again. I could see him reckoning how things would look with me rather than sullen and scarred Samuel behind him as he stood publicly among Washington society. His lips pursed; he gave the slightest nod. I closed my eyes to the inevitable.

"You are right as usual, dear wife. Always my wisest advisor."

When I looked again, he was kissing her forehead. Her hand lay upon his cheek, but her eyes bored directly into mine. Maybe the look contained some charity, but mostly what it said was that her husband's needs *always* came first.

"James," Tyler said over his shoulder. "Go and pack your necessities, and tell Samuel he needn't bother."

He still had my lamp, so I turned and staggered out into the darkness again, the first clumsy steps on my way north. I might as well have been sold.

⫸— ⫷

When I returned to the kitchen, the biscuits were in the brick oven and Mel stood before it, her hands on her hips. Before I even came up beside her, she said, "He takin' you wit' him."

"And you knew. How'd you know?" I grabbed her shoulder, half-expecting her to throw off my hand. But she didn't. She turned, and her eyes were wet and glistening in the glow of the oven. That scared me more than anything. Mel crying. I'd never imagined it possible.

She cupped her hand on my face. "You too sweet for him to leave for me." She gestured to Sally then, another of the kitchen women, to watch the biscuits, and she walked away, through the mudroom and outside.

I chased after her. "Mel, it won't be long. It's just a funeral and whatever else has to be done."

She shook her head. "World changed," she said again, then wiped her eyes and walked away.

I still insisted it was a small, brief thing. I should have listened to her.

⫸— ⫷

We rode 230 miles by train to get to Washington—a party of three, Mr. Tyler, Fletcher Webster, and me. I sat one seat behind them, at Mr. Tyler's pleasure. That kept me out of the seedy Jim Crow car at the back. The irony was, that car held some free men and women, while I was allowed in the finer carriage but only as Tyler's property.

The two of them talked some. Mr. Tyler seemed to have a lot of questions that Webster couldn't answer. Bound in my own thoughts, I didn't pay it all much mind.

When Webster nodded off, Mr. Tyler got up and paced the length of the carriage. He couldn't seem to sit still. He might have had an urgent desire to reach the city, but the train didn't care. Didn't deliver us to the outskirts of the city until after 3 a.m.; and because trains were outlawed inside the city limits, we continued to sit in our paneled carriage another hour while a team of plowhorses was hitched to the front to pull us from the yard to the B&O station. We could have climbed out and walked there faster. Mr. Tyler fidgeted and muttered the whole time.

On the hill, in the shadow of the Capitol, we paused to look out over the city. It wasn't much. We might have been standing on a pyramid overlooking a desert in Egypt for all that could be seen below. A scattering of fires and lamps dotted a black and misty plain. One single straight line of glowing dots headed off into the distance. That line, said Webster, was Pennsylvania Avenue, and somewhere along there lay the President's House, but from Capitol Hill it might have been a myth, a place that had never happened.

Tyler hired a coach, and in it we descended, me on top behind the driver, Tyler and Webster inside. It was rough and slow-going down the hill, but the avenue had a surface of pulped stone, what they called macadam, and we rolled much more briskly along that—at least, for a few minutes.

We had hardly set off when Tyler called the driver to pull up in front of a broad white-washed five-story building. The projecting marquee over the doors read *Jesse Brown*. This was Brown's Indian Queen Hotel. It housed dignitaries of all sorts, and it was where Tyler himself had stayed when the election was won, and from where he'd gone across the street alone to the Senate chambers to be sworn in as "His Superfluous Excellency," which is what old John Adams had called the office of vice president. Everybody else had been up above, listening to General Harrison recite his interminable inaugural speech in the freezing cold. Afterward, Tyler had slunk off home, his part in the election completed.

We would be rooming here until the general was laid to rest.

Despite the early hour, a colored doorman stood like a tree-trunk under the marquee, and he come out to the carriage and led Mr. Tyler inside. I remained waiting on top of the coach like one more piece of luggage, looking at the bleak expanse of the avenue stretching out ahead like a path to nowhere.

The driver remained seated, motionless. I'd have thought him asleep except for the smoke that streamed out of his clay pipe and over his shoulder. Down below, Fletcher Webster snored.

A few minutes passed. Mr. Tyler, the doorman, and a porter returned, had me untie the luggage—Tyler's trunk, and a carpetbag of my things. I started to get down, but he told me to stay put. We weren't staying. They took the luggage, Mr. Tyler gave the porter a coin to haul it inside, and then he climbed back into the coach.

The rest of the way along that straight avenue we met only one other vehicle, a small cart that crossed our path on its way down toward the canal or the Potomac itself. Wood smoke hung in the chill air, big hazy cauls of it that burst apart at our passing.

A huge toothy building emerged on our right—so many columns that they seemed to fade into the darkness. I thought that must be our destination, but the carriage passed right on by. I asked the driver, and he said, "No, that one's the Treasury Building. Well, and we gotta ride through Lafayette Park first afore you'll set eyes on the President's Castle."

The coach soon came abreast of three- and four-story brick dwellings on the right, with a street running between them, which the driver announced as "New York Avenue." Immediately we turned from them and entered the wooded expanse of the park. On the far side of it, something wide and large and gray as bone showed beyond the trees: the house. The wood smoke combined with mist off the downhill swamps swirled around so that glimpses of it looked like the mirage of a mausoleum that might evaporate before we arrived.

A fence of wrought-iron spears lined the front of the property with gateposts on either side. The gates were hung with black wreaths.

The driver got down and opened the west gate, then drove us up the carriage turnaround, a semi-circle driveway flanked by more iron posts and leading up to the jutting front of the house.

The coach lanterns threw off an anemic glow that barely reached the four front columns. Behind them I couldn't see anything much through the mist, though it looked as if a lane of the wide graveled drive ran behind them, a *porte-cochère* space. The lower halves of the columns had been wrapped in mourning drapery, which made the top halves look like giant teeth, and the porch the open and hungry mouth of a monster cloaked in swamp mist and smoke and waiting for us. Exposed on top of the carriage, I shrank back, feeling like I was a meal being delivered.

Tyler, already stepping to the ground, was all business. He passed more coin to the driver to hold him, then waited for Fletcher to get out. Untroubled by the eeriness of the place, the two of them marched up the steps into the darkness of the portico. I jumped down and followed before they could vanish altogether.

We arrived at a big door with a fanlight and ornamentation over it. Mr. Tyler tried the handle, but the door wouldn't budge. "Don't they know we're coming?" he said. It seemed a ridiculous question. No word could have been sent ahead of us, and it was about four in the morning.

Mr. Tyler pounded the side of his fist on the door and it boomed as if behind it lay a deep cavern, reminding me of the morning before. We stood, waited.

Right above me, a huge unlit lamp hung from the portico ceiling, and though no breeze blew, I swore it swung a bit; I could hear its chain creaking. I edged off to one side, away from it.

The carriage horses behind us shifted, harnesses jingling, hooves clopping. I would have been overjoyed if we'd returned to the carriage and gone back to the Indian Queen at least till dawn.

After awhile, Tyler raised up his fist again, but before he could strike, there came the clank of a bolt snapping, and the door, probably swollen by the wet air, groaned open.

A pinkish gnome holding a bedside candle by its ring blinked at us through the opening. He looked to have thrown his coat on over his pajama shirt, and I had to smile, wondering if he had been in bed with his lambkin like I had when the pounding came. I wondered, too, if she had big ears like his.

⋙ ⋘

The short doorman begged pardon but asked would we wait in the vestibule while he dressed himself all proper. Jasper, he said his name was, though not whether that was his first or last. He had short bristly white hair and his face was pink as a baby's, with patches that looked as if they must itch. When Tyler introduced himself, Jasper answered, "You'll be wantin' to see the general then, I'm sure." His speech wasn't Southern but some kind of salted British.

We were left to stand in the vestibule, lit by two lard-oil lamps on tables. There were two small fireplaces, one to each side, both of them dark, a chair beside each, and a settee for two people up against the outside wall. The floor was covered by a heavy oilcloth, tramped all over with muddy footprints. The inside wall looked like something that had been puzzled together—glass panels in makeshift wooden frames that filled the spaces between the four columns, with a single wide door in the middle.

Jasper came back after a few minutes, his shirt mostly tucked into his trousers, coat on, and carrying another lard-oil lamp. He led us out of the vestibule and into a main hall that ran east to west near the whole width of the house. Straw matting covered the floor there. "The Cross Hall," he said, as if announcing its title. The trail of all those footprints that had preceded us continued the length of it.

The soot-blackened ceilings of the President's Castle hung high above, and the light thrown off by our guide's lamp flung shadows up across them. The moldings looked to be strung thick, especially in the corners, with cobwebs. Wouldn't have been tolerated at Tyler's place in Virginia.

In the lamplight the webs seemed to flutter, and it was some moments before I realized they were moving for real. Not cobwebs then. Spiders had colonized up there where nobody could reach. Fine by me so long as they stayed put.

A few of the chairs against the walls of the broad hallway looked as old as the house itself—stuffing dangled under one seat; another was missing its back altogether. The unlit sconces above them were hung with black bows.

At the far end, Jasper drew up before a set of double doors. "The East Room, gen'men," he said, but softly, as though afraid he might wake somebody. Then he opened the doors.

An immense empty chamber lay beyond them. It stretched from the front to the rear of the house. A handful of nearly melted candles was already lit in there and fluttered with our entry. Some, on trivets, stood along the walls in between more mismatched chairs.

In the center of the room, four dying candles on tripods bracketed the corners of a draped black bier on which lay an open mahogany coffin. The candles had burned so low, the tiny flames no longer threw light over its sides.

The pathway of dried mud we were following led across a dirty blue and gold carpet from the door and back again. All those people had made their circuit just in the past day.

Jasper led our little expedition toward the bier and soon the gray contours of a body emerged from the shadows: an immobile face; folded hands crossed upon a black coat; the tips of shiny boots sticking up.

President Harrison's reddish gray hair had been brushed forward same as Samuel had done Tyler's, with the result that his head looked like the bust of a Roman emperor in the process of being unpacked out of its dark wrappings.

Then the smell of him reached us—the kind of stink that anticipates there's something dead in your path. Someone had dressed the smell up with sweet cologne, but that only made the stink more odious.

I hadn't known him at all. Surprised by the smell, I hung back.

Jasper also kept his distance. It might have been a gesture of respect or to keep out of their way, but he had owlish eyes and kept looking around us while avoiding my gaze.

The long room was so still that it seemed to be holding its breath. The windows, tall as doors, on all three sides had been covered in the same black cloth as the pillars out front. Black and white ribbons hung from the three unlit chandeliers. Black draped over the tall mirrors and the paintings mounted along the walls. Even some of the chairs stationed around the room were hung with alternating black and white wreaths.

Beyond the muddy path, the enormous carpet was irregularly spotted. The spots looked brown and sort of glittered in the candlelight. I lifted my foot and trod on one, and the rug crackled as if I had crushed an eggshell.

Beside me, Jasper whispered, "Tobacco juice."

My lip curled, I think. Imagine the great men of the land all inching forward on this path and thoughtlessly from time to time gobbing a brown stream off to the side. If someone had done that in Tyler's plantation house in Virginia, he'd have ordered me to throw them out.

Jasper kept on whispering to me like he couldn't stop himself. "Had such energy, the general did. Used ta walk to the market in the mornings, pick out 'is own vegetables for dinner—at least till them petitioners got wind of it, started laying for him in the bushes so's they could accompany 'im on his way an' make their case like. Well, it was one or two at first, but pretty soon they was assaultin' 'im by the dozens, till 'e was scared to go out alone. Had to give it up." Looking at the floor, he shook his head. "Was like the sun burnin' wif energy, the general was, an' I know he missed those days abroad." He paused as though to review what he had said, adding at last, "Most terrible fate."

These final words, spoken more loudly, echoed through the room and for an instant seemed to rattle something loose in one far dark corner.

Jasper turned and quickly headed for the door as if he couldn't stand being in the room any longer. Of course, the lamplight went with him, leaving the three of us to chase it like moths. Before we reached the doors, Mr. Tyler had passed me, Fletcher Webster hard on his heels. Might have been nothing more than the smell, but if so, that stink of rot had drawn itself together in the corner and become something that watched us back. None of us would admit it, being we were the enemies of superstition, but we lit out of the East Room and Jasper closed the doors after us, leaving those candles to die out on their own. I doubt the general's corpse would have wanted to be left alone in there without them.

Three

Vice President John Tyler walked an exhausted Fletcher Webster to the front door, thanked him for his efforts, and promised that his horse, which they had left behind in Virginia, would be returned to him at first opportunity.

Tyler turned then to the doorman. "Would you now show me to the president's office, Mr. Jasper. James, you come along too."

His slave James looked tired and ill-at-ease. Well, they were all tired, weren't they? But there was no time for sleep, not if he was to achieve his goal before Clay and the Congress interfered.

The office lay on the second floor. Jasper called it "the private floor." There were, he said, three stairways up—the main stairs on the west side of the house between the dining rooms, a narrow servants' stairs hidden from view just around the corner, and a back stairs, which they'd passed going to the East Room, and where he led them now. "My own room's under them steps, sir," Jasper said, indicating the door with his lamp as he led the way.

The second floor was laid out much as the first, with a long central hall, but sectioned at each end. The east portion was elevated a few steps.

"General Harrison called this the waitin' hall. Most days you'll find it filled up with men an' their applications, all of 'em hanging about outside your door and vying for five minutes of your time, sir. Been fistfights broke out over it."

Ahead, the exterior wall comprised mostly an enormous fanlight window through which the first colors of dawn showed. Jasper paused to look out toward the Treasury Building.

"Window on the west side just like this one too," Jasper remarked. "Was you ever up 'ere before this?"

But Tyler wasn't listening. "A shame," he said, "that so pleasant a view's going to be marred by swarms of petitioners."

Jasper pointed at two mahogany doors and directed Tyler to the right-hand one nearest the window. "This leads to your secretary's room. Petitioners is supposed to go through that room to get to you—circle through and out, you see. Will, ah, your man James 'ere be acting as your secretary then?"

Tyler laughed. "Hardly, Mr. Jasper. My son Robert will fill that role. He's on his own business in Philadelphia. One of the things I need to do this morning is send him notice." He nodded at the other door. "My office, I take it?"

"Yes, sir." Jasper rushed back and quickly opened it before he could, then scurried about inside, using his lard oil lamp to light various candles and lamps within, of which there were quite a few for so small a room, including an Argand lamp that came up so bright, it seemed as if daylight had suddenly flooded the chamber. Looking at it made Tyler wince. Jasper babbled at him the whole time. "Your secretary's room, like your bed chamber, has got a water closet in the outside corner. In case you've need of it, you don't have to face down them petitioners, ya see." He crossed to the small hearth. "I can lay on a fire, sir, if you like."

Only half-listening, Tyler muttered, "Unnecessary." He stared in disbelief at his office.

So much furniture had been jammed into the small room. A regular desk; a standing desk bolted to the inside wall across a side door; a wardrobe in the corner that had been converted to pigeonhole shelves, most of them with rolled-up papers sticking out; and tables of various sizes everywhere else. Almost every single surface was covered in documents, books, and even a map of North America. Black and white bunting had been draped along the mantel, which was about the only thing clear of papers.

He spotted an inkwell on the standing desk and wove his way around one of the tables to it. He picked up the pen that lay beside it, flipped up the lid of the well. At least it was filled. Staring into the liquid blackness, he said, "I would greatly appreciate some breakfast brought up. I haven't eaten since yesterday."

"I'll 'ave it seen to, sir," Jasper said.

He shook his head. "No. James, you do it. You need to learn the staff anyhow." Jasper turned to leave, but Tyler said, "Hang on there, Mr. Jasper. How did this room come to be in this state? Harrison was only in office a month. This looks like a dozen monkeys took up residence in here."

Jasper looked at him uncomfortably and hesitated for a moment as if weighing whether he should speak. "General, sir, 'e weren't himself at the end. Kept gettin' out of 'is bed, 'e did, and comin' here. Was always goin' on about petitions, you see. Like there was more somewhere and 'e had to find 'em."

Tyler shook his head wearily. "What I see is land grants, treaties, even here a *de novo* appeal. It's chaos is what is, sir. He's scattered things everywhere."

Edgily, Jasper answered, "I couldn't say, sir. But no one's touched the room. Nor 'is private chambers down t'other end."

"What, you haven't cleaned the room where he *died?*" he snapped. "Has it even been aired out?"

Jasper all but twisted himself up. "Staff, sir, have expressed reluctance to go into his rooms. Mr. Webster senior, 'e calls 'em all a bunch of gullible

Geechees."

Tyler snorted. "And right he is. Well, James, sounds as if you've got your work cut out for you downstairs." He blinked as if astonished. "Speaking of Webster and the others, Mr. Jasper, I will have a great many notes that must be delivered this very morning, soon as I get them writ. James will bring them to you."

"I'll see to it, sir," Jasper said, and bowed. He backed out the doorway.

"Go with him, James. Get my breakfast soon as you can. And have something yourself. This is going to be a long day."

James Christian withdrew, and Jasper closed the door.

"Geechees, indeed," Tyler said. He rummaged through the mess on the desk for a clean sheet of paper.

Four

James Hambleton Christian

I followed the doorman down the steps to the central hall again.

"Geechees?" I said. "You got actual Gullah folk on staff here, Mr. Jasper?"

"One or two. Come on and you can meet 'em all at once. You're in charge of 'em, I gather?"

"I expect, until the election."

"What election is that?" asked Jasper.

"Gonna have to be one, now that General Harrison's dead, won't there?"

He turned back to me. The light of his oil lamp made his look leery. "Can't say I had that impression from your Mr. Tyler."

I came to a halt in the middle of the hall. Oh, I'd been a damn fool lost in dreaming my dream—Robert, sent for to be his secretary; the notes he had to send off right away this morning. I hadn't understood anything at all, while Mel had seen it clear from the git-go.

World changed.

⇒⇒⇒- ⇐⇐⇐

Jasper led me through the transomed doorway at the west end letting onto the main stairs. As he'd told us, another huge fanlight filled the outside wall there. On the next landing below, Jasper said, "Here's where the general and his daughter-in-law waited till his dinner guests had been herded into the hall. Then they descended like a royal couple wiv the sun through the fanlight flowing down on 'em." His lamp revealed a hole in the plaster wall, exposing some lath.

"I'm surprised there's nobody up already," I said. "Mr. Tyler's house would be bustling by now with—" Then the smell of baking bread reached us up the stairwell.

"Nobody up *here*, no," he said. "They all think the 'ouse's still empty. Ain't nobody's told 'em what's going on, what's next. Weren't none of us expecting Mr. Tyler."

⇒⇒⇒- ⇐⇐⇐

The kitchen floor had a long yellow limewashed hallway right down its middle; overhead was a big vaulted ceiling.

The staff here was all colored. I supposed them to be Harrison's slaves.

Jasper introduced me as Vice President Tyler's body servant and told them Mr. Tyler wanted breakfast up in his office soon as possible. The woman I took to be the head cook—a big woman with dumpling cheeks— nodded that she'd heard and started barking orders at the other three women. Jasper meanwhile found a white footman in some other room and the two of them went off upstairs together, leaving me there.

Another footman, a lanky, coal-black man, came up and introduced himself as Bibb, asked if I wanted some fresh bread and coffee while Tyler's meal was being prepared. I did, and he introduced me to the cook. Her name was Weems. She stood in front of a huge cast-iron stove that filled up one of the fireplaces. Bibb called it a *ranger*. He seemed as proud as if he'd built it, and said it got that name on account of the range of pots it held, and showed me a couple sunken boilers. "We gots hot water 'vailable day and night, if'n somebody wants some tea or coffee, we git it to 'em right then. Not only that, this here was designed and installed by President Thomas Jefferson hisself."

The cook overheard. She stopped what she was doing long enough to point with a spatula at a smaller iron stove on the other side of the room. It looked rusty and considerably older. "That's the one Mistah Jefferson built," she said. "He don't know what he's talking about, like always." She turned back to her cooking, leaving Bibb to make a face behind her back. I couldn't help thinking how much life in one kitchen was like another.

"Here's something even better," he said, and snuck up beside the ranger where a curved pipe stuck out of the wall with a kind of bowtie fixture on it. Bibb turned the fixture and water gushed out of the pipe, splashing into a bucket on the floor. Mrs. Weems yelled at him, but he'd already turned it off and jumped back. "Indoor water tap. Most amazing thing."

Bibb got me a cup of coffee and a hunk of warm bread and led me along the hall to a mess room with a large table, chairs, and a couple benches in it. A window looked out on the south lawn below the house, which sparkled with morning dew. "Room used to be a lot bigger afore they installed the coal-fire furnace what heats the first floor now. 'Cross the hall, there's a room for curing meat and a cellar room full of wine and port. Then there's this one off the side of the mess. Head butler sleeps there. Rest of us in rooms down the east end of the hall by the laundry, a few under the east colonnade. Some folk go home at night though, times there's no dinner or soirée goin' on."

I couldn't understand. Folks went home? I asked, "So you all the slaves of General Harrison or of Daniel Webster then?"

That startled Bibb. He drew himself up stiffly in his chair. "We ain't *nobody's* slaves, Mr. Christian. We all free. Got our own churches, schools, our own homes. They's four thousand of us in the city here."

Going home to my own house after a day's work—I could barely credit the notion.

I sat there the longest time, no doubt slack-jawed and stupid, while I imagined walking to a cabin alongside Mel down Pennsylvania Avenue, tipping my hat to those we passed and saying "Lovely day" and "How nice to see you" while she twirled a parasol. *God*, I asked, *could you not give me that, even for a day?*

Did Tyler even suspect he'd brought me to a city full of free colored people, much less placed me in among 'em? I had to get Mel out of Virginia and up here straightaway.

Bibb was saying, "You all right, Mr. Christian?"

I came back to myself. "Fine, sir, I'm fine," I said.

"You, ah, you think your Mr. Tyler's like to keep us all on?"

"Some," I said. "Maybe." I didn't really know anything except that the cook had to go. "Do you happen to know what they gave General Harrison for y'all?"

Bibb made a sour face. "Oh," he said, "the Congress was intending to cut him off on account of that Henry Clay fella didn't like how things was between 'em."

"Cut him off?"

Before he could answer, Mrs. Weems appeared in the doorway and proclaimed, "Mr. Tyler's breakfast is all ready an' waitin'."

I excused myself from Bibb to follow her into the hall. One of the other kitchen maids held the tray out to me. "Thank you," I said.

"Service stairs are right here," said Mrs. Weems, and pointed to a doorway beside the kitchen. "Now you be sure to come back and git something more for yourself."

I thanked her and went up. The service stairs were tight and turned every few steps. It was like climbing the inside of a chimney. The whole dark way up I thought on my other life.

Tyler would soon send for Miss Letitia. Couldn't be parted from her for long. Once she gave me her blessing, he would jump to be quit of me— surely, when there was a city full of qualified butlers. Me and Mel, that's how it had to be. Maybe Mrs. Weems could stay on so they had a cook for their parties and wouldn't miss her. She could even teach Mrs. Weems Tyler's favorite dishes—those black cap apples he loved. A free community surrounded us, everything right here if I could figure out how and when to ask. Wasn't till I reached the last landing below the private floor that I stopped, struck by the realization that I was the only chattel in this entire

God-damned house.

I climbed on, full of new possibilities, and twisted like these stairs with ideas of new escapes from service to Mr. Tyler. Maybe he'd known all along about the free community here. Last thing he would want spoken of at Walnut Grove was *that* story. *Our own churches. Our own schools.*

I strode out into the middle of the hall, then paused for a second to get my bearings. The service stairs had turned me out on the west end of the central hall.

Behind me, a door came off the latch. I heard it but my thoughts were full of Mel and the possibility of some kind of free life for us, and I reacted slowly, not really even comprehending that there must be someone else in the house we didn't know of, whom Mr. Jasper hadn't mentioned. Except, there was nobody there. Just a door to a room, with a cracked inch full of darkness in the heart of which something glittered for an instant. The light liked to tug on me, inviting me into that room, and I even took a step back toward it, but the tray rattled in my hands. I had Mr. Tyler's breakfast and I wasn't about to do anything that might put me in a bad light just then—especially, I would not let his breakfast get cold.

I headed down the hall toward his office. I did glance back once before I reached the steps up to the waiting hall.

That inveigling door hung motionless and nobody emerged.

At his office, I balanced the tray, knocked on the door, and went in. He was so intent upon scribbling at the standing desk, he didn't even notice me. I placed the tray on the nearest table, which was covered by maps. Stood smartly. He still didn't react. I cleared my throat, and he looked up at last.

"Your breakfast, sir," I said. "Eggs, grits with butter, bread and jam. Black coffee in the pot."

He set down his pen. "That's fine, James. Here." He held out a stack of folded notes, maybe twenty of them. I stepped around the table. "Give those to Jasper. Tell him I'll have more. And later we'll be going to the Capitol, so we'll want the coach harnessed. I can assume there is one?"

"I'll find that out for you, sir."

"You seem more alert, James." He got up to inspect the food, took the ceramic pot and poured himself some coffee. "You like the staff then?"

"Some good folks here, yes, sir."

"Well, you'll decide who we keep and who we sack. I haven't even located the budget papers. Heaven knows where they are in this mess. Webster I'm sure will have all the information."

I kept quiet about Congress's funds.

"Figure it out quick though. We must send word back home so they can get started on their way. The country will not wait." That seemed to strike his fancy, and he smiled. "Nor shall I. 'Action is eloquence,' eh, James?"

"Oh, yes, sir." I saw again Miss Letitia writing *Take James* on her slate. Now I rejoiced that she had. Left to Samuel, God knows who would have been sent for, but it would never have included me.

I closed the door on Mr. Tyler and set off to give his notes to Jasper.

I was about to descend the center stairs he'd brought us up earlier when I glanced across at that door, which still hung ajar. I couldn't shake the feeling that I was being observed from the darkness within, the way it had felt in the East Room just hours ago. Who, though, would be hiding in this house? Some spy hoping to learn something of Mr. Tyler's plans? Surely it had nothing to do with me—I was not even his choice. Nobody here knew me.

I crossed that hall with the bundled notes in hand and shoved the door wide. It bumped the wall.

The chamber was an L-shaped room covered in green flocked wallpaper, with a big standing mirror beside the single, curtained window. The mirror must have been what had glittered at me, reflecting sunlight, though I could not see how that could be. The room was empty. It even smelled uninhabited.

I refused to be drawn to whatever mystery this presented. I was busy.

I closed the door and headed for the vestibule and Mr. Jasper.

⟫⟫⟩- ⟨⟪⟪

I returned to the kitchen for my own breakfast. Nothing as fancy as Mr. Tyler's—excellent biscuits and gravy, and coffee. Mrs. Weems poured herself some and led me to the mess. I was the only one eating—everybody else had gone off to morning chores (which I hoped included removing the linens from General Harrison's room and airing it out, even if we weren't moving in right away).

There was one other man in the mess room. He sat by himself in the corner against the wall bench. He had tight hair shot with gray, and the whole time I ate, he stared out the window as if there was nobody else in the room, as if maybe he was deaf. He wore a footman's tailcoat. The stitching in the right shoulder had come loose, and my first thought was that we would have to get that sewn up before somebody upstairs took notice.

Mrs. Weems said, "That's Isaac. Don't pay him no mind. Isaac was General Harrison's personal servant, an' he been like that since the night ol' Harrison died. Won't say nothing to nobody as to why, and Lord knows we's all asked about a hunert times."

"Asked what?"

"What it is skeered him so."

"You mean like how the general was scared by all them petitioners laying for him?"

It didn't seem to me like a matter of much import, but Mrs. Weems gave me a sharp look. "You must 'a talked with Jasper. He the only one round here thinks ever'thing's normal."

I wanted to know what she was talking about, but I just smiled, using a mouthful of biscuits as an excuse not to answer. Sometimes when you let it appear you know more than you do, folks will tell you all sorts of things they would never have mentioned. But Mrs. Weems didn't have anything to add, and I mopped up the gravy with the last biscuit while Isaac stared out the window ignoring us and she drank her coffee and fanned herself as if she was overheated.

I said, "You know, just now a funny thing happened when I carried Mr. Tyler's tray up. One of the rooms just opened, like of its own accord. And I was wondering if maybe there's someone else staying here that nobody's thought to…" I stopped talking. Mrs. Weems had gone all goggle-eyed. But not at me.

I turned to look, and Isaac was staring straight at me as if I'd said his name. His eyes were red and raw, like he'd been sitting in coal smoke the whole morning. He seemed to be taking me in for the first time. "Seen you," he said, and nodded as if I'd affirmed something.

I was about to beg his pardon, but as suddenly he returned to staring out the window as if he hadn't moved.

I put down my fork. "What in Sam Hill— You said he was scared, not scary."

Mrs. Weems put a hand upon my arm. She said, "You see that gray hair of his?"

"'Course I do."

"Well, three days past, he ain't have a single gray hair on his head. Not a one."

After that, Isaac remained stone, responding to nothing. Mrs. Weems could not explain to me how it was that she knew he had been "skeered." We talked about him right in front of him and he paid us no mind at all. In the end I didn't have time to worry about it because by mid-morning all those people Mr. Tyler had sent out notes to began turning up and I had to be on the door with Jasper to lead them into the Blue Saloon. That was my introduction to the public floor.

"These rooms is called by color mostly," Jasper explained.

Other than the two dining rooms—a small one for the family, and a public one with a table that could seat thirty—the rooms along the southside were called the Crimson Parlor, the Blue Saloon, and the Green Parlor. That great big East Room I'd already met.

Jasper said, "Folks call the crimson one the Washington Parlor sometimes on account of the painting of George Washington what 'angs in it, that Mrs. Dolley Madison saved from burnin' once upon a time. You meet 'er, be sure and mention it. She likes an opportunity to tell that story."

"Dolley Madison. She corresponds with Miss Letitia." He stared at me blankly. "Mr. Tyler's wife."

"Ah. Ta for that. I'll remember."

The room I led the visitors to was the middle one. The saloon was a big oval-shaped room. The wallpaper and most of the furnishings—save for the half-dozen chairs we dragged in there for Mr. Tyler—were blue. The tall skinny windows looked out upon a half-round south portico lined with columns.

Many of the arriving men had made up General Harrison's cabinet, and soon they would be in the house almost daily. The last of them to turn up was Daniel Webster, Fletcher's father. He was the secretary of state. Tyler and others called him "the great god Daniel." Even arriving, he seemed formidable, his mouth the very shape of scorn and his eyes blazing like they would release lightning at any moment. Tyler stood a head taller, but Webster made everybody else near him seem to shrink.

I stood at the door, expecting to be told to bring coffee or tea along, but Mr. Tyler went straight to the matter of succession. Nobody had died in office before, he said. It was up to them to set the precedent before the Congress wrestled the matter away.

"We have a quorum," Mr. Tyler said, and before they could even catch their breaths, he got them to swear him in as the new president of the United States. I understood now why he'd been in such an all-fired hurry to get to Washington.

Trays of tea and ammonia cookies were brought up, while Webster held court on the benefits to be found in Tyler's keeping "you Harrison men"—he swept them all together with a wave of his hand—in the cabinet after the funeral. Mr. Tyler looked less than certain, but he assented.

Whole thing was over and done in under an hour. Mr. Tyler was agitated to be gone to the Capitol right away.

The meeting broke up, and he had me fetch the coachman so that he could arrive in style to deliver his inaugural speech. He'd written it that morning while breakfasting.

Jasper saw to the carriage. It rolled up a few minutes later.

Mr. Tyler come out, climbed in along with Daniel Webster, and rolled off.

Left on my own, the last thing I wanted was to be cornered in the mess room with Mrs. Weems and Isaac again. Seemed like a good time for me to tour the grounds and the other buildings.

I went out under the west colonnade. There was one such wing to each side at the level of the kitchen floor, like two ladyfinger cakes extending from the house. The south side of the colonnade was an open arcade; the other side a long block of small, enclosed spaces, including one with more of those water taps for bathing and a privy. In the lawn, just out from the arcade, a small round platform of crisscrossed boards marked what had been a well before the installation of the water taps.

I strolled along under the open roof toward the stable, which had been built off the end of it, making the whole of that colonnade L-shaped.

A couple shanties beyond the stable looked like ramshackle chicken coops, though I'd seen slave quarters on some plantations that looked no better. These seemed too shabby even to keep chickens, and I wondered why they hadn't been torn down. Seemed like no one had cared about this grand house for a while.

The shacks butted up against the fence of a paddock where I supposed the coach horses was kept. Beside the paddock, a large dilapidated gate hung from a low and crumbling stone wall that girdled the upper lawn. The long south slope below the house had been mostly clearcut and was crisscrossed by numerous carriage paths. Looked like they reached all the way down to the Potomac.

The blacksmith, Absalom Lee, had a gray frizz of hair around his head and a long and horsey face as if he'd been half-transformed by working so close with the animals. He was another member of the free community and had held the position of President's House smithy now under three different men.

I introduced myself, and we talked a little. Turned out that the carriage Tyler had ridden off in belonged to Harrison's Secretary of the Navy, who might want it back now the general had died. I filed this away, thinking it bound to come in handy sooner or later.

Absalom told me that way down past the carriage paths on the south slope a canal had been cut in from the Potomac, and the land there was still swampy and malignant. The paths and the stone wall proved to be yet another legacy of Thomas Jefferson. That man seemed to have put his mark on the house more'n anybody else. Given the condition of the place, maybe he was the last one who had.

Later I strolled out along the wall. Maybe a half-dozen carriages rolled by below while I walked, mostly couples enjoying the breezy noontime sun. Women twirled parasols, and the men wore silk hats. They looked to be having a grand time.

Then, as if to prove the existence of the world Bibb had described, a colored couple dressed fine as you please rode by in their little carriage with high-stepping horses. The woman waved to me.

I stopped against the wall and watched them roll off through a free-standing stone arch to the east that I hadn't noticed before. I could feel that low wall pressed against my shins, as if keeping me on my side of the bargain.

I didn't want to look at those paths anymore, and headed instead for the east stable. It was brick and in much better shape than the other. Absalom Lee said it had been erected by President Jackson to replace the old one, but nobody'd yet gotten around to tearing the old one down.

Inside Jackson's stable were two piles of loose hay, a whole breastcollar harness in dark leather and silver studs, a couple of big padded horse collars of oak and leather, bits and saddlery hung on pegs, and a bucket of grease next to the rim of a wheel off some wagon or other with a pitchfork leaned against it. Back in one corner behind the hay sat the remains of an old horse-drawn firepump that looked like it hadn't been wheeled out since maybe the British had chased Dolley Madison out of the house. The rotting barrel on it probably wouldn't hold water long enough even to reach the old covered well on the other side of the house.

The air hung quiet and thick, with dust hovering in the beams. Up in the rafters, doves cooed. Was almost like a house in there. I sat and daydreamed me and Mel in the hay, when all at once the doves overhead flapped and fluttered about. I backed up to the door, trying to see what had riled them up.

Then a hand fell on my shoulder and I nearly joined those doves in the rafters. I swung around, slapping at the air, stumbling back into the stable.

In the doorway stood Isaac, his hands up as if surrendering. He said, "You near backed into me." His voice was croaky as though he'd been yelling for an hour.

The doves settled down, and so did I. "Well," I huffed, "I was pretty sure I was all alone here."

"You Tyler's man, same as me wit' the gen'ral. You don't know it yet, but the thing already made a play for you. You lucky you didn't take the bait."

"What are you talking about, bait?"

"Oh, my man, there's things you need to know, and I don't have lots of time left."

He was the one person who, after the funeral, would surely be turned out. In fact, I couldn't quite understand why with Harrison dead he was still here. If I had a home, I would have gone to it. Maybe Webster hadn't settled up with him yet on his pay.

He turned his attention to the stable, looking from ceiling to floor before he turned around and pulled the doors closed behind him. A moment he lingered there, head down; then he faced me. His eyes were still bloodshot and strained. "Weren't no sickness did for the gen'ral. *It* come and took him. Wit' my own eyes I seen it."

"Seen what? You're making no sense."

He shook his head, walked heavily past me, and sat down on one of the hay piles. "You need to hear the story from the beginning. When it comes back, you gon' need to know its signs. I didn't know 'em. Nobody knowed 'em. Nobody knowed to look."

When I didn't respond, Isaac gave a nod as if to say that he realized how crazy he sounded. He studied the rafters awhile as though counting the doves, then all of a sudden asked, "Mr. Christian, what you think is the single most fearful thing in all the world?"

I made no answer. I'd no intention of helping him flog his story.

A funny little smile played on his lips. Only then did he lower his gaze. "I tell you what. If I can name you the worst thing, an' you agree, then you stay and hear what I gots to say. That acceptable to you?"

I leaned against the doors. Finally I nodded, figuring the sooner I did, the sooner we were done with this.

He closed his eyes and seemed to drift off for a moment. Then he said, "The most fearful thing is when somethin' happens all round you and all you can do is watch helpless while it takes ever'body else."

His words flung me back to the day I'd returned from William and Mary College on the coach that bore Judge Christian and me home. Riding on the back, I leaned out and scanned the faces of all the servants and family lining the driveway to greet us, seeking my mother's welcoming smile. But it wasn't there. Turned out while I was gone off learning and toting for Judge Christian, she'd been sold off—sold off by the man who took her. He disposed of her just like that and refused to tell me when I begged to know where she'd been sent. Said he'd found her "inconvenient." After that he didn't care much for my presence neither, so to get me out of his house he gave me to his daughter—his daughter, who'd been my playmate once upon a time.

I thought of how fragile everything was with Mel, how easily history could repeat, which was why she and I stayed cautious and pretended detachment, scared that if we breathed a word aloud as to how we felt, Tyler or somebody would make a point of separating us forever just to punish us for thinking it. I didn't trust even Samuel. I'd told her I loved her, and now wasn't I stuck here in this decrepit house, hundreds of miles from her? You care about anything at all, it's certain to bite you. They always see to that.

I come back to myself, realizing I must have been lost in thought a good five minutes. I went over and sat beside Isaac on the hay. "All right," I said. "I'm listening."

He gave a nod. "Truth is," he said, "as you've suspicioned, I got dismissed before the gen'ral even died, on account of what I saw."

"How did you know I was thinking that?"

He made a flat smile. "Whatever you do, Mr. Christian, don't ever tell that man Webster nothin'. But *you* need to know that this house ain't right an' they folks don't see it."

Overhead, doves cooed and settled again. Dust continued to float on the sunbeams that wormed straight through the cracks in the doors. It was warm and thick and sleepy, like time in there had stopped.

Isaac said, "Saturday nights in the President's House they's almost always a soirée. Wednesdays is for the *formal* dinners."

Five

Wednesday nights General William Henry Harrison held large formal dinners as was the custom in the President's House. On these occasions he always measured up to his reputation as a talker and a prodigious drinker. In the past weeks, however, it seemed to Isaac that the man he served was drinking to escape himself, and that his talk was troubled, sick at heart, maybe even fearful.

That particular night, while Isaac dressed and coiffed him, the general abruptly commented, "Anna loves parties so." Then he stiffened and stared into the mirror as if just recalling that Anna, his wife, wasn't there.

She had been too ill to travel to his inauguration, and the bone-chilling weeks of cold that followed had kept her back home in Indiana. Harrison had been relying upon his widowed daughter-in-law, Jane, to act as his hostess.

Isaac tried to reassure him: "She'll be here soon, sir. You know she's comin'."

The general nodded tightly.

He tied Harrison's cravat then. But looking up, he found the general's gaze flicking repeatedly past his shoulder to that dresser mirror. Isaac could not help but turn around to see for himself why.

The mirror reflected back the two of them in yellow lamplight—nothing out of the ordinary at all.

Harrison brushed his hands down his lapels, made a crooked smile, and said, "There, now, Isaac, I'm ready. Let us go greet the guests," as if it was he, and not Harrison, who was troubled. He walked out to where his daughter-in-law awaited him in the hall, and the two of them descended the staircase together.

In the Washington Parlor, the president greeted his guests, declined offers of an aperitif—"I am late, and you are all hungry"—and offered his arm to Dolley Madison in her white turban and beaded gown. Sandwiched between the two women, he led the way into the dining room, even giving Isaac a wink as if to say everything was under control.

Tall folding screens had been stood up in the dining room doorway to keep the furnace heat from escaping into the hall with the doors thrown open.

The large fireplace with marble caryatids on each end of the mantel was burning brightly. It was a chilly night, but with the coal-fired furnace stoked and the fireplace ablaze, the dining room was near as balmy as summer.

The dinner guests included Secretary of State Daniel Webster and his son, Fletcher; the mayor of Washington, William Seaton, and Henry Gilpin, both longtime friends of Harrison's; and a curly-haired man who had not to Isaac's recollection attended any previous dinners.

Isaac took up his position out in the hall, in a chair against one of the vestibule columns should the president need him. From there between the screens he could see the general at the head of the table.

Others arranged themselves and took their seats. Harrison remained standing. He poured himself a glass of claret and with it pointed to the curly-haired man, who was seated down the table to his left.

"Gentlemen and ladies, I want to present to you our new collector for the Port of New York, Mr. Edward Curtis."

Everybody huzzahed or repeated the name. Harrison tossed back his claret and refilled his glass. He remained standing. "As some of you will know," he said, "Mr. Curtis here was not the choice of our fellow Whig, Henry Clay. In fact, the senator downright objected to our choice and made it plain that I was to fall in line with his wishes or else." He paused to sip some more claret. "We should enjoy this wine while Congress still allows." The guests laughed appreciatively. Isaac admired how the general could gather people's attention and hold it till it was ready to snap. The man loved to talk, that was for sure.

"Now, everyone here may have heard tell of Henry Clay's brag to some other Whig senators that he would be running the president however he likes, on account of my assurances while campaigning that I am just a simple, retired military man with no head for politics." The guests chortled. "'Why, I place myself completely in your hands, Senator,' is what I recall saying at the time. So it is just possible I left him believing he would be running the show." More chuckling.

"It thus proved necessary that I sat Senator Clay down in my office yesterday and said, 'Now, Senator, would you do Mr. Curtis here the kindness of explaining to him which one of us is the president of these United States?'"

The group guffawed and hailed Harrison, although Isaac could see Daniel Webster, seated beside Mayor Seaton, frowning. Webster was always going on about political capital, and Isaac guessed that to Webster the general had just spent a little too much.

"He did not reply to me then, but I do believe he has by now figured out the answer to this question." Smiling, Harrison sat down, and the soup was served. The dinner began. The first bottle of claret had already been emptied.

>>>> - <<<<

By midnight, having retired to the oval Blue Saloon, only Harrison, Seaton, and Fletcher Webster remained. As happened at the dinners and parties in the President's House where Dolley Madison was in attendance, most of the gathering had drifted across Lafayette Park to her house to continue their revelry there.

Fletcher Webster, smoking a cigar, teetered to the fireplace where he threw away the butt. Seaton dozed upon his chair, a half-full glass of sherry on the small table beside him. Harrison sat aslant upon the deep blue Empire sofa. Isaac had hauled his chair against another of the marble pillars of the vestibule and was himself close enough to unconscious as to be uncertain he wasn't dreaming everything he saw through the doors.

Harrison stood suddenly as if recalling an important matter, his prominent nose as red as his cheeks, his eyes glassy and unfocused. He teetered past Webster. At the door he turned back and gestured at the bottle on the floor beside the sofa. "Young man, finish that or take it with you. If I see it in the morning, I'll be green at the gills." He plunged then out into the hall like a sailor braving a ship's deck during a storm.

The words brought Isaac fully alert, and he jumped to his feet, wiping at his eyes. The general tried to wave him off. "I am fine," he insisted, and lurched away so quickly that he was at the dining room screens before Isaac could catch up.

Harrison allowed Isaac to guide him up the stairs to the private floor, where he tried to aim the general toward his corner bedroom; but Harrison abruptly announced, "No, I must go to my office first!" and dragged them off on a new course. Some notion of unfinished business had suddenly struck him.

Isaac never learned what it was. They had charged but a few feet when Harrison stopped so abruptly that Isaac thumped up against him. The general was staring off to the side exactly as he had done earlier into the mirror in his room. But this time he looked as if he was about to scream.

The door of the room across from them was swinging wide open without a sound.

The hair prickled on the back of Isaac's head. That room, currently unoccupied, was to be Anna Harrison's when she arrived.

Through the doorway he spied red flocked paper on the wall above a white dado and chair rail. The wall seemed to glitter oddly in the dark, as if the wallpaper was speckled with fireflies. A round table deep inside bore something that looked like the sort of glass dome you might put over a half-eaten cake. In the deepest shadows of the far corner, a tall and skinny mirror stood, and despite its location, it seemed to be reflecting back lamplight from the hall.

Nobody came out of the darkness.

For perhaps half a minute the two men stood there, Isaac bearing most of their weight. He was looking around desperately for a chair when the general suddenly called, "Anna?" and tore himself free of Isaac's grip. "Anna?" he cried again, and barreled right at the doorway.

Isaac sprang after him, but then a light bright as a lighthouse lamp flashed out of that doorway, so intense that even with Harrison between him and it, he instinctively threw his arm in front of his eyes for fear they would be scorched. Blinded and doubled over, he dared to look up. The door in front of him slammed shut.

He blinked until he could see clearly again in the dim hall. He shook his head.

The general was gone.

Isaac ran over, grabbed the doorknob, and pushed. The door wouldn't budge.

Hard as he could, he threw himself against it. The first time it was stone. The second time it gave as if it had never even been on the latch, and Isaac hurtled inside and nearly fell straight into the tall mirror before he could stop.

The room lay empty.

Harrison was not there, much less his wife. There was a bed, a night table beside it supporting an oil lamp, a basin, and a jug, and a wardrobe against the opposite wall that could have held at least two people. The table with the glass dome on it must have been a trick of the light. It wasn't there.

Isaac flung open the doors of the large wardrobe. Sitting on the bottom shelf was a pair of black, buckled, low-heeled pumps. Why they were in there, he couldn't fathom. He picked them up to examine them, but already knew that they were the general's. Isaac had polished those shoes that very afternoon. The pewter buckles were unmistakable. He rubbed his thumb against the waxy leather. It felt warm.

He set down the shoes, then leaned over farther and looked under the bed. Nothing.

He turned about. Deeply shadowed as it was, the small room offered nowhere to hide.

In the light from the hall, the elaborate flocking of the red wallpaper seemed almost to pulse and shift like something viewed through rippling water.

It was clear that the general had not entered, but must instead have run off down the hall while Isaac was blinded. Improbable as that was, no other explanation presented itself.

He would have walked out then, but the tall mirror bothered him. Its cloudy and tarnished surface made him take stock of the room again.

What could have flashed so brightly? Certainly not that dull glass. And where was the source of it? There was no candle lit, no fire in the hearth, not even so much as a framed portrait hanging on the wall.

He stood before it, and the mirror reflected him as no more than a silhouette, a smudge without identity.

What prompted his next action, he could not say, but he reached out to press his fingers to the glass.

The fingers and then his whole hand to the wrist passed into the smoky surface. He gasped and snatched back his hand.

The other side of the mirror—wherever that was—was as cold as if he had plunged his hand into a frozen pond.

Isaac was not aware of backing from the room, but the next he knew, he stood out in the hallway and the door was closing in his face again. It latched with a delicate click.

Like a terrified horse he bolted then, first to the president's private chambers in the corner, surely the most likely place for the general to take refuge.

The silent bedroom was lit from the candle on the mantel that had been left by one of the housemaids when she'd turned down the bed for the night. But no one occupied the room, nor was anyone in Isaac's small adjoining chamber.

He backed out and ran the length of the hall, calling, "General Harrison!" at each closed door. No one answered, neither there nor from the first floor, where his shouts surely must have carried.

He burst into the president's office, fully hoping to find the general at his desk, passed out or obsessively hunting for whatever documents he'd wanted. The room lay empty and dark, the fire gone out, cold.

He threw open the door to the small secretary's chamber in the southeast corner, then went back out into the waiting hall. He stared the empty length of the second floor. Two oil lamps lit it yellowly. All was silent. Uninhabited.

Isaac hurried down the east stairs to the first floor again, into the cross hall, where he walked its length and threw open every door he came to from the State Dining Room to the east end. Every room lay dark, every opened doorway led only to more stillness, emptiness.

He returned to the Blue Saloon. The last two revelers must have departed the moment the general went upstairs. The bottle of wine was gone too.

While Isaac hung in the doorway, the coal furnace groaned and the floor underfoot shuddered.

He must have been the only person awake in the entire house, if not the last person alive on Earth.

He could not have been upstairs but ten minutes by his count, yet even the chandelier candles were doused and the lamps blown out as if somebody had come along the hall to extinguish them the instant he and the general ascended the stairs. Only the chair he'd perched on all evening, still positioned against one marble column, evidenced that he wasn't lost inside a ghost version of the President's House.

The security of that chair spooled him. He hunched upon it, trembling, his fingers laced around his knees as he stared down at the floor like a man who hoped to be overlooked by a bear if he made himself small enough. He could neither force himself to go down to the kitchen floor nor upstairs again.

And then someone was hammering on the front door. It startled him awake. He had no idea that he'd drifted asleep on the chair. His back ached as he sat upright, and he had to hold onto the chair to stand. Stiffly, he walked to the door while trying and failing to convince himself that he had slept through the end of the dinner party and that Harrison, his employer, had kindly left him there. The whole terrible event upstairs—haunted room, mirror of no substance, shoes in the wardrobe—had been a dream. Of course it had. He would answer the door and find the president returning from Miss Dolley Madison's, or maybe tucked up in his bed already.

"I will attend it, Mr. Jasper," he called out, hoping that if the doorman had been awakened in his little room beneath the east stairs he would just roll over and go back to sleep.

In the doorway stood a bearded white man wearing a long coat, skinny as a scarecrow. Was a lamplighter, he said, and he leaned on a nine-foot dousing pole as if to prove it. He'd been putting out the lights along Pennsylvania Avenue not far from the house when he came upon an unexpected figure. "General was weaving a Virginia fence along the side of the road," he said. "I got him out here." He gestured behind him at a wagon.

Isaac came out onto the portico.

The lamplighter's name was Felton, and he led the way down the steps to the wagon. Dull lanterns hung off the sides.

At first it appeared the wagon was empty. But Felton led him around to the back, then stopped and pointed with his pole like Moses out of the Bible.

There, curled up in the wagon bed like a child, General Harrison lay muttering under his breath, oblivious of them. Mud smeared his tailcoat as though he had rolled through the swamps awhile and caught his shredded sleeves in the brambles and thorns. Small smooth rocks lay beside him, strewn across the bed of the wagon. He had indeed lost his shoes and stockings, and his feet were swollen, purple with cold.

It took both of them to get him down out of the wagon. He clutched wretchedly for the stones. One of his pockets was torn. The other spilled more stones. The general turned one over and over in his hands, then abruptly flung it away and made an awful gargling noise in his throat. He pressed both hands to his face.

Isaac and Felton managed to guide him into the house and up the stairs to the second floor. They walked him past the dreaded room, which remained closed, and into his chambers. He fell across his bed and appeared immediately to doze. Isaac left him there to escort Felton out.

Nobody else seemed to be awake, although it looked to be past time they should be. At least he would have expected to hear the noises of folks down in the kitchen—Mrs. Weems and the others. He would have gone to see, but didn't want to leave the general alone one more minute; and sure enough, after climbing the stairs again, Isaac encountered him emerging from his bed chamber and heading straight for that room. Isaac barred his way.

Tears streamed down Harrison's cheeks and he blubbered, "Anna, I have to speak to Anna! Have to *warn* her." It was all Isaac could do to turn and herd him back to his bed, softly explaining all the while that "Missus Anna" was not here.

"She still back home in Indiana, sir. You know that's so."

Harrison sobbed.

After that, Isaac did not dare leave him. He tugged the bell pull beside the bed and a housemaid eventually came up from the kitchen. Groggy and blinking, she said that all of them had overslept, as if they had drunk something or been placed under a spell. Isaac told her to send for a doctor right away.

Once she had hurried off, he lit a lamp and started to undress the general, intending to get him into his nightshirt and under the covers. He sat him up, tugged the coat off, then unbuttoned the vest and opened up Harrison's shirt. He gasped and unwittingly let go. Harrison flopped back on the bed.

Square over his heart lay a handprint like a red raw brand of five long fingers burned into the skin.

He didn't know what it was, but after that he could not make himself touch Harrison. He covered him up, then sat in a chair across from the bed and waited.

The doctor arrived accompanied by Daniel Webster—it seemed they were neighbors. The doctor immediately dosed the general with laudanum "as a precaution," he said, although Harrison was already near-insensible. So drugged, he slept through the whole next day, plagued by bouts of chills, fevers, and delirium, which came and went much like the parade of physicians who attended him from then on. One forced calomel down his throat, and another insisted to Webster that he must be bled. No one commented on the strange mark upon his chest, but the second morning Isaac saw that the handprint was gone.

Had Harrison not been dying before, a few days of skilled medical assistance and he was well on his way to the grave. He babbled still about Anna and needing to get back to "that room" to see her again.

"Delirious," pronounced Webster.

That was when Isaac made the mistake of insisting that there *was* an evil room, and he'd been inside it. Webster glowered, but Isaac couldn't help himself then. He described the aftermath of the dinner party in full. It sounded crazy to him even as he spoke. "You can go and ask that lamplighter fella, Felton. He found the gen'ral on the avenue."

Webster said nothing, but went off.

He was absent a quarter of an hour. Then, from the hall, he called to Isaac. He waved a hand about. "Show me this infernal room."

Isaac led him straight and unhesitatingly to the room down the hall. It stood open, as did all the doors on the second floor. Webster had opened them.

"What color is this wallpaper?" Webster asked.

Isaac shook his head. "It's green, suh."

"Care to try another? No? I can save you the trouble, for I've opened every one. There is no room with red flocked wallpaper anywhere on this floor. Not a one. Tall mirrors we have three, and each one is quite solid."

Isaac entered the green room and hesitantly pressed his hand to the dull glass. This was the mirror, surely. By now his hands were perspiring, and he left a moist palm print upon it.

Webster watched from the hall, arms crossed, eyes smoldering. He allowed Isaac to scurry on from one room to the next, but Isaac stopped after only a few.

He returned to Webster and pointed at the first one. "*That* was the room, I swear it. The gen'ral could tell you. He seed his wife in there. *I* didn't see her. Was him charged inside before—"

"You are a most ignorant retainer and I expect if we search we'll find that you stole the claret left behind when my son and the mayor departed, and having gotten yourself good and liquored, you either imagined or invented this wild story to cover up your failure to look after your employer. If in his inebriation he wandered shoeless out into the night—and that part of your story is regrettably all too plausible—then you failed him doubly. If he dies, it is upon you."

The last stung the most. Isaac already believed it.

"I want you to pack up and be out of this house before I return."

Webster now had to act on Harrison's behalf with the Congress. He soon departed.

The moment he was gone, Isaac returned to the general's side. No matter what the rest of the *wise* men believed, he would not allow Harrison any opportunity to reach that room again. In his soul he knew that the red room awaited him somewhere.

⟫⟫- -⟪⟪

Another day and night he remained at the bedside, retreating only when Webster turned up; and then he made someone else on the staff take his place while he hid.

Two nights later, Harrison began to jabber fearfully as if to someone who stood at the foot of his bed. At the first words, Isaac sprang to his feet.

"When did you make the sun stand still, the moon change course? Are the dead rising from their graves? No! You cannot!"

He stared where the general did. There was nothing to see.

Isaac placed a hand on Harrison's shoulder, which immediately calmed him and he lay back. He drifted awhile, lips twitching, but no more words emerged for perhaps half an hour, until out of his sleep he shouted, "No more applications!" and waved his hands to disperse a plague of petitioners, and his legs scissored under the sheets as if he was running.

The final time he woke, late in the night, he sat upright and wailed, "It's worse, much worse than they know!" then sagged back against the pillows, his head canted to the side, mouth half-open, a gob of spittle slowly spilling over his lip. An awful crackling noise emerged from deep in his throat.

Isaac tugged the bell pull furiously. When no one came right away, he rushed into the west stairwell. Another servant was hurrying up from the kitchen with a lamp, but Isaac yelled at her to have the doctor sent for immediately, and she retreated to the first floor to find Jasper.

For days Isaac had gone with little sleep. Thus when he dragged himself back up to the second floor and found the door to the general's chambers shut, he could only think that he had closed it in his rush to get help.

It opened easily, but the room lay in darkness.

No question the bedside candle had been lit when he ran for help. Now only the hall sconces behind him threw a hint of light upon the scene.

There appeared to be a dark shape hovering at the foot of the bed exactly where Harrison had imagined someone two nights past. "Gen'ral?" Isaac called. It was like a man cut out from a shadow. It reminded him of his own silhouette in the tarnished mirror of the evil room.

He could not make his legs walk him any farther.

The housemaid returned. She started to tell him a doctor had been sent for, but Isaac snatched the lamp out of her hands and thrust it ahead of him into the room.

The light, though it fell upon chairs, writing desk, curtains, and washstand, did not illuminate nor penetrate the dark form between him and Harrison. Behind his shoulder, the maid made a small noise, almost a whine.

"Sweet Jesus, save me from harm," he whispered. Then he rushed at the figure.

Upon his third step, the silhouette ruptured and scattered. By the hundreds, spiders scuttered up into the dark recesses far overhead, leaving behind a gossamer curtain, ripped down the middle where they had been pressed tight. The shredded web fluttered from floor to ceiling as if breathing.

The girl behind Isaac moaned out "Lord" now, but by then he was swinging his arms at the web, so furious in his terror that he nearly smashed the lamp on the bedstead, which would have set the whole room ablaze. He tore through the sticky strands to reach the general's side, but there was nothing left to do.

The doctor soon arrived in the company of both Websters. Isaac tried to explain what had transpired, told them to ask the maid if they doubted him. She, pressed back in the doorway, stared at them all as if they'd grown horns.

Webster silenced him. He had Fletcher escort Isaac downstairs, bellowing down the stairwell, "I informed you, sir, that your duties were at an end in this house. Yet you persist. The man you served is no more, and no one wants to hear gullible fool talk about rooms that swallow you or spiders that dress up as ghosts!"

Yet even as he called down his judgment, the Great God Daniel was trying to rid his fingers of the filmy strands of something that had clung to them from the foot rail of General William Henry Harrison's bed.

Six

James Hambleton Christian

Late in the afternoon, Mr. Tyler returned. The coach rolled up, and hadn't even stopped moving before he sprang furiously from it and stormed past me and Jasper on the portico. Jasper started to go after him, but he was already inside.

Webster remained seated in the carriage until it was fully at rest. Then, stiffly, he rose up and, holding his walking stick and with my assistance, climbed out.

"James," he said with his usual scowl. "It is James, isn't it? James, you will please undertake now to staff the *entire* house rather than the few key positions that your master originally requested." He could see I was perplexed. "The current staff is to be released. Oh, not you, Mr. Jasper, nor the blacksmith—but you are the exceptions. Everyone else. Oh, and they are not to meet, your people and theirs. Is that understood?"

I nodded.

He raised his stick then and continued on across the portico and into the house, muttering to himself, "Got himself sworn in without them, of course they punished him. What did His Accidency expect? *Accidency!*" and then barked a laugh before he stepped through the doorway.

"Well, what d'ya make of that?" asked Jasper.

I didn't answer, lost just then in contemplation: I could bring Mel here now without requiring an excuse. I left Jasper, climbed up on the driver's seat beside the footman, and rode with him back to the Jackson stable.

Mel would be coming. I wanted to cheer the Congress.

Now I had to fill every position, but so what? We would need maybe fourteen people. Scullery, housemaids, footmen, a coach driver. And a body servant to Tyler, because the last place I was going to find myself stuck living was in the servant's room off his bed chamber. No, I would be the butler for the household and have me that solitary room off the mess. Then Mel could be with me whenever she liked.

The whole time we spent backing the carriage into the brick stable, I spent enumerating and matching people from Virginia to positions in the household. Mel would want fourteen-year-old Zenobia in the kitchen with her, so I would include her. And gangly Marcellus, who was skilled at curing meats and worked well alongside them, and was also handsome and presentable for the dining room. Mel liked him too. *Mel.*

The coachman meanwhile unharnessed the two horses, held them by their reins until I finally noticed he was staring at me with a discontented expression. "You overheard Mr. Webster," I said.

"Did. All us being sacked, it's damned unfair when we all's worked hard here."

I realized that, lost in my thoughts, I might have been smiling, so now I tried to look as troubled as he did, regretful. "You know, I'm going to have to tell everybody how it is. I hope you'll ask them to allow that it's not my choice to make, nor even, I gather, Mr. Tyler's." What I really hoped was that he would go tell everyone they were not being kept on so that the bad news wouldn't have to come from me.

I said, "You go on, walk those horses down to Absalom. I'll close up this stable for you."

"Obliged," he answered, then led them off across the south lawn. I took hold of one of the stable doors to close it.

A coach rolled by on the paths below. As I closed the door, I imagined taking this coach out with Mel, driving her to market or just out for an afternoon on the banks of the river where it wasn't so swampy. We'd never even shared a buggy ride. Times she'd been called by some friend of Tyler's to come and ply her *makaya* healing with plants and poultices, one of the footmen had been sent along to drive her. Not the house—

I stumbled and caught myself against the door. I had tripped over a shoe. The coach must have rolled right over it, pushing it into a patch of mud.

It was a black buckle shoe, and that was odd. That it lay in the only mud puddle visible anywhere about was odder still. I couldn't be sure, but I thought I recognized the shoe, and I squeezed between the door and the rod of the carriage and walked back inside the stable. "Isaac? Isaac, you about?"

Dead stillness answered me. The dusty old firepump, horse collars, everything was the way it had been before. Even so, I circled the carriage and returned to the doors, where I couldn't help but lean out to peer at the East Room windows. Nothing moved there. Of course not.

I'm sure Isaac had sensed when he finished that I didn't much credit his story of Harrison's death. The door swinging open—that had happened to me already, too, hadn't it? Just meant if you stepped in the right spot, the floorboards of the hall flexed and caused a door that didn't close too well to unlatch. Nothing evil about it. Superstition and magic made folks crazy. My mother had believed there was a ghost in the slave's quarters at Tyler's plantation. It knocked on the walls sometimes to talk with her and some of the others. I was eleven, and its rapping half-scared me to death, until one early morning I came upon a stray cat outside, kicking its hind leg against the wall where it or some other cat had sprayed. Couldn't convince her—I dragged her out to show her, but the cat had run off. Nothing I could do to persuade her nor anyone else. They had invested in their ghost.

That's how I felt about Isaac's tale. I was sure he meant well, but I couldn't countenance it.

Afterward, he had started to lead me out of the stable but then drew up, his eyes wide. He was staring at the house with such fearful intensity that I leaned around the door to follow his gaze.

The tall center window of the east side of the East Room was different than the others, and looked to open onto a small balcony over the colonnade. Just for an instant I thought I saw a person standing there, holding aside the black funeral drapery to look out at us; but as quick as that, the drape closed.

Isaac beside me kept on staring. "'Spect you should gwan back now," he said. "Go be with those folk so's you learn all you needin'. I think I'll have myself a rest in here, keep me outta ever'body's way, y'all so busy wit' the funeral."

Then he focused on me—sadly, I'd thought at the time, like he knew we wasn't going to meet again. I'd given him a polite smile and gone back to the house.

Now, as I carried the shoe with me, I glanced up at that balcony window. I rinsed it off using the kitchen tap. Everybody had a look at it. Mrs. Weems and Bibb both thought it could have been one of Isaac's shoes. It matched the ones Bibb and the other footmen wore, and no one else seemed to be missing one of theirs. But we were missing Isaac himself. No one had seen him since the morning. None of them knew he had gone out to the stable to speak with me either, just that he had left the mess at some point. Bibb speculated that, knowing he could not attend the funeral, Isaac had absquatulated before Webster caught sight of him and had him evicted. I agreed that seemed most likely, but the shoe in the mud puddle burrowed its way into my doubts and followed me the rest of the day like an old dog you can't shake free of.

Seven

President John Tyler waited beside the front desk of Brown's Indian Queen Hotel just after 7 a.m. The lobby was already chaos. By train, cart, horse, and steamboat, people had been arriving for over a day for the "funeral of the president." The words sounded odd if not ominous to Tyler.

Tyler's sour expression evaporated as he spotted Webster. "Why, Mr. Secretary," he said. "Good to see you." He heartily shook hands. "I won't be but a minute."

He returned to the hotel clerk, telling him to forward the bill to the President's House. The clerk glanced at Webster as if for confirmation. Keeping his cold blue eyes upon the young clerk, Webster gave a small nod. The young man straightened right up, snapped his fingers, and ordered the luggage hauled outside.

"Your slave?" asked Webster. He didn't see him around.

"I sent him out the servants and coloreds' entrance already to secure our carriage."

They maneuvered through the clusters of travelers, none of whom knew how close they were to their new leader. Behind them, the desk clerk called, "Sold out! Ladies and gentlemen, there are no more rooms available for today!"

Webster made conversation. "You know, some of Fox's British delegation reside here."

Tyler chuckled. "Yes, I heard tell there was someone beastly in the place."

They climbed aboard their carriage. Tyler's man had seen to the luggage and climbed on the back beside it, his knees drawn up.

As they rolled off along Pennsylvania Avenue, distant cannon fire echoed in the air. The doors of the buildings lining the avenue were festooned with crepe black bows and wreaths.

The carriage soon reached Lafayette Park, slowing as it interrupted a line of people in the street. A congestion of wagons, coaches, horses, and clusters of military assemblies filled the park. The twin iron gates in the front fence had been thrown wide open, and the carriageway was already jammed with vehicles. The line of mourners through which they had cut on the road trailed out the east gate, across the park, and well up New York Avenue.

Tyler had the carriage stop at the west gate. "We'll never reach the house this way," he said, then called, "James! Have the coach go around to the west stables, and haul the luggage in through the side entrance."

He climbed out and waited for Webster to join him. Together they walked up the carriage path, weaving around the other vehicles, Webster striding with his walking stick as if it were a morning constitutional. Some of the people in line recognized him, but none knew Tyler. Webster enjoyed their looks of bemusement as Tyler strode right past them to the door. One man called out "Scalawag," and Webster half-raised his stick, but Tyler ignored or failed to attribute the jibe to himself and rapped on the door. Jasper let him in. A half-dozen more tried to push in after him. Webster simply glared at them and they backed away. He hadn't lost his touch.

⟫ ⟪

Harrison's coffin had a viewing window in it. In the East Room, two of the screens normally used to contain heat in the State Dining Room at the other end of the house had been erected to allow mourners—many of them women—a private moment with the body of a president most of them could hardly have met much less known. Some mourners placed flowers on top of the casket and the bier. Already the floor around it was piled with them. Tyler and Webster only spent a moment there. Both had already had their private viewings. This was more to make sure everything was as it should be.

They exited through the connecting door to the Green Parlor. The hall was thick end to end with milling people. Quickly, they crossed and went up the east stairs. They had only just settled into Tyler's office—substantially more organized than Harrison had left it—when Harrison's widowed daughter-in-law, Jane Irwin Harrison, was escorted to the room. Mourning clothes and a veil all but hid her prim face.

It was obvious to Webster that Tyler barely knew her. His brief conversation proved inane—how was she today, and did she think the weather would hold? Admittedly, the sky was threatening this morning; but Webster suspected that Tyler knew her husband had died of alcoholism, and could not decide whether or not to offer condolences when it had been over three years since the man's death.

In the lull of his indecision, she spoke to Tyler of how she had acted as the general's proxy hostess at the weekly soirées. "My goodness, a surrogate hostess, now there's an idea," said Tyler. He shot Webster a dark look as if accusing him of having withheld this information.

The tea arrived. Out in the park, a Marine band began playing the first of many somber tunes.

⟫ ⟪

Shortly after noon, the black funeral car arrived, a coach with leaded glass sides, and drawn by six white horses, each accompanied by a colored man wearing a turban and green jacket. Webster had hired them.

From the portico, Reverend Hawley gave a speech in which he assured everyone that at the end General Harrison had affirmed his faith in God. Following that, Webster watched as his son, Tyler, Mayor Seaton, and Secretaries Badger, Bell, and Ewing carried out the coffin to the car. Trembling, Jane Harrison followed. Some of the flowers gathered from the East Room were piled upon and around it.

Then Webster took his place beside Fletcher and they started off around the half-circle out to the park. They walked at a slow steady pace toward the Capitol. In the procession, Webster spotted ex-president Adams, members of the Judiciary, dozens of foreign ministers, commissioners, and department heads, and behind them even some of the city's fire companies. The procession was so long that by the time the funeral car reached the Capitol, the tail of it would still be in Lafayette Park.

Harrison's white horse was being led along too—the same horse he had ridden to his inaugural speech. The horse plodded along, his head low, as if he understood this was his last hurrah. *Poor horse*, thought Webster, although he felt as if his own last hurrah would be eternally delayed by his negotiations with the British in that cheerless house behind them.

Eight

James Hambleton Christian

I watched the whole of the staff leave the vestibule and join the rear of the procession. They might have been free colored folk, but they were kept as separated from the main body of the funeral as any group of slaves following their master's coffin would have been. I did not join them. I had never met the general in life, and had experienced too much of him in death. Once the staff were through the fence, I closed the front door. I was now the only person in the President's House.

⟫⟫ ⟪⟪

The windows of the president's bed chambers were open wide. The air inside no longer bore any trace of its former occupant, but was chilly.

Earlier, while the staff had waited their turn, Bibb and another fellow had helped me carry Tyler's trunk up to the second-floor hall. Now I removed my coat and gloves, and duck-walked the trunk through the doorway and over to the Philadelphia tallboy that stood in one corner, its doors ajar, and the drawers dividing top and bottom sections pulled out, emptied of Harrison's effects. Beside it was the door into the body servant's room, which as I'd suspicioned proved to be about the size of a large closet. I got my belongings and placed them on the bed in there. For my two coats and trousers, my few shirts and collars, I didn't need a tallboy. The next few days this would be my room, and I would tolerate it, knowing it wasn't a permanent arrangement. It smelled musty and unpleasant. They had aired out the bedroom but not the servant's room. I opened the window, closed the flue in the hearth, and left the door open.

Then I unpacked Mr. Tyler's belongings and filled the cupboards of the tallboy with the contents of his trunk. Where, I wondered, would we would store it? The back stairs, I'd noticed, went up another floor, and Bibb had made mention of having brought chairs in the East Room down from an attic.

Placing Mr. Tyler's dress boots in one of the lower cupboards reminded me of Isaac's story, and that in turn put me in mind of the door that had opened on me, just like the door in his story.

I closed the door to Mr. Tyler's room and started across the hall. I got maybe halfway there when the door, just like the last time, unlatched itself and drifted open.

I stopped, the hair on my neck bristling. Stood there, stuck. Reminded myself that it was the middle of the day. This had to be a loose floorboard I'd now stepped on twice. Only, this time I wasn't near the door nor the servants' stairs. The floorboards would have run on the diagonal. They didn't, and the boards under the hallway runner did not flex in the slightest.

The door had opened only an inch or two, but gave the impression that if I kept coming, it would swing wider to accommodate me. In my head I insisted *I deny such things*. But I could not move. I licked my lips.

Then from behind it came the hint of high and sweet laughter, lasting just for a moment.

It was that teasing laugh of Mel's that dared and invited me with such promise as could hardly be denied.

It couldn't be real, but my whole self wanted to rush forward to her, and I might have gone through that doorway if it hadn't been for the other sound that interrupted: pounding somewhere below. The thumps echoed all through the house, snatching me back to Isaac's lamplighter, and the moment Fletcher Webster had arrived at the plantation. I bolted for the main stairs, deciding then and there I would let Bibb take Mr. Tyler's trunk up to the attic.

Before I reached the bottom, the pounding came again. It wasn't from the front door. I stood in the hall, waiting. It came again, from the Washington Parlor. I went in.

The shapes of two figures played upon the drapery of the left-hand window, which was also a disguised door. I wondered why these visitors hadn't come around to the north entrance.

The door opened onto the curved south portico. Two men. From their sweat-darkened shirts and canvas pants they appeared to be laborers of some kind. One had wavy red hair. The other, curly black hair. He looked to me like a gypsy.

The men asked the obvious and, I thought, unnecessary question of whether I worked here at the house. Indeed I did, said I. The pride that swelled with that admission caught me by surprise.

"Well," said the red-haired fellow. He sucked on a small clay pipe. "Been an accident and we need for yas to come tell us if'n the poor wretch worked here too."

I thought maybe someone at the back of the procession had been run down. *Carriage accident* was what I was thinking.

They waited until I said, "Why, yes, sir, be happy to." Of course I had left my coat and gloves upstairs, but they were already starting down the steps, so I closed the door and hurried down after them.

We didn't go around to Pennsylvania Avenue. Instead, they walked on down the lawn, stepped over the stone wall, and crossed the carriage paths toward the river, into marshy ground. Someone had laid out a makeshift walkway of busted-up crate boards over the worst of it. Some of the wet patches under the boards remained covered in a thin icy film. I was sorry now I didn't have my coat.

As we navigated the walkway, I inquired why they thought their particular wretch worked in the President's House, and the man with the pipe explained that it was the clothes—"black coat, the brown knee breeches, and the buckled shoe." I nearly stumbled off the boards. Now I had a terrible presentiment.

We climbed up on the verge along the canal. A half-dozen people were clustered around a body, which had been laid upon the thick timbers that lined its edge. *It's some old man*, I thought.

Twenty feet distant, two workers were just shutting the nearest of the lock gates by pushing at the beams attached to the top of each one. The gates thumped as they collided in the middle to seal off the canal. The men waved to the two who'd brought me down.

The people looked at us approaching and stepped aside.

"Him and I come out this morning to open theys gates," said the pipe smoker, "and we seed this here fella hung up 'gainst 'em. Tain't very deep, but you jump off'n the middle and land on your head, deep ain't yer problem."

The skin on the body had grayed beneath the muck that coated him. The right arm was twisted up flat underneath as if the shoulder bones had separated. The threads I'd noticed unraveling at the shoulder had come away completely now, exposing the pale lining of his sleeve.

A yellowish sock dangled from one foot, wet and limp. The shoe on the other matched the muddy one I'd carried in with me from the stable.

Isaac's hair was no longer just shot with gray. Matted and half-smeared with muck, it had gone white as a powdered wig. His eyes were not quite closed, as if he was lost in some deep contemplation.

Mud—and I had wondered where the water by the stable could have come from. Had he been snatched so fast that the shoe had come off? Or had it been thrown back up there for me to find? The act of someone gloating and proud of their crime? Either way, poor Isaac hadn't absquatulated, but he sure should have.

I asked them, "How d'you mean, he was hung up against the boards?"

The smoker said, "Looked like he tripped off the lock itself an' fell, slid down head-first. That rough wood caught in his back and hung him upside down. Only his legs was showing this morning, floating flip-flopped on the surface."

While he spoke, the gypsy-looking fella knelt and grabbed a fistful of wet shirt to roll the body over and show me the shredded coat back. Splinters thick as my fingers poked out of the coat like broken harpoons.

"Wood's deep in his back, a'right. It come away with him when we pulled 'im off," said the smoker. He puffed, and the other let the body roll onto its back again. The shirt tore from being pulled on so, exposing the center of his chest. The skin over his breastbone looked reddish raw, inflamed, like it had been branded.

I leaned forward, but the black-haired gypsy pulled the shirt halves together respectfully, looked up at me, and said, "So, he *is* one a yours then?"

Distracted, I nodded. "Yes, sir, he is. The man was President Harrison's body servant. Name of Isaac. I cannot give you his last name though, as I never heard it." I was ashamed that because I thought him crazy, I'd never asked. But mostly I wanted to pull the shirt open again, to prove what I thought I'd seen.

A burn mark in the shape of a hand.

➤ ❬❬❬

I took the stairs two at a time, came around the banister, and charged into the hall. The door still hung ajar but did not move now as I raced for it in outraged fury, shouldered it wide. It banged off the wall.

The room inside was empty, cold and lifeless as a stone. The windows were closed, the furnishings sparse: a bed, a chair, a table and candle, a small wardrobe. The walls had been papered in a floral green print above a white chair rail and wainscoting. It did contain a mirror as Isaac had described, but then so did Mr. Tyler's chamber.

If I had wanted to believe that Isaac took his own life—which is what Mr. Webster and Mr. Tyler would conclude when I told them the news—how was I to account for the shoe? I felt sure the beguiler, who and whatever he was, had left that calling card as a warning to me personally: *Give thy thoughts no tongue.*

Isaac had spoken of what he knew, and someone in the East Room had watched. Someone without mercy.

Nine

James Hambleton Christian

Isaac's funeral was considerably smaller than the general's.

It fell to Bibb and me to clean and dress him for burial. The white hair shocked everybody who saw it, but I could find no trace of the burn of a handprint on his chest.

Tyler's reaction when I told him was to shrug. "Obviously a matter for you to deal with, James." He'd never so much as clapped eyes on Isaac. Besides, his son had arrived in the city while they were lowering Harrison's coffin into the Congressional Burying Ground.

Robert Tyler had come down by train from Philadelphia as fast as he could. He was to serve as his father's secretary. Mr. Robert took after his dark-haired mother, with more flesh on his face and brown, inward-looking eyes, a less prominent nose than his father's. Fancied himself a poet, having published a book of poems two years previous, which everyone in the household who could read was obliged to peruse, including me and Devonee. Can't say that I found any of it measured up to the likes of Mr. Poe or Mr. Shakespeare, although his poem called "Death," with its lines about "old Chaos and Satanic strife," might have suited Isaac's drowning.

I would give Mr. Webster his due. Despite his irritation with Isaac, he paid for the burial cart that took the body up Pennsylvania Avenue to Mt. Zion Cemetery. A Methodist church owned Mt. Zion, and they'd set aside a portion of it for colored burials. It was in the opposite direction of the hotel and Capitol, north and west across a creek, a long sorrowful walk, but like the day before, the weather held as we strode beside the wagon.

A few whites along the way made catcalls, but most paused. Men removed their hats both along the sidewalk and in passing carriages. Death was death; only drunkards and villains took any delight by it.

I was invited to join in carrying the coffin to its final resting place. I appreciated that they respected me enough to have me join in when I was all but a stranger.

Isaac had no family, so it was just the household staff and me around his grave. Not Jasper, however. He'd remained behind: "Not on account of 'im bein' a darky or like that, but I'm staying on, an' they's all leaving. I don't think they'd much appreciate my intrusion."

After we'd lowered the simple coffin into the grave and a pastor had spoken, Hannah Weems placed three dice on the ground below the wooden cross that marked it. "Isaac enjoyed playing chuck-a-luck," she told me. It was really about all anyone seemed to know of him. As Harrison's body servant, he'd spent little time in their company, and been most reticent when he did.

After we returned to the President's House, everyone gathered in the mess room. I shared what remained of Webster's money among them. He had overpaid for the cart, which might have been intentional.

Somebody opened a bottle of wine swiped from the pantry. It would never be missed, since the people who knew the quantities of wine in the cellar were all sitting right here.

We passed it around. I don't know what that felt like to a bunch of free people. To me it was reminiscent of rare evenings in Virginia when the day's work was done and the Tylers had gone off to someone else's party and we were let be. First time I ever kissed Mel had been one of those nights, up against a beech tree. Lost in that memory, I didn't pay attention right away when Mrs. Weems started speaking.

"…a sixteen-year-old with us a month back," she said. "A likely girl name of Annabelle Costin." I found her staring at me as if to say, "I'm telling this for *your* benefit." I waited for her to say this girl had drowned in the canal too. But that wasn't it.

"Second night after the general moved in, he held his first private dinner party, wi' that Mayor Seaton and some o' them big bugs outta Congress. Annabelle, she did the cleanin' up after, and got left alone up in the public dining room. Next thing, I heared glass shatter and her screamin' and she near broke her neck flying down the stairs. Bunch of us come runnin'. Something she couldn't see, she said, chased her round the big table and in the stairwell."

The bottle arrived at me again, and I paused to take a pull before handing it on. "Meanin' no disrespect," I said, "but how'd she know it was chasing her if she couldn't see it?" I tried to keep a polite tone.

"Why, it bit at her," she answered. "They was bites on the backs of her shoulders and her legs, and right through her clothes." Others were nodding in confirmation. The girl, terrified out of her wits, had quit her position that night and never come back.

Mrs. Weems had barely finished when another of the kitchen women said that twice she had seen a face in a nighttime window looking in at her. A different woman asserted the same. "Terrible face, savage as a meat axe."

Now I discovered that everybody knew these stories, and most had one of their own. Harrison and this staff had only occupied the President's House for a month or so. The number of incidents beggared belief—empty chairs that set to rocking, or whole chandeliers that suddenly doused, every candle going out at once, and even bedding that rose up on an empty mattress one night in the lamplight as if somebody was climbing out of that bed. I heard that and thought, *Who would go back into that room ever again?*

"You make it sound like Harrison brought something terrible with him," I said.

Mrs. Weems replied, "That's it zackly." Turned out she had come on as the cook in the last year of Van Buren's tenure as president, and not a single unnatural thing had happened in "all that whole year. Was nuthin' strange here 'fore the gen'ral moved in."

I nearly asked if any doors had opened by themselves, but I didn't want to admit participation in what she was describing. That house with its draughts and filth and groaning coal furnace could scare the wits out of most anybody—Jasper, for instance, high-tailing it out of the East Room just a few mornings earlier with the rest of us on his heels, and none of us willing to admit our terror. And there was the threat of the muddy shoe.

That afternoon, after I took tea up to Tyler's office, I encountered Bibb. While the others had cast their stories around the table, he'd added nothing.

Standing in the second-floor stairwell, he explained he didn't want anyone else to hear this.

"Hear what?" I asked.

Two weeks before Harrison had taken ill, Bibb said he'd been dousing the candles on the public floor after another soirée when, at the end of the cross hall, the doors to the East Room had opened on their own without a sound.

That tightened my belly. "How near were you?" I asked.

"Between the Blue Saloon and the Green Parlor, heading that direction. Them doors couldn't wait. They opened up wide like to say 'Come on in.'"

He had tried to make himself go close them, but every step nearer convinced him something waited for him in the room. I tried to keep my expression untroubled. That was how it had felt a week ago with the general's body lying in there. I considered asking if Isaac had told him his story, but Bibb wasn't finished.

He claimed he could see shadows moving inside the huge room, sliding across the far wall and behind the curtains, though he knew for a fact there was nobody there. They'd gone to Dolley Madison's on Lafayette Square. Instead of trying to close the doors, he ran the other way, past the vestibule and down the stairs between the dining rooms. After that, he refused to set foot on the public floor alone after dark. Didn't tell anyone why. Annabelle Costin had been chased off by then, so nobody had to ask.

I wanted very much to embrace the notion that folks were just scaring themselves. They all had worked themselves into a froth, same as Jasper, Tyler, Fletcher Webster, and I had done that first morning. Nothing but a case of the fantods—that's what Mr. Tyler would have said. And maybe so. Maybe all the doors in this house just wasn't hung right.

After the two funerals, the atmosphere in the house seemed to lift, like the brume that flowed up from the Potomac in the mornings and dispersed as the sun rose. I wondered if, since strange occurrences had arrived with the general, they hadn't departed with him too.

The mourning decorations still hung in place. The staff, over which I had no authority, expressed no interest in replacing the emblems of death. They were still grieving the good man for whom they'd worked and did not care in particular what the man who was evicting them wanted beyond the basic necessities, which could have caused me considerable trouble. Fortunately, Mr. Tyler was so immersed in matters of state, he didn't notice. Breakfast was ready when he came down to the private dining room in the morning, and dinner and supper were prepared on time. I did most of the serving.

There weren't going to be any parties before the family had arrived, so I moved the chairs from the cross hall into the East Room myself.

Anytime I answered the bell pull and brought up tea, Tyler and Mr. Robert went right on nattering about vetoes, disputed borders, states' rights, or something called the Caroline Affair that involved Canadians crossing the border, setting fire to a ship, and murdering a colored watchman. Robert was helping sort through the chaos of papers in the office, and kept track of Tyler's schedule, making his appointments with cabinet members, congressmen, and various petitioners in the hall. Anybody who wanted to meet with Mr. Tyler had to go through him. And it was Robert to whom I gave the list of names to be brought from Virginia to staff the house.

Their relationship appeared mostly jovial, but one morning at breakfast Robert mentioned that he'd made an appointment for his father to meet with the ambassador of Haiti that day, and Tyler let loose on him. "Robert, if you're to be secretary to the president, then you must consider the ramifications before you agree to *anything*! Do you not realize that to recognize Haiti in any way would send a calamitous message to every Negro across the land? It would undermine the very fabric of Virginia society alone. To legitimize Haiti as a free nation would be to sanction a slaves' revolution, saying in essence, 'What a great achievement.' Why, the tens of thousands of our own slaves would rise up and slaughter every white man, woman, and child across the South. Imagine you and Priscilla and Mary all murdered in your sleep. Think of it, son!"

Red-faced and stung, Robert apologized. He promised to find a way to expel the fellow.

They argued this in front of me without the slightest hesitation. I might be commingling daily with free people, but I was nothing but a contented piece of property. What could it possibly matter what I heard?

A number of times that day, I climbed up to the waiting hall to deliver trays of tea or lunch to the president's office. The ambassador to Haiti—a thin black man in a proper suit—sat politely in the hall, waiting his turn. At first he met my gaze with large eyes that questioned if I could help him, which I couldn't, but after a few hours he ceased even to look up. "I am to wait," I recited to myself, "though waiting so be hell."

Robert Tyler's solution to the "Haiti problem" was to ignore the man until he went away. But he returned the following day, mixing with half a dozen white petitioners, all of whom acted like he didn't exist. They all eventually had their audience with the president. But not him. John Tyler was *never* going to acknowledge him or his country.

It took him three days of being ignored to fully understand what nobody would tell him to his face.

⟫⟫ ⟪⟪

That third morning, seventeen-year-old Marcellus arrived from Tyler's plantation in Virginia on Fletcher Webster's horse. Riding alone, he'd had to carry a letter written by Mr. Tyler and with the official stamp of the president of the United States to protect him from being waylaid on the road by slave-traders. As it turned out, nobody had bothered him.

His arrival meant that the wagons and coaches from the plantation were on the road not far behind, and we could expect them sometime after midday.

I informed Robert Tyler of the glad news, but he was not about to interrupt his father after the dressing down he'd received over the Haitian ambassador. He went to Daniel Webster instead.

Webster was meeting with a British delegation and their ambassador, Mr. Fox, in the Blue Saloon. Robert called him out into the hall to tell him, and he curtailed the meeting at once.

I led those disgruntled men to the front door. On the way, one of them, with a sharp tapering face, complained to short Mr. Fox, "We had hardly an hour. This is outrageous, Fox!" The ambassador made no reply, at least not within earshot.

When I returned, the blue room was empty. Webster had descended to the kitchen, where he'd sent Bibb to fetch everyone. As I arrived, he was handing out envelopes to each of them—their severance money for services rendered.

Webster apologized to everyone for the necessity of their swift departure and thanked them all for their service to their country. He then shook every hand, promised them all good references, and directed me to take note—that should we receive any such requests, I was to bring them to him personally. Mr. Tyler ought to have been here doing this, I thought, but he had hardly encountered them. To him they were like Haiti. He wanted them all gone before his slaves arrived.

I found myself unexpectedly moved at saying goodbye to these people I had just begun to know. In the course of one week we had seen two men buried, and I guess that had yoked us in some fashion.

I stood and watched them collect their belongings. Bibb, for instance, owned his livery. His previous job had been at the Indian Queen Hotel and he'd purchased his footman's uniform for that position. He hoped now they would take him back.

Had they all been slaves, so much of what they neatly folded and packed would have remained behind for whoever replaced them instead of being taken along to their homes. Their *own* homes.

Mrs. Weems' final act was to prepare a cold lunch for our midday meal. She washed up, and then she left too, giving me a generous hug under the east colonnade.

"You be careful, Mr. Christian," she said, "in'is dark house wit' its secrets."

I said I would. Unlike her, I had nowhere else to go.

Part II:
O Coward Conscience

Ten

James Hambleton Christian

Late in the afternoon, two carriages and a buckboard wagon rolled into Lafayette Park. The gates were open in anticipation of their arrival. I'd been keeping watch from the private dining room window and came out to meet them.

The afternoon was cool, humid, and windy. Black funeral cloth still adorned the columns around the portico, but some of it had broken loose to snap in the wind. One length of crepe had tangled in the chain of the lantern overhead, and it flapped about like something trapped.

The carriages were rented. The buckboard belonged to the plantation and was driven by Cyrus, whom I'd selected to be our coachman.

Eleven-year-old Tazewell hung out the window on the first coach, gawping at everything. He shouted out, "James!" then flung open the door and leaped from the moving carriage, with his sisters screaming and reaching after him. Just like his father, he couldn't wait for the coach to stop.

He ran up the steps, his arms out, and I knelt to receive him. "Well," I said, "if it isn't the great Franz Liszt himself. You been practicing while I was gone?" He hugged me tighter. "Goodness, boy, you act like we been parted for years. Or is this your way of getting around my question?" I pulled him gently back, and he couldn't keep himself from a little smile. "Yeah, I thought so."

Tazewell was a sweet child, but mischievous as the devil if he had half a chance.

"Your sister performin' her lessons?"

He glanced over his shoulder. Miss Alice, his fourteen-year-old sister, was still seated in the carriage. "She did," he confided, "on account of Priscilla made her. But she didn't like it a bit."

"And she told you this?"

"No. I was spying."

"Ah-hah. You sneaked off just so you could watch." He gave me that sly smile of his again. "You won't be able to cut the didoes like that here. This house is alive all day long." He made a little shrug. He would test it and see, that much we both knew for certain. I turned him loose and he scooted into the house.

The larger pieces of luggage were piled on the roof of the first carriage. Only one person rode up top behind the driver—Samuel, who looked at me all gloomy in his coarse linen clothes. When the coach stopped, he turned away to untie the cords belting the luggage. He didn't care for Tazewell's affection for me any more than he liked Mel's. Samuel was the sort who resented any attention being paid that he didn't get equal parts of. He'd been a field slave into his twenties, and having used his wits to escape that and become a house slave, he was by nature mistrustful and proud. He would have worked out how I—and not he—had been made steward of the house, and surely view it as another snub: steward, as well as Tyler's body servant. Plus, in my good fresh white shirt and gray wool vest, I was dressed like a genteel and him like a transported slave. Soon enough he would wear his own good clothes again and get a reward he wasn't expecting from me, but for now he'd be sullen.

Fact is, they was all being transported as slaves—white folk on the inside, them up top or clinging onto the back, and the rest in the rear of the buckboard. At least they weren't chained to it. I wondered how the free coloreds like Bibb got around the city. Did they have to ride on top of coaches with the trunks and the carpetbags? They might not be owned, but that didn't mean white folk had to treat them any different. I wished I'd asked Bibb more about free life while I had the chance.

The second coach carried five women atop it and almost no luggage. They had made the journey sprawled on the roof, and riding in the wake of the first coach, they'd received a bounty of dirt and dust all the way, and as they got up stiffly now, they swatted at themselves, and the dust rose up like a plague of gnats. Round-faced and peevish Olive, skinny Zenobia, Sally, who was my age, and Ethel—everyone I'd sent for. But most importantly, at the back, Mel.

Nearly as thin as Zenobia, she stood taller than everyone else. I could look at her and almost see her small breasts and slim hips through the osnaburg cloth she wore just like the rest of them.

She bent at the waist and put her hands on the coach roof. Straightened and stretched, catlike, her sharp jaw raised to the sky. She gave me the slightest slantendicular glance to say she knew I was there, an acknowledgment that left me hollowed out.

Mel climbed down off the coach and hopped to the ground. Like always, she wore a bright headwrap over her hair that she knotted in such a way that none of the other women seemed able to imitate. She was barefoot as she preferred to go even in the coldest weather.

How a slender woman from New Orleans, progeny of Haiti, could withstand cold the way she did was beyond me. I had only known Virginia, and I liked a fire anytime it wasn't summer.

I wanted to pick her up, carry her down to the colonnade and through the door like a groom with his bride. But I couldn't even pretend it. My duties were to the passengers.

I held the door of the first coach, that Tazewell had thrown open. My other pupil, fourteen-year-old Alice Tyler, emerged first; took my gloved hand to steady herself as she stepped down. She was a pretty girl with curly dark hair, and a more accomplished pianist than her brother, good enough to entertain family, friends, and neighbors at parties.

"I'm delighted to see you, James," she said, sounding like the grown-up she was in a hurry to become.

I gave her a bow. "Miss Alice, I am twice as delighted to see you so well."

"Where's Tazewell got to?"

"I believe he went on inside, ma'am. You can inquire of the doorman, Mr. Jasper. He'll know."

She gathered up her skirts and went up the steps. She might have been practicing at being grown, but she and Tazewell still had no trouble getting into mischief together.

Last out of that coach was her elder sister, Elizabeth. Looking up at the house before descending, she said simply, "I thought it would be bigger."

I wanted to say that it wasn't a plantation house, but held my tongue, knowing that she was more than capable of complaining to her father if she thought anything said slighted her. I was just as glad that at eighteen she considered herself too old to be instructed by me on any subject.

I asked, "And how is Mr. Waller?"

"They wouldn't let him come with us," she complained. "Priscilla and mother. He wanted to ride along, have me up on his horse. They said it would be scandalous."

Billy Waller, her beau, had been the center of her universe for more than a year now. Her eagerness to be alone with him had caused plenty of trouble. Supervising her was three times the work of her younger siblings combined.

"I expect he'll come calling."

"Oh, yes," she assured me. "He has relatives in Washington, you know."

Well, I did now.

"Why didn't Father come out to meet us?"

"Expect he's trapped in some matter of running the country, Miss Elizabeth." Not that she would appreciate the one might prevail over the other. "You just go on in now. Mr. Jasper is at the door, and Marcellus is already here and can show you where your room is." She harrumphed but went up the steps.

The second coach was still closed. I peered in. The coach of my allies.

Miss Letitia lay across the width of it, a board beneath her and pillows propping her up. She held a prayer book across her middle, and her writing slate was wedged in beside her.

Across from her sat Miss Priscilla, her daughter-in-law, dark-haired in ringlets, and pale. She looked more like her mother-in-law's own daughter than did Elizabeth.

"James," said Miss Priscilla. Her baby lay in a wicker bassinet on the bench seat beside her and watched me upside down.

"Miss Letitia, Miss Priscilla, I hope your journey was not a difficult one. That's a long time in a coach."

"It was pleasant." She smiled to Letitia. "Good company always makes a journey easier. Robert is here?"

"Yes, ma'am. However, he's engaged in some business or other with his father at this moment." I knew nothing of the truth of that, but it seemed the most likely explanation. "Otherwise, he would surely have met your coach."

She gave me the bassinet. To Miss Letitia she said, "I will go see to having you taken up to your room." She glanced at me.

"Already being taken care of, ma'am." I addressed Miss Letitia: "Your room awaits. Bed linens are fresh, and the window open to air out. It's a little smaller than home, but I think it should do fine."

She nodded quickly, a gesture of hers that said she didn't want to be any trouble to anybody.

⟫⟫⟫ ⟪⟪⟪

Bald-headed Cyrus, Marcellus, the driver of her coach, and I bore Miss Letitia up the main staircase on the same board she'd ridden on. We were like a cortège carrying a great reclining queen to her throne, quilt and pillows under and around her. Her hands clutched her *Book of Common Prayer*, open to a page where I glimpsed the words, *"Oh, Lord, look with mercy upon my infirmities."*

Her room was next to Mr. Tyler's. The wallpaper was beige with a pattern of white vines and off-white sprigs adorning it. The bed was iron-framed and sturdy. We lowered her onto it.

A comfortable chair and a table with a full oil lamp stood next to it. I had brought up a copper washtub. It sat below the open window. Like the room across the hall that had opened to me, this one contained a tall Cheval glass, which was set in a marble base, and a *schrank* wardrobe with two rows of drawers at the bottom.

Cyrus and I took hold of the corners of the quilt beneath her and lifted her, while Marcellus and the driver slid the board away. Then we laid her upon her bed. She stared—it seemed fearfully—at the ceiling above her. I looked up to see what alarmed her, expecting a nest of spiders. The ceiling was fine. The plaster had a crack through it, and a few wisps of cobweb dangled down, but otherwise it was unremarkable.

The others took the board and left the two of us. I sat beside her a moment. "I know it's not as fine as the room back home."

She tried to speak, but I couldn't understand her. She patted around the quilt in search of the slate. We'd folded it in. I picked it up and offered it and the big piece of chalk, took the prayer book and closed it gently.

She wrote, *How is John?*

I said, "He's been very busy. I believe he and the Congress don't get along any too well. And General Harrison left things in a state."

She loured at this news.

"We'll have to get a cot in here for Devonee." I glanced round at the door, wondering why she had not yet shown up. By now everyone should have been inside and looking over their new accommodations. "That was a long journey," I told her, "but you're arrived now safe and sound. Do you need a necessary or anything?"

She shook her head, slurred, "No," as best she could. She had once had an almost musical voice, and she had loved to dance. In the early years after leaving her brother's service, I had played piano while she danced with various beaus. When she married John Tyler at twenty-three, I had played a waltz for them. Dancing was one of the things they had in common. Another was his ambition: She worked tirelessly for him. She had been a great one for laughter, too, and the light of it still shown in her eyes underneath the weariness of her invalided life. She hated that she was a burden.

For a second I contemplated asking her right then about giving me and Mel our freedom, but I knew better. Wasn't at all the right time. She had to be secure enough of Tyler's position to release me from mine. I had to walk a fine line here: to be essential but not irreplaceable. Our time would come—I had to believe that.

I put the matter away.

"Now," I said to her, "I'm going to leave you alone for a bit while I go find out what is keeping Devonee. You'll be all right?"

She rubbed the slate, wrote, *Thank you, James,* and then below that, *Dickens?* Her eyebrows were up, hopeful. It made her look like the little girl I'd grown up alongside.

I grinned. "Did they remember to pack *Oliver Twist* among your belongings?"

She gave a nod. Evenings I often read to her, and she was quite taken with the works of a British author by the name of Charles Dickens.

"All right then," I said. "I'll come up after supper." I gave her hand a pat, and placed the prayer book under it before I left.

Across the hall, the door did not so much as rattle.

Jasper was manning the front door as always. "What happened to everyone?" I asked him.

"The president's still up in 'is office an' Mr. Webster's in the Blue Saloon wiv—"

"No, I mean, where are the… Where's the *staff?*"

"Couldn't say. They can't come through this door—not the entrance for their kind."

Their kind. I had to remind myself that for him, my association with Tyler and Webster magically excluded me from bein' *their kind.*

I hastened down the stairs to the kitchen level. The hall was empty, the whole floor quiet. How could they not be here?

I went out the west door.

Below the colonnade there they all were, spread across the lawn. Sally, Olive, and Devonee were nearest. Seated against the pillars as if they had all the time in the world, they gave me big-eyed fearful stares. Across the hillside by herself, Mel sat on the ground, propped on her hands as if taking in the pleasant afternoon. Between us, the rest stood in clusters. Even Marcellus, dressed now in his proper livery and gloves, stood jawing with Tall George Washington, another of the household footmen I'd picked.

I turned to Devonee. "What are you doing here? Your mistress needs you upstairs right now."

She didn't answer right away but looked down the slope at Mel. Finally, she said, "We cain't go in there."

"Can't— What are you talking about?" Farther down the hill, strangers rode along the paths in their carriages or on horseback, none seeming to pay the slightest attention to the dozen or so slaves salting the lawn. Devonee kept watching Mel as if expecting instruction.

I glanced up at the windows of the dining rooms, at the big fanlight, fearful I would find Tyler or his son or even Miss Priscilla staring down at this scene.

I started toward Mel, but I spoke up so that all might hear me. "Why isn't everybody inside? Miss Letitia's lying up in her room alone and needing Devonee. Marcellus was…"—I turned to him—"Did you show Miss Priscilla her room, boy, before you come out here?"

"Yes, sir," he said, but he couldn't meet my eye.

"Well, where is the *luggage?* Still up by the carriage turnaround? You people must be in an all-fired hurry to get sent straight back to Virginia and put on the block!" I took off my gloves and slapped them against my thigh. "And me along with you!"

Mel patiently watched me approach.

"What is the *matter* with everybody?"

"James Christian," she said, "we can't none of us go in that house."

A group of men lounged on the south portico. That would be the party meeting with Webster, the British or the French—in my growing panic, I couldn't remember.

Right about then, Samuel bulled through the west doorway. He hefted a big stone jug in front of him that he held up for Mel to see.

She rose then, lissome as a gown, and glided on up to the house. Everybody fell in after her. I made a point not to look at the southside porch. Marcellus and I walked up beside Samuel. Sally, Olive, and Devonee got to their feet. Others crowded around behind us.

Mel had Samuel set down the jug and remove the big cork stopper in it. I was tempted to ask her, *You got Samuel doing for you now?* But I didn't want to have that conversation in front of everyone else neither.

She stuck her hand inside the jug. She announced, "First I got to call on Legba. Doors are t'resholds, and he the *lwa* in charge of all them gates and crossroads, and it no good crossing wit'out him."

Crossing what? I wanted to ask.

She couldn't possibly know any of the stories about this place. What could she have sensed on her own, without even going *inside*? She stared me down. We were in the part of her life now that I made it a point to avoid.

Mel was what the whitemen called an *obi*. Her mother and some New Orleans witch had trained her in the *makaya* arts—the things like pine vapors and sassafras teas and salves; but they'd taught her other skills too—ones that used dolls and figures and charms to call on certain dark gods and the like— things that I went out of my way not to hear of.

Vodou.

How many times I had turned a blind eye to the more witchy craft. I knew the healing and the *vodou* were inseparable—that her way with plants was only a part of it, and that the rest involved spirits and demons and a whole assortment of rituals that could have gotten her sold if not killed had the whitefolk heard about it.

The field slaves back home called her Mambo Mary, a name I was sure they'd made up. They were the sorts of brutes who swore that the devil takes the form of a singing blackbird so he can lure colored girls into the cotton fields and snatch their virtue. Funny how that old devil always turned into one particular man if you hunted him down and caught him. The Tylers called her Mary Elena, on account of they'd already owned three Marys when they purchased her. The rest of us had called her Mel from the day she arrived.

Just as Mel had no use for my quoting Shakespeare at her—calling her "my nightingale," or whispering in her ear that "the very instant that I saw you, did my heart fly to your service"—I would skedaddle when names like Bondye and Simbi were breathed and I knew she was going to go make a charm or level a curse at somebody. Not knowing about it was the only shield I had.

More than once I had purposely walked away rather than learn about her darker arts so I that could answer truthfully if Tyler ever raised the matter with me: "No, sir, I know nothing of it." She knew I did this to protect her.

Now I needed for her to get everybody in the house before the whole of the upstairs learned what was going on down here. I'd no time to argue it or to pull foot.

"Fine," I said. "Call on your Legba. Bless this door and get it done."

"It's not so simple as that."

She drew her arm out of the jug. Cornmeal spilled from between her fingers.

"This t'ing," she said, "already met you, James Christian, and it don't care about you bein' in the house, on account of you be like the mister—you don't recognize it even if it stare you right in the eye."

Well, I thought, that was insulting—to be already dismissed by the evil that put everybody else here in peril while bein' considered the same as Tyler.

She turned to the doorway, bowed her head. I could just see her lips moving in some kind of silent recitation.

Turning her fist as she leaned down, she opened her little finger and created a flow like out of a funnel. In the dirt below, a bright yellow cross formed. In each of the cross's four sections she drew a circle, and then inside each another cross. She grabbed more meal, laid a vertical line and three stars to the right. At the top and bottom of the cross she painted leaf shapes and curlicues and two more stars. Then with a third handful of meal she made more curlicues on the left and one final star. The silence of her chant grew to a whispered hiss of unfamiliar words. I took a step back.

The first night she came to my tiny room in Virginia, she'd walked around it, naked and whispery, making signs in the air. Afterward, lying next to me, she said gravely, "You bound to me now, James Christian," and I'd laughed on account of she didn't need any magic to accomplish that and ought to have known it. But I replied, "Yes, my nightingale," and she made her awful face.

Whenever somebody came to her for aid—when she made a potion or a poultice—that quiet, breathy stream of words would accompany its fashioning, and I couldn't have said if they were the same ones or something different for each complaint. That was as much as I knew or wanted to know of *vodou*. She could have been saying anything in my room. After she had made that face, I whispered back to her, "Being your slave what should I do but tend upon the hours, and times of your desire?" She told me to stop talking like that, and yet her eyes had gone soft and tender.

Now she dusted her hands together and hefted the jug. "We can go in here now, we got his permission. But don't smear Papa's *veve* or you undo all the protection it accord us."

They all believed utterly in Mel and this yellow bunch of lines and circles and stars. Stepping carefully, everyone hoisted trunks and bags and followed her inside.

They didn't get far. Mel knelt down in front of the entrance to the west stairwell and set to work on the bricks with more cornmeal. When she finished, the group set down their belongings in the vaulted crosshall and followed her along the brick pavers.

I carefully stepped over the *veve*.

My sense of existing outside them grew palpable. We didn't belong together, them and me. They disrespected my book learning, did not care what I could call up and recite. It was of no use to them. And I had little respect for their foolishness.

I glanced down at the stairwell floor. The same *veve* as outside. People was going to have to step carefully not to kick it there. Sooner or later somebody was bound come down those stairs—Tazewell would if nobody else beat him to it.

I followed at a distance. The scullery, the meat curing room, pantry, cellar, the enormous kitchen itself—each threshold now bore a cornmeal *veve*.

In the kitchen, Mel had poured cornmeal before the door that exited under the north portico, but then she'd drawn other shapes in the hearth ashes and on the ledges of the square, mullioned and barred windows, and the surface of the ranger. Not just doorways then.

She inscribed some kind of blessing on each surface she encountered.

Everyone moved out of the kitchen to the sleeping quarters. Maybe she was dusting under each bed. I would have gone to see, but a voice from back down the hall sharply called my name. I cringed even before I turned.

Miss Priscilla Cooper Tyler stood and waited at the end of the hall.

She had come down the west stairs exactly as I'd feared someone would. She kept glancing down at the floor beside her with her arms folded the way women do when they're about to list all your defects. We was all 'bout to get rowed up Salt River for certain if I didn't give a satisfactory explanation of what she was glancing at.

At least she had seen the *veve* in time to lift her skirts and step over it.

"What is this, James?" she asked. Her gaze focused past me at the far end of the hall. "What is going on here?"

"Ma'am, did the baby travel well?"

"Mary is just fine, James. I have Elizabeth looking after her," she said, "and Alice is sitting with her mother in the unaccountable absence of Devonee."

"Well, you know, I brought Sally along in part because she's so good with babies. Any time you need her." With that I had used up everything I could think of to forestall having to answer. Then, in the midst of my panic, she considered the floor beside her again. She had no inkling at all what it was.

In Virginia, I had encountered a few *veves* in the slave quarters, even painted on a couple trees, but never near or in the main house. The kind of evil that came and went there was just how people were.

"James?" Miss Priscilla asked.

"It's a blessing, ma'am, a blessing upon this house." She looked past me. I prayed that everybody would remain out of sight.

Then I thought of something. "It's like what that German farmer Mr. Tyler knows up Pennsylvania way painted on *his* barn?" I wasn't certain she knew the man I was speaking of, but I hoped.

Her expression remained skeptical. "We'd no blessings like this at Mr. Tyler's house."

"Well, no, ma'am," I said, "we don't need any. House and the outbuildings were blessed long before you arrived. This is a new place with lots of folks comin' through it every day, and, well, you and I both know Hell is empty and all the devils are here."

I was sure she would recognize the quote. She had famously played about every heroine Shakespeare ever created, before Robert Tyler swept her from the stage and married her.

Her face softened into a slight smile, and one hand brushed at the dark ringlets covering her ear. She said, "Hmm… I fear that may be quite true. Robert has told me how it came about you had to replace the whole staff. With this Congress, we likely need every blessing we can get." She dismissed the *veve*. "It seems, because of Letitia's infirmity, that I will be acting as hostess at these…levées." What Washington had called soirées, we knew as levées in Virginia.

"You must feel honored, ma'am," I said.

"More like terrified would describe it, James."

"General Harrison's daughter-in-law did the same for him, on account of his wife was back in Indiana."

"Truly? I wish I'd had opportunity to speak with her."

"I did talk with her some, Miss Priscilla. She said she got good advice on the subject from Dolley Madison."

She blinked a few times. "Oh, what a very fine idea. We'll have to go see her."

"Yes, ma'am. Sounds like we should."

Her mood had shifted toward the positive. We were out of danger for the moment. "How long do you expect this will be here?"

"Oh, not very long, ma'am. Just till everybody settles in."

We could not have these figures scattered around in the open. I would need to find a better solution. "I'll get Devonee upstairs to Miss Letitia quick as I can," I said.

"And have you figured out where everybody goes yet? You and I must agree on the best placement. We have to make this work, James, for Mr. Tyler's sake."

That was a subject I could speak to at some length. "I surely have, Miss Priscilla. I had to do that just to compile my list for Mr. Robert to send. I've placed Olive, Ethel, and Zenobia to work with Mel. 'Tall George' will serve as a footman, assist me with bringing meals up from the kitchen, and polishing too. There's a lot of silver and brass in the house could use a good cleaning, and an awful lot of mirrors. And if Cyrus can't drive the coach, or we need a second driver, George is also handy for that. Sally and Deborah going to be the housemaids, along with Devonee when Miss Letitia doesn't require her. Marcellus will cure the meat same as back home, and he can assist with all the state dinners too—I know from what Harrison's folk had to tell, you're gonna have a lot of 'em." *From what* Isaac *had to tell.* "Seems that's how things get done here, at dinners and parties. Marcellus will make a fine footman, do you proud." As an afterthought, I added, "That Mr. Jasper, of course, already has his job on the door, so that's one we don't have to bother after."

"What about Mister Tyler?" she asked.

"Samuel, ma'am, will be his body servant. If I'm tending to the household, I can't be going off with Mr. Tyler everywhere he travels. My place needs be here." *With Mel.* "Samuel can double as another footman at the levées when we need him, since he'll already be accompanying the president."

She shook her head, and for a moment I thought she was disagreeing with my arrangements. But she said, "The *president*. It is still amazing to me, James, that this has happened."

"Amazing to us all, ma'am," I answered. "Amazing to us all."

➤➤➤ ◄◄◄

Once everything had been protected to Mel's satisfaction, she settled right in learning the kitchen, seeing what produce had been left for her, and then preparing her first meal using that cast iron ranger. The rest worked hard to make up for the delay.

Tall George, Samuel, Cyrus, and I hauled all the family's trunks into the house and up to the private floor, where Tyler was still meeting behind closed doors with the daily string of petitioners.

Down on the kitchen floor, everybody had their assignments—mostly the same or similar duties to what they had performed in Virginia.

Samuel was dumbfounded upon my telling him that he would be Mr. Tyler's body servant like back home, and that he would have his own room off Tyler's chambers. I think he couldn't believe I had done him such a courtesy, but with his suspicious mind it didn't take him long to work out the cause. As was his habit, he rubbed a finger up and down the scar on his cheek. Then a sly look came over him. "Sure," he said. "You got her all to yourself down here, ain't you?"

Mel and Zenobia, working in the kitchen, heard none of this, but some of the others watched to see what would happen.

"That's your thanks, is it?" I said. "I didn't have to name you at all. Could'a left you back home where you'd be no headache for me, and brought Passmore instead. So, if you got an issue with the situation, you let me know now, so's I can send for him right quick to take your place. You have a problem, I can fix your flint for you right easy."

His eyes went hard as diamond, and I half-expected him to try and land a sockdologer on my jaw; but in the end he backed down. By now Mel and Zenobia had come out to see where everybody was. Samuel took them in, a muscle twitching in his jawbone. He turned on his heel and marched off upstairs.

Young Marcellus, though he was watching Zenobia, leaned close and whispered to me, "Why *didn't* you leave him back home?"

"Passmore's an awful body servant. Would have ended up with Samuel anyhow, or worse, woulda been stuck in it myself."

Nobody else voiced a complaint about their assigned position in the household.

»»»—«««

That evening the family ate by candlelight in the smaller, private dining room on the north side. Mel had prepared a kind of burgoo from what lay in the larder. Marcellus shaved a good portion of an aged ham he found hanging up to accompany the makeshift stew. Zenobia and Ethel managed to punch up some flatbread to serve.

Near the end of the meal, Miss Priscilla caught my eye and gave me a nod to let me know it had passed muster. About then the baby started crying, and she and Robert left the dining room to put Mary to bed. Elizabeth rose quietly and followed them.

I dismissed Marcellus, but remained standing myself in case Tyler or the children required anything else.

Tyler was acting all lord of the manor now. He smiled at his two children, but spoke to me: "Everything's running smoothly, James, and I am pleased to say so. Why, I expect in a day or two you'll find time to start giving these youngsters their lessons again."

Tazewell groaned like any boy who'd been hoping for a summer free of instruction.

Tyler was teasing his children. The only people getting lessons in the next few days were the staff. I said, "I expect your father means music lessons, Tazewell."

"But we don't even have our piano!" Alice objected.

Tyler replied conspiratorially, "Oh, that's all taken care of. Isn't it, James?"

"Ah, yes, sir," I answered, though I had no idea what he was talking about. Mr. Tyler did not elaborate. He chortled a bit as he stood, excusing himself then to go spend time with Miss Letitia.

Back home he had liked to sit with her of an evening, just describing his day, sometimes asking for her advice. I expected he would have more need of her counsel now than ever. Some nights he read to her, as Miss Priscilla and I did. Most often she wanted more to hear about all those things in which she used to participate. It was a way for her to remain vital.

He and the children had just headed up the stairs, when there came a crash from the far larger public dining room on the other side of the stairwell. I ran round the stairs to the room.

Olive knelt by the sideboard where a lamp was lit. She held a tray of silverware that she had cleaned, but she had spilled half of it on the floor. Her eyes were near as round as her face, but seeing it was me, the look of terror soured, as if I'd had some hand in scaring her.

I crouched to help pick up the cutlery.

While I faced the floor, I asked, "What happened?"

"Nothin'," she replied. I looked up but she turned her face away. "I jist clumsy."

Whatever else I thought of Olive, I knew her to be steady and not easily distracted, never mind clumsy. That was one of the reasons she was here.

We gathered everything off the floor and rose up. She kept her eyes straight down at the tray. Then, as if hearing her name called, she was compelled to glance at the wall mirror over the sideboard beside her. It was one of those pieces in the house in need of polishing: a girandole mirror with a pushed-out surface. Like the bottom of a bowl, it captured a distorted image of the whole room. A number of the parlors had them, with gilt trim in the style of rope, and a wide-winged eagle set as if perched on top of the frame.

"I'll go down, wash it all agin," she said and, clamping the tray between her hand and her hip, she reached out. "You hand me my lamp?"

I did. "Olive," I said. "You sure you all right now?"

"I tol' you," she snapped, then swung around me with her tray of silverware and headed for the stairs.

I shook my head. I hadn't been anything but respectful. She had no cause to be snippy.

That's when out the corner of my eye I saw movement in the girandole mirror.

It had to be the effect of her lamp retreating toward the stairs, drawing the shadows along behind it, but those thick shadows flowed across that mirror like sideways-running ink, blotting me and the room out altogether.

Eleven

"The essential thing that is expected of you," said Dolley Madison to Priscilla Cooper Tyler across her teacup, "is that you behave the great lady in all circumstances. You may be a surrogate for poor Letitia, but you must be as proper as if this was your own castle and, by extension, your own nation." They were in Dolley's pearl-gray parlor.

She glanced at Priscilla's "man," standing stiffly by the door. James, was it? He was one of the household slaves, of course, although she could not be certain of the name. She had seen him in the Walnut Grove plantation house once, maybe twice. His mixed blood made him striking, a sculpted nose and face almost European and exotically handsome, really. His propriety reminded her of her own slave, Paul Jennings, that she had been forced to sell to Daniel Webster for cash.

Priscilla set down her china cup. "Is that how you beheld it in your tenure?"

"Oh, my dear," Dolley replied, and patted at her bejeweled turban as if she had felt it slipping. Her eyes glinted with mischief. "It was all so nascent then. Our nation and the business of being in charge of it. We learned as we went along from one crisis to the next, although we did certainly rely upon formal dinners and soirées as you will." She leaned back on her wide lavender settee. "I doubt you will have to flee an incursion by the British, although there's such saber-rattling over the burning of the *Caroline* that I wouldn't rule it out."

With the turban, she wore a green beaded shawl and a high-necked white gorget like a man's cravat. It was her customary outfit, and these days, thanks to her profligate son and his disastrous financial schemes, the only one she owned. She was not penniless; yet, she worried what it said about her status that she accepted money from Paul, her own former slave—not even Webster's money, but out of his own earnings.

Her Quaker upbringing scolded her that she should be humbled by his compassion toward her plight; but she'd long ago cast off dour Quakerism for handsome James Madison and ball gowns and society life. Pauperized or not, she must continue to reign as the queen of Washington.

Priscilla, who was truly a lovely young woman, was simply the latest princess in the President's Castle requiring her help. Just as Jane Harrison had before her. They all needed Dolley's advice.

But Priscilla was speaking. "…heard talk of it. However, Robert will not discuss the matter. He claims it's statecraft, wherein women have no place."

Dolley clucked her tongue. "Your husband ought to know better. If necessary, you must instruct him. You will shortly play hostess to the various involved parties—why, Ambassador Fox and the British deputation have practically taken up residence in your house beside Daniel Webster. The more you are informed of incendiary situations, the better—and this one is *most* incendiary."

She set down her own teacup.

"A British man has been arrested and held in New York, charged with murder. His name is McLeod and he was a conspirator with a group who rowed a boat from Canada, boarded an American ship, the *Caroline*, tied up in our waters, and set it ablaze above Niagara Falls. In the process, they murdered a watchman. It is being treated as seriously as if they'd killed Fletcher Webster."

"How awful."

"The crime is, certainly, but the British through their ambassador have already made it clear that if this man McLeod is found guilty and hanged—as he richly deserves—they will consider it an act of war and retaliate in kind."

"So I should be particularly cordial to the British ambassador."

Dolley Madison laughed. "Fox *and* his entourage. Listen to everything that goes on around him. Gather snippets and imputations, gossip. As a simple female, your presence dismissed by them as it seems to be by your husband, you will soon find yourself possessed of information that neither your husband nor John will have heard nor could have extracted, hmm?

"Use all of your talents, my dear." She lifted her hands and for an instant struck a dramatic pose. "I've seen you on stage, at the National Theatre—your Ophelia, and your Lady Anne to your father's Richard III—so I know for a fact you have the necessary skills. Letitia, if she were up and about, could not accomplish what you can in this role. You will wander among the audience and they will not even suspect you are acting."

Priscilla Tyler blushed, and while she did not deny the compliments, she said, quietly, "Theatre's all in my past."

"Nonsense. It's a talent that you *must* apply. Hold them spellbound with your beauty and your charm, and they'll celebrate you as in Russia they celebrate Catherine II." She leaned forward like a conspirator. Colluding with these young women made her feel so young again. Their energy fed her. "Now, tell me, when is your first social event? We are late in the season and must get your calendar started."

Dolley's energy galvanized Priscilla. With more excitement than she had shown so far, she replied, "Saturday, the week after this. At least, that's my hope."

"Good. You'll want to organize as many soirées and dinners as possible before the swelter of summer drives everyone out of the city. The marshes become absolutely noxious. Now, my own little parties, they fall on Wednesday evenings, as they have since my own days in the President's Castle—I always held them in the Yellow Drawing Room then. President Harrison scheduled *his* dinners for Wednesdays so that the attendees could simply walk across the park to here afterward. Something you might suggest to John, as he may want to end them early to spare Letitia the cruelty of festivities she cannot attend. Now, you must appear at my two little parties prior to your soirée in order that we may excite expectations. Also, don't dismiss your theatre connections either—bring actors and poets and writers to the castle for these parties whenever you can. The arts and performance are essential." Then she leaned back, her hands in her lap. "Culture."

She turned her gaze upon the handsome slave again, pointed at him without lifting her hands.

"Your man will have the staff inculcated by then?"

Priscilla turned in her high-backed chair. "James?" she asked.

Dolley congratulated herself that she had correctly recalled his name.

"Yes, ma'am, they will be ready," he said. "We could take it on right now if everything wasn't still dressed up in mourning black."

He had a most pleasant voice, too, and the comportment of an educated man. Oh, if only she could afford him. She could have hired him out everywhere and made a tidy income.

The way he looked at Priscilla, Dolley could tell there was some harmony between them. Less mistress and slave, closer to friends. It put her in mind of her own servant girl, Sukey, all those years ago, the two of them gathering up all the silver in the house, dumping it into her bulging reticule, and fleeing barely an hour ahead of the British soldiers. Dear Sukey, so long gone now.

She realized she had drifted off in memories and that Priscilla was looking at her cautiously. Had the slave said something more? She didn't think so.

She covered her uncertainty by proclaiming, "Your other single most important duty will be to return every invitation made upon you or Letitia. Anyone who leaves their card at the door, calls upon either of you, or even sends a note. Once you have the rhythm of it, you must set aside two or three mornings a week to board your carriage and pay your calls in kind to all of them.

"You needn't stay very long—planning the soirées will consume your time." She couldn't help grinning. "With various members of Washington society, that will be to your advantage. You will find yourself conversing with quite a few hard-of-hearing spoons."

It was a moment before Priscilla understood. She smiled broadly. "I shall consider myself forewarned."

Yes, Dolley thought. She was lovely and much better equipped than that daughter-in-law of Harrison's. "One visit and you'll know who I mean," she said. "You'll soon have a list." She picked up her teacup again. "Some you cannot appease and others you dare not indulge, but you will have to visit every one, all the same."

Twelve

Like the three floors below it, the attic floor of the President's House was laid out with a central hallway and rooms off both sides. It was the graveyard of broken things. Furnishings from past presidencies had migrated there: chairs with missing legs, divans with ripped covers, unused rolls of wallpaper, tarnished serving dishes and cracked china; chests, wardrobes, broken mirrors.

To Tazewell it was a treasure trove, a secret world. Every room was musty, cluttered, and uninhabited, providing endless perfect places for Alice Tyler to have hidden.

In the parlance of the game they played, Tazewell was "it," and he crept down the hall, looking into each chamber, straining to catch the tiniest noise—a creaking floorboard, a rustle of cloth, the scrape of a chair leg.

It wasn't until he was halfway along that, in a crossbeam of light, he caught sight of small footprints in the dust. Someone walking on their tiptoes. His sister had ducked into this room.

Stained linen curtains hung limply across its dormer window, giving the emptiness a brownish glow. Sunlight haloed the old material.

Tazewell lost sight of the footprints and edged farther in, maneuvering to get the wan light to reveal which way she had gone.

Bunk bed frames had been built along the wall adjoining the next room—wood frames and slats but no mattresses. Nowhere to hide beneath them. A large rusting iron ring bolted into the wall caught his attention, and another one on the far side of where the brick chimney protruded. They reminded him of the rings through which chains were passed in the slaves' quarters at Walnut Grove—for the field slaves, his father's foreman had explained, some of which couldn't be trusted not to pull foot. But there weren't any field slaves here. At least, not any longer. There was, however, a butter churn against the wall big enough to crouch behind, but Alice wasn't there either.

Tazewell scratched his head, wondering how the churn had got all the way up here from the kitchen. What if President Washington himself had carried it? Then he remembered his lessons with James about the second war with the British and knew that couldn't be the case. Andrew Jackson then, maybe.

He lifted the linen drape and turned around. The new light spilling in revealed another half footprint in the dust of the doorway to the next room.

On the far side of it, a stool lay long overturned. He spied another smudge there—kidney shaped, and the curving dots of toes. No heel mark: She was leaping, trying to leave as few prints in evidence as she could. It amazed him she hadn't thumped the floor loud enough to alert him when she jumped. He carelessly nudged the stool aside and heard a small noise from deeper within the room.

He had her now and no doubt. He leaned cautiously around the jamb until he could see all of the room.

It had been fitted with more bed frames. Another iron ring hung from the wall. More discarded items were strewn through here: a standing trunk, valises, an oak cradle, two chairs with tattered seats hanging down like moss; and a couple of hoops from a game of graces. They leaned against a busted tip-top table like the one in his mother's room back in Virginia. So much stuff that Alice hadn't been able to hop around or through it. The spoor of her bare footprints led right behind the large trunk.

On the floor beside the stool lay two broken pieces of a candle. They had half-puddled onto the floorboard. Carefully, Tazewell crouched down and pried up the larger piece, and the other came with it, articulated on the wick. He took aim, and then flung the candle underhanded beyond the trunk. As quickly, he pulled back out of sight.

The candle landed with a loud bang in the middle of all that silence, and Alice came charging out of hiding to run smack into Tazewell.

"Boo!" he shouted, almost drowned out by her squeal, and tagged her. "You're caught!"

Alice clutched her hands over her heart. "Oh, you devil!" she called him. She had her mother's thick dark hair. She lunged as if to make a grab for her brother, but Tazewell danced out of her reach.

He laughed his triumph in her face and skedaddled out into the hall. "Start counting," he called.

She kept one hand on her breast and leaned against the door. "Oh, I will, but let me catch my breath, you gave me such a fright."

Tazewell grinned at that news. The longer it took her to regain her composure, the more time he had to hide. He ran for the stairs.

Alice had to count to one hundred before giving pursuit, and she wasn't sure she could calm herself enough to do it. Why, she had almost swooned because of her little brother. She coughed now from all the dust they had kicked up. *He* had kicked up. Crossed to the dormer to let in some fresh air.

When she pulled back one of the old curtains, it tore, loosing even more dust. She sneezed twice, fanning the air, then lifted aside the rotting curtain more delicately.

In the dirty surface of one of the panes, she read her own name: ALICE. It had been scratched there as if with a nail. "Ha-ha, Tazewell. I am not afeared," she muttered. Just like her little brother to take the time to frighten her even more. He must have had his pocketknife with him.

She let go the drape.

Righting the stool, she sat down and rubbed furiously at her nose. Then, more calmly, she began counting aloud: "One...two...three..."

Beside her, the iron ring that was screwed into the wall rocked slowly in its rusty collar. She forgot to count a moment. She was quite certain she hadn't come anywhere near it. That was...odd.

"Oh well. Four...five...six..."

⟫⟫⟩ ⟨⟨⟪

Tazewell tried to hide in his mother's room. It was the last place Alice would think to find him because it was so outrageous. He planned to climb inside the big double-door schrank in there; but Devonee was on hand, bathing Letitia, and when he unlatched the door and attempted to poke his head into the room, she jumped up in outrage, shooed him out, and slammed the door.

Alice must surely have reached one hundred by then and had probably heard the door slam. Tazewell crept to the stair hall and listened for the echoes of her steps above. Nothing yet. He could try to hide in his father's bedroom next door, but Alice would catch him for certain after that noise.

He imagined he heard her shuffling feet on the third floor, and he hightailed it down to the first floor without a backward glance.

From the stairwell he peered the length of the cross hall.

The public floor bustled with activity. Deborah, whom he thought of as *the Indian* because she was part-Cherokee and never spoke, was removing the wreaths adorning the wall sconces, while Tall George worked a pulley to lower the nearest chandelier so that he could untie the black bunting decorating it and maybe replace the candles. Sally, on her knees, was scrubbing at the woven mat covering the floor in front of the vestibule. It was filthy with muddy footprints.

Tazewell crept along past them, hoping to go largely unnoticed or at least unremarked upon. But as he neared the middle of the hall, he heard yelling from within the Blue Saloon, and suddenly the door swung wide and three men came backing out, pursued by a bellowing Daniel Webster. "Oh, I am *well* acquainted with Congressman Gilmer's opinion of me—'blackguard and debauchee' were his exact words." He stalked them into the hall, forcing Tazewell to dodge their uncertain path. Webster yelled, "You may inform him, gentlemen, that my opinion of him is nowhere near so *elevated!*"

The men bolted for the door, passing Sally. She cried, "Be careful, Tazewell!" as he skittered out of their way and fled down the hall to the East Room. Behind him Webster continued yelling.

Alice, meanwhile, had descended to the private floor. No footprints there to guide her. He might be hidden in any room, and she looked for more evidence of him, going slowly along.

A door to one of the unoccupied rooms hung ajar. She had started toward it when downstairs a commotion erupted.

Daniel Webster's voice rang out, chastising some congressman. Alice considered Webster a terrifying man. She would never want to be yelled at by him.

Then Sally all of a sudden called out to Tazewell.

Alice turned from the open doorway and hurried down the east stairs.

"And damn Virginia for producing him!" Webster shouted. The front door slammed shut.

Alice stopped at the bottom of the stairs. Webster stood directly across the hall. Upon seeing her, his expression slid from the blackest of storms to the warmest of smiles in a heartbeat. "Why, Miss Alice. I hope I didn't shock you. I do apologize for my sharpness with these…" He gestured as if to say there was no reasonable word for them. "Are you interested in affairs of state?" His brow lifted. "Or are you looking perhaps for your brother?"

She cleared her throat so that her voice might not shake in his presence. "The latter, sir. I allow as we're hiding and seeking."

He nodded, and his fingers played upon his belly. He stepped closer to whisper to her, and seemed not to notice that she leaned away as he did. "Seek and ye shall find your reward in the East Room." He gave a wink and walked back across the hall into the Blue Saloon.

Alice, certain now of her prey, all but skipped to the East Room door.

Inside, the huge room lay dim and uninviting. It smelled as if maybe a rat had died behind the baseboards. Closing the door softly behind her, she pressed against it and took stock.

This was where the body of General Harrison had been kept for days on end. No wonder it smelled so awful.

From the doorway, she could identify where the coffin had been. A wide swath of dirt curved out across the enormous carpet to a set of trestles draped in black crepe—forming something like a narrow table in the middle of the room. She visualized the line of people shuffling up to the coffin and then away. Sally was going to be scrubbing for days in here.

Most of the other furniture had been pushed off toward the sides. Chairs lined the yellow walls, as if for an evening of dancing, although she knew better.

Her father had told the family about the funeral—in particular of how the general's horse had walked along so gallantly in the procession. She loved horses. She had asked what would become of him, and father had assured her that "Whitey" was on his way home to Indiana. She wished she had been there to see him.

This long room was still hung everywhere with the black drapery being removed by Deborah and Tall George from the hall. Crepe covered the four huge mirrors, the paintings, and the three cut-glass chandeliers.

The four fireplaces were black, but black was their usual color. Black drapery covered all the tall windows, even the set in the middle with the fanlight window above. What illumination there was came through those fanlight panes.

Tazewell might be behind any of the drapes or even crouched under that covered trestle, or...

But *there* he was.

Pretending to be a piece of furniture sheathed in the same black drapery, he must have climbed up on a chair in the hope that he would look like a bust on a pedestal, or a tall candelabra—there were four of those over where the coffin had been, all covered up. It would have worked as a disguise if he hadn't moved. No doubt he expected her to go looking behind the curtains, at which point he would jump down and scare her again or run from the room. Well, she would show him. She was going to sneak right up on him and scare him back for the way he'd terrified her upstairs.

On tiptoe she continued across the room; but after maybe a dozen steps, the wood creaked under her toes. She cringed. In that great empty space, the sound was as loud as a pipe organ. She expected Tazewell to bolt, but he didn't move. The black material trembled ever so slightly. Nervous, or was he laughing? He could be such a critter sometimes.

All right then. Of course he knew she was in the room. Probably could see a little through the black cloth—it wasn't much thicker than a heavy veil. Maybe if she didn't make straight for him, he might think she hadn't seen him. She gave the bier a wide berth. The floor creaked again, but she pretended not to care. She was headed to the fireplace beyond him, as if she believed he might be hiding in the hearth, or in the deepest shadows way down the room. She wanted to get behind him.

Keeping her distance, she circled to the outside wall. The way the funereal cloth spread out in the middle, she was sure now he'd gotten up on a chair or small table.

She edged along the wall, close against the curtains, and made a show of peeking behind one or two as she passed him and moved on to the fireplace. She lingered beside the corner of the mantelpiece, pretending to ponder what she should do next while she gave a careful sidelong glance his way.

Beyond him now, she imagined him straining to watch her. No doubt he waited breathlessly for her to continue to the south end of the room. That's when he would dash for the door and make good his escape. Let him think it was going to happen that way.

She leaned down as if to peer up inside the hearth, and surreptitiously picked up a long-handled embers brush. She held the brush at her side, sidled along, and pulled out another window drape. Trapped where he was, all he could do was listen to her moving away.

Alice just wanted one good swat. That would teach him. That would be enough. She did, after all, like her brother most of the time.

She gripped the brush in front of her, in both hands, took another step away from him. The floor creaked again, but that should only convince him that she had missed him. Now before he could even jump she would grab him. The cloth hung almost to the floor, but she knew her brother's height and fixed on exactly where to hit him.

She took a step toward him and was overcome by the sensation of his eyes upon her, even though she hadn't seen him turn. But she didn't care: She had him.

Alice raised the brush and walked fast at the shape. Even as she cocked her arm back to swat him, the curtains beneath the fanlight rippled, and Tazewell stuck his head through them.

They saw each other, but Alice had already swung the embers brush.

Tazewell cried, "Alice, don't!"

The wide brush snagged the black shroud and snapped it into the air.

Thirteen

James Hambleton Christian

"She is so very right," Miss Priscilla said out of the blue as we rode in the coach the short distance across Lafayette Park. Cyrus drove, his bald head shining in the sunlight.

"Who is, ma'am?" I asked.

She gave me a smile that forgave me for not keeping up with her private thoughts. "Mrs. Madison, of course."

"Of course. And what is the thing she's right about, ma'am?"

"Why, the application of my acting skills. I can do so much good for Mr. Tyler at the dinners and levees we're going to have, and in visiting people. It's quite possible that some of those attending will not be on good terms with him, or will want something from him that he refuses them."

I remembered the Haitian ambassador in the waiting hall, too shamed to meet my gaze. *Yes,* I thought, *there will be quite a few of them.*

"I expect some will apply to me as a kind of intercessor, a sympathetic ear. That is the role of hostess—to seem always ready to listen, or advise..."

"And then to tell her husband and father-in-law what she has learned," I finished.

"It would be my duty, don't you think, James? To inform my...my father-in-law?" She tried to smile, but could only bend her lips to it for a trembling moment before giving up with a deep sigh.

I almost said aloud, "What a sigh is there! The heart is sorely charged," which was a line from *Macbeth* spoken by a doctor secretly beholding the conflicted Lady Macbeth, which role I knew she had performed.

It wasn't that her husband was cruel to her, at least not in a way you could point to. But he was the very opposite of his mother and father. They both delighted in the theatrical, Mr. Tyler in particular with his quoting of Shakespeare about any time he held forth on a topic. And before she'd been laid low, Miss Letitia and he never missed an opportunity to dance at a levée. Mr. Robert had inherited the sourness somehow without the sweet.

Even though he had married an actress, he considered acting a profession beneath the family's station, and insisted that his wife "forswear any further association with theater people." The entire household of Walnut Grove plantation had overheard *that* argument. At the time, he and Miss Priscilla had been married only a month.

She sought guidance from her mother-in-law, who upon that particular occasion had let her down. "A wife," Miss Letitia instructed, "must conform to the shape of the role her husband makes for her." That was what *she* had done for Mr. Tyler—lived her life for the cause of his advancement. She expected Priscilla to do no less. It mattered not that Robert Tyler had married Priscilla Cooper, the well-known *actress*. That title was to be folded away like a wedding dress.

Priscilla had capitulated, though it sure froze the core of her.

When later she'd learned that I could recite Shakespeare verbatim, she asked for my accompaniment whenever she went out calling, and on the road away from him we had recited any number of scenes from *Macbeth*, *Hamlet*, and a host of other plays, sometimes taking circuitous routes to our destination that we might finish. I only spoke the words. Even rolling along in an open coach on a hot day along the James River, Miss Priscilla inhabited them. I would have watched that woman play any role on stage. She was born to it, and her husband had smothered that part of her as surely as Othello had suffocated his Desdemona.

It was a golden opportunity: To revive that part of who she was in such a way that it could not be objected to. After all, the doyenne herself, Dolley Madison, had advised her to pull out all the stops and make free use of her gifts on Mr. Tyler's behalf. I could bear witness to this.

Thus in the few minutes it took us to cross the park, I found myself colluding with Miss Priscilla the actress against Robert Tyler. I can't say the idea displeased me.

>>> - <<<

An empty wagon drawn by two horses was tied up to one of the iron posts near the portico, with two boards angled out the back of it to the ground.

"What do you suppose that's about?" she asked me.

Whatever it was, it had distracted Jasper, who should have come out directly we arrived. The front door did not open.

I climbed from the coach and helped Miss Priscilla down. The horses of the wagon ahead of us looked around as if wondering what we might be up to behind their backs. I hastened ahead of her to the door.

Inside, just past the vestibule, a teamster stood leaning on a large canvas-covered object, and he was regaling Jasper and Tall George with a tale of how he had come to Washington "not two days ahead of the Natchez tornado of last year, what kilt the rest of mah whole family."

Jasper spied us and reacted immediately, scurrying past the marble columns. "Apologies, mum. George an' I just 'elped this fellow carry your new piano up inside, and we was just catchin' our breaths like."

"Oh," she said in delight, "the piano, how wonderful! We shall have music, James, at our first levée!"

She hurried straight to it, the other two men stepping away. I noticed a bucket and a rag on the floor matting beside the vestibule, and wondered where Sally had got to, since she had been cleaning the hall alongside George, and he'd gotten pulled into helping because he happened to be handy. Cyrus had been driving us, and it hadn't occurred to anyone to go get Marcellus or Samuel to move a piano. I could see how it had all happened—not that it mattered, since Miss Priscilla had noticed nothing but the piano itself.

"We should install it in the East Room," she said to me, "and then call the children down, don't you think?"

At that moment, someone in the East Room screamed.

"Alice?" Priscilla said, and started to run.

Galvanized, I thundered ahead of her and threw open the doors.

Across the dim room, Tazewell knelt beside his sister, who lay unconscious on the floor. One of the black mirror drapes half-covered her, and a fireplace utensil poked out of it, lying on the rug. Tazewell looked up at us with such agony that I thought he must have struck her.

I hurried across the crackly blue and yellow carpet, crouched opposite him, but immediately leaned away. The air around Alice reeked like the back end of an outhouse. "What happened, Tazewell?"

Priscilla made a sound of revulsion beside me. I glanced up to find her with one hand over her nose and mouth, and fanning the air with the other.

He said, "She— I looked out of the curtains and it was right here in front of her. I called, 'Don't, Alice!' but she'd already swung the brush." He was close to tears.

While he babbled, I tugged the black drape off her. She didn't appear to be harmed in any way. The utensil was one of the long iron-handled brushes for sweeping up ashes. A strange grayish gelatin lay on the floor beside her. It looked like a lump of gravy that had congealed. With the drape off, the smell was even more awful. I had to close my eyes to the stench, and I let the drape settle over it again.

Miss Priscilla asked, "*What* was right in front of her, Tazewell?"

He didn't reply, and couldn't meet her eyes. The boy worshipped Priscilla. All at once he launched himself at me and wrapped his arms about me. He pressed his face into my coat. He said, "The *thing*," then looked up at us with pleading eyes. "I thought it was a vase and she was going to smash it."

I traded a glance with Priscilla. His answer hadn't made things much clearer. Finally, I peeled him off. "All right, you gotta let me tend to her now." I gave him a pat and a nudge toward his sister-in-law. She pulled him to her hip and he closed his eyes and hugged her tight.

Tugging off one white glove, I pressed my hand to Alice's face. "She's not fevered," I said, and noticed that the bristles of the fireplace brush beside me shone with the stinking gray muck. "What the devil?" Whatever it was, I wasn't about to touch it.

Gently, I shook Alice but she didn't awaken. After carefully moving the brush, I scooped my arms under her and picked her up. Her bare feet were filthy but only with the common dirt of the floor. I stood. "Let's get her upstairs away from this."

Miss Priscilla gently brushed Alice's hair from her face. Her eyes were moving under the lids, but she didn't wake up. Priscilla and Tazewell led the way across the room and out. Tall George, Jasper, and Deborah waited outside the door. Cherokee Deborah looked on flatly as if this sort of thing happened every day. Softly, as I passed her, I said, "Go get Mel."

Upstairs, Mr. Robert stood in the waiting hall with some men. He saw us emerging from the stairwell and excused himself, striding down the steps and quickly over. To me he said, "What's happened here?"

Miss Priscilla answered. "She's fainted, Robert, that's all. They were playing a game and she fainted."

To Tazewell, darkly, he asked, "What sort of game?"

"Hiding and seeking, sir."

Robert nodded as if that explained something. "Too much playing," he said. "Not enough lessons." To him, apparently, we should have taken up their lessons the moment they arrived. "Priscilla, you will let me know when she's awake. I won't mention it to Father. It would have him worked up over nothing. No word at all to Mother either."

I answered, "Not my place to say anything to anyone, Mister Robert, sir."

"Of course not, James. I didn't mean you." He scrutinized Alice, traded admonishing looks with Miss Priscilla and Tazewell, then went back across the hall.

Priscilla's cheeks were scarlet. I pretended not to notice, and carried Alice off to her bed. It struck me odd that she still remained unconscious. Usually, it seemed to me, women swooned momentarily, and mostly for effect.

I had Tazewell sit in the chair between her and Elizabeth's beds. Miss Priscilla perched on the end of the bed. The boy looked terrified. At the very least his elder brother had implied he bore responsibility in some way for this situation.

"This thing," I said to him. "What did it look like?"

"It was just there for a second," he said. "Looked sort of like a person dressed up to be a ghost. I seen it when I snuck into the room, too, but I went to hiding in the curtains and didn't pay it any mind. I heard Alice come in, knew she'd missed me, but I couldn't tell where she got to, and when I looked out to see, she was swinging that broom."

"Why?"

He didn't know why. But on some instinct he had cried out to stop her.

Miss Priscilla clearly comprehended no more of this than I did. I said, "All right then. She whisked the crepe away and you cried out. What was under it?"

He thought, squinted as if he couldn't bring the memory into focus. "Like greasy smoke off a lamp with too much wick. And weaving side to side sort of, like it was alive." He looked at me. "It had eyes."

Priscilla said, "What?"

"The thing was *looking* at her. I swow, I could tell it was. And then it looked at me, and then it was gone like maybe it didn't cotton to being yelled at."

"You scared it off," I replied.

"Why doesn't she wake up?"

Before either of us could answer, Mel came in. She carried a small brown glass phial with her, and she was barefoot like the children. She smiled and bowed to Miss Priscilla before crossing to the foot of the bed, from where she considered Alice for a moment. "May I?" she asked Priscilla, who nodded and stood up to let her pass.

Mel went down on one knee beside Alice. Carefully she held the phial close to Alice's face and then waved it under her nose.

Eyes still closed, Alice started, her head pushed back hard into the pillow, and her eyelids fluttered wide open. She thrashed and for a moment looked as if she might scream again.

Tazewell whispered, "Oh, sis." He clutched at his knees like to hide behind them.

Mel got up and let Priscilla slide in on the side of the bed.

"You're all right, dear," Priscilla said. "You're in your own room. You just fainted and we brought you up here."

Alice cast her eyes over the walls and ceiling as if fearful she would find something there. I watched Mel watching her and then scrutinizing the room too, but more slowly. "We were playing hide and seek," Alice said suddenly, as if she hadn't been able to remember.

"Tazewell told us what happened," I answered. Mel turned to give me a look and I knew that, later, I would be repeating it to her. "But we'd sure like to hear your rendition."

After thinking for a moment, she answered, "He was supposed to find me first. He scared me the way he likes to, then ran off."

"Where was this?"

"In the attic. He even scratched my name in the window glass up there to spook me some more."

"I did not!" he cried. "How'd I have done that?"

"Your pocketknife," she said, with something less than certainty. "I saw—"

"I ain't got it on me, Alice. I never did it, really and for true."

"It's all right," Priscilla assured him. "That's not important." She turned back to Alice. "So you came down from the attic. What happened in the East Room, sweetheart?"

"Mr. Webster told me Tazewell was in there. I went in and right away I was sure I saw him. He'd got up on a chair pretending to be one of those crepe-covered candlestands. It shook like he couldn't stand still. I thought he was laughing at being so clever."

"But it wasn't *me*." He was pleading, sure we intended to blame him.

I gave her a nod, but put a finger to my lips. I wanted Alice to keep going.

Priscilla said, "So you took that fireplace broom to give him a good swat."

She nodded enthusiastically.

"But then it wasn't your brother," Priscilla prompted, and Alice's eyes grew round again and her fingers laced and unlaced nervously.

She brought her knees up and hugged them the way Tazewell had, trying to hide. "It hung up in the air where the crepe had been."

I asked, "What did it look like, Alice?"

"Like something smeary. It *jumped*."

"And you screamed?"

"I don't know, maybe. When I woke, I smelled it. I thought it had me," she whined.

Gently, Mel said, "Was just this to wake you, child," and held up the brown phial.

Smeary—that put me in mind of the shadows that had flowed across the girandole mirror trailing after Olive.

"Miss Priscilla," I said, "would you excuse me? I want to take a look in the East Room."

I think she wanted to come too. But she said, "All right, James. Sally's down the hall looking after the baby. Can you have her bring Mary to me? She's overdue for her feeding, and I should remain here, I think."

"Certainly, ma'am." I bowed and stepped back.

Mel followed me out. Robert wasn't in sight in the waiting hall, and we went quickly to Miss Priscilla's room, told Sally to take the baby to Alice's room, although Mary seemed to be asleep. Then I led Mel to the tight service stairs and up to the third floor.

I hadn't been there till then. We exited into another hall with rooms to each side. It was cloying and warmer than the rest of the house, smelling of a closed space that never got aired out. Tazewell's footprints were easy to follow and led us into a room with frames for beds but without mattresses, and being used for storage of broken furniture and odd items, such as a butter churn. We both noticed the rings in the wall. We weren't the first slaves in this house then.

Mel pointed to where his footprints intersected with Alice's. Hers led to one dormer window in particular. We followed them and drew back the torn linen drapery.

The window was smudged, dirty, but otherwise unmarked. There wasn't a scratch anywhere in the glass, despite this had to be the window Alice meant.

Mel didn't seem in the least surprised. She calmly licked a finger and drew one of her *veve* figures in the dirty pane. While she did, she asked to hear Tazewell's version of what had happened.

I described it as he had, including his insistence that the shroud had eyes. She pulled the linen back into place in front of the dormer.

"So you goin' to believe me now when I tell you there something in this house wit' us?"

"Say that I do. What is it I'm believing *in*?" She shook her head, didn't know. I asked what she thought it could be.

After a minute, she answered, "What I think— I think if Tazewell had not been in the room wit' Miss Alice, that thing would have her right now."

When we reached the East Room, there was nothing on the carpet under the black crepe. Even the smell of it had faded. The piano had been rolled into the northeast corner, and Jasper swore that nobody had touched the crepe nor even gone near it.

Fourteen

Mel had learned the basics of her craft from her mother, who had been taught at the altars of *vodou* in Haiti as a child.

At twelve, Mel had been sold away from her family into a household in New Orleans and put to work in a kitchen. When a grease fire burned another of the kitchen maids, Mel had quickly fashioned a poultice. Everyone later agreed that her skill had saved the poor woman's arm. Because of it, the cook took her to a St. John's Eve bonfire in the city where she introduced her to a witch named Marie Laveau.

Madame Laveau's craft differed greatly from what Mel had learned from her mother. For one thing, it incorporated many Christian elements. The *lwa*—the gods called upon for aid and protection—had transmuted and expanded. Madame called them *mystéres*. Mel did not question Madame's teaching, nor did she accept it at face value. Instead, she absorbed everything, but shaped what she learned, pouring it together with what her mother had taught her and creating her own alloy.

Rather than being incensed by this, the witch was impressed. "*Vodou* is always personal," Madame Laveau told her. "Always it comes out of you, becomes your power, your energy—that is what you got to reach for. You got the very instinct, girl, for reaching. Ain't nobody can teach you that. All the others I teach, they don't do that. Makes you good and dangerous if you want to know. Makes you a healer, makes you a witch." After three years, Madame declared her a *mambo*, a name that followed her back to the house, where the slaves took to calling her "Mambo Mary." Although she did nothing to provoke anyone, there were some among them who feared her after that, and they whispered slurs against her that finally reached the ears of her owner.

At eighteen, and despite being an excellent cook, she was sold off to prevent further discord, arriving at Tyler's plantation. Cautious about revealing herself now, she limited her work to curing and easing folks' suffering, gaining a reputation as a healer that reached beyond the plantation slaves to the households of Tyler's neighbors, who sought her both for advice and curatives. *Makaya*—a talent with plants and herbs—was viewed by the white gentry as special knowledge, a science, and not witchcraft. She had refrained from practicing *vodou* except as necessary, and then in as solitary a way as possible. She did not wish to find herself accused of anything again. More than that, she had dared to feel something for someone, and did not want to be separated from him ever.

But this house…this new house *craved* her darker arts.

>>>> <<<<

Dawn was a good hour off when she came walking up from the marshes. Across rutted carriage paths and between saplings she hauled a large flour sack over her shoulder, the neck of it tied off tightly because the things she had caught were not all friendly with each other much less with their captor. The river rat might well have chewed its way out if it hadn't been paralyzed by the cottonmouth she'd taken.

Daniel Webster had called the area down around the canal a "swamp," but it was no swamp, nothing like the bayou country she had known as a child. Louisiana—there were the real swamps.

She carried the sack under the south portico and through the doors to the furnace room. Coal rooms had been added on both sides of the metal monstrosity itself. The furnace was like a fat spider laid on its back, its legs— the ducts—splayed across the ceiling, anchored in the hollow spaces beside various hearths in the first-floor parlors. She had noted the vent in the wall beside one hearth of the East Room when she and James went to look for the remains of what had terrified Alice. She did not know what was in the house nor how it had come to be there. Until it had stalked the children, it had been nothing more than a sensation, like something watching from dark corners, and she had driven it from the ground floor without effort. With the near-assault it had shown purpose, even cunning, and while that didn't tell her what it was, she knew it could manifest. In physical form, if cornered outright, by her reckoning it might be destroyed.

Mel carried the sack into the coal room to the right of the furnace. The coal in here had provided most of the fuel this past winter, shoveled up by a fireman, whose job was to stoke the furnace. But he had been let go with the rest of the staff. James wasn't sure he had even clapped eyes on the man. They wouldn't require another until winter. She felt confident nobody would intrude here.

In the back, she'd cleared a space, heaping two piles of the coal between which she laid a board, a makeshift table that she could work on in secret. Laid out upon the board were a mortar and pestle, a small tin box, a large clay bowl already half-full of necessary ingredients, assorted feathers from birds, which she had collected mostly in Virginia, and a dozen small, stitched squares of red calico and burlap. A bucket sat on the swept floor next to the board, along with a lard oil lamp borrowed from the men's bunk room. Pushed into the layer of coal beside her was a single large stone with a concave surface—her *pe,* her altar stone.

The flour sack wriggled some more when she set it down in the bucket, but she wasn't ready for the snake. It must be sacrificed at the right moment in the ritual.

From the tin box she drew a lucifer that she struck against the bricks. She lit the lamp. The thick greased wick spat to life.

A half-hour longer she worked, grinding up items in the mortar: bones and shredded skins, dried leaves and berries. She knew her proportions, knew most of all that none of what she was preparing would have much efficacy without the final ingredient—the one that couldn't be had easily. Too many days had passed since the children had been terrified out of their wits. While there had been no further manifestations, today she hoped to acquire what she needed well before Miss Priscilla's first levée.

Standing, she picked up the lamp and slapped coal dust off her skirt, then went back out and around the behemoth of a furnace and into the vaulted brick hall. As Mel stepped out, Ethel was coming along from the west, a small basket dangling from her arm. A heap of eggs showed over the top, gathered from the chickens penned down past the stables. Ethel was a Gullah woman from Charleston, where John Tyler had purchased her the year before. She had a thick torso and an underbite that pushed her lower teeth between her lips. She made James crazy with her talk, most of which, for all of his learning, he could not understand. His frustration amused Mel, who got on well enough with her. Ethel had some knowledge of Gullah healing ways, called *ashay*, which agreed for the most part with her own *makaya* arts.

In the warm kitchen, Zenobia had finished fashioning two loaves of sourdough and slid them into the baking hole in the older brick hearth where Jefferson's rusting iron stove squatted; she poked at the wood burning below it. Watching Zenobia work was like watching herself back when she'd arrived in New Orleans, and it was strangely comforting to see. People even sometimes thought the two of them were sisters until they got close and saw how Mel was more than twice her age.

Mel said, "You can handle the family's meal all right, boil them eggs?"

"Yes'm," Zenobia said. She glanced at Ethel, who was already getting a pot off the shelf as if anticipating that she would be making the eggs. Ethel waved her hand down by her side without turning, as if to say *Go on with you*.

Mel set down the smoking lamp and picked up her large wicker basket. Quietly, she told Zenobia, "I'll be awhile at Centre Market this morning. Hopin' for the *maudit* today. Everything else is ready."

Zenobia gave a solemn nod. "I hope it's there," she replied. "After that thing what hunted Miss Alice..." She glanced back at Ethel filling the pot from the wall tap, ignoring them. Zenobia was more than Mel's kitchen helper. She was her apprentice in *vodou*, her *hounsi*.

"Later on, when we got everything, you'll stitch *ouanga* so I can see you got the talent," Mel said with a smile. "Don' let that bread burn now."

She walked out the east door. Dawn was coming up gray this morning. Pausing, she crouched to touch the small *veve* she had painted at the base of the outside wall the night before. It was dry, and on that white stone, nearly invisible.

James had brought her the small bucket of limewash and a brush. "This doesn't mean I warrant any of it," he'd said so solemnly that she'd had to turn away before he saw her smile. "You got to sweep up all the cornmeal before someone other than Miss Priscilla stumbles on it." That was as close as he came to admitting that he wanted her protections in place. After what had happened with Alice, he finally accepted that *something* was wrong in this house and that Mel's defenses were warranted. She knew it was hard for him to embrace belief in such things; but like his incomprehension of Ethel's talk, his attempts to frame his relationship to the unholy amused her enough that she would tease him about it later.

She had painted the more permanent *veves* unobtrusively low to the ground next to every exit and entrance on this floor, and on the underside of the table in the mess, and in every room. Even in the doorway of James' room and the one beyond it where more crystal and silver was stored—he might not believe, but he'd put up no argument to her protecting him as well.

She had some sympathy for his inability to acknowledge powers outside his control. His whole life—like hers, like everyone's here—was outside his control, but more complicated than most. He was a slave tethered to his own half-sister, robbing him of any autonomy. It was like being owned twice over. Plus he'd been educated in ways that had little meaning to the rest of them, so that he often seemed more like their owners than like them. He tended to judge folks harshly, which she forgave him. Being of neither sphere, above or below, he was much like her. But he did try to understand, and she loved that about him even as his obstinacy challenged the life they might have together.

Leaving the house, she walked out across the lawn and under the strange eastern gate standing by itself like the doorway to an ancient temple that had crumbled to dust.

The stalls of the market would shortly be bustling with activity. She had a list of items to acquire for the family's meals, including chard to accompany the fricandeau she planned for their supper and fruit to make the sauce, some melons, and jarred peaches if she was lucky. She was also on the lookout for ingredients for dishes she intended to make for the levée, three nights hence.

>>> ⫷⫷

Mel wandered among the stalls in the long open building of Centre Market.

Someone could have piloted a steamboat under its roof, which was covered with moss so thick it hung off the eaves in places. It was where nearly everyone in the city went for their fresh meat, fruits, vegetables, and cheeses. Old farmers called it Marsh Market, the name it had gone by back in the days before the canal had been dug. One fishmonger, who looked like he had been here from the beginning, had explained: "Tiber Creek run right through here where you all are standing, and the fishmongers used to keep their fish fresh and alive in baskets they submerged in the creek right behind they stalls." He pointed at the floor. "Nowadays we gotta have a runner to retrieve the fish if we run out, which we're most likely to do, and we pay someone to watch our catch and make sure nobody gets into the baskets in the meantime. Practically has to be a family business if you don't wanna get honey-fuggled."

Today she didn't need any fish, filling her basket with root vegetables, squash, honey, herbs, the asparagus she had wanted, and three lovely jars of peaches.

Mel paid for her purchases with money Daniel Webster had provided. She was careful to write down each item and its cost, a list she was to give to James each week so that he could keep a record of expenses as he had done at Walnut Grove.

She covered the basket with a cloth and set out below Pennsylvania Avenue toward the canal, crossing Louisiana Avenue into Haymarket Square. Unlike Centre Market, Haymarket was an open area selling everything from the hay that gave it its name to livestock and wagons. Men shouted out prices, auctioneers trilled bids, and hucksters with small wheeled carts preached the curative powers of their various nostrums.

Among the stalls on the far side of these quack peddlers was the one she sought—a dark little recess selling the usual vegetables and fruits, but also offering candles, holy bread, pig bristles, and other assorted essentials for those who knew what to ask for, much of it not on display.

The woman seated there was a small and shriveled creature with tightly curled gray hair. She was smoking a little corncob pipe that she'd carved herself. She had promised to acquire what Mel sought: *maudit*. There was, she'd explained, a retired old *houngan* who lived all by himself out on the Chesapeake and received supplies from ships coming up from the Antilles. While she didn't think he practiced *vodou* himself anymore, he was a reliable supplier of all sorts of hard-to-find ingredients, but especially *maudit*.

Ingested, the root was poisonous. It came from the *figuier maudit* tree, which thrived on the islands—on Hispaniola from where her parents had fled—and in Africa. Her charms would not be half so efficacious without it.

When the old woman saw Mel, she stood, and her face lit up. She bent down below the small counter, covered with horseradishes and cabbages. When she stood back up, she held in each hand a thick section of scraggly root. She laid both on the counter.

They looked like horseradish's larger cousins, with yellowish bark. The two pieces combined were about as thick and as long as her forearm. They would do very nicely for Mel's needs.

A breeze stirred, kicking up dust around the market. The vendor named her price. Mel wasn't surprised: such rare ingredients did not come cheap. She drew from the pocket of her skirt a $2.50 Liberty gold piece. It had been given her by one of Mr. Tyler's neighbors for curing his daughter's pneumonia. She placed it on the woman's palm. The old vendor took the pipe from her mouth and drew the coin close as if she'd never set eyes on a gold piece before. She shook her head.

"I cain't repay you but half ob dis," she said.

Mel swept the two chunks of root into her basket. She replied, "Then you keep the other half as on account. This will not be the last t'ing I purchase from you."

The old woman clamped her teeth around the pipe stem again, nodded, and sat down. The gold coin had already vanished from sight.

Mel leaned nearer and asked, "Can you speak the name of the *houngan*?"

The old woman closed her bony hand over Mel's wrist, drawing her down until her ear was beside the vendor's mouth. The tobacco smoke smelled tart like sour cherries. Very softly, she whispered so that no one else could hear. Then she slid her fingers down and squeezed Mel's hand in fellowship.

If a woman needed this much *maudit*, the old woman knew, then something very bad had invaded her life.

Fifteen

James Hambleton Christian

That Wednesday night, the family had a dinner of fricandeau, after which Mr. Tyler spent some time with Miss Letitia; Miss Priscilla fed her baby; Miss Elizabeth probably wrote another love letter to Billy Waller; and Mr. Robert had Alice and Tazewell reviewing their history lessons, reading about the Boston Tea Party. During that lull, down in the mess room we all ate our meals, except for Cyrus, the coachman, who'd taken ill. Mel had made him something to calm his stomach.

Not long after we'd eaten our own fricandeau, the elder Tylers, including Miss Elizabeth, joined their father and headed off by coach to Dolley Madison's Wednesday soirée. I knew that this was Miss Priscilla's first opportunity to promote her own upcoming Saturday party. Dolley, I was certain, would look after her.

Once they had all gone, we settled in for what I hoped would be a quiet night.

I climbed straight to Miss Letitia's room to read some more *Oliver Twist* to her. As I sat down, I glimpsed her slate and the message she'd scrawled upon it for her husband: *Tell Dolley to come see me.*

She saw me reading it. I said, "You know, she *will* be here for the levée on Saturday. Going to be quite the party, I believe. You'll have all of Washington society lining up at your door to see you."

She turned her head with some effort to glance past me to where the tall mirror stood. My presumption was that she worried how she would appear, and I jumped in to reassure her.

"I'll speak to Devonee and Sally, and I promise we will get you into your finest fashion for it."

She blushed, but her gaze, still troubled, slipped to the mirror again as I leaned forward and picked up the book from the table beside her, causing me to glance around. All I saw was myself in the glass.

⤜⤛ ⫷⫸

Awhile after Devonee arrived, I came to the end of a chapter and closed the book. "More tomorrow," I promised, then left Miss Letitia to go check on the children.

Tazewell was asleep in his room, lying on top of the covers. I blew out the candle across from him.

Miss Alice, like her mother, was a book lover, and was reading a collection of stories by Nathaniel Hawthorne when I came in. Beneath the rug, the floor creaked. She started, wide-eyed for an instant.

"Oh, you gave me a fright, James," she said.

I asked what she was reading.

"It is a story about an old woman who has been widowed twice but now has agreed to marry the man she first loved in her girlhood. Only, when he meets her at the altar, he is a corpse, dressed for the grave, and all those in his party are mourners, and the wedding coach a hearse."

"Sounds grim to me," I said.

"They are both finding love upon the threshold of the tomb."

"I take your meaning, Miss Alice, but that won't be a problem you'll ever face," I teased, and she blushed like her mother as she closed the book and scurried to bed. As I turned down the wick adjustor on her Argand lamp, borrowed from the East Room, I said, "Tomorrow we take up piano lessons again. You worried still about being in that room?"

She shook her head but I could see her uneasiness.

"Tell you what. I'll go look in there right now and make sure it's all quiet. How'd that be?"

"Thank you. Thank you, James."

"My pleasure, Miss Alice." I didn't let her see any of my own unease about that room. I went out and down the east stairs.

⤞ ⤝

In the cross hall the lamplights still burned, although the whole floor appeared deserted, doors all closed. The hall smelled as if someone had been smoking in one of the parlors. Maybe Jasper was enjoying a cigar out on the south portico or somewhere. If so, I truly didn't want to attract his attention. I took one of the unlit candles off a side table in the stairwell, lit it, and walked carefully to the doors of the East Room.

I opened one. In the opposite corner, a candle was burning on the floor. But there was more light than that, and I poked my head in. Candles were lit in all four corners of that long room.

In the center of the rug, beneath the dark chandelier, stood Mel.

She was still as a statue, her eyes huge. I was reminded of the shade that had watched Alice from under a black shroud. I slipped inside and closed the doors.

A small wicker basket sat on the rug beside her. She was holding something in her hands, at her sides. Behind her, curtains gently fluttered and I realized she had opened every window around the room, even the glass door leading onto the promenade atop the east colonnade.

I strode up to her. "What are you doing in here?"

"Don't you interfere, James Christian. I only got time before the Tylers come home from their party to secure this room."

"If you're caught here doing any of this, it's the end of you for sure."

"Oh, and you think I don't know that?"

"Mel—"

"If you going to remain, you do as I say. You worried for the children, then let me work while you listen by the door. Whatever happens, whatever come, you stay there, and blow out your candle. These ones goin' to attract the seven twins, and you don't want them coming to you."

Seven twins. I'd never heard her speak of them, and had no idea what it meant. I gestured with my head. "What have you got there?"

She showed me her left hand. She held what looked like a loosely rolled cigar, the end of it already charred as if half-smoked. That explained what I'd smelled out in the hall. On her right palm she had a square pouch of red calico that looked greasy, like whatever it had been stuffed with was leaking.

Mel lowered her hands again. "Go stand by the door and do not speak another word until I'm done."

There was a lot I wanted to ask—and knew better than to do so—but I returned to the hall doors, opened one a crack. At the far end of the hall, Marcellus walked along, putting out the last of the lard oil lamps on the side tables. He'd taken over Tall George's hall duties tonight.

I quickly shut the door again and pressed my back to it. At least, I thought, the smell of those spent candles would mask the tobacco scent I'd noticed.

Meanwhile, Mel had lit the cigar off the southeast corner candle, and she'd slung the wicker basket over her shoulder.

She started walking and half-stepping along the long outside wall of the room, a kind of slow dance during which she waved the tobacco in swirls through the air and, under her breath, began singing very softly in skritchy syllables somewhere between a prayer and a spell. She called it a *priyè*, and I'd heard its like a few times before from her at Tyler's plantation, but outdoors and in the night. I'd made a point of not finding out about it; but watching pressed tight to the doors, I felt like Odysseus against the mast, transfixed by one of the beautiful sirens who was taking her sweet time getting around to me.

Her slithery glide took her close to the wall. She rubbed the calico pouch across windowsills, over lamps, under tables, up the side of the black fireplace mantel, and then across the huge mirror above it. She stretched up on her bare toes and fit her hand around behind the mirror. She stepped back, staring at herself there a moment. Then she sashayed away with a new pouch in her hand. She sang and made more signs until she reached the upright piano; then she crouched low behind it and another pouch disappeared. She reached into the basket for a third as she rose up.

By the time she reached the north end and turned to start back along the inside wall, the curtains on all three sides of us were swelling and flapping from some late breeze. I thought the guttering candles would go out, but they didn't. If anything, they seemed to be burning brighter than the Argand lamps on the mantels, none of which was lit nor the oil-lamp chandeliers nor the wall sconces. How could candles cast that much light?

Mel sidled up to the doors, and passed the pouch around and across their surface, and then past me as if I wasn't there. She waved the burning tobacco, blew it in my face, but her eyes seemed rolled up under her lids. I didn't know how she was guiding herself. Her singing never stopped. She touched every shiny surface, everything metal, even the fireplace tools.

At each of the four fireplaces, she leaned down and reached up under the mantel. I knew there was a lintel shelf in the throat of the firebox, and I guessed she was placing one of her pouches on each of them. I half-expected her to drop something into the round furnace duct cut out beside it.

Once she had completed the circuit, she moved out into the middle, where she swirled the cigar in elaborate motions up under each of the chandeliers. The smoke, I thought, appeared to shape itself into insubstantial *veves* as it floated in among the glittering glass.

Finally, she returned to the center, set down the basket, and laid the stub of the cigar across it. She knelt, drew a small bottle from out the basket, unstoppered and poured it over her hands, washing them a moment. She picked up the stub again, blew on it, and then pressed her hands together around it. They burst into blue flame. I gasped and started to run to her, but hadn't taken two steps before the flames were gone, and Mel was just a dark shape.

The four candles had gone out as well. The curtains what had bellied out now hung motionless.

She got up. "James," she called in a whisper, and I ran to her, took her hands. Rubbed them. They felt smooth and unblistered. I sniffed one.

"Rum?" I said.

She nodded. "Ogun's pleasure. Now we can go."

I didn't know who Ogun was, nor cared to find out. "Where?" I asked.

"Back down to the kitchen. These parlors all are protected now. Private floor—that one's going to be much harder."

"Protected against what?" I asked.

She picked up the basket. "Against whatever it is that's comin'," she said. She turned and headed for the interconnecting door to the Green Parlor. I hurried after her, and we made our way through the parlors and then quickly across the dim hall to the service stairs. There we went separate ways. My duties were to ensure that everything was in order upstairs and here for when the family returned from Dolley Madison's.

Mel went down to the ground floor, to safety.

➤➤➤ ❴❴❴

Tyler's party still hadn't returned by the time I retreated downstairs. It was nearing midnight. The parlors and dining rooms was closed and quiet, and no trace of any rituals that had taken place in them. Not even the tobacco smell remained above the stink of lard oil.

I felt as exhausted as if I'd performed the rites myself, but I could honestly say to Alice tomorrow morning as we sat at the piano that she was as safe as could be in that room now.

The kitchen was dark and no lights showed at the far end of the vaulted hall. Everyone had gone to bed, and I did the same. But the door to my room hung open and I knew I hadn't left it that way—I didn't like anybody peering in there while they ate in the mess room. I edged into the doorway and held the candle up in front of me.

First thing I noticed was the white shift draped over the fan-back rocker beside my bed. Then I spied the wicker basket resting on its seat.

"Mel," I said, and she rolled over to face me. Naked, she leaned up on one elbow, and patted her other hand upon the mattress beside her. She smiled like a cat in cream.

I closed the door behind me and set my candle on the washstand. Then I undressed too. I looked at her all the while, at the wicker basket, which I could see still held something. I pointed toward the chair. "More calico pouches?"

"Called *ouangas*," she explained.

"Do I want to know what that means?"

She huffed. "You helped me hide them an' you don't want to know what they are? You are a very stubborn man, James Christian."

I grinned. "So you like to remind me." I got into bed beside her. She stared back as eagerly as if it was our first time. When she studied on me that way, I could not imagine anything other than being pressed against her and deep inside her. Mel could make me forget that any other world existed.

She liked to begin slowly, with tiny bites and nibbles, while I rubbed my palms in circles over her small breasts till they stood tight at the points. Her hair was wet, her back too.

"How'd you get so wet all over?"

"Used a tap inside the east colonnade. You pull on a chain, a waterfall pours down on you, cold as if ice melted to make it."

"That's a shower bath for the men upstairs," I objected, "Mr. Tyler and Mr. Robert."

She made no reply, and before I could lecture her on using it she reached down and took hold of me and I forgot my words, my intentions, everything but her touch. I just went where she wanted to go, and from then on there was nothing else but Mel for a long, long time.

Even when I had wits of my own again, all I could do was lay entangled with her like we was two vines grown from foot to headboard. Awhile later, I leaned up and watched her in the light of the candle. The sharpness to her face never went away, even in the soft pillow of sleep, but as if she could feel my eyes describing her, her own sly eyes opened and stared back.

"Them *ouangas* is charms. Talismans," she said, as if our conversation had never ended. She reached down to the basket.

Turning back, she held up a different object, far more elaborate, looking like a cloth turnip wrapped in ribbons and cords, and sparkling with sequins, tied off with feathers that stuck out like roots. "This a *pakét kongo*. I made some for *makaya*. With the right leaves, these can be for healing. This one's for something else, something that *ouangas* don't do. I put one of these in the blue room and one in that East Room, in one of the fireplaces."

"What's it do? Keep someone from coming down the chimney?"

She rolled over and put it back in the basket. "James. Always teasing to hide your fear. The thing is hereabouts, but I never knew such a one before. I'm thinking there's a *bokor* somewhere about."

"You know I don't know what you're saying."

"And you think you don' want to."

"You think I'm scared—but what I'm scared of is having to say what you do. Mr. Tyler asks me, I want to be able to say, 'Why, Mary Elena, she just cookin' y'all's food, sir, she not doing nuthin' with magic that I's heard of.'"

She snorted. "You don't speak like that to nobody."

"And would you like it better than, 'The very instant that I saw you, did my heart fly to your service'?"

She held her lower lip in her teeth a moment, then slowly shook her head. "I don't want you soundin' like anyone else," she said, and pressed herself to me again.

After that second time, I know I slept. I awoke when she climbed out of the bed.

"Time to go, is it?" I asked. That was our old routine, back in Virginia, her going off to start the morning, me lighting candles and lamps. Mr. Tyler was an early riser.

She stood, grabbed her shift. The candle had nearly gone out. She took another from the table drawer beneath it, lit that and turned back to me. Her eyes shone with that candlelight, laying bare what she felt, and I smiled back sleepily, warmed by it.

I watched her maneuver the basket up her arm and open the door. The mess was outlined in the dimmest gray light coming from the barred south window. I expected her to disappear, to close the door after, but she stopped there as if unable to go.

I'd been ready to roll over and go back to sleep. "What's wrong?" I asked.

"There's a man sittin' here," she said.

That brought me full awake. I was on my feet and pulling on my pants before I even knew what I was doing. Slid up my suspenders and pressed up behind her.

There was just light enough to make out the whole room. It was empty. I said as much.

Mel pointed to the bench on the far wall. "He just sittin' there, staring through the window like he wishes he was out instead of in. Air 'round him is glowing like there's a candle behind him instead of the wall. I never seen the like." She glanced at me. "This man is dead."

Hard as I stared, I couldn't see anyone, but I didn't want to. I knew already who it was. "Describe him," I said anyway.

"A smooth face, though his hair's an old man's, an' he look to be soaked through like he been in that shower bath after me. He's missing one shoe, and his yellow stocking hangin' loose from t'other foot."

"Isaac." I didn't mean to say his name out loud, but maybe I wanted to ward him off, to deny him. How could *she* know about him? He'd been buried before she ever got here. I had to tell her then, everything—how he had sat on that very bench while I heard about the Angel of Death coming for Harrison, how he'd told me about it himself up in the stable, and how he had later drowned and I'd had to identify him.

"This man never killed hisself," she insisted.

"They pulled him from the canal down below us. I saw." When she didn't respond, I said, "All right, you tell me what happened to him."

"Something found him. Same thing as was huntin' Alice."

Curtains and funeral drapes in the East Room. "Why's he here still?"

Instead of answering, she reached into the basket and took out the charm that looked like a turnip. She walked toward the bench, holding the *pakét kongo* out on her palm as if offering something to eat.

"Won't you drive him away with that?" I whispered.

"Only drive away the thing what's got its claws in him." She drew up sharply. "He's pointing at you, James." She asked the room, "What you want wit' him?"

I strained to see even an outline of a man. There was nothing at all. I leaned forward.

She gasped and jumped against me, yelling a string of words. I caught her shoulders, heard her yell, *"Dambala Wedo!"* There was a phrase I'd heard before.

A minute went by with neither of us breathing. Then she went and sat at the table, placing the basket and the bulbous *pakét kongo* before her.

What had happened? I wanted to know.

When she had asked him what he wanted, he'd opened his mouth to reply, but what she thought was his tongue had turned into a great gray snake twisting its way out of his gullet.

"Him's eyes went big and round with fear and he grabbed at his throat. That snake wasn't of his making. Was no true snake at all, and come at me. When I called on Dambala, it burned up green and was gone, but it took the man with it too."

"Why?" I sat beside her. "Make this make some sense."

"Isaac is trying to give you counsel, to warn you. The thing won't let him." Her eyes sought overhead, for a ghost on the ceiling or maybe one wrapped around a furnace duct for all I knew. She started to stand but I grabbed her arm.

"Why's he trying to speak with me? I hardly knew him, and all his people are gone."

"I don't know, James."

"You said...you said you thought there was a *bokor* hiding in the house. What does that mean? What's a *bokor?*"

A glint sharp and wrathy shone in her eyes. "*Bokor* is a sorcerer. The very darkest arts." She placed the *pakét kongo* back into the basket. "What else would I need all these for?" She drew free of me and I let her go. They would be expecting her down the hall in the kitchen. We had slept a few hours at most.

I edged around the table to the bench where Isaac had supposedly sat. Directly beneath that spot, the gray light slanting through the iron-barred window shone on a large puddle of black water.

Sixteen

Letitia Tyler lay propped up on pillows on her bed, wearing the formal green gown in which Devonee and Deborah had dressed her, her hair coiffed and curled across her forehead. Alone in the room, she trembled, the sensation of being watched so intense that it was like ants crawling over her skin.

When Devonee tramped in with her supper tray, Letitia pushed the slate across her gown to the edge of the bed. On it, with all the control she could muster, she had written, *Someone in here with me.*

Devonee read it and hastily set the covered tray on the table. She put her hands to her mouth.

Letitia had seen that Devonee sensed the presence too—the way her eyes darted every which way just before extinguishing the light or turning down the lampwick beside her cot.

"You want I should get somebody? Who you want, missus?"

Letitia dragged back the slate, turned it over. *John,* she wrote.

Devonee wrung her hands, nodded, said, "Yes, ma'am," then hurried out, leaving the food on the sidetable.

Letitia patted the covers for her prayer book, then weakly clutched it to her breast. At the edge of her vision across the room, the surface of the tall mirror roiled like the dark clouds of an approaching thunderstorm.

Then John came marching in from his chambers next door. His hair was brushed forward and pomaded. He wore the tailcoat that made him look so official and upright. "What is it, dear, why did you send Devonee?" he asked. He sat beside her on the bed, put his hand to her brow. She'd run a fever earlier in the day, likely from being carried down to the shower bath and washed in that fiercely cold water. But she had insisted. "Your fever's abated," he informed her.

He lifted the cloth from the tray, looked over the food: a plate of roast veal garnished with parsley and lemon slices, and a squash puree, plus his favorite confection of baked apples smothered in sweetened wine sauce—called black caps. It was, in miniature, what their marvelous cook had prepared for the levée itself. The aroma made her stomach gurgle.

"Oh, this looks delectable, my dear. Such wonderful fare. That Mary Elena is a huckleberry above a persimmon, isn't she?"

She pressed her head back against the pillows propping her up to see the mirror, how it had become flat and dull in his presence.

John turned around as if in anticipation of someone else entering. He seemed nonplussed that Devonee hadn't returned with him.

Letitia tried to get hold of the slate again, but he snatched it up and read her message. Glanced again out the door.

Irritated, he said, "Of *course* you want someone in here with you. Of course you do. I do not understand where the girl has got to." He turned the slate over and read his own name. Sighed. He gave her back the slate. "Oh, my dearest dear, I wish I could sit with you tonight as well, but you know this is the *first* levée. And here you are made all beautiful yourself. I wish we could walk downstairs together, hand in hand like in years past in Virginia. Already right now there are ambassadors and congressmen and so many others down on the public floor. Seaton's here, you know. And your dear friend Dolley will be arriving at any moment, and surely will come up to see you right away." He pressed his hands together. "But this night of all nights I cannot be your companion here." He glanced around. "Where *is* that Devonee?"

Letitia had smeared out his name and begun to write *Not Devonee* in its place, but paused to think how to phrase what she wanted to say so that he would understand. Unfortunately, in that pause he read those first words.

"Oh, I see." He looked her in the eyes. "Well, we'll take care of that, won't we?" He squeezed her hand, stood up stiff and furious.

That was the moment Devonee came rushing in again. John did not stop, but forced her back into the hallway. Letitia tried to call to him, but he didn't hear.

"Listen here, Devonee," he said. "You are to find someone else to stay with my good wife this evening. She has expressly said she does not wish your company, and I can well understand her misgivings. How *dare* you leave your poor mistress alone."

"But, Mr. Tyler, sir, I left her to git you."

"And did you think I would be able to feed her with all that's going on tonight?" He made a huff of irritation. "We will discuss this tomorrow after I have spoken to James on what ought to be done with you." He walked back in and yanked on the bell pull beside Letitia's bed.

Devonee shook her head. There was no one downstairs to answer it. Letitia groaned, helpless to intervene. John glanced back. She raised her hand. He leaned down and squeezed it. "Don't you worry, my darling. I won't have you left alone." Then he turned and marched off down the hall.

Devonee came in finally. "I told Mel," she whispered. "But she cain't do nothin' now either, on account of the party. You know that she knows about things what aren't right and how to fix 'em. She swore she be up soon as she can. I had to go tell her, missus. You know I'd never as run off an' leave you alone."

Letitia nodded. And she knew that Mary Elena was a healer, her reputation such that even their neighbors on the James River had sometimes sent for her aid. Letitia wasn't sure she would have characterized that as "knowing about things that weren't right," but her thoughts were interrupted by the arrival of Elizabeth. Dressed for a gala affair, her daughter did not disguise her frustration at being sent from the party, and coldly stated, "You're supposed to get gone, Devonee. Papa said he doesn't want you in here tonight."

Letitia chalked one word on the slate: *No.*

Elizabeth stared at it as if she couldn't divine its meaning, then gave her mother a big smile as if nothing was out of the ordinary. "You want me to feed you, Mother? Why don't I do that. It smells awfully good."

Letitia looked from her to Devonee, who put her hands out as if to say, "That's all right," then backed from the room.

Elizabeth picked up the cutlery and began to slice the veal into small bites.

⟫⟫ ⟪⟪

She was wiping the corners of Letitia's mouth with a napkin when Dolley Madison arrived. Beaming, she rapped on the wainscoting as if she hadn't been seen. "Oh, my dear Letitia," she said. "Look at you, if you were downstairs you'd outshine us all."

Dolley was dressed in her usual shawl and turban. As the room contained only the one chair by the bed, she insisted Elizabeth should go downstairs and have some punch. "In fact, send one of your admirers up to give us some punch too. I'm sure your mother would love a little punch, hmm? Wouldn't you, dear?"

There was no point in objecting. When Dolley Madison decided, you agreed. It had been thus as long as she'd known the woman.

Elizabeth bent over her. "I'll send Alice up after awhile, Mother." She kissed her cheek, then slipped around Dolley, who stood as immobile as a statue.

"Headstrong girl, always has been, hasn't she, dear? Really, I am greatly impressed that she was considerate enough to give of herself this evening, the way she gallivants. I suppose it's because young Mr. Waller isn't about."

Dolley plumped the cushion before sitting in the chair.

"So. I like how they fixed your hair. The curls really do suit you. You're absolutely radiant."

Letitia reached for the slate. In feeding her, Elizabeth had pushed it aside. Dolley reacted to her movement by grabbing the tablet first and reading the message on it.

"Oh, I quite agree. There should be someone in the room with you all the time." She looked behind her, at Devonee's empty cot beyond the wardrobe. "Did John make your girl go to the soirée?"

Letitia pressed her head back in the pillows and gave out a small moan. She wiped her husband's name from the slate, held the chalk at the ready, but finally set it down. She strained again to see the mirror. It reflected Dolley now, her white turban in particular, glowing like the moon set on its points. Dolley twisted in the chair to see what had caught her eye.

There was nothing to be gained by trying to explain to anyone what was going on when she didn't know herself. Even if she could express it, John would attribute it to the fever, or worse, begin to suspect that her mind was succumbing to the strokes. But she knew with all certainty of a prayer that had Devonee not kept her company every night, what was swirling in the mirror would have claimed her already. There was no way to make them understand that.

She set down the slate and drew her *Book of Common Prayer* to her, wrapped her weak arms around it to clasp it to her bosom. She closed her eyes and recited, "*O God, make speed to save us. O Lord, make haste to help us*," until Dolley placed a hand upon hers.

"There is great solace in prayer, isn't there? It's *absolutely* where to put your trust—would you like me to recite with you, dear?"

Letitia opened her eyes, shook her head. Dolley meant well, but…

"Then let me distract you from your woes." And she launched into her prediction of how successful tonight's event would be based on those she had invited alone. British, French, Prussian ambassadors, and "even a few New England Democrats who have no particular reason to socialize with the likes of Virginia Whig John Tyler. Priscilla is going to do you proud. I've heard already that she took my advice to heart and has begun paying calls about the city on your behalf."

She was interrupted by the tall young kitchen slave, Marcellus, who was dressed in his footman's costume and carried a tray with two cups of punch on it. Dolley delightedly retrieved the punch, and the boy left without a word.

Now armed with punch, Dolley talked on about all sorts of matters—in particular the way Henry Clay was twisting arms to gain passage of his federal bank bill, and of some trial in New York that she considered would escalate into another war with the British. John had mentioned neither of these things to her, but when he was sitting here he tried to put behind him the day-to-day drudgery of the office.

It wasn't long before Alice appeared in the doorway. She politely greeted Dolley and explained that Elizabeth had told her to come up to spell Mrs. Madison.

Dolley said, "You are very sweet, dear." She took her glass of punch and stood. "Letitia, I'll bring the women of Washington up here tonight if Priscilla doesn't lead her own coalition first." She squeezed her hand, then asked Alice to accompany her into the hall.

The two of them spoke too quietly for her to hear, although Dolley did glance her way once or twice. Were they discussing her condition?

Letitia's attention was drawn again to the cloudy mirror, but its depths remained still. No doubt the frustrated presence had given up on getting her alone. At least she had achieved that.

>>>- <<<

Alice sat beside the bed with Letitia's Bible open in her lap.

Between interruptions by the women—mostly congressmen's wives—accompanying Dolley to meet Letitia, they had read some from the *Book of Prayer* together. Letitia had been told something of Alice's fright in the East Room, and though John and Robert both dismissed it as "the two children spooking themselves by playing amongst gloomy funerary items," she wondered if it wasn't possible that what had frightened Alice was the same thing tormenting her. Could this presence move around the house? If so, it obviously enjoyed terrifying her family. And why? What had they done?

Letitia lay with her eyes closed while her daughter read in a soft, clear voice from the Book of Ruth: "The Lord grant you that ye may find rest, each of you in the house of her husband. Then she kissed them; and they lifted up their voice, and wept."

When she did not continue with the next line, Letitia opened her eyes.

A slender black woman had entered the room, carrying a large flat bowl. It took her a moment to realize it was their cook. Rare to encounter her—she hadn't even seen her on the journey up from Virginia.

Mel said, "You been here a good long time, Miss Alice. Go be with your father awhile. I know he wants to show you off to all them people. My chores are done and I'll look after your mama." The woman had some power. Her words acted as instructions upon Alice, who closed the Bible, kissed Letitia on the cheek, and then left the room.

Mel sat down where Alice had been. She had a sharp face, shrewd in the older sense of the word. The bowl she held contained a thick, steaming broth, which she placed on the bedside table with the dinner tray.

Letitia stared at Mel's hands. They were dirty.

Noticing, Mel told her, "I had to make a special charm in a hurry for you between all the cooking. You got at least three hundred people down there tonight. Didn't know if I would ever get away." She smiled.

She reached beneath her apron and brought out a green calico object wrapped in red ribbon, stitched with sequins, and with black feathers sticking out the top. Cupping it in both her upturned palms, she held it out before her as if offering it to her mistress.

Letitia groped for her slate, but Mel ignored her, stepped to the center of the room, and then turned in a slow circle with the object extended. She didn't stop turning until she faced the cloudy mirror. "He been here wit' you," she said.

Amazed, Letitia stared as Mel sashayed over to the mirror, her moves like some sort of dance, as if she was taunting her reflection. She had begun to hum quietly a tune that prickled the hair on Letitia's arms. Gooseflesh.

Upon reaching the mirror, Mel spat onto it. Then, still cupping the glittering charm in her other hand, she pressed one finger into her spit and pushed it around into lines and squiggles, spit a second time and drew stars into the quadrants she'd formed.

The sense of the impalpable presence dissolved. Letitia sighed deeply, realizing as she did what a latent tension had been clinging to her.

Mel turned from the mirror, smiling. "Devonee told me about your visitor. Comin' to know him, sweet woman, I'm chasin' him all through this house. Him's driven from the first floor. Before long up here too. When others are with you, he disappear, don't he?"

Letitia closed her eyes in assent, gave her head a nod. Her cook knew everything.

"But he always comes back after, and we going to stop that."

Mel turned, gripped the charm, and pushed the oily bottom of it around the edges of the mirror until she had made a full circuit. The smear it left hardly showed at all, like a light coating of oil.

"Legba guard this mirror, close the doorway."

She drew across it with the greasy charm.

"But we can't keep closing it all the time. So we got to do more to keep you safe after. Now, you do as I say, all right? I can't lift you out your bed, and I got to push up the mattress. When I do, you gonna roll to the wall for me. You can do that?"

Letitia nodded. She could.

Mel began removing the various pillows that propped her up, piling them in a line along the wall. "Going to put this *pakét* deep under you. If someone like to find it when they change your sheets, then it can't protect you. So we make sure they don't."

She slowly pushed up the side of the mattress, shouldering it off the slats of the frame. Letitia, arms folded, embracing her prayer book, tipped onto her side and rolled almost face down against the pillows. Her slate and chalk tangled in the bedclothes. She felt the lump of a hand slide beneath her, under the mattress, then found herself rolling onto her back again.

It took Mel only a few moments to rebuild the pile of pillows and hand Letitia the slate and chalk.

"There now," she said as she straightened out Letitia's dress, and tucked her hair back into place. "Your visitor will have to go somewhere else after this. Can't stand what's protecting you now. But you feel him back again, you tell Devonee to come get me right away. We want to be rid of him everywhere."

Yes, wrote Letitia. *Get him gone.*

Mel laughed. She picked up the bowl, saying, "Now you need to eat some soup to help you rest."

There wasn't much of it. She ate it all. It was strangely sweet, and she couldn't recall having ever eaten it before. At the end, she felt more alive and safe than she had since being placed in this big dark house.

About then, Elizabeth returned. Nervous, and apparently frightened that she had succeeded too well in shirking her duties, she told Mel, "I didn't know Alice had come down. I feared we'd left her alone. Didn't mean to."

Letitia tapped on her slate. Wrote, *It's all right.*

Mel said, "I made her something so she can sleep. You don't have to worry about her no more tonight."

Elizabeth crossed to the chair and plunked down. "I don't care, I'm not leaving her unattended the rest of the night."

Nodding, Mel carried away the bowl and the dinner tray.

Letitia reached weakly for her daughter's hand.

"The levée was simply grand, Mother. I met all *sorts* of people—a roguish French attaché, and there's an Englishman who's intoxicatingly wicked. Such blue eyes. Of course I didn't *do* anything about the way he beguiled me. I could never betray Billy. But there's nothing wrong with being a little coquettish, is there? Priscilla dazzles all the men with her presence, and that's with Robert right there at her side. I didn't even do that much."

As Elizabeth droned on, Letitia drifted off. Whatever was in that soup worked exactly as Mary Elena said. Now the room was safe, and she no longer had to worry at all.

Seventeen

James Hambleton Christian

All night long Marcellus and I led guests through the house from the north door to the East Room. The cross hall was thick with people, a flowing river of them with us sliding through the ripe currents. Sometimes arrivals would spot friends and turn aside, and we might find ourselves leading nobody at all, our charges swallowed up, already lost in a crowded parlor, the etiquette of their being announced tossed aside, and we would wrestle along to the East Room to hand their card at least to Mr. Robert or Miss Priscilla, so that they were aware of the person's presence. This left Mr. Tyler free to hold conversations, move through the various rooms, smoke a cigar in the Blue Saloon alongside other cloudbound smokers and those dipping a pinch, sharing a spittoon, or debate Texas statehood in the State Dining Room.

Tall George and Samuel walked through the raging frolic with trays of tea cakes and tarts and slivers of almond cheesecake that were snatched from them as if by locusts. Deborah offered lemonades for those who did not desire the champagne or decanted wine, mostly women. Sally and Olive and Ethel spelled each other in making sure the dining room offered enough platters of food, and cutlery and plates for everyone, though Sally mostly watched the sleeping baby upstairs.

I saw and heard only snippets throughout the night—arguments over granting statehood to Texas, or whether "that McLeod fella" should be hanged. I didn't know anything about what had fallen out upstairs until, coming back from the East Room, I glimpsed Devonee setting a tureen of cauliflower puree upon the table in the State Dining Room, and made my way to the west stairs before she did.

"What are you doing here?" I asked her, and was rewarded with the whole story of "Miss Letitia's *haant*"—a Gullah word she'd picked up from Ethel—and the repercussions of informing Mel. It was possible that Mr. Tyler would insist Devonee be replaced come tomorrow, and we would have to confront that as it came.

Later on, while I sought one of those straying sheep whose calling card I held, I entered the Green Parlor just as a half-drunk Georgia congressman in an untidy yellow vest and coat caught sight of Deborah passing by, and shouted above the din, "We's bein' served by a goddam Injun!" I changed direction to intercede, intending to require her services elsewhere, but Mayor Seaton got there first and politely drew the yokel away. Deborah passed me, and from the hard look in her eyes I guessed it wasn't the first time that night somebody had demeaned her. Seemed that among our statesmen, poltroons and bumpkins were well-represented. Then again, I doubt any Georgia congressman would have given a damn for her.

Deborah had run away from a household outside Brunswick. She'd stolen a pressed white shirt and made her way north by getting passage on a boat, carrying that shirt on board as if delivering it to her master. There had been other runaways on the boat too. As the story had come to me, she'd given that shirt to one of them. Later on, up the coast, the boat had run aground near Beaufort, and she and the others had been chased down by men with dogs. That white shirt had been like a beacon in the night, and the men had set their dogs on the fellow she'd given it to. Desperate, she gave herself up, but they gleefully let the dogs tear him to bits. She hadn't spoken a word since—anyway, not in all the time she'd served in the Tyler house even under provocation such as the Georgia yokel.

⇶ ⬿

By midnight, the levée moved on to Dolley Madison's house. People swarmed out and across the park like a hive of bees.

Before leaving, Mr. Tyler took me aside. He was positively grinning. "James," he said, "I want you to give all the staff a bit of their own frolic for the excellent job they've done. You're all to finish the veal, have a bottle of wine, be proud of how you have represented us this first night." He made no mention of Devonee and the earlier incident. I was fairly certain then that we would hear nothing further of it.

"Yessir," I said. "Thank you, sir."

Tall George got hauled along to drive the family across the park, as if they were royalty who could not be so put upon as to have to walk to a destination they could see from here. Samuel accompanied them.

The veal was carried down to the mess with other leftovers and spread across the table. We were all free to eat and enjoy ourselves now that we were all exhausted.

Mel came in with Zenobia and Devonee. I shook my head at them, got up, and walked back into the hall with Mel. "We come so close to trouble with this, and it's lucky for Devonee that Mr. Tyler's over the moon tonight. He could as easily have told me to send her back to Virginia or worse, but for the moment he's forgotten, and I expect I can get Miss Letitia to advocate if it comes to it."

"Wasn't her fault," Mel said. "Miss Letitia was terrified. That mirror in her room is another threshold. Devonee obeyed the missus, then quick come to tell me. The mister wasn't going to do nothin', and it needed fixing."

I wanted to ask how many times was it going to need fixing? How long before she got caught in the act of warding off what nobody had clapped eyes on? But I didn't. She had protected Miss Letitia this time.

⟫⟫⟩ ⟨⟪⟪

Everyone ate and celebrated. Most of them, dog-tired, soon turned in. I'd tossed my coat in my room, unbuttoned my vest and rolled up my sleeves, and wandered the first floor, carrying a bottle of claret with me while I assessed the damage we would be cleaning up in the morning.

Plates and cutlery lay scattered about through all the parlors, broken stemware, and here and there a spittoon that had been knocked on its side. There would be a lot of laundry—napkins and tablecloths—a lot of scrubbing. About every carpet would have to be hauled outside and beaten.

I strolled out of the Blue Saloon onto the south portico. I was intending to deliberate alone, but spied Cyrus and Marcellus sitting on the curving right-hand stairs, and I walked down, edged around them, then squatted down on the landing, stretching my legs out, which made me groan.

I handed the bottle to Marcellus above me. He took a pull and passed it to Cyrus, sitting above him. Cyrus still had on his long tailcoat from being the coachman all evening, but he'd taken off the white gloves he'd worn while handing people down from or up into their carriages. The moon gleamed on his bald skull, shadowing the smallpox pits in his face as he reached to hand the bottle back down.

He leaned forward on his thighs. "We was discussing that Paul Jennings—Mr. Webster's valet."

"Uh-huh," I said. "Don't believe I saw him."

Cyrus said, "He come along with Mr. Webster tonight, but he stayed out front. We got to talkin'. You know he used to be Dolley Madison's slave but she sold him to Webster on account of she needed money?"

"I've heard something of it."

"Jennings told me old Dolley expects to be the queen of society till the day she dies. Always has plenty on hand to drink for these soirée evenings though she is church-mouse poor. Ain't got nuthin' but her house, and Jennings says he been givin' her money outten his own pocket, on account of Mr. Webster's lettin' him earn his freedom, paying him a full salary, same as he would a hired white servant."

Marcellus took another pull and handed me the bottle. "Maybe we oughta look into if we can all git bought by ol' Webster," he said. "I could do with some money of my own."

Cyrus guffawed. "You wantin' to buy Zenobia something pretty?"

"Maybe."

I told them how I'd overheard Ambassador Fox in the Green Parlor this night saying we'd all be at war soon, and that if the British won, they intended to abolish the "peculiar institution."

"Then we *all* git free," said Marcellus. "No need for Websters."

Cyrus snorted and rolled his head back and forth. "Boy, that won't mean nuthin' to Tyler. He just haul us all back to Virginia. James, you know it too, you been in his service longer. Virginia ain't never giving in. Different if you get up north maybe. But down on the James River they gonna go right ahead sellin' your family and you don't have no say."

"Cyrus, quit your damn picking on Marcellus." I knew that at ten Marcellus had seen his older sister sold on the block to help fund one of Tyler's senate races. Cyrus knew it too.

But Marcellus raised his hand, capitulating. "Naw, he's right, likes of Tyler ain't goin' to be persuaded by no Britishmen." His words were starting to slur together.

I drank and gave the bottle to him again. "We'll all go north then," I said, "and to hell with 'em."

Now Cyrus laughed at me. "Oh, that's jist fine for you, Mr. 'I Talk Their Talk.' You kin go anywhere an' slide right on in. You're light enough and educated enough, they kin almost pretend you's not of the colored persuasion."

Cyrus was good at getting under anybody's skin; usually I shrugged him off, but the wine made me bold and irritable. I answered, "I got more education than most of them, and they don't like being reminded of it nohow, same as most colored folk don't like it neither, 'cause they think I'm talking just to show off. Whatever way I turn, nobody likes it, and they want me to act stupid so they can feel comfortable with it." I shoved my sleeves down and fixed the cuffs up again. "There ain't anybody forgets my persuasion, Cyrus, not for one goddam moment."

I stood then. My legs wobbled and I leaned against the railing.

Cyrus began to laugh, and after a moment so did Marcellus, and then so did I, as if laughter was a breeze blowing down the stairs.

I pushed away from the rail. "I do bid you gracious gen'men a most excellent evening and I thank you for sharing my wine. Last of all the Romans, fare thee well," I said, and made a big sweeping bow to them. As I started to turn away, Marcellus tilted his head back to look at Cyrus.

"What you think of that?" he asked.

"Right snooty, I say."

"Ain't he just, though? Next thing, I bet he runs for office."

"That Henry Clay better look out."

I waved behind myself at them, refusing to get drawn back in. Exhausted and inebriated, I wandered under the portico and to the furnace room door. In the deeper darkness I almost didn't see the thing on my left, and had taken a half-step past it before its shape registered. I backed up.

Nailed into the wood at the height of my elbow was a small doll made from rags and twine.

I had seen such figures before, once when a field hand had died in an accident at Walnut Grove, and once on the gate of a slave cemetery along the James River.

It was a poppet.

I wiped a hand across my face and stumbled inside. In the furnace room, I nearly struck my forehead on one of the low metal ducts. I stooped under it, then headed to the kitchen.

It was all dark, no one there, but the women's dormitory room still glowed from an oil lamp. I marched along the hall to the doorway.

Some of the women stood or sat in dishabille, and Deborah was stark naked. For one instant I glimpsed the whip scars on her back before she turned and held up her shift. They all glanced from me to Mel. She was still dressed for kitchen work and was reclining, lying with her bare feet up on a pine wardrobe beside her bed. There were two wardrobes in the room, as well as a couple pine tables, a long bench, and some chairs.

"Mel, I need to talk to you," I told her.

She rolled out of bed without a word, grabbed the chamberstick off the table beside her, and came out into the hall. She passed me and kept going, leading the way through the furnace room and out the door. Knew already what had me agitated.

She waited for me there. In the candlelight, I could see that the poppet was green and how she'd stitched on button eyes and a mouth. "Do you want to find yourself sold on the block tomorrow, Mel? What are you *doing?*"

The more I got worked up, the calmer she became. "It's for Isaac," she said. "His spirit needed guidin' out of here. I trapped him in, James, with the *veves*. I got to help him find a way out. Him's in fierce danger."

I bowed my head and told myself that I had caused this. I hadn't put a stop to it the other night when she saw Isaac's ghost, when she pulled out that charm of hers. A tiny voice in my head reminded me that she had *seen* Isaac without even knowing of him, but my hot fear-driven temper drowned it out. "This ain't Greenway," I told her, forgetting that she hadn't been bought by Tyler till after he'd sold that plantation. "This ain't laying a cure on a bunch of superstitious field slaves."

It was like I'd slapped her. I hadn't meant it to sound that way, as if I thought all of her cures were nonsense, but I couldn't stop myself now.

"Mel, this is nobody's grave, and if the white folk see this, they'll *know* who it was fashioned it. Tyler will ship you back and sell you to make an example, you and Devonee both. Even Miss Letitia won't be able to save you,

you embarrass that man."

She gave a look that asked how I thought she didn't know the risk.

"If you… If I lose you, lose you to this house—"

"Them upstairs folk don't come through this door, James. You know that, 'least when you're sober, you do."

"You can't be sure. Miss Priscilla saw the cornmeal *veves* because *she* came down here. They'll hire themselves a new furnace tender."

"Not before winter. You barely believe what's going on in this house anyway, so good at talkin' yourself out of what you know, what you saw with your own eyes, that water."

Under the bench. That puddle. Why was it there? Why did it have to be there?

"Isaac never getting free of this place without my help now." She gave a nod at the poppet. "I called Maman Brigitte to come take him, soon as she can."

"And how long is that—how long till Maman Brigitte responds?"

"It's not going to take till winter," she teased.

"Mel, please. Tell me."

"Today maybe, or tomorrow. She got to come when she's called this way, to carry a soul home."

"Two days," I said. "All right. But she comes or not, that's the last day. After that I'm taking it down to protect you. Protect *us*." I wanted to wrap my arms around her; even half-drunk I knew she would push me away.

She gave me a look both sympathetic and pitying, then walked back inside. The light of her candle bobbed through the furnace room and was gone.

In the dark I glared at that spiked poppet, sorely tempted to rip it away now. But I didn't. I had promised, and could only pray that the "upstairs folk" continued to adjudge this a servants' entrance. Maman Brigitte, whatever else she was, had damn well better come soon or it wouldn't be Isaac who left here.

⤞ ⤝

Two mornings later, while Mel was at the market, Zenobia found me upstairs in the family dining room where Sally and Ethel were clearing away the family's breakfast dishes.

"I thought you'd gone with Mel," I said, but could see right away that something was wrong. I'd an awful premonition. "What's happened?"

"You need to come." It was like she didn't want to tell me in front of the other two. They had stopped to watch.

"Finish up," I told them and followed after Zenobia.

In the stairwell she spoke over her shoulder. "I was with her, and she sent me back to tell you a supply wagon's comin' with a side of beef. Be here soon now."

"Uh-huh, but that's not what you didn't want to say."

She shot out of the stairwell and down the brick hall, where she entered the furnace room, bobbed down going under the ducts, and led me outside beneath the south portico. She stopped there, and with a dip of her head indicated the ground at my feet.

I peered at a whole lot of green flecks, some bits of animal fur and sinew, and what looked like snake vertebrae, all half-stomped flat. Then I saw a button. I wheeled about.

The naked, rusty spike impaling the poppet projected from the wood where Mel had nailed it up. But the poppet itself was what we were looking at. Someone had ripped it to shreds and ground it into the dirt.

Mel hadn't done this even though I'd told her it had to come down today. None of the family nor Webster could be responsible either or I would already have been taken to task over it.

Somebody else had done this.

"Right now, go inside, ask everybody if they saw anyone out here at all this morning, no matter who." She took a step, and I added, "If any of them were out here yesterday, last night, find out if they noticed whether the poppet was still nailed up."

Zenobia went inside. I walked out from under the porch. From the stable at the end of the west colonnade, down the sloping grounds to Jefferson's stone wall, and all the way to the brick carriage stable way up on my left, there was nobody in view. One carriage rolled past far down the hill, a couple out for an early ride before the day heated up. They had the paths all to themselves.

I ran up the steps where I'd sat drinking wine. The doors from the three parlors onto the portico all stood open, letting air flow through the house. I could hear Mr. Webster declaiming in the Blue Saloon. A dozen or so men sat in there listening. The other two parlors were empty this morning. I went down the other steps, and had just reached the landing when the wagon Mel had sent came rolling through the old east arch, headed straight for me. I would need George and Marcellus to help carry in the side of beef, and I would need the record book from the kitchen pantry so that I could write down all the purchases. Mr. Tyler was unhappy with the price of food from the markets, and he wanted an exact accounting of every single item that came into the house. That had to be the first order of business, not the torn-up poppet.

In came bags of buckwheat, rice, corn, and sugar, ham hocks, snap peas, potatoes, onions, and other root vegetables, jugs of vinegar and molasses—everything including the side of beef we'd been told of was hauled inside. I wrote it all down.

By the time I stood in the hall paying the driver and taking his receipt, Mel came in carrying a thirty-pound mackerel past me and into the kitchen. She swung it up onto the wooden counter as if it weighed hardly anything, grabbed a bucket and a long thin-bladed knife, and then began to gut the fish. The entrails she scooped into the bucket at her feet.

The driver watched in awe until I saw him out through the furnace room to his wagon. I was about to go back in but glimpsed Mel walking across to Jackson's stable. She had that knife in one hand, the bucket in the other. I headed after her.

On the far side of the stable, she dumped out the mackerel guts. There were feral cats that roamed from Lafayette Park all the way to the Potomac. The offal was her treat for them. They did a real good job keeping the river rats from making it as far as the house. Mrs. Weems had told me about them, though I didn't recall telling Mel. She just seemed to know.

I called out to her, "Didn't Zenobia find you? You need to come right away."

She dropped the knife into the empty bucket. "Told her I would be only a minute. What is so terrible wrong now?"

Around and under the south porch we went. Zenobia already waited in the open doorway.

Mel walked straight to the spike, brushed her hand over it. "I know you didn't do this and nor any of the upstairs folk." She knelt and dug free the button I'd noticed earlier. A scrap of cloth was still stitched to the back of it, but embedded under the dirt.

"Mel—"

"He's sending a clear warnin'." She seemed almost pleased. "Made him furious, James, look how he tore it up. Riled him to find it, when it ain't even directed at him."

"At who?" I asked, but remembered the word even as I spoke. "The *bokor.*"

Her eyes slid to meet mine. "You beginning to see a little."

"You're saying that your sorcerer, the one scaring Alice—"

"And Miss Letitia."

"That's who did this?"

Mel nodded. To Zenobia she said, "You already asked. They tell you no one saw anybody under here, not yesterday or today. Not so's they recollect."

Zenobia replied, "That's so."

I asked, "But *who* is he? Can't you make...something to reveal him?"

"It's not simple like that. This one is powerful, dark as midnight. Might be he can hide in shadows. You could stand right beside him and not know it. Might be he was at the levée, but not down here."

I exchanged a glance with Zenobia. She seemed as confused as I was. "Why not down here?"

"Because this made him angry. Wasn't expecting any interfering wit' his big plans. In General Harrison's house, was nothing in his way. Been teasin', scaring us for the fun of it—like them feral cats playing with a rat they caught. Whatever he is, now he knows it's not like that. Won't be so easy this time."

Zenobia swallowed. "He's goin' to hunt us, ain't he?"

Mel dug her toe in the dirt, pushing loose another shred of cloth. She looked up at us both. "He already is," she said.

Eighteen

Every other week or so, Jasper, the doorman, left the President's House and spent a day and night with his daughter, who lived in the city with her husband and child. On those occasions, Tall George Washington and James Christian shared his duties on top of their own, and for one night nobody occupied his small under-stairs apartment on the public floor.

Mel needed such an evening in order to seal his room—the last on the public floor to be protected. She waited in the service stairwell for him to leave, but then stayed there awhile longer.

Upstairs, baby Mary was crying. Her mother cooed to her until the baby fell silent, but Mel waited a quarter-hour after that. Sometimes Priscilla strolled the halls while Mary drifted to sleep. Tonight, though, there was no sound of footsteps and floorboards: Mother and daughter had stayed in their room.

Mel crossed the vestibule and entered Jasper's room.

The space was smaller than the one James had occupied at Walnut Grove, and it took her little time and less tobacco to make a circuit, paint the air, whisper the words, and find a place to hide one *ouanga*—down behind a loose jamb board in Jasper's cramped, triangular corner closet. His two formal outfits hung there.

Outside, a storm was brewing, but as yet only the wind had arrived. Mel left Jasper's door open, crossed the vestibule, and opened the front door. The wind pulled the smell of tobacco out into the night.

Lightning flashed distantly. She had closed the door and returned to Jasper's room before the sound of thunder followed. She pinched the wicks of her four candles, then placed them in the flour sack she'd brought along.

Rather than exiting into the hall, she crept across the vestibule, through the pantry and family dining room, to emerge in the main stairwell, from where she could see the length of the first floor. Everything was dark and silent. *Good.*

She started to turn away when a pale shape floated out of the east stairwell and into the hall, dwindling. It seemed vaporous, and Mel thought she was beholding another ghost. The shape hesitated before the East Room, then disappeared. It had gone into that room.

Quickly, silently, she strode after it along the matted floor. Lightning flashed again, lighting the empty parlors. She reached the East Room doors and paused.

Would it be Isaac? It couldn't be the thing that lurked in mirrors—not if her *ouangas* were still in place. She fingered the cord of the fetish bag she wore around her neck, her protection and power. She had to know what she had seen. Quietly, she opened the door and slipped into the East Room.

A drape in the north corner fluttered where one of the windows was cracked open. Thunder rumbled outside, well-removed from the lightning that had caused it. The storm was far off yet.

Most of the chairs were still lined up along the side walls from the levée. The upright piano was a solid, identifiable square shape in the middle. Something pale was just visible beyond it. Mel set down her flour sack.

She circled wide around the piano, and the pale form emerged. It sat in a chair in front of the exterior door to the promenade, the same place where Tazewell had hidden from Alice.

Closer now, she saw that it was a woman in a nightgown, but partially covered by the darker drape. An awful dread grew in Mel as she stole nearer. She gritted her teeth.

The woman's head was thrown back as if she was staring at the ceiling overhead, her throat white and bare, an offering. Her dark hair dangled behind her.

It was Priscilla Tyler. The drape was pushed out strangely around her. It described a body as if someone stood cloaked within it, hovering over Priscilla. Drapery hands pushed the nightgown from her shoulders, exposing her breasts.

Lightning flickered again.

The drape had pulled into something like a head that bent now as if to suckle at her breasts. Words were being whispered, feathery allurement.

There was no ghost here. There was something far worse.

Mel sprang to the curtain and tore it aside. It flapped like some huge bird of prey, whipping, snaring her for a moment, and then opening wide. The glass door behind it hung ajar. Outside, the top of the colonnade made a flat bare strip of light. Empty. Whatever she released, it had been no one.

She closed the outside door as more thunder rattled it.

Priscilla's eyes were rolled back in her head. Her expression leered, a horrible depraved grin. She breathed hoarsely. Her fingers opened and curled.

Mel berated herself for failing to protect this door when she had sealed the room. She could surely find somewhere on the stone outside it to scratch a *veve* to ward him off, but wondered what good it would do. There were open windows everywhere. This huge room alone was full of them. And he was immensely powerful, more than she had appreciated. Maybe more than she could appreciate. This room seemed to be a hub for his activities though. Did he lurk in here, reach deeper into the house from here?

Mel stood beside Priscilla. Carefully, she pulled up the nightgown, covering the wet milky breasts again.

Then she shook her awake.

Priscilla Cooper Tyler, still facing the ceiling, blinked a few times, and came to with a jolt. Fearfully, she looked around herself, focusing at last upon Mel beside her in the dark. "This is the East Room. Why am I in the East Room?"

"You was just sleepwalking is all, Miss Priscilla," she lied. "I happened to see you in the hall."

"I don't sleepwalk."

"Well, tonight you did. Let me help you back up to your bed." She drew Priscilla to her feet, then guided her around the piano. Lightning flashed. Carefully, Mel asked, "What do you remember?"

"Um. Mary was crying. I got up and fed her." She glanced down at the darker spots on her nightgown. Not much time had passed.

"Do you remember returning to your bed?"

Priscilla's face pinched. "I...I must have— I remember dreaming. There was dancing. Here, in this room. A levée. Everyone was whirling around us."

"Who was with you?"

Priscilla shook her head. "I couldn't see him. Masked—I think it was a masked ball. His hands were... Oh Lord, I can't speak of this."

Mel opened the door into the hall. "It was Mr. Robert, surely."

Priscilla sobbed. "No."

Mel placed a comforting hand on her shoulder. The skin burned hot as with fever.

As much as Mel wanted more details of the charged dream—especially the identity of the masked partner—she could not be so malapert. She had already inquired as much as she dared. But she'd beheld the rind of the dream and could guess the rest.

From the look on Priscilla's face, Mel doubted she would be able to sleep tonight for fear of being taken again, but in her room was where she belonged.

She walked Priscilla up the stairs. In the doorway to her room, in the candlelight, Mel glimpsed her husband and baby, both asleep and unaware.

She returned to the East Room to retrieve her flour sack. Lightning flashed, answered almost immediately by rumbling thunder. She closed the open window, paused to stare out again across the pale promenade atop the east colonnade. Rain was splashing down onto it now.

Despite the charms she had placed, the protections she had invoked, no one in this house was safe. Not even in their beds. Not even in their sleep.

Nineteen

James Hambleton Christian

Tall George held onto the pulley line that lowered the chandelier in the Washington Parlor while I inspected the cleaning that he and Marcellus had given it. The glass sparkled in the Wednesday mid-afternoon light.

We were expecting a dinner party of forty that evening, and it was already a sticky, humid day such that I couldn't help wondering how many more dinners and levées we would have before the awful summer heat drove most of the government out of the city. I recalled Dolley Madison warning Priscilla about the heat.

The door into the Blue Saloon was ajar, and through the crack I could see just two of the members of the British delegation—Ambassador Fox and a Mr. Cruickshank, who looked to be asleep, kept upright by leaning on his walking stick. I knew Webster was in there too, but for once he wasn't orating.

The hall doors creaked, and I turned to find Samuel coming in. He said, "Mister Tyler would like tea brought up for himself, Mr. Robert, and the secretary of the treasury."

"I'll see to it," I replied, then told George what a fine job he and Marcellus had done with the chandelier. When I turned to leave, Samuel had already withdrawn.

I took the service steps down to the kitchen. Mel was working alongside Zenobia, Marcellus, and Ethel on the preparations for the meal. They had the north door and every iron-barred window open to let in air.

I filled the teapot with hot water from the ranger. Mel gave me a sidelong glance but said nothing. She had been quiet the past few days, and hadn't visited me at night; I guessed she was planting her charms around the house. I wasn't about to ask.

As I set the cups on the tray, Ethel suddenly spoke to me. "You ansring dat bell fum up 'n Missuh Tyler's awfice, arnsha. Uh t'awt I'd go, but showly 'e redduh hab you." She grinned, showing the spaces between her teeth. I shook out that Gullah talk for what she was telling me: that Mr. Tyler had rung the bell in his office at least once and nobody had done anything about it. Mel looked my way and then Zenobia, but they added nothing. They were busy preparing his state dinner. The task of chasing after the ringing bells belonged to someone else.

The kitchen was Mel's domain, but at some point we were going to have to have a discussion about the importance of responding to those bells when we heard them. Sooner or later it was going to be about something more important than tea. I added leaves to the pot, took the tray, and headed upstairs.

>>>- -<<<

From Miss Letitia's room came the sound of baby Mary crying and her mother trying to sing-song her into stopping. Miss Priscilla had a pleasant voice, and the sweetness of her cooing to her little one accompanied me down the hall.

Save for Samuel on his chair, the waiting corridor lay empty, and that surprised me. It was a rare day when nobody had some petition or other to shove under Mr. Tyler's nose: a demand for water rights, or statehood for California, or how somebody'd lost everything because their bank had failed and they expected him to fix it. Maybe it was the mugginess of the hall that had driven them all away.

Samuel sat stiffly against the glow of the huge fanlight window as if I wasn't there. Fine, I thought, at least we weren't going to argue.

I balanced the tray on one hand while I opened the door.

Inside his office, Mr. Tyler sat conferring with his son and Mr. Ewing, the secretary of the treasury. None of them looked terribly happy. I heard the words "federal bank" as I set the tray down on the nearest table on top of a map of New England where a big section had been circled and labeled *Maine*. Then I stepped back and awaited my instructions. Sometimes Tyler liked tea poured for everybody and other times not.

Without looking up from the discussion of banks, Mr. Tyler said, "We rang three times, James."

"Yes, sir," I replied. I was prepared for this, courtesy of Ethel. "Nobody was in the mess this afternoon, as we're preparing for this evening's event. I was just now seeing the first-floor chandeliers are cleaned and the candles replaced. Got here fast as I could after Samuel found me."

Mr. Tyler looked up then. "No one to spare, I see. All right, well, thank you, James."

I bowed and stepped out into the waiting hall, feeling like I'd been told off.

Samuel continued to stare at nothing as if I wasn't there. Mr. Tyler's shortness had me galled enough now that I'd had about enough of his conceit.

I was all set to upbraid him when, on my right, the door of the secretary's room began to open. My first thought was that some petitioner had stolen into the secretary's room and Samuel had allowed it.

I took a step toward the opening door.

The light in the waiting hall shifted as if someone had thrown a curtain across that immense curved window, except that I could still see the muntins between the panes, and the stables in the daylit distance. But here in the hall the air seemed to congeal, going dark, and I remembered Mel saying how her sorcerer could use shadows.

Before I could collect myself, something rushed at me from the secretary's chamber—a silhouette.

I didn't even have time to blink. A black curtain closed over me. Skritchy words whispered at my ear, like Mel's breathy chants. Something grabbed my arm, stung my wrist between my shirt cuff and glove, and the black curtain dragged me to the bottom of the world.

Next thing I knew, a pretty white woman with auburn curls was doing her best to lean over me in her boned bodice and blue taffeta dress. She was speaking, repeating a word over and over. My name. It was a moment before I recognized the sound of it.

My one foot had pushed up the side of the rug. But when had I sat down, and why on the floor?

"Miss Priscilla?" I said. My mouth hardly worked. It was like I had never spoken her name before.

"James," she said again.

With her help I managed to sit fully upright.

Beside me, a door opened. I looked upside down at the head that poked out. Robert Tyler. "What is this?" he asked.

I tried to explain what had happened, but the only memory I could find was of Mr. Tyler dismissing me.

"He wanted some tea," I said to Miss Priscilla, which made hardly any sense nor answered for anything.

I'd one time seen a field slave name of Albert Moss kicked in the head by a horse he was trying to shoe, who had come to himself after a few minutes and couldn't remember the whole of the day, never mind the horse. The memory had been kicked clean out of his bruised skull. What had kicked me?

"Yes, we got our tea," Robert said to his wife. He gave her a look that I read as him telling her to deal with me herself. The door shut. I twitched at the sound.

"Did you fall?" Miss Priscilla asked. "Samuel, help me with him. Can you get to your feet?"

She tugged lightly on my arm. I rolled to my knees and stood, wobbly. I had to lean against the wall in order to identify "up," but I did remain on my feet. Samuel hadn't moved.

"Apparently so, ma'am," I said, although I wasn't so sure. My head pounded like my heart had surged up into it and was attempting to climb out through my left eye.

I went to press my palm against the pain. That's when I noticed the drop of blood on the cuff of my cotton glove. I peeled it back. Saw a dark spot on my wrist. Looked as if I'd been bit by something. The spot was swollen, like a bee sting.

Overhead were all those spiders up in the corners. Had one dropped down when I came out of Tyler's office? I glanced outside again, recalling how my first time on this floor I had compared the fanlight windows at each end to spider webs.

Then, for an instant, darkness wrapped me up again. A glove closed around my wrist—one white glove clutching another. The door of the secretary's room. Somebody wearing white gloves.

Miss Priscilla held onto me. I must have nearly fallen, but the image remained. White gloves.

The footmen wore them. All of us did. Samuel was wearing them, sitting in his chair.

I hissed his name. He blinked a couple times, turned his head to look at me.

"How'd you git up here?" he asked. "Where's Mr. Tyler's tea?" He stared at Miss Priscilla in confusion, looked around himself. "Where's all the men what was in here?"

"It's all right," I said. "He got his tea." Something had gotten to Samuel too.

White gloves.

Jasper at the door wore them. He could go anyplace in the house and not be questioned, and he led people up here to the waiting hall all the time. But if he was on the door, he couldn't be in that room. And why would *he* attack me? Had I been attacked? Or was someone taking hold of me, easing me down so I didn't fall. Except, Jasper wasn't here, was he? Hadn't been. Who then?

The men with Webster: Were they wearing gloves? Their hats had been off, at least Cruickshank's and Fox's—all I'd seen. No gloves. They would have been laid over the brim or dropped inside. Had they even worn hats? The petitioners now—where had they all got to? Samuel didn't know, nor I.

My brain seemed to be running crazy, jumping from one idea to the next, unable to fix on any point. Then Miss Priscilla said, "What is happening in this house?" and her words stopped the whirl of my thoughts.

She wasn't posing a question for me. She was staring out the fanlight window as if asking the world outside, which was just as well, because right then nobody inside could have helped her.

Miss Priscilla walked me down to the kitchen, and it was good that she did. I'm sure I would have fallen if I'd tried to navigate the stairs on my own. We were halfway down the main stairs when I remembered. "Samuel came to get me to bring up the tea," I told her.

"He seemed dazed."

"Yes, ma'am," I replied. I started to say more, but lost the thought.

Olive, Ethel, and Zenobia were in the kitchen, Zenobia in front of the ranger and stirring something with onions in a big pot. Ethel stood at the table out in the middle of the room. She was slicing a pile of reddish potatoes, but seeing us she put down her big knife and ran up. She took my free arm and with Miss Priscilla walked me over to a stool against the wall. The other two stopped and watched.

The stool scraped on the pavers as I collapsed there. Zenobia held her wooden spoon up as if she'd forgotten it was in her hand.

Olive asked, "What happened to you, James Christian? You take a tumble?" She should have been asking Miss Priscilla, but where she'd come from, slaves weren't even allowed to address their masters directly, and she couldn't shake that fearful training. Didn't dare even make eye contact.

Before I could think to answer, Mel walked in from the meat curing room. She was wiping her hands down her apron, but she stopped in the doorway, taking us all in. A peculiar look passed between her and Miss Priscilla.

She came around the table and Ethel. Before she even reached me, Miss Priscilla was explaining that she'd found me on the floor outside Mr. Tyler's office. She didn't address Mel by name. It was like she was speaking to an equal. Maybe, with what had happened, she just forgot herself.

Mel took my wrist. She must have seen the bloodstained glove. Pushed it back and pressed her finger against the swollen puncture there. I jerked away, hissing.

She raised up the finger, a clear drop of blood on the tip. At least, I figured it to be blood. After considering it a moment, she put it to the tip of her tongue as if she was testing a recipe. Her eyes closed a moment, and she said, "I'll take him. He'll be all right now."

Miss Priscilla nodded and said, "Thank you, Mel," and again that look passed between them. Another time I might have pressed for an explanation, but right then I couldn't even keep up.

Miss Priscilla stepped back. For a second she was an actress who'd forgotten her lines. Her hands clasped and pulled at each other until finally she said, "Then I'll go. Oh, and Samuel upstairs may have fallen victim to the same thing."

I lowered my head and listened to Miss Priscilla's shoes hurry away on the bricks, then the boards.

Mel's hands closed on my upper arm. She urged me off the stool. I lifted my head, looked in her eyes. "You come wit' me, James. I'll take you to your bed. You need to lie down for a time. You been poisoned."

"My duties—"

"Zenobia, I just left Marcellus in the meat room. You tell him to go back up, check on Samuel outside Mr. Tyler's office."

Mel hauled me along the hall like a sack of potatoes, through the mess and into my room.

She dumped me onto the bed, settled herself alongside me, and said, "It wasn't to kill you, this poison, or you would have been dead upstairs. So one thing we know is, he doesn't consider you no threat to him—and you should be glad that's so."

"Maybe. Or maybe he wasn't ready to kill anybody today."

She replied, "Mmmm," as if the interpretation didn't matter. "Right now you tell me everything as best you can recollect."

I tried, but with hardly more clarity than before: Samuel telling me they wanted tea, carrying the tray up, surprised there were no petitioners as if Mr. Robert had come out and told everybody to vamoose, and Samuel staring across the hall like I wasn't there. "I thought he was just being ornery, but it was like he was asleep with his eyes open."

She wanted to hear all I could remember about the glove that held my wrist. "Was white," I said. "Like mine, or Jasper's, or most of the men who come through here every day."

"Miss Priscilla—where was she when you come out of the office?"

"Don't know. Been with the baby, I think. Earlier, Mary was crying, but I don't recollect hearing her when I come out. Anyway, why? Miss Priscilla wasn't wearing gloves. And how would she stick me with something?"

"No," Mel said, then added, "but what brought her to you quicker than Mr. Robert could open the door?"

"She heard me fall?"

"Or she saw it. Might not know if she had."

"What's that mean? I saw the looks passed between you two."

At first, she didn't say anything, but seemed to be warring with herself over giving me an answer. Then she replied, "I am going to share a confidence wit' you, because it might be important, but you can't say nothing to nobody about it." She told me about Priscilla's sleepwalking.

"Like the thing Alice saw," I said. "I thought you'd protected that room with those charms and chants."

With a sardonic glint in her eye, she said, "Oh, so now that you been snakebit, you're more interested in the snake, hah, James?"

"That's right. Now I am."

"Then listen. This sorcerer, he looks like anybody. You, me, Mr. Tyler. And he got access to this house so he can come and go. Was here before us. Isaac told you, so we know it for certain."

"Mrs. Weems too—she was Harrison's cook, was here a time for Van Buren before him. She said nothing like these things happened before the general arrived." I thought on that a moment. "What if it's Jasper?"

"Jasper," she repeated in a way that expressed her doubt of it. "You had that same post at Mr. Tyler's plantation. Were you free to roam through the house?"

"You know I wasn't."

"Days you was on the door, you had to be spelled just to go teach the children their piano."

I saw her point. "Tyler didn't have one tenth the visitors neither."

"So, I would never say no of Mr. Jasper, but if it's him he has a very hard time of it."

I could see her point. We could guess the identity all day long and not come any closer. Even Daniel Webster would fit the bill. He had been here all along, and was on hand nearly every single day, had access to every single room of the house. He was in the house now. And hadn't Isaac warned me to tell him nothing of any strange events in the house? Yet the Great God Daniel—why would he have killed Harrison? It made no sense.

Mel held my wrist. "This was done by the *bokor*. But him's put something from the darkness in this house called a *tebo*. A thing under his control, like a demon what he owns. He brought it into bein', and hid it here before we even arrived."

"*Tebo*," I repeated.

"A hateful shadow," she said.

"Everything's darkness and shadows. Shadow of what?"

She made a shrug. "Whatever's in the vessel he used to make his *tebo*. The charms I'm layin', the *ouangas*, they block its way back to that vessel. More I do that, I think, the weaker it gets."

"You *think*?"

She laughed at that. "It's not as if I encounter its like every day, James Christian. This is something spoken of in abstractions. Even Mama Laveau never saw nothing like this. I can trap the *tebo*, but the sorcerer still gon' get in."

"All right, but why the secretary's office? He might have been caught. If Mr. Robert had gone there for something—"

"Then it would be Mr. Robert lyin' on the floor and not you. I think he was searching for the charms. It's him tore up the poppet, for sure. He knows his *tebo* can't go everywhere anymore. Maybe he can't see it, but he can feel it." She sounded triumphant to have caused him such inconvenience.

"Wait," I said, and tried to sit up. My head swam and I lay back down. "'Searching for the charms'? You already put *ouangas* in the secretary's office?"

"And in the president's office too. Hid 'em deep. *Tebo* got less room to get at Tyler every day. Can't touch him in his office or his bed now. Samuel helped me wi' that."

My jealousy of Samuel flared like a lucifer when she said it, though if she'd told me what she intended, I would surely have argued against it and she'd have gone to Samuel anyway. She was taking terrible risks, and Samuel offered some protection—only he didn't. Something had been done to him, same as me.

Until that moment, the strange goings-on had been like some sort of game—we were being teased the way Mel had said. Even finding myself on the floor and ministered to by Miss Priscilla seemed less than diabolical. I had been knocked aside—dosed to lay me out but not to kill me. Somebody strolling under the south porch had torn up the poppet. Something had given Alice and Tazewell the fantods but only spooked Miss Letitia, who was as helpless as anyone could be. Where was the express threat in it? John Tyler constituted more of a threat to my long-term happiness.

Now here was Mel treating things like her version of hide-and-seek, but it was no game at all. Taunting this shadow master, her life more than anyone else's was in peril. She was meddling in his scheme.

"If I could, right this minute I'd pack you off back to Virginia," I said.

"You think that would save everyone here, you fool man?"

"To hell with everyone here. It's you I care about, not them."

She sighed. "You're lying and you know it. You love them children like they's your own blood. Your half-sister too. You don't want nothing happening to them. And they all been picked out as targets."

"Maybe. But I'd give 'em all up for you." I held her tight against me, and we both stopped talking because we would only argue if either of us said one more thing. I wished I'd heeded Isaac.

My whirling thoughts went from protecting her to wondering why it had become necessary. There was something I couldn't make sense of; my mind wouldn't stop working at it, which must have showed in my agitation, because Mel drew back and asked, "What's eatin' at you, James Christian?" She closed her thin fingers around my hands.

"This sorcerer," I said. "If he's so powerful that he killed General Harrison and Isaac, then why is he waiting now? Why not strike right away when we arrived? He had Tyler and me in the house a full week with no one and nothing protecting us. Why'd he let that opportunity pass?"

"Didn't know it was going to pass, did he? Wasn't nobody to save the general. And that man didn't have no family to frighten."

"But he did—a wife, only she took ill in the winter and never made the trip here from Indiana to join him."

"Else she would be dead now too." She reflected upon that. "Maybe that's how come he waited a month with the general. And maybe he got tired of waitin'."

"He *wanted* the family here?"

She nodded slowly, thinking it through. "Wants to harm everyone. Wants suffering. This is punishment."

"But for what? Who's he quarreling with?"

She couldn't answer that any more than I could. Harrison and Tyler had campaigned together, traveled and made speeches together. But what could they possibly have done—what crime could they have committed—that had brought down this plague upon both their houses?

Twenty

Among all the rooms on the private floor of the President's House, the so-called Yellow Library remained mostly neglected and unused by John Tyler. It had begun life as a ladies' drawing room, and was oval in shape like the Blue Saloon one floor below it. Owing to its general disuse, Mel had put no protections in place there.

The wallpaper was newer than in much of the house, with a bordering of vines along the top and bottom and between each faux-marble panel. The three large windows, beneath the south portico roof, overlooked the south lawn and its carriage paths. The drapes were drawn aside with tiebacks, emphasizing the curved sweep of the valences. In the center of the room hung one large elaborate chandelier matching those in the hall outside. The fireplaces of white Carrara marble had a naked maenad in relief on each end supporting the mantel, above which, as in many of the rooms, hung a large mirror, rectangular in this instance and in an ornate gilt frame.

On the day that John Tyler was required to meet with Secretary of the Treasury Ewing and an entourage, the Blue Saloon was occupied by Daniel Webster and the British delegation.

In Tyler's view, Webster was either a glutton for punishment or a saint. Every proposal or concession Webster made was met with objections. Sometimes it was that feist dog, Ambassador Fox himself; other times it was the tall man, Cruickshank, with his waxed mustache and his sneer; and still other times, if it seemed Fox was about to capitulate, the youngest of his attachés, Lord Ettryne, would either stir Fox up into a froth or say something inflammatory to Webster.

At least half the meetings thus far had ended with one side or the other walking out. The advent of summer heat and humidity did nothing to improve the negotiations; they continued to occupy the oval saloon.

For reasons even he would not later be able to explain, John Tyler elected to hold his meeting with Ewing's group in the private-floor library rather than in one of the other parlors downstairs.

>>> - <<<

As he awaited Ewing and the advisors that Ewing insisted he must hear, Tyler scowled at the soot-smeared ceiling above the chandelier. The whole private floor was going to ruin, and he cursed Henry Clay in particular for withholding the necessary funds for upkeep. The soot on that ceiling would not be scrubbed nor any of the ceilings whitewashed this year. No repairs—and many were needed—would be performed unless Tyler capitulated on Clay's pet project: a new federal bank to replace the one dissolved by Andrew Jackson. Otherwise, if Tyler wanted repairs, he could spend his own money on them.

It was extortion, pure and simple, and Ewing had been cowed and bullied into supporting it. Tyler knew exactly what and who was behind Ewing's "urgent" meeting. The longer he sat in that godforsaken oven of a room, the more his spine stiffened. All three of the windows had been opened to pull in a breeze, but no breeze was evident. By the time the seven chairs were occupied, the men facing him in a half-circle, their backs to the maenads of the fireplace, he was nearly seething.

It started exactly as Tyler had expected. Ewing took the line that Clay had surely spun out for him: that the nation desperately required a new federal standard, that states could not be entrusted with financial decisions on a national scale, and that the current, rudderless situation had already resulted in the depressions of 1837 and '39.

Almost immediately, Tyler held up a hand to interrupt the speech. "By your argument, Mr. Secretary, we're already in a state of chaos. If that is truly so, I am far more persuaded that both the Bankruptcy and Homestead Acts will resolve this without violating the superior rights of the states."

"Chaos is hardly hyperbolic in the face of two such financial disasters," Ewing agreed.

Tyler replied, "I know that Mr. Clay has persuaded you with his rhetoric. I will tell you what I am certain of, sir. That I behold in this circle Clay men and perhaps one or two Harrison men. Nowhere in this body do I see the face of a single *Tyler* man. Or might you point one out to me?"

Ewing stood and attempted to placate him. "Mr. President, let me speak for all of us here in reminding you that your predecessor was guided by the will of this cabinet in steering the ship of state. You should do likewise if you don't wish to find yourself adrift. Harrison men can also be Tyler men"—he paused to glance around—"and would be if given cause."

"Cause, in this case, meaning I hand Henry Clay his victory."

Then one of Ewing's men, seated on the end toward the windows, stood to speak.

When Tyler looked his way, the sunlight streaming through the window slewed on him as though the sun had suddenly cartwheeled across the heavens. An intense beam flared in the looking glass above the mantel and, like a lighthouse beam, it struck him full in the eyes so suddenly that he had to raise his hand to shield them.

In the slits between his fingers, shapes slid through the light. He lowered his hand enough to peer narrowly over it, and found himself staring back from inside the glass, hand similarly raised as if to hail himself—except, in the mirror where his hand's shadow fell across his face, it was all red, as if his scalp had been slashed, peeled back, and blood run in a sheet all the way to his collar. He squeezed his eyes tight, tried to squint only at the advisor, who remained standing, speaking, the words, whatever they were, lost on him.

The man's head had turned into that of a rabid dog. With his yellowed teeth bared, he sneered triumphantly, and foam dripped from the corners of his mouth. His voice was a drone, a growl of contempt.

The core of Tyler's rage boiled over, pounding like a hammer in his head. "You show adamantine cheek, sir!" he yelled.

Men gasped. The light swung across Ewing and the rest of them.

Tyler beheld them for what they truly were—pink-eyed rabbits, grasping voles, grotesque animal heads stuffed into collars. He guffawed at the revelation. Hadn't he known it all along?

"How dare you," he accused, "tell me how I'm to be governed. I *alone* am responsible for my administration. Not you fleas from another dog, and nor that cur at the far end of the avenue!"

He swung away from them and the excruciating light, but caught a sidelong glimpse of movement in the mirror: his own blood-drenched reflection mocking him with a grin and a wagging finger.

At some remove he understood that the mirror, hung where it was, could never have reflected him to begin with. The delighted doppelgänger didn't exist.

The light shifted again, as if shutters had been thrown up over the windows. His eyes watered. He flung an awful look at the shocked Ewing, who no longer had the head of some vermin. Dared another glance at the mirror.

It reflected only the chandelier and the corner of the wall behind him— what it ought to have shown all along.

His head throbbed now as if the sutures in the skull would split. He lurched away from the group, headed for the door, mumbling an apology. Two steps before, the light poured straight through the window and captured him. He pressed his forehead against the door. His sweaty fingers slipped off the handle. Confused, jumbled, his eyes squeezed shut, and his world beset by enemies and sneering doubles, he pawed at the handle again and managed somehow to throw the door aside and stagger into the hallway.

Blind, Tyler slid along the wall with his eyes tightly closed against the pain. Someone spoke—had Ewing followed him? He waved the voice away. He needed Robert; Robert should have accompanied him instead of dealing with the morning's petitioners. Ewing would never forgive him for this outburst. Webster would quit, too, after this. Why wasn't Robert with him right now? What could be more important? But Robert wasn't dealing with petitions. He had left that morning for business in Philadelphia and New York. Tyler had *sent* him, to find cheaper suppliers for their food—meat in particular. The Washington markets were outrageously expensive. It had only been a few hours. How had he forgotten?

Robert was gone. Who remained in this city that he could trust? "I need Tyler men," he sobbed.

He had to rest, had to lie down. The sides of his skull must have been compressing, crushing his brain—that's how it felt. The harsh light had set in motion some terrible disequilibrium, the worst headache he had ever known, the sort that could twist your entrails and bring up your breakfast. He started to call for Robert, again reminded himself that his son was absent. Where was Samuel then, he wanted to know. Samuel should have been perched on a chair outside the yellow oval. By God he would whip that impudent Negro for abandoning his post. If he could just reach his room and lie down awhile—were they *all* against him?

The wallpaper was soothing against his cheek, but the wall seemed to stretch on and on.

>>>> <<<<

He dared not open his eyes again. Felt his way along. Surely by now he ought to have come to his wife's door. It should have been ajar, Devonee or someone sitting with her. No, hadn't he intended to dismiss Devonee? He couldn't recall why. He would now though, along with Samuel, soon as he had his wits about him. Once this horrible pain released him.

Confused, he tried opening his eyes a little, but the glare was so severe, the colors pinwheeling and fractured, that he closed them again immediately. Tears squeezed out.

He lost the wall that was his guide. His hands pressed against nothing for a time as he shuffled forward, and then his hips struck something, and he gripped it—a railing—before he lost his balance. A stairwell, it had to be. Surely the one between the dining rooms, in which case he had missed his own door as well as Letitia's. In his misery, the house seemed to be shuffling itself to torture him.

He sank down, bowed his head. He pulled his coat over it, heard himself whisper, "God, show me mercy."

Almost at once hands took hold of him. He cried out and swatted at them, but a voice said, "Mr. Tyler? *Sir?*"

"James!" He dared to open one eye enough to confirm that he wasn't hallucinating; made out the shape of James Christian kneeling beside him.

"What are you doing, sir? What has happened to you?"

"Terrible. Attack. My head." He emerged from the coat like a turtle out of its shell. The fit seemed to abate somewhat, as if the nearness of his wife's slave had the power to ameliorate it.

"I thought you were meeting with Secretary Ewing."

Then the fit surged back in the form of a buzzing that drowned out James' voice as though a hive of bees filled his head. It lasted only a few moments.

James was explaining: "...came and informed me, said you'd suffered some sort of attack."

"Oh, Ewing. I fear I have spoken terrible words. Atrocious words." He hesitantly looked around. He was on a landing, but not the west stairs and not the private floor.

"Mr. Ewing has said nothing to that effect, sir."

"No?" What if he hadn't spoken any of it? The leering double in the mirror that seemed to have taken possession of him—that couldn't have been real. Had *any* of it been real? The sun whirling across the sky—surely that was hallucination. But he *had met* with Ewing and those advisors. *He had.*

A raft of cooler air rose through the stairwell as if someone had opened a door far below, and the throbbing slid from his forehead to his temples. His vision cleared.

"Is it done with me, d'you think?" he asked.

"Well, sir, in case it is not, perhaps you best lie down."

"I was trying to find my room. I lost it."

"Yes, sir." In James' simple words he heard the withheld observation that he was nowhere near his room.

Tyler allowed himself to be lifted to his feet. "James, my dependable...servant." The cool air fluttered up the stairwell. His hair, pushed askew, trembled in it. "Blow me about in winds," he said.

"You must be better, Mr. Tyler, if you can be quoting Mr. Shakespeare."

"Heh. And you would know. You always know." He leaned on James and they returned to the private floor from which he had escaped.

The doors of the oval library hung open. The empty sliver of room beyond still looked intensely bright. *Harrison men and Clay men*, he thought. "They surround me, my enemies."

"Which enemies are those, sir?"

He didn't answer. James, for all his education and the parlor trick of his ability to memorize text, could not possibly comprehend the vagaries of politics, the subtle ways that men could promote their own interests whilst pretending to yield to your own. *Clay*, of course, perfect example.

He changed his mind then. "Let's not go to my chamber. Take me to my office. I will recover by losing myself in work. I shall find my solace there."

"You're certain of that, sir?" James' green-gray eyes sought some assurance from his own.

"Yes, James. And I don't want Letitia to know what has occurred here. We mustn't trouble her with my brief illness. You understand?"

"Yes, sir, Mr. Tyler, I do."

From down the hall to the right came the wail of the baby. It seemed obvious that his daughter-in-law and her infant were sitting with his dear wife. Where was— But, oh, yes, Robert was traveling. Why could he not hold onto that fact?

He looked ahead at the waiting hall, saw perhaps a dozen silhouettes up there—men pacing in a slow circle before the fanlight window, all with scrolls of paper, folders. "But, James, how will we get past the petitioners?" he asked.

James Christian looked where he was looking, blinked a few times, then with a concerned expression, faced him again. "Mr. Tyler, sir, there are no petitioners. Because your son is gone to New York, Mr. Jasper has turned them all away till next week."

Tyler looked again, and the waiting hall was empty. Through the fanlight window he saw clouds and blue sky. No one blocked his view. There were no men in the corridor. A noise, a whine, escaped from him, and if James Christian hadn't had a hold of him, he might have collapsed there in the hall.

They walked unsteadily forward, then up the steps to the waiting hall and into his office. Tyler grabbed the edge of the table covered in maps and sank down trembling into one of the chairs. The window was open. It was cooler here on the east side of the house.

Ewing, the advisors, the flock of petitioners—what was real? Slowly, he shook his head back and forth. "It's what Hamlet said, isn't it? 'There's nothing either good or bad—'" He faltered. Couldn't even remember the full quote.

"'But thinking makes it so,'" James recited for him.

He massaged his temples. "You speak like a book, James. Today we're angry at each other and on no account."

"Sir?" James asked. "Who's angry?"

Tyler waved off the question. "You can bring me some tea now. I would be much restored."

"Yes, sir, I will do that." Yet James hesitated as if concerned to leave him alone.

"Oh, and another thing, James. Find out what happened to Samuel. He should have been in the hall outside the library when I exited." He raised his head to stare James in the face. "You tell him, he does that again, I shall sell him and have you find..." James was eyeing him with worry again. "What is it now?"

"Sir, as I told you, it was Samuel came and found me giving Miss Alice her piano lesson. You'd dismissed him. He *was* sitting in the hall, and he knew something was wrong, Mr. Tyler, but he didn't know what."

The wind seemed to go out of him then. He sat loosely, hands curled in his lap, a marionette on broken strings. Finally, he said quietly, "How—how is she coming? Alice? Does she play well, do you think?"

"She plays most beautifully, sir."

"We will have to…have to get her to play at one of the levées, but in the fall when it isn't so God blamed hot." He looked up, smiled jaggedly at James. "My good wife was right in choosing you to manage the President's Castle. I don't believe I've told you how much I appreciate the way you've steered it."

For a long time neither of them moved, almost until Tyler began to wonder if he had said any of that aloud. Then James replied, almost begrudgingly, "Thank you, Mr. Tyler. I will get your tea now."

It wasn't until James had closed the door and left him alone that Tyler realized his headache had abated. He crossed his arms on the table and laid his head upon them. To lie down and rest forever was all he wanted.

Part III:
Secret Service

Twenty-One
James Hambleton Christian

Over the next weeks the heat and humidity wrapped us up like a blanket of wet wool. Our formal serving attire itched and stuck to us. The washing of our clothes became a nightly task, and the shower taps in the colonnades saw a lot of surreptitious use after the Tylers had retired for the night. Finally, to the relief, I think, of everybody, Miss Priscilla suspended the levées.

Usually by then the whole of the Congress would have left town, but not this summer.

The morning after Mr. Tyler's "headache" episode, I'd been sent to the Treasury Building with a note for Secretary Ewing. He sat behind a desk wide enough for three people. He was a portly man with a bald, egg-shaped head fringed with hair and thick sideburns, and had pouchy eyes like maybe he never got enough sleep.

He waved the letter while telling me that none of the things Mr. Tyler was apologizing for had happened. "President Tyler suddenly went, well, catatonic," he said. "Transfixed. Wore this stricken look, and just stared at the mirror behind where we sat. Then he up and headed out the door. I thought he might have been taken ill. When he didn't come back, I went out, and his man down the hall said he was indeed indisposed."

"Yes, sir, was some sort of terrible headache that just came on him."

Ewing claimed to have a nephew who suffered blinding headaches, but hadn't realized "they afflicted John." He had me wait while he wrote a letter in reply, urging that the meeting reconvene at the earliest opportunity because Clay was hellbent to get his victory if he had to give the entire Congress heat stroke to do it, and they must be prepared.

Mel had by then finally put her protections in the Yellow Library and the two guest rooms. The only floor now that had no protection was the attic. Trapped amidst the debris up there, the *tebo* could rage all it wanted. She didn't care, she said. Wasn't going to latch onto anybody now.

Mel took to leaving all four entrances to the kitchen floor propped open. Cooler breezes flowed in from under the porticos and the open colonnades, and often that brick, vaulted space proved to be the most comfortable in the house, even despite the heat thrown off by the ranger.

The second, smaller stove finally rusted out to where it was unusable. Mr. Robert, returned from Philadelphia, came down and confirmed its decrepitude. He took some measurements and said he would look into replacing it.

The children, when not outdoors, began staying down on the first floor, notably in the East Room, where we kept all the big windows open. If there was a breeze, in the afternoons they would go out onto the east promenade, shaded by the house. Alice and Tazewell went about barefoot, and sometimes Elizabeth as well. The girls shed layers of unmentionables, their crinolines and corsets. Only Miss Priscilla continued to dress in formal outfits, as she continued to drive out for social calls.

Elizabeth, unhappy because Billy Waller had not written her in weeks, petitioned to go back to the plantation for the summer. Nobody trusted that she wouldn't get into mischief if she did, and Miss Priscilla could not chaperone her, but Miss Elizabeth didn't give up making her case at every opportunity.

With the formal dinners and parties suspended, all of us had less to do; even during the day, fewer petitioners turned up to be escorted to the waiting hall, and Daniel Webster had broken off his talks with Ambassador Fox and the British delegation. No headway had been made in their negotiations.

Before he left the city, he turned up in Mr. Tyler's office. The door through to the secretary's room was propped open, as were all the windows on the east and south sides of the two rooms.

I brought up coffee. Webster was complaining about Fox and his delegates. "I've penned a letter to my good friend Lord Ashburton to petition the British government for permission to overthrow Fox and step into the breach. Otherwise, John, I shall be snared in this negotiation until the end of time. Ninnies to a man, the bunch of them." He then inquired what Mr. Tyler had decided to do regarding Clay's bank bill. I didn't hear the answer. Mr. Ewing had already come a second time with his advisors. They had spent hours with Mr. Tyler in the Blue Saloon (Mr. Tyler never again used the yellow oval library for anything). The doings of Henry Clay seemed to be the only topic of the summer.

Congress caved and finally passed his bill in the dead heat of July. The moment it was resolved, they all fled the city.

By the end of August, President Tyler had vetoed it.

It wasn't until then that I realized I'd been paying far more attention to all the political shenanigans and had stopped expecting another attack by the *bokor* or his invisible, mirror-dwelling demon. We had gone for two months and nothing more had happened.

I let myself think that maybe Mel had beaten the sorcerer of shadows. That, or, like the members of Congress, he had melted away in the heat. Either way, if creeping demons were gone for good, that was just fine by me.

Twenty-Two

Mel was carrying a basket of radishes, cucumbers, eggplants, shallots, and onions across Pennsylvania Avenue from the Haymarket toward the Centre Market that Saturday when she spied the president's carriage pulled up outside Brown's Indian Queen Hotel.

There were surely many reasons why the carriage might be there so early in the day, and she wasn't privy to the workings of the president's office, save for what James mentioned.

Trouble was, she was nearly certain the men had been breakfasting at the house when she left, and that Mr. Tyler had intended to spend the morning with Miss Letitia. Only one other person made regular use of that carriage.

It was late August, and Mel couldn't imagine who might have left a calling card directing Priscilla Tyler to the Indian Queen Hotel. Surely, anybody who made their residence here through the spring would be long quit of the place by August. That, coupled with the absence of the *bokor* these past weeks, pushed Mel to walk along the avenue, near enough to establish that the head of the driver with its frizzed halo of hair belonged to Absalom Lee. He appeared to be dozing, sitting tilted to the side. That suggested he'd been here awhile.

Tempted as she was to stroll up and wake him, Mel only went close enough to confirm his identity. Then she headed back toward the market.

This would be a perfect afternoon, she thought, to bake up a skillet of cornbread and carry it on down to the stables. What with one thing and another, she just had not seen enough lately of Cyrus and Absalom Lee. She was sure they were going to have lots to talk about.

>>> ‑‑<<<

Sally swept the straw mat in the cross hall, which allowed her to keep an eye on everything on the public floor for Mel. It wasn't long before Miss Letitia was carried down the main stairs with the family following ceremoniously in her wake. President Tyler held the family Bible under his arm. James and Samuel, supporting Miss Letitia, both gave her a glance as they passed, no doubt wondering why Sally had chosen to sweep the floor now.

About the time the procession reached the East Room, there came a knock at the north door, and Jasper welcomed in the Reverend Addison from St. John's Episcopal Church. He was here for his weekly Sunday service with

Letitia Tyler.

What had started out as a brief event each week held in her room, over the past months had grown into a family service. The heat of the summer necessitated that it take place now in the cooler, larger East Room. Only Elizabeth, who had finally won approval to go home for the month of August, was absent. After the service, the Tylers would no doubt impose a little longer upon the reverend as usual. The lemonade and cookies were already prepared.

A minute after the reverend arrived, the sound of James playing the piano echoed through the house, accompanied by the family's solemn voices.

Sally set aside her broom and went quickly down the serving stairs to the kitchen. She hurried up beside Mel. "They's all in there now," she said.

⟫⟩- ⟨⟪

As she expected, the State Dining Room was deserted.

Mel knew where she had placed the three charms in here. It took her only a few minutes to ascertain that the two *ouangas* were missing. She guessed that the *pakét kongo*, out of sight behind the circular wall vent beside the fireplace, remained. Otherwise the room probably would have seen some sort of activity already. The two lesser charms had definitely been removed.

When had it happened, and who had taken them? She feared she already knew.

Yesterday's cornbread conversation in the west stables had proved enlightening, if troubling. Both men had had occasion to drive the coach to Brown's Indian Queen Hotel numerous times, beginning as early as May, and as she'd suspected, always for the same passenger.

Priscilla Cooper Tyler.

Neither Cyrus nor Absalom had the slightest idea who she might be calling upon. There had to be folks living at the hotel who attended the levées: no doubt congressmen and foreigners, diplomats without a legation. But who might be residing there now?

Cyrus had commented, "I can tell you, on the way to the hotel, she keeps herself to herself. Not one word. But after and once we're down the road a piece, it's like the sun come out again. When she's quit of that place, she's like always, sweet and talkin' up a storm all the rest of the way round the city."

Mel wondered if Priscilla Tyler herself even knew who she visited at the Indian Queen.

Tearing her poppet to shreds outdoors would have proved no problem for the *bokor*. But wandering through the house while looking in cabinets and behind wardrobes was another matter. The one time they knew of that he'd tried to hunt on the private floor, he had nearly been caught. It was far less risky to send an agent to do the seeking—especially an agent who was not out of place anywhere in the house.

The *bokor* would think himself clever and his retaliation unknown.

Mel would replace both charms, of course, but she would also have to inspect every room again; not just down here, but upstairs as well.

More importantly, she must watch Priscilla closely from now on, something she could not do from the kitchen. Mel needed help.

>>> <<<

"He's moved through the house, seen how things fit together, the way the people join. He seen things we haven't noticed," said Mel as she strolled along.

It was a gray and sultry afternoon for a walk across the lawn. She'd had to wait until James had finished with the children—their piano lessons, and a short spelling bee, which Alice won by spelling *mischievous*. Now she and Tazewell were busy with their arithmetic problems, and for a time no one would be looking for James.

Mel walked opposite him, with Deborah and Zenobia between them. Deborah walked beside her, face cast down, always silent and somber, contemplative. The buffer of her silence helped Mel. She could often sense what Deborah was thinking. And Deborah, like James, worked mainly upstairs and went everywhere during dinners and levées.

"This man," she said, "already knows his power's been contained, and he don't like it at all. Already found some of the protections, just like he found the poppet I nailed up. Him's hunting through the house now. In the dining room he found two, carried them away." James looked worried—not surprising given his pillow talk of how he was so sure she had defeated what he called "the sorcerer of shadows." She'd let it go, though she'd known better.

"Maybe he done all this searching while the levées was going on, made it easy for him to be in the house. Explains why it's been quiet through the summer. It means when the levées start again, first thing him's going to do is look to see if I found him out or not. So I'm going to let them *ouangas* stay gone."

Zenobia and James gave her much the same incredulous look.

She grinned. "Oh, I gonna hide more, just not in the same places. I want this man to think he maybe missed some the first time. Keep him thinking him's in charge long as we can."

She faced Deborah.

"When them parties start again next month, you and James got to watch for the man who watches everything else."

They circled past the crumbling eastern arch to Pennsylvania Avenue.

"What if he doesn't come back when the levées begin again?" James asked. "What if he's pulled foot because he *does* know someone's on to him?"

She shook her head. "You believe a man what's gone to this much trouble—killed the general and struck at Mr. Tyler—that he's going to just quit on account of a few *ouangas?*"

With obvious and heavy reluctance, he answered, "I suppose not."

"The longer he believes him's safe, the more we can watch for the signs of him. Whatever he turns out to be, we got to be ready."

"Whatever he turns out to *be?*" James repeated.

They were heading toward the east colonnade now, but Mel slowed, deep in thought. She understood James so well. There were elements of her skills he could reconcile: the healing salves, the teas, soups, and potions. Protections, poppets, even the *veves* for which he had acquired limewash, he accepted mostly because they pacified everyone else. He ignored how their power might shake his world. It did not intrude upon his day. Even having been assaulted directly, he'd seen nothing but a shadow, one that had robbed him of any possibility of perceiving it otherwise. He'd been stuck by something and poisoned. It took no magic to explain that. James would believe, provided he could ignore what he believed.

Abruptly she realized that all three others were standing together, eyeing her with concern. She had stopped walking. Also she had not answered his question.

She said, "Before I knew Mama Laveau, there was a man back in New Orleans who come to her on St. Anne Street, asking to be trained in her arts. Her husband had just died, and maybe that caused her to misjudge the man and be persuaded.

"He thought, on account of he was a man, that he deserved more power than she had, that he would take all she taught and become the most powerful *bokor* ever had been seen. She didn't recognize this about him, and so she showed him more than she might have. More than she should have. Mama had dangerous books kept hidden, but she lay with the man and she told him about them.

"For awhile he learned from her, but he grew tired of the effort. Why go through all that trouble when books could guide him? He stole one, a book that contained the darkest spells. He hadn't learned even enough to know what those spells cost."

"What did they cost?" asked Zenobia, wide-eyed. Mel had never told her this tale, but the first thing she'd ever taught Zenobia was how every act of magic came with a price.

"The man lived on Coliseum Street. You go to the Quarter today, you won't see no house there, just dirt that's all gray with some kind of rust. Nothing grows in that dirt, and no one will build there. His house and him, they up and disappeared one night, and nothing remained but that book lying on the ground. Mama Laveau took it home, and maybe she destroyed it, I don't know."

James said, "I don't see that answers my question."

"Mmm. What I'm telling you about is *vodou*—what I know. This, what our sorcerer of shadows calls down—I don't even know the shape, the name of it. He got the darkest powers, just like that book. Can seize people from outside the house. Can send his demon *tebo* into rooms like a ghost any time he chooses…least until I came. No telling what he is, but what I know for sure from Mama Laveau's story is that the power he got came with a high price what he already paid. This man's soul was forfeit a long time ago."

"Way you make it sound, we might as well run for our lives right now. Who here's gonna forfeit their soul to match him?"

She wanted to assure him that it wasn't hopeless, that together they would destroy the *bokor*. The truth was, until she knew more about their enemy, she could not be sure of anything at all.

"For now there is nothing to do. The *bokor*'s absent and his *tebo* is at bay. But when the parties start up again, he'll come back, and he'll mean to finish what's been left undone."

Twenty-Three

James Hambleton Christian

The first we learned of the Coffeehouse Letter was when I answered the door of the President's House to a small white boy younger than Tazewell. He was dressed in a formal black coat with white collar and cravat, and his blond hair was bottle-curled. He handed me a letter sealed with wax.

"For the president," he told me, then immediately turned on his heel and marched off as stiffly as a soldier. He must have practiced that a few times, I thought. I didn't see a carriage waiting nor anyone else.

Jasper was having his midday meal downstairs and I was standing in for him. I carried the letter upstairs. Baby Mary was crying, and Elizabeth, who'd returned from Virginia, was helping Miss Priscilla with her as I passed their room. Samuel watched me approach from where he sat in the waiting hall, so I knew Mr. Tyler was in his office.

He stood at President Jackson's standing desk, with Robert seated in front of the other desk, behind him, neither of them so much as lifting a pen. Something was wrong, and that was for sure. Mr. Tyler glowered at the envelope in my hand. "Another resignation?" he asked. "That would have to be from Webster, since the *rest* of the cabinet has already quit me."

"Father—"

"I will not change my mind, Robert. Clay's bank bill gives the federal government far too much say over commerce in the states." He grabbed and started tearing at the envelope as he spoke. "Grant that, and I set precedent. A government of northern Democrats would have the power to curtail"—he paused and stared at me—"our peculiar institution everywhere all at once. Anyway, now I can replace my cabinet with men I want on board. *My* men."

He unfolded the letter. His eyes lost their hardness, his mouth went slack. A kind of soft horror strangled his voice. "Where did this come from?" he asked.

I told him of the child messenger.

He shook the paper at me. "No child wrote this."

I leaned forward for a better look. Robert was on his feet and across the room immediately, shoving his way between us. I had to peer around his shoulder.

The scrawl might have belonged to a child, if not the words: "Tyler, you ar the enemy of all of us, you traterous dog. Yore life is forfeit." It was unsigned. I straightened up, picturing the park again as the child had marched off. There had been no one thereabouts.

"It's a naked threat," said Robert.

"Yes, it is. And by someone who can conveniently spell 'forfeit' but not 'traitorous.'"

He had hardly said that before there came a rapping at the door of his office. I was closest, so opened it. Samuel stood there. He held a stack of a dozen more envelopes of all sizes. He said that Tall George, while sweeping the floor of the portico, had found them leaning against one of the pillars, and not finding me at the front door had come upstairs. Samuel all but smirked in suggesting I'd not been at my post. Unfortunately for him, no one in the room cared. We were all consumed with the envelopes. One was tied with string, a couple were just folded-up paper, and the others, like the original delivered one, were formally wax-sealed.

I took them. "Thank you," I said, and closed the door on him, then carried the letters across the room.

Mr. Tyler looked at the folded ones before he began opening the others. After another few he didn't bother with the rest, handing them to Robert, who slit the remainder, opened them, finally gathered them in a pile that he placed on a table away from Mr. Tyler.

Each one threatened him with death. Some promised slaughter to the entire family. Two swore to blow us all up. Bombs would be planted or thrown.

"Give them to James," Mr. Tyler instructed his son. Then to me, "Show these to Daniel Webster. You must fetch him from home right away."

⟫⟩- ⟨⟪

I explained the situation to Jasper and he returned quick to the front door. Absalom Lee hitched up a wagon in no time and the two of us rode off across Pennsylvania Avenue to Webster's house.

Paul Jennings, the slave Webster had bought from Dolley Madison, answered the door of the rowhouse. He was nearly as light-skinned as me, with a squarish face and long sideburns and a small black mouche beneath his bottom lip.

Before I could even state my business, Webster strode out of the parlor. The look on his face told me he knew something of the situation already. It was like everybody had disappointed him. Reading the stack of threats, his face tightened even more. He returned them to me, went into his parlor again, and came back with a one-page leaflet. He said, "John must anticipate the worst. And you must tell him all I'm about to tell you so that he will understand." He handed me the leaflet. "This is the cause of what's happening. They're calling it the Coffeehouse Letter."

The leaflet named John Tyler a traitor to the nation and urged the people to rise up against him and throw him out of office by whatever means proved necessary.

Webster gave me the whole story. "A Whig by the name of John Minor Botts distributed that shortly after the president rejected the bank bill—so fast, in fact, it's my opinion he had it ready to print well before the veto came down. Fact is, the whole Whig party is John Tyler's enemy now, and they've abandoned even the principles of civil discourse. I have already drafted my response to this, assuring them that they could have made no more grievous error in judging your master's character. At the bottom, it is Clay and his overweening pride. The man will never be president, nor will he have his way despite this attempt at forcing the matter. John says you have a flawless memory. Can you retain all of that?"

"Yes, sir."

"Good. I will not go with you. Rather, I shall pursue other avenues of objection. But, James, you *must* convince him to arm himself. Bring in guards, soldiers if necessary. He should send for Seaton. There's no telling what will come of this incitement to treason, although no mistaking it's Botts who is the traitor."

He dismissed me then and went to dress in order to deliver his reply. Jennings gave me a worried look and as I departed said, "You all take care, Mr. Christian."

I can't say I much looked forward to returning to the house without Webster, much less having to deliver his warning myself. All of a sudden, notions of sorcerers, *vodou*, and magic seemed harmless and irrelevant—unless in some way this letter was another form of assault from the same source. *Who is Botts?* I wondered, and my mind ran away with itself: Had he been at the levées? Had I seen him, introduced him, and now had no recollection of him because he'd wiped it away? How was I to look hereafter upon those swirling mobs of people who attended Miss Priscilla's parties and not spy villainy in every face?

»»»- -«««

On our way back, Absalom and I drove around a dozen or so people what had gathered in the square at Vermont and K Street. Loud and more than likely corned—one of 'em even threw an empty whiskey bottle our way while he shouted at us, but we'd already passed them all on the dirt street by then, and they didn't come tearing after us, didn't really seem to know quite what they was doing besides standing up drunk.

Past Dolley Madison's house, a different group was heading across the park, but these were five well-dressed men, didn't look particularly hell-bent.

Glancing at them, I was pretty sure I did recognize a couple from the levées. I wondered if they numbered this Botts among them.

Once in the drive, I jumped down. Absalom steered the wagon on around to the stables, and I went up and through the front door. It seemed like an occasion for breaking protocol. Jasper let me in.

I told him, "Looks like we're having company, and maybe more than we want."

He peered nervously out the righthand vestibule window, replying, "He's 'aving 'is dinner now," and without looking away nodded vaguely toward the family dining room.

I thought, *Well, he'd better eat quick.*

⫸ ⫷

While I was at Mr. Webster's house, Mr. Tyler had fed Miss Letitia and then descended to the dining room to share a meal with the rest of the family. When I entered, he jumped up and came around the table to me, instructing everyone else to continue without him, despite which they all, even the children, stopped eating and stared after him at me. Robert had gotten to his feet but was told to stay. I made myself smile to disguise the nature of things from them.

Sally and Olive, standing by to serve, watched warily as Tyler turned me about and propelled me ahead of him back into the vestibule. He sought for Webster there, confused that it was just me and Jasper, and I had to tell him, "He did not accompany me, sir, on account of right this moment he is delivering a response."

"A response to what?"

"To this, Mr. Tyler, sir." I handed him Botts' leaflet.

He read it over, and then again. His expression grew more incensed by the moment. "Webster knew of this and told me nothing?"

"I don't believe he's known of it long enough to share it, Mr. Tyler." And there I was, covering for Daniel Webster, which I'd never have expected to do. I explained then what he'd told me of the Coffeehouse Letter, and how Mr. Tyler and the Whig party was at odds now. Was more than just the members of his cabinet opposing him.

"Botts." Tyler spat the name. He only grew more agitated in hearing all of it, and he was about to say something choleric, but was interrupted by a loud knock on the door. Jasper hurried over to answer. His motion seemed to tug Tyler along in its wake.

The five men we had passed coming back from Webster's stood clustered there on the portico. The one in the front announced himself as Charles Ingersoll of Pennsylvania. I did recognize him when he said that, but

Mr. Tyler had done already and stepped forward. "Gentlemen," he said, all friendly as if he hadn't been apoplectic mere seconds before.

They were a group of Democrats, whom the Whigs called "Locofocos" after the matchsticks, which I guess was supposed to mean they were hotheads. Ingersoll stepped forward and extended his hand. Mr. Tyler reached forward like he was going to shake his hand but stopped. Mr. Ingersoll was holding another batch of letters. "These were propped outside the door," he said.

Mr. Tyler drew his hand back as if from hornets. I reached over with my white-gloved hand and relieved Mr. Ingersoll of them so that he could shake Mr. Tyler's hand properly. The other four men pushed in to do the same, surrounding him.

"What is this, sir?" Mr. Tyler asked, kind of unfriendly in the circumstances, though he did shake everyone's hand.

"President Tyler," said Ingersoll, "we wanted to shake the hand of possibly the only man in Washington willing to stand up to Henry Clay."

Mr. Tyler blinked in dismay at that, and took a half-step back. "I have to tell you, gentlemen, it is not Clay himself that I oppose, you understand—"

Ingersoll interrupted. "Of course, sir, it's the principle upon which you stand. We acknowledge that. We respect that."

Right then I imagine Mr. Tyler wondered what party he belonged to. However, as decorum dictated, he welcomed them to follow him to the Blue Saloon. They walked through the door in the glass partition, and Mr. Tyler instructed me to send Robert in to join them, and have sherry and glasses brought up right away.

I handed the letters back to Jasper. "We'll give these to Mr. Robert. He's collecting them. Will you tell him he's wanted in the Blue Saloon?"

I went down to the cellar, retrieved an unopened bottle of sherry. "Things are very strange today upstairs," I told Mel as I carried it past her, "even without your shadows and demons workin', I think."

"What is it going on?" she wanted to know.

I arranged a tray of eight glasses just in case any others joined the men.

"I can't be sure yet, but you'd best keep everyone down here once they've cleared the dining room."

I carried the tray and bottle upstairs.

Taking their sherries, the Locofocos raised a toast to "the brave John Tyler." He and Robert exchanged a fretful glance. Before any of them had a chance even to drain their glasses, there came a crash and a shriek from the other side of the house.

I set the tray down on a table near the door even as a startled Mr. Tyler said, "James, find out what that is." As I opened the door, however, Samuel barged in, plenty agitated.

"Mister Tyler, sir," he said. "They's a mob out front calling for your life, sir!"

A shot punctuated his announcement. One of the glass panels separating the vestibule cracked, and something thumped into the wall not far from the open door. Samuel stepped back to look, and I joined him. A musket ball or the like had dug a hole in the plaster.

Voices outside cheered the shot. Others yelled profanities wrapped around the name of "Tyler." A rock crashed through one of the front vestibule windows and thudded across the floor there.

"My God. Priscilla!" Robert cried. He charged for the door.

Mr. Tyler exclaimed, "Go with him, get the children out of there." Samuel and I took off full-chisel after him. Robert ran through the vestibule, while we dashed into the stairwell and came through the adjoining door, the quicker route.

Miss Priscilla had Mary in her arms and was already circling the table. Tazewell had drawn back a curtain and boldly stared out the window. The shouting was louder from here. Sally was gone, but Olive, who had been clearing away the plates, was pressed up against the sideboard.

Robert burst in from the vestibule and ran to Priscilla. "Get the children," he told Samuel, who immediately stepped in behind the two girls, while I jumped for Tazewell, who seemed transfixed by the mob.

"Come on, now," I urged him, taking him by the shoulders and turning him away. As he moved, I saw a figure running along the drive hurl something straight our way. Instinctively, I swept him into the corner, and a rock shattered the glass where we'd stood a moment before. Alice shrieked, and the rock skittered along the table, upended a bowl, and then fell to the floor. I didn't have to encourage him to leave after that. He sprang to catch up with his sisters.

Olive seemed not to know what to do with only half the dishes and silverware cleared to the sideboard. I grabbed her. "Leave it," I said, and pushed her ahead of me. "Go tell Mel to block up the north kitchen door. Sooner or later the rowdies will figure out it exists."

The family all headed upstairs. Olive dove into the stairwell and down. Only Samuel and I remained. I said, "You should go with them too. Keep them safe up there."

He looked daggers, but for once not at me. We shared a common enemy. "I want to *do* somethin' to them people," he said. The vertical scar on his cheek was suddenly livid, angry. "Y'understand?"

"They get through that front door, you're gonna have your chance."

His expression changed to something like delight in the contemplation of it. He charged up the stairs.

I called, "Samuel, see if Mr. Robert has a pistol he can bring us in the saloon." Then I ran to the vestibule.

Jasper cowered beside the door, not knowing where to stand. The rowdies had already shot through the top panel. But he saw me and stood up halfway. He gripped one of the fireplace pokers. He said, "Get out of it before they see you through the window and kill you." Even as he spoke, another shot was fired and we both ducked, but either it was into the air or the shooter was too drunk to hit the house right in front of him. More shouts for Tyler to come out and face justice; fists pounded on the door. "It's locked for now," Jasper said. "Go on with ya!"

I ran to the Blue Saloon again.

The Democrats had opened a south portico door and were making to leave.

"No, sir, stop them!" I shouted.

The men all turned. Tyler came at me in a fury. "You forget your place, James," he snapped. That was true, and if they'd been Virginia Whigs, I'd have been whipped later for my effrontery. He added, "I told them to escape while they can. There's nobody on the south lawn. They can send for help."

I *had* acted without considering my place, the limits baked into me, mainly because I wanted to survive, and I could either hold my tongue and maybe get killed, or else risk offending him and them and get sent home after. At least I'd be alive.

I said, "Mr. Tyler, sir, we need these men to rout that mob before it gets bolder. You send them off, you'll have to face them louts directly and alone, else they'll soon be corned enough to break in here no matter what anyone does. Mr. Webster wanted you to send to Mayor Seaton but you don't have the time for that now, sir. They're upon us."

"What do you propose?" asked Mr. Ingersoll. It took me a long moment to appreciate that he was asking me and not Mr. Tyler, who was also surprised. Between Ingersoll and me, he had to wrestle his ire under control.

When I didn't answer directly, Tyler said, "Well, James? The man asked you a question."

"These good gentlemen came here to offer you their support," I said, "and now they can show you. If they confront that mob instead of you, it will fold like a bad hand of cards."

"And how do you figure that, James?" Ingersoll asked.

"I witnessed the mob gathering earlier, when Mr. Tyler sent me to speak with Mr. Webster. They was a loose and cowardly bunch spurred to act by intoxication. Right now they think they're having their way of it. They want Mr. Tyler to step out onto the portico and face the music. If you all march out there instead of him, they won't know what to do. They got no plan and no skill to make one when things don't go their way."

Ingersoll considered me a moment, then replied, "That's quite sensible and probably true." To Tyler he asked, "John, do you have any guns?"

As if that was his cue, Robert Tyler entered through the Green Parlor door. He carried two weapons. I knew of the Allen Pepperbox, which he kept in a drawer in his desk. The other gun I had never seen before. It was much larger, with a long single barrel. Seemed none of the other men had seen it either. Robert explained, "It's a prototype. Called a Paterson. I was given it while I was in New York. Fires five shots, and it's loaded. Manufacturer hopes we'll arm our soldiers with them."

The Democrats gathered around, wanting a look at the gun. They had drunk down some courage of their own, I noticed, polishing off the bottle of sherry. Ingersoll took the formidable Paterson, and one of the other men accepted the Pepperbox. I'd stepped aside, to the doorway into the hall. I opened both doors for them, and Tyler tried to lead them out, but I pressed a hand to his chest and shook my head. He stared down at my glove against his coat as if it was the most infernal outrage that I had dared touch him, never mind in front of these men. There would likely be consequences, but he was not the general leading his forces into battle. He still did not seem to understand what both Ingersoll and I plainly did.

"Please, sir," I said, "you mustn't let those folks so much as see you or they will rally and storm the house. Allow Mr. Ingersoll to stand for you. You should go be with Miss Letitia and your family. Mr. Robert too."

Robert put his hand on his father's shoulder as I drew mine away. "James is right, sir. You should be with Mother." Ingersoll echoed that sentiment.

With everything decided for him by someone else, Mr. Tyler stepped aside and allowed the men out into the hall, but his eyes continued to burn with shame and he would not look at me.

The five men strode across to the vestibule. Mr. Tyler watched until they were all through the glass divide. Then he let his son haul him to the stairs across the hall.

Jasper, still wielding his poker, was all too happy to open the front door for the Democrats. The crowd roared.

Then the Locofocos stepped out onto the portico, brandishing their weapons, and the voices outside fell into confusion and silence.

Jasper and I peered through the broken window.

Ingersoll held his gun at the ready. He thumbed back the hammer to make his point. The sound of it seemed loud as a cannon. The other man aimed Robert's Pepperbox at a seedy lout straight with a musket in front of him, who immediately sprang away and down the steps. The mob looked like maybe two dozen people, most of them men. Some held stones, others sticks, and a few had torches though it was not yet dark—maybe they were expecting to set the house afire. A couple others also brandished muskets and must have done some of the firing.

One at the back, probably emboldened with so many bodies between him and those guns, shouted again for Tyler to come out.

Ingersoll answered, "No one is coming out, but someone is going in the ground if you don't all leave *now*." He marched straight at the fellow in front of him. "Maybe you!" he called.

The rowdie backed up so fast that he went right over the edge of the steps and fell into the group below him, dragging three more of them to the gravel.

That acted like a signal to the congressmen. They fanned out across the portico. The crowd couldn't be sure if they all had guns or not and gave ground everywhere, scurrying out of the carriage lane and back as far as the wrought-iron fence. The Locofocos stayed on the portico, poised like giants over them. Ingersoll shouted, "Go home, the drunken lot of you, and be glad you aren't being hanged for *treason*!"

Maybe being called traitors when they had been having all the fun of it persuaded them. At the back people were already fading across Lafayette Park. Ingersoll stood his ground as if at any moment he might pick one of them and shoot just to make his point.

The intimidation worked. The rabble slunk off into the night. One of them flung his torch as he fled, but it bounced harmlessly off the steps and then lay sputtering.

Beside me in the vestibule, Jasper exhaled and said, "Them men just saved all our lives."

"I know," I told him. "Let's hope they aren't going to have to do it every night from now on."

Twenty-Four

More envelopes appeared overnight, in cowardly fashion left anonymously outside the front door. Jasper was both dismissive of such low behavior and relieved that he hadn't required to accept any directly. After the mob, it was too easy to imagine being a target in that doorway, reaching for a letter only to be shot in the belly.

He only opened the door now with the greatest reluctance, and while standing at the side. When Mayor Seaton softly knocked, he almost did not answer.

Seaton, thickset and with a fierce visage second only to Daniel Webster's in Jasper's opinion, looked dismayed at the handful of letters he held.

"Just lyin' there, were they?" asked Jasper. "The cowards."

He took the letters, let Seaton in, and paused to look out across the empty park. It was cooler this morning.

"If you'll follow me, sir. Mr. Tyler's in the Washington Parlor." He led the mayor across the hall.

Tyler greeted Seaton and, frowning, took the letters Jasper held out to him. "Where is James?" he asked.

"Gone to fetch a glazier, I believe, sir." *Which you should know since you sent him,* Jasper thought.

"Of course." He crossed to the bell pull. "Whoever comes up, have them bring us some tea, Jasper."

He said, "Yes, sir," and backed out, leaving the door ajar. Jasper took a seat in the cross hall against one of the marble columns. From there he could attend the front door, catch whoever came up to answer the bell, and listen to the conversation in the parlor.

It was only a moment before Tyler shouted, "Here, look at this, Seaton!" He shook the letter. "'Die you dog.' How do you like that?"

Seaton shuffled through them. "Dear Lord," he muttered after reading a few.

"There are more, up in my office. Some far worse than this."

"And it all began with Botts' leaflet?"

"So says Daniel. He should be here soon."

Seaton said, "He came to me yesterday to draw up a warrant against the man, but I have it on good authority that Botts has already skedaddled back to Henrico County. In any case, arresting Botts won't persuade any of the hooligans who shot up your porch. They don't answer to him. I doubt the coward will even confess provocation."

"What am I to do, Seaton? Can we not call upon the police?"

The mayor answered, "Honestly? Like as not, for a mug of beer the Washington police would look the other way if not directly join in the rabble."

Olive came out of the service stairs. Jasper stood, told her they wanted tea brought up to the parlor. She nodded and went back down.

In the meantime, Tyler had torn open more envelopes. "Here. Another bomb threat. Look at this—they threaten me and the whole of my family."

Seaton said, "This one promises to burn the President's House to the ground."

"I am sorely tempted to move everyone back to Virginia this very afternoon. Deliver them to the train station before anything further happens."

"*These* are the nation's true traitors," Seaton replied, and Jasper nodded to himself in agreement. "Forgive me, John, I know I'll sound like one of Clay's supporters, but is there no way you could consider changing your position, compromising even a little on this bank matter? I heard that Ewing had offered an alternative—"

"Compromise with *these* sorts?" He slapped the envelopes. "You said it yourself, these people aren't governed by legislation."

"No, of course—you can't give in to such intimidation. The lid is off the box."

"Soon we will have to host those infernal parties week after week again. How can I have people I don't know in my house when any one among them might stab me or throw a bomb? Henry Clay's men, all unsounded yet and full of deep deceit. I would be Julius Caesar for their knives."

Olive returned, carrying a tray. When she left the parlor, she closed the door after her, thereby eliminating Jasper's ability to hear what was said. He got up then and returned to his post in the vestibule. He looked out the window. A few figures now clustered on the far side of the park. Of course, people strolled the park all the time. It didn't mean anything, or so he tried to convince himself.

Awhile later, Seaton emerged from the Washington Parlor. "Let me see what I can do," he called back to Tyler.

Jasper let him out. If anything, the mayor looked more indignant than Webster.

James returned within the hour. He had secured a glazier's services, but the man couldn't come for a day or so. Jasper thought maybe the man knew there was no point in repairing windows that were just going to be broken all over again.

Instead, Cyrus and Samuel were tasked with loading a wagon with boards from the stable. They carried them in through the front door, laid them on the oilcloth, then started nailing them up across the broken windows. Jasper stood beside James and remarked, "Like watching someone nail the lid on your coffin, ain't it?"

Tyler came out to inspect the work, looking grim and exhausted. "Send Webster up when he gets here," he said, then headed up the east stairs to his office.

⇛ ⬺

Jasper spent the latter part of the afternoon looking out around the boards nailed over the vestibule windows. He tracked the growing clusters of people in Lafayette Park. Their numbers ebbed and flowed; some gathered, talked, pointed at the house, but many who strolled past seemed confused by those that sat or loitered there. He kept hoping to catch sight of who was leaving the envelopes; but as if they were aware of him, no one approached the portico when he was watching.

A few hours passed, and a buckboard wagon came rolling across the park and turned into the curving carriageway. The small groups of people in the park watched it pass among them. They didn't seem to know what it represented any more than Jasper did.

Three rough-looking men occupied the buckboard. The driver was a hulking orange-haired brute wearing a raffia top hat that looked to have been kicked along a dozen dusty streets before he'd set it on his head. Beside him sat a much smaller man with black hair, and in the back was a pale scarecrow with his arms folded and his cap pulled low. He might have been asleep.

The wagon drew up on the carriageway but not in the carriage lane beneath the portico. The shorter man jumped down, and Jasper considered whether he shouldn't run to the family dining room and yank the bell pull to get James or Samuel up here, at least have one of those pistols on hand. But he dithered so long that the short black-haired man reached the front door. He knocked, and if a rapping at the door could be called insouciant, his was.

Jasper opened the door a few inches, all set to leap aside.

Lean and standing hardly an inch taller than Jasper, close-up the fellow had shaggy, oily hair shot with a few early strands of gray. His black eyes were sharp with mischief. He'd a scar across the bridge of his nose, a silver ring in one earlobe, and where his patchy shirt was rolled up, a mermaid tattoo curled around his forearm. His trousers were indigo-dyed canvas. He smelled, oddly, of smoke, and the curve of his mouth bore the same insouciance as his knock.

"I'm here ta see the president," he said. *Irish,* Jasper thought.

Jasper's inclination was to slam the door and sound the alarm, or at the very least inform the fellow that he'd come to the wrong entrance for a tradesman; instead, he masked his own trepidation, remaining stiff and superior on his higher step. "On what business shall I say?"

"On business of Mayor Seaton's. My name's Renehan, Martin Renehan, and I was directed to come here by no less than the mayor hisself."

"Are you the glaziers then?"

Renehan's lips twitched and for an instant he grinned. "That wouldn't be me area of expertise, no. Maybe if you just let me talk to your man, we can sort it out, hey?"

Jasper flicked a glance at the other two roughs, still in the wagon, and then across the park at the loose clusters of rowdies. Would anyone be so bold as to name Seaton? He thought not.

Cautiously, he opened the door and let the man in.

Renehan stepped across the threshold. He looked up at the toothed molding, the chandelier, the fireplaces on either side of the vestibule, and the oilcloth covering the floor. Jasper was about to have him sit, when from the family dining room there came the clinking of silver and chinaware. He excused himself and quickly passed through the anteroom into the dining room, where he found Zenobia and Tall George setting the table for a late afternoon's repast.

"George," he said, "quick, go upstairs and find Mr Tyler, tell 'im there's a man 'ere for 'im sent by the mayor."

He returned to the vestibule. Renehan was inspecting the marble columns and the glass panels that separated the foyer from the cross hall. He glanced at Jasper. "Quite the palace, innit?" he commented, and grinned as if they were well acquainted. "I see this pillar here took a slug. Musket ball?"

Jasper made no reply, just nodded and returned to the door, then crossed to the window to make sure no one else was approaching the house. Peripherally, he tracked Renehan's inquisitive circling of the vestibule.

Noises from the dining room seemed to draw the Irishman to the anteroom door. He hung in the doorway and asked, "An' who might you be, darlin'?"

Jasper started for him, but heard Zenobia reply, "I don't know you, mister, what you doin' in here?" Past Renehan he saw that she had a meat cleaver in her hand. Jasper smirked, half-hoping the bogtrotter would try something with her.

Renehan raised his hands in apology or to show her they were empty, and said, "I didn't mean to interrupt your business, girl. Lovely to make yer acquaintance."

At that point, Tall George and John Tyler came from the main stairs into the vestibule. Tyler carried Robert's Pepperbox pistol with him, making a point of holding it along his thigh as Renehan crossed the vestibule to meet him. Renehan noted the pistol and drew up.

"Y'all are from Seaton?" Tyler said.

"I am, sir." He introduced himself and held out his hand. It was dirty, and two of the knuckles scabbed over. A scar ran over the back of it to the thumb joint. Tyler hesitated, but then took his hand. "The mayor sent all three of us." He tipped his head toward the door. "Me mates and I are Frogtown lads."

"Frogtown?"

Zenobia came out of the dining room and stood in the anteroom door beside Jasper. Tyler caught sight of her. "Zenobia," he said, "go find James and send him up."

Renehan turned his head. "Lovely to meet ya…Zenobia."

Blushing, she lowered her head and ducked back into the dining room. Tall George took her place, a proper footman awaiting instruction. Jasper warranted he would be more difficult to flirt with.

Tyler asked, "What is Frogtown, Mr. Renehan?"

"A fire company is what it is. Frogtown's the fire company south of the Capitol."

Tyler blinked. "Seaton sent… You're a fireman."

"All three of us, and about as good at starting 'em as we are at putting them out. And I can affirm we hold our own when them Swampdoodle, Liberties, or English Hill lads dispute the provenance of any blaze in question."

"I apologize," Tyler said, shaking his head. "I have no idea—"

"Ah, well, there's a great deal of competition with the other fire companies, ya see, to be the ones what put out a fire. But the boundaries are often a bit sketchy. We sometimes fail to see eye to eye."

"Really?" Tyler replied, the sound of it halfway between amused and taken aback.

"And your Mr. Seaton, the mayor, he indicated you might be wanting to employ a few…"

"Hooligans?" Tyler offered. He glanced at Jasper as if for confirmation.

Jasper nodded. Oh, that was the word for this one, all right. But given the growing number of people in the park, he wondered if perhaps Seaton didn't have a point.

Compelled at the thought, he returned to the window and was shocked to find two large men lumbering straight across the portico with a crate between them. Renehan's mates were still seated on their buckboard, although watching with some curiosity as these new men out of a second wagon reached the door. The nearest knocked forcefully.

Tyler half-raised his pistol. That was good enough for Jasper. He drew open the door with himself behind it.

The two men barreled through the opening with their crate. Tyler took a step forward as if to bar their way if they came much farther.

Oblivious of the gun, the men set the crate on the floor just inside the door and groaned from the exertion. They straightened up, confused to be met by so many people. The nearest one had a ginger beard. The other, squat and lumpish, put his hands on his lower back and stretched. He started back out again without a word or any apparent interest in the customary gratuity for a delivery.

"Just a minute," said Tyler. "What is this?" He pointed the pistol at the crate.

The ginger man seemed to see the pistol for the first time. "Eh, no idea, sir," he said. "We was instructed to deliver it and then go. Paid us at the other end, they did."

Tyler stumbled back from the crate. "My God, it's a bomb!" he yelled.

Upon those words, the delivery men bolted out the door. Jasper slammed it after them, then dove for the entrance to the east stairwell and his room.

Tyler himself leaped back through the doorway in the glass panels and pressed against the pillar that formed one side of it. Tall George fled into the anteroom and must have kept going. The word "bomb" echoed through the house.

Martin Renehan lunged into the anteroom after Tall George, but re-emerged immediately with Zenobia's meat cleaver in his fist. He knelt before the crate and swung the cleaver, splitting the corner board with a single blow.

Jasper cringed, expecting an explosion to follow. He thought of his daughter near Georgetown, feared how he would never smoke a bowl of tobacco in her parlor or bounce his granddaughter on his knee again. But nothing happened.

Tyler had slid around behind the pillar.

Renehan struck the crate over and over until metal sang against metal.

Jasper peered around the doorway. Tyler was leaning into the vestibule now too.

Renehan had hold of the smashed crate boards. He ripped them away until he had revealed a good portion of the black iron thing they concealed.

Small handles graced the front of it, and some circular scrolling decorated the top, which was edged with a curled lip. The one visible bottom corner rested on an iron clawfoot. Jasper crept into the vestibule again. What sort of bomb had feet and scrollwork?

At that point, Daniel Webster came barreling out from the east stairwell and nearly knocked him aside. Right behind him followed Robert Tyler. Priscilla and James Christian arrived from the cross hall, but Tyler stopped her from entering the vestibule. James edged around her.

Everyone around Jasper watched as Martin Renehan fished a torn sheet of paper out from the wreckage of the crate and looked it over. He barked a laugh, then rose up and formally held the paper out to President Tyler. Jasper walked over beside James to see.

President Tyler read aloud: "To Robert Tyler. Please accept scale model of proposed new stove for your kitchen, Charles Kent, Yards Foundry." He lowered the page and gave his son a dark look.

James Christian coughed loudly to hide a laugh. Jasper used him to hide his own grin from the Tylers.

Renehan set down the cleaver, gouged and dulled from striking the cast iron model so many times. He got to his feet. "I don't believe it's any sort of a—" He stopped, beholding Priscilla Cooper Tyler for the first time. Jasper saw the almost reverent look on his face, his gaze so naked that she blushed and turned toward James. Jasper thought, *This is trouble.*

The others were staring at Robert Tyler and didn't notice.

Renehan cleared his throat, then said, "So, it's a wee stove for the faeries then." He grinned

Robert Tyler frowned at the accusatory looks from all around. "One of the ovens downstairs has rusted out, Father," he explained, and made a point of ignoring Renehan. "We need a new one, and I took care of it. I saw no reason to trouble you with the details. Webster—" he gestured across the vestibule "—has it in the budget. I'd quite forgotten all about it. Didn't know Yards was delivering it today. They should have said."

The front door swung open then and the two firemen who'd accompanied Renehan in his wagon burst in only to appear disappointed to find no fight in progress. The huge one in the hat announced, "Had ta circle the wagon on account of them delivery men, Martin," as if someone had asked him a question. "Saw them two fleein' fer their lives, so we hot-footed it, hey?"

The third fireman stood tall and sullen behind him. He had the sort of fishbelly-pale skin that to Jasper always looked unwashed.

Tyler stared down at the half-revealed stove and gave a slight, embarrassed laugh. He folded up the paper. "Well, it is not a bomb, is it, Mr. Renehan, but it might well have been, given the threats that have come so thick yesterday and today, and with those drunken dogs out there in the park. You hesitated not a moment, while I—while *all* of us…"

He brushed down his coat, straightened his cravat, and handed the Pepperbox pistol back to his son. Now he fairly beamed at the fireman. "My apologies if I was surly with you before, young man. I would like—that is, your country would like to hire you along with your—your Frogtown confederates to join our company. Mr. Jasper here and James can assist you with accommodations. You'll all board here most of the time, naturally. Who knows when another stove might need to be catawamptiously beaten into a jelly, hmm?" He smiled as though having made a remarkable joke, shot another glance at his son. "Mr. Webster there will see that you three get measured for suits. Two apiece, Daniel."

In the stairwell doorway, Webster nodded.

Renehan made a face as if he smelled something unpleasant. "Begging your pardon, Mr. Tyler—suits?"

"You must be attired appropriately for the President's House, to blend in at levées and dinners. That is where most of your efforts are likely to be focused, I think. You'll join Mr. Jasper here at the front door, and other times, like James"—he gestured at Christian—"you'll mix among the guests, all with an eye to our safety."

"Oh, I see. Bodyguards, is it?" Renehan winked at his comrades.

"Yes, well, we won't use that word or Congress will never agree to the funds, now will they, Daniel?" He frowned. "Some of them would delight in seeing me shot, an idea they are currently promoting to the more inebriated among our citizenry." He gave a nod toward the park.

Jasper said, "Well, if they're on the door wiv me, why not call 'em *doormen* then."

Everyone looked at him. His face grew warm.

"We do 'ave a considerable number of doors in this 'ouse is all I'm saying."

Renehan repeated it. "Doormen." He laughed. "Sounds a wee bit too respectable for the likes of us. What d'ya think, lads?"

He took in the whole vestibule again. Robert was kneeling, inspecting the dinged-up model stove, and Renehan allowed his gaze to rise as if naturally to Priscilla again.

Jasper watched her match and wither him with her own stare. He thought James was recognizing the staring contest too.

Tyler interrupted. "One more thing, Mr. Renehan, if you would." He wore a self-deprecating smile now. "Let's not mention to anyone how events unfolded here today, hmm? No more fuel for their fires? Even fairy-fires?"

Renehan drew a finger across his lips. "Oh, mum's the word, sir. We'll consider it a...*secret* service we've done ya." He grinned.

Nothing but *trouble,* Jasper told himself again.

Twenty-Five
James Hambleton Christian

The Frogtown firemen were persuaded to stay for supper. My expectation, on account of they was white men, was that they would eat upstairs with the family; but however indebted Tyler felt to Renehan for saving him from a stove, it didn't serve to level them in any particular way. The firemen would be eating at *our* mess table.

The family's meal was a cold supper. Outside, a thunderstorm shook and flashed. It had rolled in about the time they sat down, and because of it they got to eat in peace with no rocks heaved at the windows and nobody screaming outside. Everybody was hoping the matter was finished. Even so, Mr. Tyler asked me to come take his place reading to Miss Letitia after we finished our supper. He wanted to keep an eye on the park.

The other two firemen were named Osbert Drummond and Eli Garvine. Drummond had the unkempt orange hair and straw top hat. Garvine, the lanky dead-pale one, seemed ready to boil most of the time. He didn't sit until the other two had, as if he wasn't committing to anything. He smelled like old meat, and I don't know how those two tolerated being near him.

Downstairs we had cornbread, and spicy beans and rice with some ham hocks, which was a lot more belly-filling than what Mr. Tyler had chosen for the family.

Renehan planted himself between Mel and Zenobia. As he sat, he commented, "You two have to be sisters." It was anything but an original observation, but Zenobia got all shy and shifted on the bench to put some space between him and her. "Back where I come from, Zenobia, they used to let girls young as you work in some awful places, and sometimes those lovelies got tossed out in the street. I'm glad to see that's not the case with all the beauties here." Then he winked at her.

I have no explanation for why that man's line of hogwash worked on the women around the table. They laughed and giggled. He had some sort of gift for tickling them. Even stone-faced Deborah was sly-smiling on him.

You could not say the same for the men. Garvine and Drummond all but ignored him, giving the impression they had heard it a hundred times already. Marcellus watched him dispiritedly, probably trying to figure out what the man did to make Zenobia titter and blush and say, "Stop now, mister."

Mostly Renehan seemed to make fun of himself while he talked, telling how on board the ship over from Ireland, he'd been awful seasick and had tried to retch out a porthole just as the ship took a wave, and had instead drunk down half the ocean; and how the first time he'd confronted a house blaze, he'd caught his trousers on fire before he'd even got off the wagon. Anyone walking into the mess would have thought he and the women had all been together for years.

Then I went to spell Mr. Tyler.

I knocked, although the door itself was open. Mr. Tyler glanced up at me a moment; then he read a little more.

"'To tell the truth, the good lady's opinion had been not a little influenced by her brother-in-law's appeal to her better understanding, and his implied compliment to her high deserts; and although she had dearly loved her husband, and still doted on her children, he had struck so successfully on one of those little jarring chords in the human heart (Ralph was well acquainted with its worst weaknesses, though he knew nothing of its best), that she had already begun seriously to consider herself the amiable and suffering victim of her late husband's imprudence.'"

He marked his place and closed the book, then leaned over and kissed Miss Letitia. He said, "I hope you don't feel the victim of my imprudence," and she smiled and placed her hand on his cheek.

He got up, passed me without a word. He wasn't openly belligerent, but wasn't making it a secret that he remained aggravated with me for speaking on my own the day before when propriety dictated that I advise him and thus allow him to lead. Either I should get used to terse and dismissive treatment awhile, or I was going to have to apologize, perform some act of penance.

Mr. Tyler walked to the middle of the hall. Samuel started after him, but Tyler stopped him, saying, "Go turn down my bed and get the room ready, why don't you, Samuel?" Samuel came sullenly back past me.

There was a narrow center corridor that ran perpendicular to the hall between the children's rooms, ending in the window directly over the front door. Mr. Tyler had put a chair there. That isolated window would become his private observation post.

Thunder shook the window in Miss Letitia's room. The storm was still upon us. Personally I hoped it would drown the *miscreants*, as Mr. Tyler called them—send them like rats floating along the avenue and into the Potomac. If I'd had *bokor* powers, that's what I would have done.

I'd seen them gathering after the doormen had arrived. I counted more of them than the night before.

The breeze pushed along by the storm was almost chilly. Before I sat beside Miss Letitia, I leaned past the mirror and closed her window. "Maybe the summer heat's finally quit us." I took up the volume of Dickens from the table and turned up the lamp. "This is the most recent one, isn't it, Miss

Letitia? If the man doesn't write another novel soon, we're going to have to go back to *The Pickwick Club.*"

She seemed amused by that. I opened *The Life and Times of Nicholas Nickleby* to where Mr. Tyler had stopped, and began to read.

⤷⤷⤶- -❬❬❬

The thunderstorm I'd put my hope in blew itself out by the time I had reached the end of the chapter, and sometime after sunset, the mob came back through the park like wolves wandering out of the woods.

I stood at the boarded window beside Jasper and watched a couple of them stand a makeshift gibbet on the lawn. They'd hung an effigy of Tyler on it, his name painted on a plank around his neck. In the dimming light they set the thing ablaze while one of them tugged on the rope to make the stuffed figure seem to jerk and twist like a live man.

I gritted my teeth against a bile of memory that rose in my throat: I was nine years old, riding in a wagon beside my mother and three other slaves. The three was chained. They'd just been purchased at the slave market in City Point. My mother and I had been put unchained in the wagon by Colonel Christian to make his new purchases feel safe and calm in his possession. Must have been ten miles out from Cedar Grove plantation when we smelled the hanging man; a few minutes till we came upon him. He was strung up in a pignut hickory. Was nobody around, so that he seemed weirdly like a feature of the woods, some freakish black and seeping natural formation dangling from a big gray tree. He was so thoroughly charred that I wouldn't have known whether he was black or white except for the sign hung round his neck, scrawled with the word *Runaway.*

The effigy of John Tyler stuffed with cotton batting couldn't come close, but it exhumed the awful stink and sight lodged in the ventricle of memory.

I could about sense Tyler directly overhead in his narrow little hall, like a French king staring down at the rabble come to get him.

Footsteps came running up, and the three firemen crowded in behind us. Seeing the gibbet, Renehan muttered, "Sweet Jesus." Then brightly to the other two, "Seems we got us a fire, and ain't that our calling, lads? So, James, we'll want to be comin' out the back. Might need a few items, too, if you got 'em."

"Mr. Tyler has a couple pistols," I replied.

He shook his head. "Oh, we want nothin' like that, now, do we, Eli?"

Garvine gave him a cunning look.

I led them down through the furnace room, where Garvine scooped up a short-handled coal shovel as he passed by it. Once again the south lawn remained empty. Garvine swiped the air a few times with his new shovel.

We marched along the west colonnade to the stable. As we arrived at the stable door, Absalom Lee jumped up with a mallet. He thought the mob had come for him until he turned up his lamp and saw me. He hadn't eaten with us, so didn't know the doormen. I made quick introductions while they looked around. Renehan took a fancy to Absalom's big mallet and asked if he could borrow it. The carrot-haired Drummond poked around in the straw until he found an axe handle leaning against a side wall. He came back, hefting it with such a look of joy, I wouldn't have been surprised if he'd asked it to dance.

Renehan went up to him. "Now, Osbert," he said, "you don't do a thing 'less I tell ya, right?" He gave me a wink and leaned in closer. "Osbert's me half-brother, James. He's a bit slow, like his old man was, and you can't bend him once his course is set. Ain't that so, Osbert?"

Osbert just continued to smile like a happy child in a beat-up hat.

I led the three of them around the stable and then up the incline to the carriage circle. Someone's wagon and horses were tied up to an iron post there. Renehan pressed my shoulder and said, "Far enough for you, James. You stay safe. This is our business now." They walked out onto the carriageway. I crouched beside the wagon and watched.

Their business now. Earlier I'd endured listening to Webster and Tyler agree to pay these men an annual salary of hundreds of dollars for their business. It made them and their actions legitimate, I supposed. Like a police force. Nobody would lynch them for anything they did.

They strolled over through the fence and deep into the park to seem to enter the mob from behind, like new recruits joining in the fun. The gibbet fire revealed about fifty people on or near the steps of the portico. Nobody paid the trio any mind. Lots of people had weapons. As well as rocks, I counted two muskets, a sword, boards, and a few brickbats.

More rocks suddenly pelted the house, and more windowpanes shattered. Even the fanlight above the front door got smashed this time. The walls and the columns thumped and thudded under the assault. People yipped and howled and called out threats at the top of their lungs.

Renehan and the other two wove in among the rest, working their way up to the front of the crowd by the gibbet and then onto the front steps, where the columns cut off my view of them.

A moment later, the mob's roistering bawls changed to screams, and somebody went flying off the portico and into people below.

All of a sudden people were leaping from every side of it. They fell over the iron anthemion rails, tripped down the steps, dove out of the port cochère. Scattering madly across the drive, they sprawled over one another, but scrambled up right away and fled into the night. Two ran along the carriageway to the west gate but didn't see me.

A man with a rifle and a torch come racing toward the wagon, Garvine at his heels. The man must have sensed he couldn't get away; suddenly he whirled to swing the rifle butt behind him. Garvine struck it aside with the shovel. It tore out of the man's grasp and into the gravel. The man tried desperately to batter him with the torch, but Garvine thrust the coal shovel up into his jaw. The torch flew and the man plunged over backward onto the driveway, tumbling into the horses. They whinnied and backed up, flinging him aside. He crashed down, his face bursting a puddle left by the storm. The rolling torch sprayed mad sparks everywhere, but remained lit. In a panic, the horses jumped, snapped the rein tied to the post, and tore off with the wagon, careening across the carriageway and through the park.

The fool man tried to get up, but Garvine, grinning like a pasty demon luxuriating in Hell, swung that shovel again, once, twice, and the man curled up, still. Calmly, Garvine picked up the torch. He stared sidelong at me a moment, as if he might have a go at me. Then he turned and walked fast back into the fray. He was in his element, which is to say plumb crazy.

Others seeing him striding at them veered toward the park as if the threat of him carried on the wind. A thrown rock brought one of them down, and I saw it was Drummond who'd thrown it, laughing and jumping in place as it struck home. Renehan had crossed to the gibbet. He kicked it over, and with that, the onslaught ended.

I counted half a dozen bodies on the ground, motionless or crawling, a few wailing.

The mob had been smashed in no time at all. I wanted to share in some vindication, but it wasn't in me. I thought of Samuel, angry and frustrated, wanting to do something to these people, and I felt the same way. But all we could do was watch.

The mob had scattered in a frenzy. The last few torches reached Lafayette Square. The carriage semi-circle in front had fallen dark. Muskets, sticks, rocks, a couple guttering torches, and half a dozen bottles of courage lay on the ground. Renehan, wreathed in smoke like some hopping Irish myth, stomped out the last of the gibbet fire.

The doormen met up on the steps, where they contemplated their handiwork. Garvine had found a corked bottle that hadn't been drunk when it was dropped. He took a pull and passed it to Renehan. They laughed and divvied up the lumps they had personally brought down, like Indian braves counting coup.

I walked up the carriageway, reaching the steps just as Tyler opened the door and heartily welcomed the three back inside. He'd been watching it all.

The door slammed and I was alone with the debris, the broken, and my envy. Those men could take on a mob without fear of consequences or reprisals. Kill with impunity, protected by the highest power in the land. God, I thought, to be so victorious.

I stared up at the wounded mansion, and counted all those inside it whose lives I would gladly have protected at the risk of my own. Instead, I got dressed down even for trying. Appropriate then, I suppose, that I ended up standing out there in the dark, in the shadows, watching it all as if through glass.

I walked away, back to the stables. Garvine's victim that I'd thought dead groaned as I passed. He might have been dying, but I felt nothing one way or the other for him. A half-hour before, he'd have killed me without hesitation.

I found Absalom and Cyrus had come up from the stable to watch too.

"Them boys done up that mob good," Cyrus said. I failed to find a voice with which to join his celebration.

Back inside, Mel was sitting in the mess room with some of the others. Nobody was eating.

"We all right?" she asked me.

"If you mean, is there no more mob, yeah, we all right." I sat down. I kept looking inside myself, trying to know what to feel.

Olive said, "We lucky them men come along."

It was an innocent remark, but it set me off. "We're lucky that mob didn't come up from swampside yesterday," I said, "else none of us'd been spared. They'd have stormed in past the furnace and about slaughtered us while Tyler skedaddled across Lafayette Park. Bombs and mobs and white men out for blood—*that's* real. That's what's gonna kill the likes of us, not some shadow what slides around in mirrors just to scare idiot *women*." I stared hard at the table and bit off the rest of what I wanted to say. One by one everybody else left.

That night I lay in my bed, hot and angry and frustrated. I should have apologized to Mel, to Olive. Rate I was going, pretty soon I would have to apologize to everyone in the house.

I was undone by knowing that I would never have the freedom to act as those firemen had. Defend us? I couldn't even keep one of us from being sold off if Tyler decreed it. My whole life was trying to keep me and Mel together.

That night I hated those firemen for saving us. I hated everyone for it.

>>>——<<<

Next morning, some smears of blood and the charred remains of that gibbet were all that remained of the previous evening's events. Absalom and I dragged the pieces down to the stable. Lafayette Park was almost empty, and no groups gathered throughout the day.

The doormen, as we called them now, settled in comfortably straight off the reel. Marcellus had removed himself to the stables during the height of the summer heat, boarding with Cyrus and Absalom Lee. One night in bed Mel told me the real reason he'd done so was to avoid being tempted into sin by sleeping so near Zenobia. In his eyes, I supposed I must be past saving.

That left Tall George Washington all by himself to be inconvenienced by the presence of the new trio in the men's sleeping quarters. Only Eli Garvine made a fuss, standing out in the hall and braying that he would "not sleep beside no *neegra!*" Who did he think was listening to him?

Renehan intervened though. "Eli, you go sleep in that corner by yerself then. Osbert and me'll bed over there at George's end. Anyway, he smells three times cleaner 'n you."

Nobody gathered in the park the next night. But two nights later, they tried to start up once again. A much smaller group, no more than a dozen, congregated. They weren't boisterous and hadn't drunk enough courage to start hurling rocks before the three doormen marched straight out the front door and into the carriageway, juggernauts of murderous intent. Those twelve people scattered like leaves blown on the wind and did not return.

We were troubled thereafter by no other mobs.

≫— —≪

I found it perplexing at first that the doormen hadn't been put in the empty rooms on the second floor, until at the next state dinner I happened to be serving the chilled soup when the new secretary of the Navy, Upshur, commented that "it's a damn shame when you got to surround yourself with a few *mudsills* to protect you from the rabble." Renehan was standing right outside the dining room. He couldn't have missed it.

Later I found him alone in the mess, and I sat beside him on the bench. "I confess I didn't understand why you got relegated to the kitchen floor," I told him, "till I heard Upshur."

Renehan looked me in the eye and laughed. "Oh, he's the one then called us *mudsills?* That's halfway polite from his like. You saw it through your eyes, and you thought 'cause we're same color as them we belong upstairs. But they recognize us as lowlifes sleepin' drunk in the gutter, where they can climb outta their carriage and step on us so as not to get their boots wet. Even your employer and that Mr. Webster, they think it whether they say it."

"My *employer*," I said. "Now, that's you seeing us through *your* eyes. That General Harrison who was president before? He had hisself a staff of free colored folk from the city. Mr. Tyler, on the other hand, didn't want to spend his own money."

Renehan chewed on that till it came clear.

"Perfectly reasonable mistake, Mr. Renehan. But save for you three gentlemen, it's all slaves down here."

He rubbed a knuckle across his teeth.

"Sure you want to continue consorting with us?"

He still had no reply.

I started to rise.

He said quietly, "We'll be on hand so long as they don't want to get their boots wet. Of course, we'll steal the silver if they leave us alone for five minutes up in the pantry."

I leaned on the table. "I'm the one who counts the spoons, just so you know."

"Fair enough, Mr. Christian. Whatever you do, though, for the love of Christ, don't tell Eli he's sleepin' wit' slaves. I'll have to drown him."

⤖ ⤕

That was his gift, making light of serious things. The only woman in the house unaffected by his folderol seemed to be Miss Priscilla, and the more she refused to acknowledge him, the more he dedicated himself to chipping away her ice. It was like my own relationship with Mel, except that, as I had to remind myself, he was attempting to beguile Mrs. Robert Tyler. He remained respectful enough in his overtures that nothing came out and he wasn't dismissed. She never said a word to her husband, which made me wonder whether for all her aloofness, she didn't maybe enjoy his attentions a little bit too.

Eli Garvine was the one that bore my attentions. After his fuss about George, he refused to eat with the rest of us in the mess. He would carry his food outside, usually through the furnace room and under the south portico. Later in the fall, he ate his meals in beside the furnace or sometimes alone on his cot. It turned out he had skill with coal-fired furnaces, and when the weather turned cold, Webster, instead of hiring another person, made Garvine the furnace tender. He was a fireman again, and most nights, save for soirées, he didn't have to put on fine clothes or mingle upstairs, leaving that to Renehan and his brother. He was the color of coal-dirty milk anyhow, pretty much how he'd looked upon arrival. At least now he smelled more tolerably like smoke.

I came to understand that Garvine was contrary by nature. He complained about the suit he had to wear, the food he ate, who slept in the room, and even about Jasper being considered a doorman and getting the same pay, when Jasper was the only *actual* doorman in our midst. To have a conversation with him was to listen to him cavil over whatever topic you were discussing.

Renehan ignored him—the result, apparently, of a lot of practice. "He's one of those men, hates life itself, like it didn't reward him with all the things in the world he knows he deserves, so he's got to pick at everything instead. Can't help himself."

I worried at that description, which could easily fit me too.

A few days later, it was Jasper's next furlough to visit his married daughter. I offered to take his place on the door that evening, to give him some extra time with his family. He thanked me, and within a half-hour, had changed his clothes, packed his carpet bag, and gone.

I sat in his vestibule chair that evening, listening to the house itself: the muted voices of family, the thumping of running footsteps overhead, probably Tazewell's, after having said goodnight to his mother in her lonely room.

There were no sounds from below. Nothing moved that shouldn't have: Chandeliers didn't swing. Doors didn't open. Nothing crawled out of the twin fireplaces in the vestibule to swallow me up.

When it was time, I doused the lights and walked down to my bed, still speculating at the absence of *bokors* and demons and ghosts. Maybe they'd been depending on the mobs. Might be those doormen had done more than they knew. Leastways, I hoped so.

Twenty-Six

A few weeks after employment of the doormen, Daniel Webster arrived at the president's office to be greeted by Tyler with the announcement: "The mobs are finished, Daniel."

Robert sat at the maps table, and Webster supposed they had been discussing it, obsessively.

"I'm sure you're right," he replied.

The week before, Tyler had vetoed a second Senate bill—of fiscal corporation—and in the aftermath no mobs had gathered. There *had* been consequences: Clay had seen Tyler expelled from the Whig Party; following on that, the entire cabinet, save for Webster, had resigned in a single afternoon.

Somewhat surprisingly, Tyler's response to this was delight. "I will finally have my Tyler men advising me. The devil take Clay."

Tyler men, thought Webster. Like Upshur, the new secretary of the Navy. He cringed at the thought of working with such "Tyler men."

As he'd promised to do, Webster had sent off a letter to his friend Lord Ashburton in England, begging him to sail to Washington and wrest negotiations from the contrary Ambassador Fox. The two of them could surely hammer out some satisfactory agreements, and then he would be quit of his obligations, free to flee Tyler's cabinet as fast as he could. As it was, the Whigs were barely tolerating his continued service to "His Accidency."

The mood in the house, however, had regained something like a state of calm, and just in time for the return of the social season, with its concomitant dinners and levées. The shattered windows had been reglazed, even the fanlight over the front door. If it weren't for the damnable trial of Alexander McLeod for murder, everything would have been manageable. That one trial threatened to tip the entire nation into war with England.

➤➤➤ ◄◄◄

Most of the dignitaries in the city attended the first levée of the fall, including the British delegation. The trial was on everyone's mind. War would destabilize more than just British and American comity. Members of the Spanish and French delegations as well as various congressmen were also on hand in the Blue Saloon, where Ambassador Fox, puffing on a cheroot, leaned upon the ivory handle of his gutta-percha walking stick and expounded: "War is on the horizon, gentlemen. It's a simple fact. If this American court finds a British citizen guilty of murder next month, what choice will we have? Think if it were one of *your* citizens."

Webster scowled. Really, the man's ego beggared belief. "Your pitiable British 'victim' is a *self-proclaimed* murderer. It's not as if we trumped up a case against him. It's your people crossed into American waters, and not the other way around, then murdered a watchman—"

"Only a *colored*," interjected Representative Owsley of Kentucky.

Webster glowered at the asinine interruption.

Fox added, "Even were I to grant you that McLeod is a drunk and a loud-mouthed simpleton, you lot can't even put him at the scene of the events. He's a scapegoat."

"Must I point out that the trial is taking place in New York, and not here in this house?"

Fox puffed on his cigar. "If you feel the need. Of course, then I must point out our remarkable steam-powered warships, even now sailing the Atlantic off your coast. Imagine what they'll do to your navy. Who is the new secretary?"

"Upshur," said Webster. "He's in the East Room if you wish to speak to him." Looking up, he saw John Tyler enter the room.

"No point," said Fox. "After this war he'll be out of a job."

Webster sighed heavily. Oh, to be rid of this little barking dog and his arrogance.

The Spanish delegation bowed and stepped back, giving Tyler a straight lane to the ambassador. Behind Fox, a few of his own saw Tyler and cleared their throats to signal him; but Fox wasn't done declaring: "As for your invitation to Ashburton—yes, I know of it, Mr. Webster—should there *be* war, you can be certain milord will not sail to your rescue."

"Nor to yours," said Tyler.

For a moment Fox faltered. The long ash spilled from the end of his cigar.

"Should you all declare war because you don't like the conviction and execution of your man, McLeod, I swear that you personally will find yourself clapped in irons and marched straight out of your embassy and into a cell, where you shall remain a hostage of the United States for the duration of the war, whether that be months or years. What Lord Ashburton does or does not do won't be your concern."

Fox yanked the cigar from his mouth and spluttered. Members of his delegation spluttered with him. "Outrageous!" "Of all the cheek!" Then Lord Ettryne began to laugh. This unexpected reaction poured cold water on their outrage, and even Fox glared at the fair-haired lord. Ettryne had proved contrary and so cold in negotiations that until that moment Webster hadn't considered him capable of laughter.

Ettryne's blue eyes impaled Fox and Tyler over the rim of his champagne glass, before he closed them and downed the last of the drink. He set the empty glass on the nearest tray, held by James Christian.

"Oh, Fox," he said, "you and he are like two cigars. I've no idea which of you puffs up more. Don't fume, for God's sake. If he's as good as his word, we'll sail up the Potomac and pound this whole pestilential city flat with our guns."

Featherington, one of his compatriots, cried, "Hear, hear!" and the others quickly echoed that huzzah. They shook gloved fists at Tyler and Webster. The nearest clapped Ettryne on the back, which seemed to annoy him. He took a silver-topped blackthorn walking stick from beneath his arm and pointed it ahead to clear the way in front of him.

He paused before Tyler. "Threats beget threats. Whatever we might think of Ambassador Fox, none of us will leave him to rot under *your* authority. Good night to you, sir." He strolled out of the room. Most of his delegation followed after him.

Fox stood a moment longer, his face working, as if he was trying to come up with something to add that could top Ettryne. Finally he marched out at the tail of his group.

The Spanish minister, Argaiz, leaned in toward Webster. "I thought that little man was going to declare war on you right here," he said.

Webster answered, "I'm not certain but that he didn't."

Twenty-Seven

James Hambleton Christian

The levée of October 16th was a real frolic. After the weeks of saber-rattling and posturing and proclaiming, the matter of war was defused when the New York jury acquitted McLeod. The news took four days to arrive. Afterward, the whole government, it seemed, was in the mood to celebrate.

People poured back the claret and sherry, the sauternes and punch, by the bucketful. There was a good deal of shouting, too, as though we'd let loose one of those September mobs into the house. At one point I spotted Tazewell crouched on the landing of the east stairs, watching the people stroll the hall. I gave him a wink. "Don't get caught," I warned him, but let him stay. Expect if I'd been him, I would have spied on that levée too.

Ambassador Fox and his entourage turned up in the company of Dolley Madison, which I guess meant that all was forgiven. If anything, the British deputation looked a bit disappointed.

The celebratory mood must have infected that congressman, John Minor Botts, too, because he snuck in amidst a group of Whigs. But the man who had called Mr. Tyler a traitor was hoping for too much remission.

I had seen, and must have introduced, Botts at some point in the previous season. A short man, he had the dissolute look of someone who had been to a few taverns before arriving. His gray hair looked to have been combed with a picket fence and his chin hadn't seen a razor in days. Had he been on his own, I might have thought he'd rolled in off the avenue, intending to filch a bottle or two, but he hid out in the middle of the group of congressmen.

When I led them into the East Room, Mr. Webster was standing nearby. He glanced around at them, and his cold eyes sharpened almost at once. He walked straight to Garvine, standing beside the punchbowl table, and whispered to him. Garvine turned, grinning at the cluster of Whigs. He gave Webster a nod, then walked past me to the other side of the doors, where Drummond stood, looking bored. Renehan must have been in another room.

While the two doormen conferred, Webster crossed to where Mr. Tyler stood with Robert and Misses Priscilla and Elizabeth, and spoke to him. I swear Tyler's head nearly spun off as he came about.

Garvine and Drummond closed on the Whigs from two sides and all the sudden slid in among them. The ones at the rear stepped back, seeing what was coming. There was a brief commotion. Then the doormen turned around and Botts turned with them. Those two held him in the air with his feet kicking and his right hand trying ineffectually to swipe his walking stick at Garvine. He howled for someone to come to his aid. The other Whigs not only made no move to help him, they scattered. Garvine fairly cackled as he brushed past me.

Down the cross hall they went, Botts shrieking and people jumping aside, more spilling out of the parlors, including Renehan, who when he saw the situation just leaned against the wall and watched.

They turned and entered the vestibule. Botts' cries for aid quickly faded.

I walked back down the hall in their wake. Renehan gave me an inquisitive look. "Man who wrote the Coffeehouse Letter," I said. Took him a moment to recall the cause of his hiring. Then he guffawed.

I returned to the front door. Jasper was owl-eyed. For all he knew, it had been an assassin. "What the 'ell was that about?" he asked, as the other two returned. They were tugging their jackets straight.

I noticed Garvine had removed his white gloves, and blood streaked the knuckles of his left hand. He saw where I was staring, looked down at his own hand, and deliberately licked the blood away. "Not mine," he told us. The two of them walked back into the hall as though nothing out of the ordinary had occurred.

Mr. Botts put in no further appearances.

»»»-«««

Later that evening I was sitting on my bed. I'd a candle burning on the table beside it, next to a book by Mr. Edgar Allan Poe, though it didn't even identify him as the author but claimed to be the autobiography of a man named Pym. It was a fanciful adventure, and I had read it to the point where a mutiny had taken place. I was looking forward to reading some more before I turned in for the night.

I had my shoes off and my braces down, and my shirt unbuttoned. That was when Mel came in from the dark mess room like some wandering spirit. My first thought was that she had come to lie with me. In the absence of any strange occurrences in the house the past months, she'd spent more of her nights with me—but one look told me otherwise.

I got to my feet. "What's the matter?" I asked. "What is it?"

Her face drawn tight, she said, "*Ouangas* are gone—the new ones."

It had been so long since she'd mentioned them, it took a second before I comprehended what she was telling me. My heart sank. I'd been so sure we were all done with *veves* and *vodou*.

Trying to remain calm, I asked, "Where?"

"Public floor. The blue room. I been checking them every week. This the first time they gone."

"Maybe Tazewell or Alice found them. I mean, how many—"

"Ain't the children, James." She sat down on the bed, her arms slack. She stared at the floor, not at me. "I told you he wouldn't run off, this man."

She seemed certain he had been in the house tonight, and of course none of us had been following her instructions to watch for a man who scrutinized everything. Anyway, half of Washington had been in the house. It would have been impossible.

"You thought he left town for the summer, and maybe so," she said. "But I think he was waiting for the war. I think he was countin' on it to do his work for him."

"And now it ain't coming."

She nodded.

I tried to sift through all the people who had passed through the front door tonight, but it was hundreds, and I hadn't seen them all. Maybe Jasper had. Once upon a time we'd speculated that it was Jasper himself we should be watching. Now I fairly trusted him.

I thought about Botts, the man who got evicted. He hadn't even made into the Blue Saloon before they threw him out. Ambassador Fox had though. And Argaiz, the Spanish minister, most of the French delegation, and a goodly number of the Whigs who hated Tyler, including Henry Clay— or had he been in the Green Parlor? I tried to remember everyone, where they was standing when I saw them; but I kept coming back to that little man Fox, the man Webster called a feist dog. How spiteful he had seemed, like he resented the verdict, and he had gloated upon the threat of war, goaded Tyler with it. He'd been expecting it, like Mel's *bokor*.

Before I could name him, Mel said, "Tonight was everybody here. Next week it maybe won't be like that, make it easier for you."

"Easier?"

"You and Deborah both, I told you, you're my eyes on that floor. *Bokor's* found the new *ouangas*."

I sat beside her, wrapped my arms around her. "You told us he might think he'd just missed them before. That was why you put them in new places. So, put more in new places, right? Doesn't have to be now. Stay here tonight with me, Mel."

She slipped out from my embrace. Holding her was like trying to hold onto the water flowing out of that kitchen tap. "Can't. Have to go tell Zenobia and Deborah too. We got to watch everything closer." She darted out of the room then so fast that the candle guttered, leaving me alone in the dark, my arms circling a ghost.

I didn't want to start watching the shadows again. The hell with Fox and sorcery revenge. On a day when everyone else had something to celebrate, why couldn't I?

Twenty-Eight

Elizabeth Tyler was sitting at her mother's bedside and chattering away excitedly when Tall George arrived to announce that Billy Waller awaited her down in the vestibule.

She jumped up. "Oh, he's here!" she cried. She flapped her arms, turned about, not sure what to do. Leaned over and kissed her mother, who tapped her slate sharply, then made Elizabeth wait while she wrote, *Be more lady-like.*

Elizabeth lied and said of course she would, then scurried out of the room. She didn't want her mother to read in her expression that she already had a plan for what she intended to do with Billy at tonight's New Year's Eve levee.

⟫⟫⟫ ⟪⟪⟪

Probably the only reason Father had agreed to Billy's coming was that he'd been too distracted to give the matter much thought. Critical matters of state were once again overwhelming him.

The matter of some big trial in New York had been resolved to everybody's satisfaction, and Father had been greatly relieved. But he had hardly drawn a breath when a slave brig navigating from Richmond to New Orleans had been overrun by the slaves. They had killed their owner and thrown his body overboard, then chained up the crew, and sailed the brig into Nassau Harbor on New Providence Island, which belonged to the British, who had promptly declared the slaves free men and hailed them as heroes.

She knew this, because it was all Father could talk about with Robert over dinner for days, and he had on two occasions even dragged them all into the State Dining Room so that his secretary of war, Mr. Spencer, and Daniel Webster and some others could talk and plan.

The awful man, Fox, was threatening to go to war with him again should the slightest action be taken to recapture those slaves under Britain's protection. Father was furious, and it was clear that Ambassador Fox was relishing his predicament because he had threatened to chain Fox up just weeks earlier; and Henry Clay and the congressional Whigs were stirring things up again too, branding Father and Webster cowards or worse for not sailing into Nassau Harbor, declaring war, and retrieving those slaves, which were, after all, someone's property.

Father had complained to Webster, "If I cry 'Havoc!' to placate Clay's

Congress, I will plunge us into the most awful war from which we have just only escaped. The guns of the very same steam warships as before lie just off our coast. I would have to be mad!"

It was during this time that Elizabeth quietly and demurely petitioned that Billy be allowed to attend the New Year's Eve party, and her father in his distraction had said, "Why, dear daughter, whatever you desire, you have my blessing, but right now the menfolk are terribly busy," and he'd patted her shoulder and gently propelled her from his office.

Triumphant, she had begun then and there to formulate a plan by which she and Billy would disappear unnoticed for hours and she would finally have her way with him.

>>>- -<<<

Billy looked like a young dandy in his checkered waistcoat and vest, gloves, and a beaver hat that made him seem taller than he was. In the time since she had seen him in August, he had grown something approaching a beard. It was so thin that his pink skin showed through save for one brown tuft beneath his lower lip, which reminded her of the mouche that Daniel Webster's body servant sported. The changes in her beau excited her—how dashing he would be when his full beard came in!—but she restrained herself from any expression of what she felt, allowing him only a token kiss to her cheek there in front of Jasper and the other early guests coming in out of the light snow.

She let him take her hand and they strolled, quite the proper couple, into the hall and to the festively decorated East Room. A chamber string group had set up and was performing. Robert and Priscilla stood beneath the north oil-lamp chandelier. With the Argand lamps lit on the four mantels and reflecting out of the mirrors, the room was brighter than she'd ever seen it. She identified Mayor Seaton and his wife, and the new secretary of the treasury, Walter Forward—presumably in the company of his wife—among the small cluster of early arrivals with her brother and Priscilla.

She and Billy sat beside the inside hearth next to the furnace vent that was prodigiously pumping out warm air. More people arrived. The doorman Renehan took up his station just inside the open hall doors. James and Tall George took turns leading people to the room and announcing them. Shortly, her father arrived, having been upstairs with Mother, she was sure. She led Billy over to him right away, and the two men shook hands. Mr. Tyler seemed bemused, as though he didn't recognize the name—and more likely the face—any longer.

For an hour or so Elizabeth and Billy danced reels, drank punch, and chatted with everyone. The room filled up rapidly, couple upon couple being announced at the door. People danced, sat, stood, strolled, and the room warmed considerably with all of them in it.

Elizabeth picked her time, waiting until Priscilla was occupied with a group of Washington ladies. Then she walked over to Alice and told her to inform Priscilla that she was going to give Billy a tour of the house. Alice was preoccupied, being chatted up by the well-groomed son of somebody or other. Did Mother know?

Elizabeth led Billy across the room, and they left through the door into the Green Parlor and kept going. She took him through the fogbound Blue Saloon full of men puffing on cigars, and into the Washington Parlor; made him look at the painting of George Washington "that Dolley Madison rescued from the British way back when she lived in the house—that's before it was set fire to," and on through to the State Dining Room, where the long table was laid with a variety of meats and dishes and desserts set out alongside bottles of claret and sauterne, port and sherry. Billy, who hadn't eaten a thing all afternoon, lifted a piece of ham on a serving fork, but she pulled him away before he could lay it on a plate, and he hastily stuffed it into his mouth. Zenobia, setting a warm pie on the table, watched the two of them duck into the stairwell. It was clear enough to her what Elizabeth was up to, and she shook her head, grinning.

The first-floor tour officially complete, Elizabeth led Billy to the second floor. A small line of people stood in the hall outside Mother's room, awaiting their turn with her. Dolley Madison happened to emerge just at that moment, and Elizabeth had no choice but to lead her beau over and introduce him. They remained with Dolley a few minutes, but she wanted to go downstairs, and Billy offered his arm and escorted her while Elizabeth waited impatiently. He seemed to take forever, and she suspected he'd been asked to lead Mrs. Madison all the way down the cross hall to the East Room. However, when he came back, he was chewing another piece of ham. He'd been hungry and had dived into the dining room again. Any other night, she might have thrown a fit, but now she just tugged him along the hall.

Nobody was looking, so she pulled him into the narrow corridor that Father used to look out over Lafayette Park. She gave him a passionate kiss. Then another. Not surprisingly, he tasted like ham.

She whispered, "We don't really want to see the *kitchen* floor, do we?"

He stared at her, agog, shook his head.

She led him back out, and along the hall, but then drew him into the east stairwell. "Wait right here," she said. She kissed him again and hurried back into the hall.

One of the doormen, the tall unpleasant one, Garvine, was coming down from the waiting hall. His gaze shifted, and she knew that he must have seen Billy in the corridor as he passed. But he didn't stop. He gave Elizabeth a nod that could have been considered lewd, and kept going. His fingernails, she noticed, were black. He'd been down in the coal room earlier, firing the furnace. Probably with the house so full of people, they didn't require the extra heat, and he was back to being father's thug. Still, he ought to have scrubbed his nails. She would complain to Robert about it if he said anything about her being with Billy. Garvine passed the line of people outside Mother's room and entered the stairwell without even a backward glance.

She hurried into Priscilla and Robert's room. Sally sat there watching baby Mary sleep. Elizabeth grabbed one of the unlit chamberstick candles. She had already made up her excuse. "I'm giving Billy Waller a tour of the house and it would have been improper to go into my room for a candle," she whispered, as if that explained her need for a candle in the first place. She lit it from the fireplace. Sally stared after her in such a way that Elizabeth knew she hadn't been deceived. But, really, what could Sally do? Wasn't her place to say a word about anybody's behavior. Besides, she couldn't leave the baby alone.

Back in the hall, Elizabeth returned to the east stairwell. First, she leaned over the rail, making sure no one was coming up. Then she and Billy, who was finally getting the idea, scampered up the stairs to the disused third floor.

Almost nothing had changed there since Tazewell and Alice's adventure. Dust and cobwebs coated most everything. None of the rooms was heated, but the heat rising through the stairwell from two floors below kept the hallway fairly comfortable. The thought of the chilliness of the rooms excited Elizabeth: She would need someone pressed close to keep her warm, wouldn't she?

She walked purposefully through the darkness to a door at the west end and entered the north corner room she had previously selected. The room itself was deep and narrow. Toward the rear, almost all the way to the windows, stood an old striped backless Madame Récamier sofa. It looked to be an identical twin to the one in the yellow Washington Parlor on the first floor, except that it had a rip across the cushioned headpiece. Upon discovering it, she'd thought it had to have been waiting there for her.

The hall door, when she pushed it wide, bumped against a large mirror frame leaned up behind it. The glass had cracked from one corner down the center. They picked their way past a heap of broken wall sconces, around small tables, and even one wagon wheel. A section of brickwork jutted from the middle of the side wall where a chimney stack extended up to the roof. The stack also threw off warmth from the fire burning two floors below. Around the far side of the chimney was a door leading into the next room.

Near the Récamier stood a wirework mannequin, headless and armless, with wooden calves and its feet painted black to resemble boots. Like everything else in the room except the sofa, it was dusty and strung in place.

She kept Billy from closing the door. "It'll draw more warmth in," she told him. "Besides, no one else is going to come up *here*." Nevertheless, she wanted to make haste. Her plan had worked!

She set her candle on a crate, turned her back to Billy, and said, "Quick, help me," then tried to reach around her sides. She needed him to unfasten the tight bodice of her green satin dress if they were to have any delight at all. With cold fingers he worked clumsily while she pushed down the flounce along her neckline and then worked her arms out of their sleeves. Finally, together they lifted the dress up and over her head.

Billy handed it to her, and she, with a wicked smile, draped it over the mannequin.

Underneath the dress, a bone corset rode on top of her petticoats. The corset wasn't drawn too tight on her thin frame, and she left it on rather than take the time to unlace it, too, instead concentrating upon undoing the ties of the petticoats, and soon enough she'd pushed her way out of them. Her chemise hung to her knees, her pantaloons visible just below them. She set to work on Billy then. Tugged off his coat from behind, trapping his arms as a tease until he worked each one free. While he wrestled with that, she undid his vest. She left him to thumb down his braces and undo his fly buttons while she climbed onto the Récamier. Even though she had swatted it two days earlier, this caused a billow of dust. She got down again, padded over to the windows, and opened one halfway. Warm air whooshed past her and out the opening. She closed the window until it was just the tiniest slit.

She turned to find that Billy had his pants halfway down, and she hurried back onto the Récamier, took her position up against the curled torn headpiece. She put her feet up on it, revealing to him the cutout in her pantaloons, and thrilled to his eager reaction upon beholding it.

With his trousers down to his boot tops, he clambered up onto his knees between her legs. She reached out, undid the button flap of his drawers, and slid her hand inside. Her hand was cold and as she closed it around him he made a gasp, and his eyes went wide and adoring. She drew him out, drew him to her, guiding him as he fell upon her. Her brocade-slippered feet pincered his waist. His hands closed over her small breasts where the corset pushed them up, his lips pressed hard upon hers. She touched the tip of himself against her mound. He groaned and tried too late to drive himself into her, but she hadn't let go, and continued to hold on as he shuddered and let loose. He lowered his head against her shoulder in embarrassment.

After a moment, she tenderly said his name and drew her hand out from between them. She wiped it along his drawers. "You got my arm all wet," she whispered, but her tone was teasing, and he lifted his head. She let him know with a look that she wasn't about to have things end here. This plan had been too much effort to hang upon the cusp. Elizabeth had decided they were going to do it and that was that.

Her naked desire inflamed him again. He leaned up on one elbow to let her breathe under him, and uttered the first syllables of his undying love for her while he tried to work himself to the ready for a second time.

The door to the hall slammed shut.

Elizabeth gasped, her body bucking, almost throwing him off. Billy sprang away, onto his knees. He stuffed himself madly back inside his drawers, twisting around to see over his shoulder where Elizabeth was looking.

She thought sure they'd been caught, and waited for whoever stood on the other side of the door to reveal themselves.

When after a full minute no one called or flung the door open, Elizabeth got to her feet. For a moment the diamond-shaped hole in her pantaloons was right in front of Billy. Then she scurried back to the window. "Probably having this open did it," she said. "Too cold in here now anyway."

She latched the window tight.

It *was* cold. Her breath puffed in the glow of the candle. As she made her way back to the sofa, that glow seemed to be closing tighter. The corner of the room nearest the door had gone all black, as if the light no longer reached there. But that couldn't be right.

Billy glanced around as if he sensed it too. Even where he knelt was growing dimmer, yet the candle, looked at directly, remained unchanged.

A formless shadow was slowly, steadily swelling into the room. It was coming from where the broken mirror had stood behind the door. That mirror was no longer visible.

Elizabeth ran to Billy. "Get up!" she said. "Hurry, now." She scooped up her petticoats and reached for her dress.

The mannequin lurched and slid away from her, alive. Billy, with one suspender strap up, gawped after it. It tipped and fell over.

The room had gone as cold as an iced-over pond. From the absolute blackness in the corner, something crashed hard enough that it shook the floor. One of the small tables came skidding out of the darkness there, tilted onto one leg, and then shot away, along with one of the sconces, as if something invisible was flinging aside the debris as it came for them. It *was* coming for them.

Elizabeth stood transfixed with terror. Not so Billy. Clutching her wrist, he yanked her after him. He snatched the candle, kicked aside the crate, and made a beeline for the door through to the next room. The abandoned Récamier suddenly clattered about like a wild horse. The material covering it tore wide and stuffing belched into the air.

Elizabeth screamed and bolted past Billy, flung open the door and leaped through, straight into a wall of cobwebs—only, they weren't cobwebs.

They were spiderwebs, layers of them that shredded as she swung and batted, spilling dozens if not hundreds of small black creatures onto her, over her bare shoulders and down inside her chemise. She shrieked and dropped her petticoats, swatting at herself, spinning dizzily. Billy danced about, slapping at himself too. A small table rested upright beside him. He slammed down the candle so that he could swing both arms, thrusting his hands through his hair, slapping his shirt. The entire room seemed to be thick with webs and swarming horrors all the way to the door.

Tiny legs on her skin skittered down into her bloomers now. She whined in bestial yips, jumping this way and that as if she could escape them and all the prickling sensations, pushing her hands down under her unmentionables.

The other room had filled up with darkness. Then something roared out of the open doorway—a smoky, deformed shape, eyes as cold as midnight. A tendril of it whipped around the candlelight beside Billy, and he threw himself headlong away from it, crashing against her.

She tried to run, but something caught her by the hair and snatched her back on her heels. Billy grabbed her flailing arm, but got tugged off his feet too. He yelled her name. The sound came out like a cry stuffed against a pillow. Out of the dark mass something slashed his shoulder, and he howled.

The thing had them both hooked.

The hall door ahead swung open suddenly, so hard that it bounced off the wall. A light floated into the room. It quickly closed the distance to them.

The grip on Elizabeth's hair relaxed, and she tumbled to the floor. Billy went down on top of her. They both scrambled up, ready to bolt in any direction, to find Mel standing there, her expression chiseled by the light of her own oil lamp, wide-eyed and fierce, as terrifying in her reaction as the thing cut out of darkness. In her free hand, she gripped an object the size of a large stone, and as she approached them she whispered a chant that rose and fell like a song.

The candle Billy had slammed down ignited again as if it had never gone out. It threw long shadows around them and even back into the room they'd fled. Elizabeth scuttled away, prepared to strip off her unmentionables, only to realize there were no spiders on her anywhere.

Standing before them, Mel said to her, "Oh, you fool child." She surveyed the room, the ceiling. "But it's my fault as much as yours. Him's been up here in this empty place all this time. Wasn't used for nothing, till now."

She slipped by them without explaining.

Like a ghost floating through the debris, she passed into the next room. Called out, "Come now, get your things and go quick from this floor."

The lovers followed her, attached to the safety of her light. Elizabeth collected the discarded green dress off the mannequin. He got his coat and vest. Mel said, "Go back through the other room and out. Mustn't go near this mirror."

Billy made to leave, but Mel turned him about. She pulled aside his torn shirt to look at his shoulder. It was red with welts like from a whip. Blood dotted his shirt in three lines. "I got something for that," she said. "You come see me."

He shrugged it off, defensively saying, "I'm all right." He closed the collar of his shirt again, then turned, faced her. "What was that, Miss Mary? What was it?"

"Take your candle with you," replied Mel.

⋙ ⋘

She waited for them to leave before she returned to the other room. A small round table with a broken leg leaned against the wall near the Récamier. She pulled open its single drawer. Sure enough, the *ouanga* she'd placed there after Tazewell and Alice's adventure up here was gone. Even up here, the *bokor* had hunted.

Anyone could have accessed this floor at any time. She would have to secure all the rooms up here now. Whoever her enemy was, he was thorough. He missed nothing and left nothing to chance.

The cracked mirror beside the hall door reflected nothing more than her oil lamp's flame now. "This is where you come out, hmm?" she said to the invisible entity. She turned in a circle. "This whole floor is full of shiny places for a shadow demon to hide. But not here no more."

She took the *ouanga* she held and smeared it down the dusty surface of the mirror, then using the greasy mark it left, she drew a small *veve* on each side of the diagonal crack. A ratlike squeal rushed from the room and down the hall.

She had mostly neglected this floor. Her efforts had driven and sealed the *tebo* up here. Relegated to these shadows, cut off from its physical form and its master, the *tebo* had been directionless. Elizabeth and Billy had walked straight into its lair. She should have known someone would. They were lucky Zenobia had seen them.

She could not hide anything in the table again. If he came looking, the *bokor* would find it there immediately. She glanced around.

The wagon wheel with splintered spokes caught her attention. She made her way to it, leaned over, and carefully stuffed her *ouanga* into its rusting black hub, then stepped back. Even with the lamp held close, the *ouanga* wasn't obvious. Good. Make him work harder to find it. She had no doubt he *would* find it. He was clever and careful, this sorcerer. And nobody watched this floor.

"*Bokor* let you be cut off, expecting the war to give him his revenge instead. What is it he got planned now it's not coming? Why he want to harm these people so bad?"

Whatever the answer was, she was going to force him to come up here if he wanted to turn his dark creature loose again. With more charms she would push it into one room, one mirror or broken brass fixture—trap it, maybe even glimpse its true nature.

Mel turned about, holding the lamp high to illuminate the whole room. It lay absolutely still. Dust was settling once more.

She closed the door after her. Could she seal all the rooms up here? Paint *veves* around? She doubted anyone would notice. Trap the *tebo*, maybe find its body and destroy it. That would set back the *bokor*, force him to act directly instead of through his surrogate. Either way, he would have to come here himself to release his demon. If they watched—she and James, Zenobia, Deborah, all of them—they might finally know him.

She was going to need more *maudit* root, though, and right away. They were very close, almost upon him now.

She took her lamp and left. The entire third floor settled into darkness.

Three rooms down the hall, where Tazewell and Alice had once played hide and seek, the lefthand door of a discarded wardrobe creaked open, and something darker than the darkness slid from the small mirror hung on the back of that door and swelled to fill the unprotected room. The master had destroyed the barriers there.

The thing gathered itself and flowed to the door like a lengthening shadow, then triumphantly out into the hall, where no protections were laid to stop it.

Lying inside the mirror, it had absorbed the conversation taking place. Words had passed into it as into a conduit, echoing from this room to the distant room of mirrors, where its other half lay, confined by the master.

In the bowels of the house, on the kitchen floor among the slaves, the witch had remained anonymous, impossible to single out. Now, though, thanks to Billy Waller, she had been given a name.

Miss Mary.

"Miss Mary," jeered its other half, parroting the voice of Billy Waller.

"Miss Mary," it would shortly tell the master.

Twenty-Nine

James Hambleton Christian

With the New Year's party still raging, I went down to the cellar to fetch some more bottles of wine, and discovered that Zenobia was alone in the kitchen, stirring a pot on the stove with a wooden spoon, and no sign of Mel anywhere. Zenobia tried hard to be too busy with the soup pot to pay me any mind, and that's when I knew there was trouble.

"Where is she?" I asked. She kept stirring, slowly, leaning over the pot as if she might dive in. "Zenobia, not telling me doesn't help."

She made up her mind then, set the spoon down and faced me. Out came the whole story—how in the dining room she had seen Miss Elizabeth with Billy Waller in tow sneaking up the main stairs, and then Garvine had come down a few minutes later and gloated that he'd just watched "Elizabeth and her feller off fer a screw up to the attic." Remembering what Mel had said about leaving the attic to the *tebo*, Zenobia had hurried to report Garvine's words. "Mel called herself a fool for not seeing it coming." She planted Zenobia in the kitchen, took the oil lamp off the cutting table, and then ran out—first to the furnace room and then up the service stairs. "I guess so's nobody'd see her."

By the time she said that, I'd already set down my bottles and was running for the same tight twisting stairs; unseen up to the private floor and out into the central hall. No one was about as I ducked into the east stairwell. By then I think I'd conjured a thousand terrible fates for Mel, but none of it came close to the tableau awaiting me in the stairwell.

Miss Priscilla in her bright blue dress almost filled the space. She took a step back in surprise at my approach, which inadvertently revealed Miss Elizabeth tying on the last of her petticoats. Behind her Billy Waller held her green dress over his arm. He had on his jacket, but his vest was half-unbuttoned and his shirt buttoned up wrong. Priscilla stepped over to cover her again. Where, I wondered, was Mel?

"Were you looking for something, James?" Miss Priscilla asked it as if she thought I was part of whatever scheme the two lovebirds had cooked up.

"Ma'am, fact is, Zenobia said she'd seen these two skulking off, and soon as she said that I guessed something was up, so I expect I was, ah, doing the same as you."

"Oh, I didn't find them." She glared at Elizabeth. "They found me, right here before I got any farther along." The defensive look on Elizabeth's face was the equal of hers—two gorgons trying to turn each other to stone. It was hardly the first impropriety at which Miss Elizabeth had been caught, and even standing there without her dress on, she was not about to admit that what she'd been up to was even objectionable.

We might have been there a long time while they faced off, if Billy hadn't stepped in front of her and announced, "I am hereby proposing that I wish to marry Miss Elizabeth Tyler."

Elizabeth, petticoat ribbons loose in one hand, stopped and stared, her mouth agape. She had not known of this proposal. Her cheeks flushed with color, a smile pulled at her lips, but trembled, unable to hold its shape, while her eyes filled up with tears.

Miss Priscilla looked from one to the other of them, and once even back at me as if to make sure I'd heard the same thing. Finally, gathering herself up, she said, "Mr. Waller, that is a noble sentiment under the circumstances. However, the person to whom you must put such a proposition is right now downstairs dancing the Boston Waltz in the East Room."

He nodded hastily and began closing his buttons, but she stopped him with a raised hand.

"I think I would not make my proposal while *either* of you is in dishabille. Would you not agree, James?" She turned to me, still smoldering but a little amused too. "Let's give them a few minutes," she said. "But no more." Then she walked past me into the hall, and it was clear I was to follow. What I had seen, I was about to be instructed, was not to be shared with Mr. Tyler or Miss Letitia.

As a result, I never reached the third floor or Mel.

⟫⟫⟩ ⟨⟪⟪

Billy Waller's request for the hand of Elizabeth Tyler became the event of the night. Her father announced it to all and sundry, drawing as he did so often upon the bard in a toast: "God bless thee and put meekness in the mind, love, charity, obedience, and true duty!" he called. Given Miss Elizabeth's nature, I can only assume the advice was directed at Billy.

After father and daughter had danced, the two of them went upstairs together to tell Miss Letitia. Devonee informed me later that she burst into tears on the instant.

That hopeful announcement concealed from the family everything that had happened. Neither Elizabeth nor Billy spoke of the awful events on the third floor or of Mel's interceding to save them—in fact, the entire episode wasn't mentioned again outside the kitchen. And once again, I had cause to envy someone else's circumstances. Billy could properly ask for the hand of the woman he loved from Mr. Tyler any old time at all. The idea gnawed at me.

⟫⟫– ⟪⟪

"No question he has been up there," Mel told me and Zenobia.

She had now spent three nights hunting through the third-floor rooms, carefully placing the few remaining charms she had, but discovering as well that those she'd placed way back last spring, after Miss Alice's fright, was gone.

"But ain't there nothin' to tell us who he is?" asked Zenobia.

She shook her head. "About everyone in the house was up there getting chairs and settees for the New Year crowd. If the *bokor* left any tracks, they're all lost."

"What about the first floor?"

"Some are gone again—private-floor ones now too. Least a couple."

"How?" I asked. "How's he got access on the family's floor?"

"New Year's Eve, James, that one had access everywhere."

I reflected on that levée. Webster had been up in the president's office at one point with a group of men, most of them out of Congress; dozens had queued outside Miss Letitia's room, women and their husbands mostly. And those were the people I'd seen, people who weren't *trying* to hide.

Yet something about the obvious explanation troubled me. How could this man hunt for hidden objects while he was in the company of others? During levées people were hardly left alone in any rooms. The man might be able to sniff out a charm here or there, but he couldn't very well open every drawer, pull mirrors away from the wall, or feel under tabletops without looking foolish and conspicuous. I might not have noticed someone studying a crowd, but I couldn't have failed to see someone gouging out a seat cushion while reaching for one of her pouches.

Mel listened patiently to my skepticism. She didn't seem surprised by it—more, in fact, as if she had already turned the same arguments over, and been left with similar doubts.

In any case, she had run out of her *maudit* root, which I gathered was critical to making *ouangas*.

The next morning I woke to hear her whispering to Zenobia in the mess: "The old *houngan* on the tidewater, if he don't have some stored up for the winter, I don't know where we going to look."

There was a pause. Quietly as I could I crept to the crack in the door.

The two of them were seated at the table, both dressed in blue bonnets and heavy cloaks. Two wicker baskets sat on the table. They looked like twins, neither older than Zenobia. Early light from the south window spilled across them. Then the furnace rumbled like a distant storm, and I glanced at the empty bench under the duct. I wondered if Isaac's ghost had ever found his way free of this house. Mel hadn't spoken of him since her poppet had been torn apart.

I walked in. "What is this?"

Zenobia gasped at my intrusion as if she'd forgotten I slept right here.

"We going to the markets," Mel said. "If anybody ask, we going to get cream for to churn some butter, 'cause we almost have none an' we all know Mr. Tyler likes him sweet cream."

At the sound of that, I went suddenly grum. "*Maudit* root," I answered.

She didn't pretend otherwise, but stood, brushed her fingers across my cheek. "If there is any to be had, then we need it here. Even so, going to be days before it comes. Can't wait for another levée to let him in."

"But you don't think that's how he's doing it any more'n I do. Something more is going on here."

She nodded, lifted her basket. "Won't know what it is till we see it. Whatever I think, meantime, we got to protect things as best we can."

I put on my boots, pulled up my suspenders, and hurried after them. They were at the eastside door with their little baskets, looking from behind like two Quaker girls.

I couldn't explain why, but I didn't want her out of my sight. In my head was Billy asking Miss Priscilla for Elizabeth's hand. It wouldn't leave me alone.

I chased them under the colonnade, calling her name. They stopped.

A shower stall door was open, and from the spout high on the wall icicles hung down like claws. Mel had turned back. She looked more amused, maybe pleased, than annoyed, even as she said, "What you wantin' now, James Christian? You trying to freeze to death out here? You not even wearing a vest."

"Don't go," I said. "Or wait and let me dress and come with you."

Her eyes shifted back and forth, reading mine. The amusement on her face changed to a look of regretful acceptance, as if she credited that everything to follow was pre-ordained. "Now, James," she said. She stepped to me, put her gloved hand on my cheek. Then she said the oddest thing: "You keep this house in order for me till I come back." She tilted her head to get the bonnet brim out of the way. Kissed me.

Marry me, I wanted to say. *Right now, this minute, come back inside.*

She drew back. Zenobia looked on, her eyes full of worry. Mel's words must have rung strange for her, too, but like me she was used to doing what Mel said and trusting it would all be fine.

I remained there, imprisoned behind the columns, shivering with cold, my teeth rattling, until they had walked beneath the old eastern arch and been swallowed up in the gray mist coming off the canal.

>>>> ◄◄◄◄

Sally and I arranged the place settings for a late-afternoon family dinner. Daniel and Fletcher Webster and some other cabinet members would be in attendance today, we'd been told, so we were laying everything out in the public dining room. The dinner would include half a ham, various puddings, and a dish of black-eyed peas with winter onions. Marcellus, Ethel, and Olive were at work on the dishes. Mel was going to make her black caps for dessert—Mr. Tyler loved those sliced apples.

I had hold of a bunch of butter knives, and Sally was complaining that the heat from the furnace vent was making her nose itch, when someone behind me said, "James."

I turned about to find Martin Renehan in the doorway from the west stairwell. I knew when I saw his face that something was wrong. He said, "Ya need to stop doin' that right now and come with me."

I set down the knives. Sally said, "What..." but never spoke the rest of it before whatever was peeling off Renehan silenced her.

I expected him to lead the way down the stairs but instead he took me into the hall and out through the vestibule. Marcellus, at the door, held out a coat for me, his face gone tight as leather, his fearful gaze trying to avoid mine. I thought, *Why aren't you down keeping an eye on that ham?* And where was Jasper all of a sudden? He'd been on duty when the Websters arrived.

The two hearths had fires blazing in them, normal and welcoming, and all of it felt wrong.

Outside in the carriage lane of the portico, Cyrus stood at the bench of the buckboard wagon. The two horses pawed the gravel, their breath smoking like they'd arrived here from Hell.

Renehan climbed up beside Cyrus, then reached out to me and said, "Come on, man." I took his arm.

Cyrus drove the wagon down past the east stables. We shot across Jefferson's carriage paths, through the arch, and onto C Street, heading east. The wind off the river flayed us, and brought tears to my eyes. The wheels roared over the stones. We had no gloves nor scarves. The sky over the river had gone thick with clouds, and was the color of halfway-to-twilight as if most of a day had passed unnoticed. I looked at Cyrus staring hard at the street ahead. Renehan, between us like something taut and ready to spring, met my gaze with no solace.

Just when I thought certain we were heading for the Centre Market, Cyrus wheeled around and down Louisiana to the canal. We thundered past canal boats and skiffs floating, tethered at canalside.

Ahead, people—maybe a dozen—clustered near where a small barge had been tied up. A grizzled old white bargeman in a bearskin coat stood on its flat deck, with one foot up on the rail, watching everybody, smoking his pipe.

The crowd turned at our approach. They were mostly colored folk; more of Washington's free people, I had no doubt. They was stomping and walking in place to stay warm, but at our careening arrival, they shifted, a couple stumbling aside. In the opening I glimpsed a bit of that blue, enough that I jumped down before Cyrus had come to a stop. I shoved past everybody, and they cleared the way.

And then I couldn't move.

Scarcely any patches of the bonnet shone blue any longer. The rest was almost black with blood, a tent over her head.

The wicker basket lay trampled beside her, and strewn around it a few heads of cabbage, beets, some purple turnips, apples. I think I may have asked, "But where's the cream?"

In the distance lay a second basket, vegetables all tumbled out. "Zenobia?" I said. I wanted this to be her. I insisted on it.

I looked around, needing Mel to step out of the crowd, haul me aside, and explain what had happened. But Renehan answered, "Back at the President's House."

The words didn't make sense. "No, this is—"

"Zenobia got away, man, thanks to her. That's how it is we're here. You were upstairs, she couldn't find ya in the kitchen."

Did I give some kind of sign? He caught me as I dropped, lowered me to my knees. I slapped at his hands. Didn't want help or comfort.

"No." I heard the word, but I didn't think I'd said it out loud.

The people around me—they had stayed there in the freezing cold to bear witness. Renehan let me go, but other hands—hands I didn't know—came and pressed my shoulders, patted me, pressure of sympathy, kindnesses I didn't want because they hemmed me in over her body, made me be there when I needed to be upstairs, in Tyler's office, insisting, "I am hereby proposing that I wish to marry Miss Mary Elena in your employ," and he would stare back at me like a dead mackerel.

A colored boy no older than Tazewell came up in front of me and told it. I guess Renehan asked, I didn't, but the boy knew somehow that I was the one needed to hear it.

Mel and Zenobia had been returning from the market. They walked fast along the canal, he said, like they already knew to be in a hurry. The boy had been going the other way, and right after they passed him, two men came from up by the hotel. The men swooped down on the women, knocking the boy aside, so intent in their purpose, they didn't even seem to notice him. Two more strode up the path from the canal and heading this way, the four of them hemming the women in. None had been obvious even a minute earlier.

The old white man on the barge interrupted the boy's telling. "Those four'd been standing around beside the canal a good half-hour afore, acrost the way where them crates be. Hadn't troubled nobody else in all that time. But I was watchin' 'em as I couldn't figure out nohow what they's up to and they's sich scalawags and that was certain."

Two behind and two ahead—Mel would have been aware, known what was coming. Why hadn't she run?

The bargeman went on. "One girl, that 'un, she start to chanting. I heerd her clear. Didn't sound like no prayer, not beggin' or nothin'. More like somebody calling up all the rage they can git at.

"One of the uglies in front come at 'em first. That chantin' gal pushed between him and the other girl like to protect her, and when he took hold of her she bawled something that, so help me, called down lightning right outten the blue sky. That was something I never seed. Dropped the feller where he stood and t'others jumped back. She yelt at that other girl to run and flung her basket at the second man's legs, tripped him up, give her a chance wit' him too. But them two behind her, they'd been carrying clubs under they coats. They moved swift. Those men beat that poor child, stove in her head and kept right on beating her once she fell. I didn't move, like to be as still as a pole so's they wouldn't notice me. Whatever she done to that first man left him thrashing and blind. I mean, was *smoke* comin' out where his eyes'd be. His friends dragged him off 'tween 'em. Was his wailing brought most of these folk here, except for the kid and those two inebriates behind him. Too many for 'em to kill I 'spect, and made them four run away quick 'stead of chasin' the other girl." The bargeman drew on his pipe, nodded as if satisfied. "Yep."

The boy said he saw something appear out of Mel when she struck the man down—a black cloud, he said. No, argued the man behind him, it was for sure a *bear*, while the other drunk insisted it was the devil himself had blasted that man's eyes. They set to arguing, all of it nothing but noise from two red-eyed bummers.

"Yes," I said to I don't know who, "she can handle herself." I was up on my feet and walking back and forth now, like the glass wall of the vestibule stood in front of me and I couldn't go beyond it.

A couple of the people in the crowd edged around me. They were going to move her to the wagon. I jumped at them. "No! Nobody touches her, nobody moves her. She can—she has...power..."

A hand gripped my shoulder. Renehan's. I flung it off, my own raised in a fist. "You," I said. "You can pick up an axe and smash anybody! *I* want that. Me. She's the best of me, you understand? They killed—"

Cyrus stepped in front of Renehan and let me hit him once before he clamped his thick arms around me. "She's dead, man," he said. "Now you gotsa stop." He didn't let go until I sagged into him. Let me back down. I crawled on hands and knees.

The bonnet covered her face, and I knew better than to look under it. I squeezed my eyes, recollected how she tilted her head to lean in and kiss me beneath its brim. If we could just stay right there.

I scooped my arms around her. Her body, always so rawboned and hard, was hinged loose like a marionette. A hollow bag of bones and all that was Mel had gone off somewhere. Thousand miles gone. *I should have sent her back home.*

I pressed my face against the bonnet. "You're the best of me, Mel. You know that. The best of me." I kept repeating it, like I thought it would wake her. All those dark mornings she slid out of my bed so as not to wake me when she went to start the breakfast. All those times where I pretended along with her.

All her witchy ways, her magics and potions. Where was the magic to set this right?

It started to snow a little.

Renehan and Cyrus wanted to help me, but I wouldn't let them, didn't need them. She weighed less than an angel.

I carried her to the rear of the buckboard. Her head flopped toward me but I couldn't look. I stared up over the wagon while I tugged the bonnet across her face. On the rise along Pennsylvania Avenue above us, the backside of Brown's Indian Queen Hotel was all lit up and festive, though there wasn't a sound coming from it. It was like everything was happening in some world where I no longer existed.

>>>- -<<<

After that it was all terrible.

Zenobia blamed herself for Mel's death so much she'd torn at her hair, leaving blood where she pulled it out, screaming that she should have died instead. In my heart I agreed. I couldn't even speak to her.

Deborah stayed with her in the women's room, clamping her hands to make sure she didn't harm herself further. Couldn't let her near the kitchen.

Renehan went up and reported it all to Mr. Tyler. When he returned, he cornered me in the brick hallway. "We'll sort these bastards, James," he insisted. "Me and the lads will, make no mistake." I must have nodded to show I heard him, because he left me alone, which was what I wanted. I didn't want to hear how *he* was going to punish the killers. He didn't understand.

The whole house with its stalking demon could have been sucked down into Hades for all that I cared. All I had any spirit for was Mel. I'd laid her body out on the mess table and wouldn't let anyone near her. Closed the door so it was just the two of us.

I undressed her, tore the sheet off my bed and laid it beneath her. Got water from the spigot in the kitchen in a bucket. Ice cold, but it wasn't like she would mind, and I hardly noticed. I washed her down with a sponge, and there was pink water and the pink sheet and pools all over the floor. Sweet Jesus, how they'd destroyed her.

At some point Tyler was bellowing my name off upstairs. I don't know, maybe it was dinner time and I wasn't there making that God damned ham appear for him. I don't know who took care of him, but he stopped yelling. I'd have killed him if he'd walked in just then. This was all on account of trying to protect him.

Awhile later—might only have been minutes, might have been days— Miss Priscilla said my name, but real close behind me. She'd come in, and I hadn't heard the door. I heard her gasp beside me, breath all sawtoothed. She moaned awfully. Maybe she'd seen the cord I'd tied around Mel's head that was holding it together. She made thick noises in her throat, tried to speak. "Oh, dear God, James, I'm... I am..." Whatever she was trying to say, awhile later I looked around and she was gone.

After that there wasn't a sound out of Tyler or the house. But I swear now I could feel the thing that didn't belong, that dark creeping monstrosity, as though Mel was letting me have her senses now that she'd no use for them.

It breathed slow like a thing gone into hibernation deep in some black cavern where you'd better have sense not to follow. The house was dead. Was the family all up there eating their meal alongside the Websters? Did the feast include the black caps? It'd be the last time Tyler would ever taste them. Last time for everything.

Somebody passed through the room, going into mine, into the cupboard beyond my room where more glassware was stored and—a couple steps down—a small second cellar. There was port in there. I don't know who took over my duties that night. I didn't look. I fell asleep in a chair beside her, just rested my head in her ice-cold palm.

They all left me alone with her. Mel lay on the table wrapped in osnaburg cloth. We'd half a bolt of it, but I don't remember getting it or removing the sheet. I stitched her up in that stiff cloth like one of her dollies.

Next thing I knew, Zenobia was beside me, crying and holding out a cup of black coffee and telling me it was time to take her, that things had been made ready. "We got to, James," she said. I recalled she'd given me the needle and thread.

That day was warmer, like maybe I'd sat in there all through the winter.

Instead of snow it rained, which melted the patches of snow remaining in the shady places. At Mt. Zion, a grave was already dug and waiting. Samuel told me Tyler had paid for it.

Zenobia led me through the vestibule, out of doors, and then trudging along behind the wagon up the avenue. I felt like the general's horse following along. Wondered if I'd be sent home after.

The preacher spoke his piece, saying, "God shall wipe all tears from their eyes; and there shall be no more death, nor crying, neither shall there be any more pain: for the former things are passed away." Across the hole, Miss Priscilla, Tazewell, and Alice stood among Olive, Marcellus, Samuel, and everyone else, even Devonee. I wondered who was doing for old John Tyler this day since his entire household stood here at the grave. Even Renehan. But then I saw that he stood in back, his face near hidden under a silk and baleen umbrella, Drummond and Garvine there, and Dolley Madison by his side in Miss Letitia's place, I suppose. It was Elizabeth who was missing, who'd remained behind with her mother. Someone had to.

I was all set to change my opinion of Tyler right then; but afterwards, after we'd filled in the hole and started back down to the road, I heard him ask Dolley to help him find another cook. "If the replacement proves dear, we'll sell off a few back in Virginia to cover the cost, so don't worry yourself about that." It was essential, he said, that he get someone of Mel's virtuosity in the President's House.

Mel's virtuosity. He had no idea at all.

The rest of that day kind of blurred, as if the rain hovered around me, keeping the world outside. That night I didn't think I would sleep. My bed knew her, and it had held onto her smell for me, both sanctuary and curse. She lay in the bedclothes, her skin warm and slick from the kitchen heat. I buried my face between her breasts. And all of a sudden I found myself sitting up, gasping. It had been real. She'd been next to me. The clean sheet I'd put on the bed was drenched with her scent.

I got up. Walked out to the mess, hopeful and half-expectant, but she wasn't at the table. Wasn't on the bench where Isaac had sat. I must have left a candle burning there, or someone had. It was almost burned down.

I realized I was still dressed from days ago on the canal path. My shirt was stained pink from washing her, and spattered with her blood. Stubble rough on my chin.

I sat in the same chair where I'd slept next to her. That other time Isaac had been there, where I hadn't seen one sign of him; but *she* had known. How could I be sure she wasn't there now? More likely she sat right there giving me the eye like she always did for being too proud and cocksure and wrong about everything. I just wished I knew where to look.

"Mel," I said. I stared at the low candle, expecting maybe a flutter of the flame. Nothing happened. "I know if there's anybody in the world can come back, it's got to be you. You were far from finished, way more than Isaac, and he came back."

No answer.

"I wish—" I stopped. Instead of saying what I'd started to, I said, "I wish you could tell me who it was did this. Where you are you must know who that *bokor* of yours is now. You could give me a sign, write it on a mirror someplace. Is it Clay? Fox? Some other bastard? Old Webster maybe? He's here most every day. I know it's someone in the house. Someone sent those men. You could show me. Couldn't you, Mel?"

A shadow loomed in the doorway, and I jumped to my feet. "Mel?"

The shadow came closer. The candlelight caught her sharp Cherokee cheeks above the pale nightdress.

"Deborah," I said.

She sat down at the end of the table. I sat again too. Her black eyes stared at the table as if she could see Mel's body there.

Then to my surprise she slid her hand over and took mine. Tears slipped along her cheeks, and she still stared at the table. Well, Deborah never spoke, so I accepted that we would sit here together until the candle melted away. It wouldn't be all that long. The furnace groaned, probably cooling down without Garvine tending it in the night.

A raspy soft voice said, "She loved you." It was a second before I realized it was Deborah. I just stared at her. Her eyes finally shifted from the table, boring into mine. "She loves you still."

"Don't." I winced like she'd burned me.

"The worst is death, and death will have his day."

Deborah speaking was boggling. Deborah quoting Shakespeare at me was something on the far side of a miracle. "Where did you learn that?" I asked.

Her hand on mine was ice cold. She blinked at me, shook her head, then got up and left.

"Deborah."

She glanced back over her shoulder. "She isn't the only one." Then she was gone, her feet pattering down the cold hall.

Right then I was so hollowed out, I didn't comprehend what that meant. The very worst thing had happened, just as Isaac had named it, and nothing could ever be so terrible, and nothing could ever be good in the world again.

A minute later, the candle finally guttered and went out. In darkness I got up and returned to my bed and the cocoon of Mel's scent. All that I had left of her.

Thirty

Four days after Mel's murder, Martin Renehan walked back and forth in the waiting hall between the president's office and the secretary's room, too fidgety to sit among the four petitioners awaiting their turn. Jasper came barreling out of the east stairwell. They saw each other in the same moment, and Renehan jumped down the two steps to the center hall. The petitioners posed no threat to John Tyler. They were two Pennsylvania Quakers, a plantation owner up from Georgia, and a man who owned a stockyard outside the city and hoped to convince Mr. Tyler to purchase beef and pork exclusively from him.

Jasper said, "'Ere, there's man at the front door for you."

"Dignified man?"

"Naw, rough and tumble sort."

"Good." He clapped Jasper on the shoulder. "Let me do you a favor and man the door awhile, and you stretch your legs a bit more leisurely. Feel free to keep an eye on these dangerous Quakers, if you will."

Jasper laughed, thanked him. The men in the waiting hall looked their way.

Renehan hurried down the stairs and across the vestibule. He anticipated a member of his old Frogtown fire company; but the man who stood on the portico was a stranger to him. He had thick brown hair and was wrapped up inside a long bearskin coat. A low-crown buckram hat floated on his hair. There *was* something vaguely familiar about him.

He stepped near and held up his hand, displaying the back of it, which bore a tattoo of a liberty pole sporting a Phrygian cap.

"Swampdoodle, init?" Renehan said.

"Name's Branden."

"I do believe you and I have altercated over a fire up Maryland Avenue."

Branden grinned, revealing a missing front tooth. "I do believe you're right, sir."

"What is it I can do for you, Mr. Branden?"

"Y'all gots it backwards. We, that is, Swampdoodle, we got word through yer company that you's looking fer four toughs might have perpetrated a crime in yer district. That so?"

"'Tis." He couldn't keep from showing his excitement.

"One of them was afflicted, I'm told." He touched his fingers toward his eyes. Renehan nodded. "Well, one of our company happened to be in

Wentworthy's Tavern up on H Street t'other day when a wagon come careening up North Capitol and drew up long enough to discharge two of its foursome. Two rough *b'hoys*, it was. One had a coat over his head and was caterwauling for all he was worth. The wagon with t'other two shot on north without you could draw a breath."

"H Street."

"Yep. Them two didn't go into Wentworthy's neither, but up the side stairs. There's rooms up above the tavern."

"Definitely *b'hoys*, now?"

"Oh, yeah, young, and near halfway as mean as a Swampdoodler."

Renehan smiled back. "Oh, I doubt that," he said. He pulled his hand from his pocket and dropped a dollar onto Branden's palm. "I am very much obliged that you took the time to come tell me."

Branden pocketed the money and tipped his hat. "See y'all at a blaze then, Mr. Renehan." He turned and walked down across the carriage path and into the park. Only then did Renehan allow himself to shiver at the cold.

Garvine would be down in the furnace room. Renehan figured he would love an excursion outside.

Heading for the west stairwell, he spotted Priscilla Tyler in the Washington Parlor. Her plump daughter was on her lap, and Priscilla was reading her a book titled *The Child's Pictorial Preceptor*.

"Mr. Renehan," she said, and set aside the book. Mary turned to look at him and babbled something. She reached in his direction.

"Do you think she'll remember any of it?" he asked.

Priscilla smiled in spite of herself. "Mostly, she wants to chew on the corners."

"I know the feeling," he replied.

Her look chided him for his innuendo, but she said, "That man you were speaking to out there." She nodded toward the vestibule. He realized from where she was sitting she could see through the glass barrier and straight to the front door.

"Fireman from a different company than mine," he told her. "Had some news for me. And Eli. Right now I've got to go speak with him."

At Garvine's name, her expression soured.

He was about to turn to the stairs, then stopped. "By the way, if you happen upon James, would you tell him for me that I believe I've found the men responsible for Mel."

"Oh. Dear God, Mr. Renehan. You are not—"

"It's why I'm looking for Eli. We got us two *b'hoys*."

"I'm sorry. Boys?" she asked.

"B'hoys, with that bump in it. It's what they call young toughs trying to make a name for themselves by proving how ferocious they are."

"Really."

"Oh, indeed. That mob attacked Mr. Tyler, there was a few in there. The ones that do all right now, they grow up to be firemen." He said it without a trace of humor. "So, Eli and I have a little excursion to make. James might want to know."

"Surely, you should tell Mr. Tyler and my husband, have them send police."

"Begging pardon, ma'am, I don't see as how that's of any advantage. By the time all that got arranged, this lot'll clear out, if they're even there still. They're *gobdaws* to have stayed around this long." He hesitated, then added, "I am leaving me brother upstairs to fill my duties so that your father-in-law won't notice the absence, as I'm not bothering to ask permission, for all the reasons we just discussed. So I'd appreciate if he didn't learn of it just now. Won't be very long."

Mary burbled and managed to get her fingers on the edge of the book. Priscilla gently drew her back and reached for the book again. She didn't look at him as she replied, "I won't say anything regarding your whereabouts."

"Thank you."

"Come back whole though, won't you? Mr. Renehan?" Her eyes met his then.

"It's me lifelong ambition, Mrs. Tyler." He ducked his head and turned away before she could see his cheeks flush.

>>>- -<<<

Renehan changed clothes. Garvine, having been stoking the furnace, didn't need to. He was dirty with coal dust and in his regular clothes. They took the wagon from the stables. The back of it still bore blood stains from Mel's body.

With Garvine at the reins, they rolled up New York Avenue and then down Massachusetts in case anyone might be keeping a lookout. A wagon coming in from the wrong direction was less likely to attract anyone's attention. Most of the way there, he was picturing Priscilla Cooper Tyler's expression as she told him to come back in one piece. It was not his imagination that there was something between them, and more than propriety allowed. He experienced the rare sensation of being someone's champion.

Wentworthy's proved to be a seedy grog shop a few doors in from the corner. H Street was a surface of muck and manure, some of which their wagon wheels sprayed across the lower rows of small windowpanes that adorned its front as they drove past.

Garvine pulled the wagon to a halt halfway along the block, and tied the reins to an iron hitching post, and they walked idly back.

A narrow door next to the tavern entrance led up steep stairs to the second floor, exactly as Branden had described. The street was deserted. They went up as quietly as possible.

A hall of four rooms ran front to back, with a door at the back that likely let down to a communal outhouse somewhere. They paused at the top of the steps and listened.

Renehan thought Garvine must have tramped in a layer of street manure, but neither of them had much muck on their black boots. As they started cautiously down the hall, however, the smell took on greater substance and specificity, until it was a wonder anybody sober could have navigated the hall and not had their gorge rise. The stink was definitely worse at the back.

There were only two doors to choose from. Renehan gestured to the one on their right for Garvine, and he went left.

Garvine put one hand against the righthand door and shoved. There was no lock and the door swung wide upon a small room. Renehan hadn't even opened his door, but didn't have to now. The death stench poured out of the open doorway like a soul fleeing Hell.

Inside was a table and two chairs, a dead cold fireplace, and a curtained-off nook to the back. Behind the curtain were two small beds framed out from the wall. The body they'd been anticipating lay on the nearest bed, and had probably been dead since the day he assaulted Mel. As firemen, Renehan and Garvine had seen more than their share of bodies and burns. In death this young man's face remained tight with agony, his jaw twisted open as if in the midst of howling. Both eye sockets were charred, weepy with yellowish fluid, and devoid of eyes.

"Called down the lightning from a blue sky, did she?" Renehan said as if to the body. Garvine stared at the corpse as if impressed by Mel's work.

Of the second man there was no sign. "Prolly run off already, ya think?" Garvine said.

"I'm not so sure as you," replied Renehan. He kicked a one-dollar carpet bag out from under the other bed. Drawing back the sheets he found a wool vest and a cap. Given the cold weather, he couldn't imagine anybody leaving their hat behind.

They went out into the hall, closing the door. "What about t'other rooms?" asked Garvine.

"We'd best look, I suppose."

The other three rooms proved to be unoccupied and, by the look of them, unrented. That at least explained why no one had complained of the stink.

They walked down the stairs and outside. Renehan turned to Garvine. "I want you to stand here and count to fifty, then come in and stick close by the door like you're not sure you want to be there and ya don't know me. We'll see what fish we hook."

He opened the tavern door and went in.

The interior defined the cheap grog shop. The plank flooring was half-dirt, most of it tracked in. Kegs were being used for chairs around most of the tables, although along the wall opposite stood a couple benches that looked like stolen church pews, one to each side of the small hearth, where a fire was crackling.

A half-dozen clients sat around the room, most of them near the fire. One group of three had the air of men who'd been pouring back ale for so long they were even bored of being drunk. A couple sat side-by-side on the back pew. The woman sized him up. He could see she was thinking she might have more luck with him than with the red-nosed inebriate beside her.

Casually, Renehan went over and leaned against the bar. He'd already taken stock of the one other patron in the place, who sat alone in the cold front corner pew beside the mud-smeared little windows, wrapped in a worn, brown wool coat too big for him. A *b'hoy* to be sure—scruffy and mean-looking, probably seventeen or so. His long greasy black hair curtained half his face. He kept his chin aimed at the empty whiskey glass on the tiny table ahead of him, but his eyes connected to Renehan's with a strained resignation.

Wentworthy was a toothless barman with a spitcurl of bear-greased hair. He slouched over to the bar near Renehan. "What ya having?"

"Two jars of Philadelphia porter," he answered, then asked loudly, "And I was wondering if you might have rooms to let upstairs for two men."

The *b'hoy* twitched at that.

The door opened and Garvine came in. He was bundled up in his black coat, his hands dirty, fingernails black with coal. He threw a glance at Renehan. He'd seen the *b'hoy* too.

It was unlikely the young villain wouldn't have worked out that two new strangers could not be a coincidence. One of his hands withdrew from the table and slid down into his coat.

When he made to stand, Garvine instinctively stepped toward him. The *b'hoy* drew a knife, rose, and clutched the edge of the little table as if he might fling it up as a shield.

"Hey," Renehan said, drawing his attention. "There's no leaving here save as your friend did upstairs unless you put away that Arkansas toothpick. We're bothering you for some answers is all. Bought you a jar if you'll have it. Whiskey if you'd rather. Now, what do you say?"

The rest of the clientele had stopped whatever they were doing.

Wentworthy started to interrupt, but Renehan cut in. "*They* haven't smelled him yet, but they're going to soon enough when he starts leakin' through the ceiling."

The *b'hoy* didn't drop the knife but he sagged into himself, putting his back against the glass as if he couldn't stay upright without the support of the table. He considered his blade as if he might cut his own throat. "Shoulda pulled foot, like Burgee and Hoat. I knowed it." He flicked his head to toss some of the hair aside.

Renehan relaxed as the first jar was set beside him. "Burgee and Hoat the pikey bastards what dumped you here, were they?"

"Hoat said it was good money. Easy pickins."

Wentworthy set down the second jar as if nothing out of the ordinary was happening, but he moved to the far end of the bar without asking for payment.

"Not so easy after all then."

The *b'hoy* looked up through his strands of hair. "What'd she do to him?"

Renehan turned and picked up the jars to show that he had no weapons and no ill intent. "Did Hoat happen to say who it was procured your services?"

"Told Phil."

"Phil'd be upstairs, I s'pose?"

The kid nodded and flicked his head again. "M'brother."

"Then I grieve wit' yas. I've got one of them meself, needs constant lookin' arter."

The *b'hoy* sighed, caving in now. He pushed his hair out of his face again, and Garvine, who'd edged closer, sprang and caught his wrist. The knife spun from his grip and across the bench. Garvine raised a fist, but Renehan snapped, "Eli!" The big man frowned but uncurled his fingers and lowered his arm. "He can't tell us nothing if you smash his head in, and the other's done talking forever. Here, for Chrissake, take one of these jars and give it to him."

As he reached toward Garvine, a shadow rippled across the smeared and distorting window panes, someone passing by outside. There was a sound, the smallest tinkle of glass, so soft that no one really noticed.

Garvine let go of the skinny wrist and took the jar. Immediately the *b'hoy* lurched away. Garvine twisted in a crouch, sloshing porter, ready for the kid to grab his knife. Instead, the *b'hoy* seemed to throw himself back against the pew, and his head slammed against the nearest pane so hard that it shattered. His shoulders pressed tight, upward, and he made a choking gargle, pitched forward over the table and rode it to the floor.

"Jesus, he's having a fit!" Renehan yelled at the same moment that Wentworthy shouted, "You pay for that table, you hooligans! Gettin' me a constable!"

Garvine slammed down the jar and bent to pull the kid upright.

The pew and entire front corner erupted in blue phosphoric fire. Garvine yowled and reared up, eyebrows singed off, face as red as sunburn, his left sleeve and hand engulfed in the weird flames.

Renehan flung the remaining porter across his arm. Still folded around the table and now consumed in fire, the kid shrieked and gasped horribly as if he was sucking down the flames, and his heels thundered against the pew. Renehan turned to the barman. "God's sake, man, give us something to put it out!"

Wentworthy sprang around the far end of the bar, scooped up a bucket of ashes from beside the hearth, knocking one of the drunks aside. He scurried up and flung the ashes over the flailing corpse, an explosion of powder and charred wood. The whole front of the tavern vanished in the cloud. Renehan and Garvine coughed and swatted at the air. Ash covered everything, but the blaze was out. The stink of cooked flesh filled the bar.

Renehan ducked and knelt, reaching to turn the *b'hoy* over, but stopped. He could hear the body sizzling as if the blue fire was scalding it from the inside out. His jaws clamped shut, and he took hold and rolled the *b'hoy* off the table. The wood had burned black and hunks of skin and tissue remained glued to it. The whole front of the body was nothing but blackened bone and glistening fluids.

Behind him, Wentworthy stammered, "But—but he weren't on fire more'n seconds!"

Garvine, gray-faced as a specter, collapsed on one of the kegs. He hissed, pressing his wounded, blistered arm against his belly. Looking at it, he said, "Holy God," through his clenched teeth.

Renehan crossed himself as he got up, but he was thinking how much this was like the victim of Mel's magic lying dead upstairs. He half-wondered if she hadn't somehow managed to strike him down from beyond the grave.

Then he noticed the cracked window pane beside the one the kid's head had smashed, and recalled the sound he had only registered unconsciously— the plink of breaking glass. There was a tiny hole in the center of the crack, smaller than his littlest finger. A shadow had rippled across the windows...

He flung Garvine aside and leapt out the door and into the street, the muck, with ash like a vengeful wraith flowing after him.

There was no one anywhere on the street, and nothing to be seen but their own wagon halfway along. He swung about and raced out onto the broader lane of Capitol Street.

It lay as deserted as if all the inhabitants of the city itself had evaporated.

Part IV:
Late Eclipses

Thirty-One

Letitia Christian Tyler clung to God, her rock, as she was sat up, pushed one way and then pulled the other by Sally and Devonee as they worked her nightgown up and off her. She tried to banish all thoughts of her body, the indignity of its exposure to them with her useless breasts, her loose and scarred belly, her hairy thighs. The two girls pretended in their own way not to see her as they sponged her with hot water from the copper washtub much as they might have a horse. It was different, more elaborate, than her usual toilet. This would be her first public appearance since entering this inhospitable house.

In the end, only God watched over her. He saw her in her nakedness and her shame, and did not withhold His blessing. "He will not let your foot be moved, and He who watches over you will not fall asleep." She recited her *Book of Common Prayer* from memory, her lips twitching until Sally took a cloth and cleansed her face. Then she held her lips pressed tightly together.

Next Sally brushed her hair out and then began to coil it elaborately while Devonee dressed her in a linen chemise, bloomers, stockings, garters, and one good layer of petticoats, but no corset—she couldn't bear being cinched anymore. The silk dress she would wear hung in the schrank behind the girls, a pale blue gown as befitted the mother of a bride.

A bride. Oh, those words almost brought tears to her eyes. Her Elizabeth was marrying William Waller on this final day of January, and that would set matters to rest.

The family thought Letitia didn't know about the indiscretion that had taken place on New Year's Eve, but she had been, she thought, quite crafty in the questions she had put to Priscilla and Robert and Mr. Tyler. Individually the scribbled-out questions were innocuous enough, or at least allowed each person to tell her something without having to reveal too much. Mr. Tyler had tried to pretend that he knew nothing of the matter by saying, "Honestly, my dear, it was Priscilla who came upon the two of them upstairs. She's insistent that nothing untoward occurred beyond that Billy had imbibed too much punch and boldly asked *her* for Elizabeth's hand first. I know how nervous a young suitor can be, now, don't I?" He'd chuckled. "Everyone ensured that he was sober and presentable before he approached me down in the East Room."

Priscilla had offered a little more, but Letitia knew how to read her household, and she knew when they were obfuscating. Plus, she held no illusions regarding Elizabeth's unruly behavior. More than any of her children, she prayed that Jesus would guide Elizabeth. This marriage was surely His answer: Elizabeth would become a wife and settle down.

When she was coiffed and dressed, the girls lay Letitia again on the bed and withdrew.

For a few minutes she was by herself, and she could hardly recall the last time that had been the case—probably way back on that night when everyone had misunderstood her terror of this room…everyone save for Mary Elena. *Poor Mel.*

In her thoughts she recited: "The angel of the Lord encampeth round about them that fear him and delivereth them."

Mel had surely been Letitia's angel. No one else had even sensed the evil presence in this room. Only she had understood and driven the devil out. Certainly her methods were unorthodox, but she was a healer—Letitia had seen that herself years ago, when Alice had the croup and Mel had made her some kind of special broth that cured her in no time—and wasn't healing a power granted by God? Didn't God place in those plants the power to cure just as surely as he had bestowed the knowledge of them upon Mel?

What would she do going forward? Should the devil return now, who would protect her? Her angel had been *murdered.* Though no one told her much, Letitia speculated it might have had something to do with the mob attacks back in the fall.

A minute later, James, Samuel, and the gangly beanstalk, Tall George, came in to carry her downstairs.

James and Samuel gripped each other's arms to make a seat for her and bore her from the bed like a child between them. Sideways, they maneuvered out the door and along the hall, with George at the back to brace her upright. They were going to carry her into the East Room like a queen. They went carefully down the stairs, and James whispered, "I am pleased for you today," but his eyes remained distant and sad. Both he and Samuel seemed taciturn. A month had passed since the terrible murder, but the entire house still seemed to be grieving for Mary Elena.

She knew James had been bent upon asking to be released from service to her family—a release she alone could give as he was her chattel and not Mr. Tyler's. He had never quite found the way or the time to ask, but she'd known him since they were children. She understood him. He had served so exceptionally, even becoming learned; but learning, she thought, had only made him unhappy. It was exactly why so many men, including her husband, argued against teaching slaves to read and write, why laws were passed against it. She, of course, dependent upon her body slave's ability to read, appreciated that there were sometimes sound reasons to educate them too.

James was a very good reader. He invested the works of Dickens with far more life than did Mr. Tyler, though she would not have admitted it. John had never quite taken to James, despite showing him off occasionally by having him recite something to guests, or teasing Shakespearean quotes from him, amusing parlor tricks; and though James always performed obediently, she sensed his unhappiness, even resentment, in doing so.

But it wasn't just learning, it was love that had made him want to rise above his station, planting ideas about freedom in his head. He thought he would run off to the North someplace with Mel, that they would make a life together. Mr. Tyler's stated opinion was that slaves, like children, were taught early on how the world was circumscribed, and were only happy within those limits. When they attempted to press beyond their limits, they realized only grief and disappointment. "Why, you free a slave," he'd said, "before you know it, they'll be at your front door, begging to be taken back because the world is too much for them."

She knew James would have asked for Mel's freedom along with his own—a request Letitia had dreaded. Mr. Tyler would never have consented. Mel belonged to him, and as she was surely the best cook in any house on the James River, he would never have manumitted her to James. He'd said any number of times that any slave capable of putting in a day's work was worth keeping; although he usually said that right about the time he needed to sell one off to finance a political campaign.

Now that Mel was dead, none of it mattered, and she was comfortable admitting that she could never have freed her guardian angel either, not after the devil had watched her out of that mirror.

The flow of her thoughts was interrupted as the trio carried her along the cross hall. Despite the matted floor that always made her think of an old cabin, the hall was festooned with gay white ribbons, the candles all burning in the chandeliers. She was whisked not to the East Room as she'd expected, but into the Green Parlor beside it. There, out of sight of the groom, Elizabeth stood, being fussed over by Deborah and Sally, all under the direction of dear Priscilla. All the preparation stopped as Letitia was carried in. Elizabeth burst into tears and ran to her. Unable to contain herself, Letitia began to cry as well. Of course, they hadn't remembered to bring her slate, so she could not express herself beyond slurring a few words, which no one seemed to comprehend, and gasping incoherently. A tiny bit of spittle ran over her lip, and Elizabeth took the handkerchief with which she'd been wiping her eyes and quickly dabbed it away, saying, "Oh, Mother, I'm so happy. So happy." Letitia nodded in reply. She hadn't seen this parlor before. It was all green and gilt, with silk-bottomed chairs and a lovely mahogany writing desk in the corner, and a big chandelier, all lit up like the ones in the hall and dazzling.

She got only a glimpse of it, for Priscilla hugged her, and then they carried her through the door adjoining the East Room.

They were a few feet into the room before the guests, expecting her to be brought through the main doors, realized that she was there in the middle of the entourage. Those who'd been sitting jumped to their feet, and everyone burst out in applause as though she was the cause of the day's celebration.

Chairs had been lined up facing a small platform in front of the hearth. Letitia was delivered onto one of the front center ones. She tried to make eye contact with James, but he kept his head down as he withdrew.

Mr. Tyler would sit beside her once his part was completed; Dolley plunked down immediately like a sister on her left, and like sisters they wept together. Something akin to an informal procession took shape behind Dolley, and one by one people came up to say hello: members of Mr. Tyler's new cabinet, their wives (some of whom she had met when they'd come up to her room during recent levées), William Waller's family from Leesburg, a few congressmen and their wives, Daniel Webster and his son, and then more society people whose names she could not remember two minutes after meeting them, so overwhelmed was she by it all. It hadn't been so long since she had moved among them herself, vivacious, laughing and dancing reels with her husband. It seemed as if only months had passed, but it was years now, wasn't it? But, no, she would not let herself slip into self-pity. This was a day for showing nothing but joy. She was not one to wallow in despair.

The wedding proceeded. The groom took his place. James played the piano as the bride entered on her father's arm, looking glorious. The Reverend Addison, who attended to Letitia's private worship most Sundays, presided.

At the point where he asked if there was cause why the two children should not be joined in wedlock, a deep groan came from behind him. For a moment everyone stared, transfixed, at the fireplace. The sound came a second time, and Letitia identified the source as the round vent beside the fireplace. "The furnace," whispered Mr. Tyler, and he then repeated it to the row behind them. The echo of flexing ductwork was a noise that had become familiar to him. She turned her attention back to the reverend and the nearly united couple. And then it was done, and her headstrong daughter was Mrs. William Waller.

A cake awaited them all in the State Dining Room. Despite her increasing exhaustion, Letitia let herself be carried there and set beside the warm fire. In her weariness she thought for a moment, *Oh, what a fine cake Mary Elena has made,* before remembering with a stab of loss that it wasn't so.

Some of the same people who'd greeted her in the East Room came up to congratulate her again. The nodding, smiling murmurs of gracious thanks quickly wore her down, and she tugged on Mr. Tyler's sleeve. He understood, of course. He had her carried back upstairs. Robert assisted this time. James was not there.

Coming into her room, she watched the tall cloudy mirror in the corner. It reflected only the end of Devonee's cot and the edge of the schrank. They placed her on the bed, where the mirror was no longer in her line of sight, thank the Lord.

Dolley came in as quickly as the men left, and a few others who still wanted to wish the mother of the bride much joy. She put on a friendly façade. At least now she could write *Thank You* on the slate and let it speak for her.

Elizabeth came last, her new husband in tow. A carriage was ready outside to take them and the Wallers to the train station and away to Leesburg.

Letitia wept anew and Elizabeth wept holding her, both knowing that she was leaving her family for good. Letitia remembered her own experience the day she had departed with Mr. Tyler. Of course, James had come with her then, and in a way his presence provided a sense of connection to the family. Elizabeth would not be leaving with a slave of *her* own. The Wallers would supply her and William's servants.

When everyone had withdrawn and before the girls came to undress her, Letitia lay upon the bed awhile unattended. Her eyes almost closed. And then all at once she sobbed a great ragged breath, fresh tears spilled from the corners of her eyes, and she dragged her prayer book from the bedclothes and clutched it to her bosom.

Praise God, her daughter had escaped this accursed house.

Thirty-Two

James Hambleton Christian

"I got word on Burgee and Hoat," Martin Renehan told me.

I was alone in the mess with the Argand lamps from the private floor that I was cleaning and topping up with whale oil. The family, which is to say everyone but Miss Letitia, plus Samuel and Sally as servants, was in Philadelphia where Mr. Tyler had been invited to celebrate the birthday of President Washington. It was something of a reprieve for me. Tazewell, Miss Alice, and I had been working daily on music that their father wanted them to perform at a levée down the road.

Renehan had on a new thick double-breasted pea jacket against the February cold. I set down the bottle of oil. "Back in the city, are they?" I stared down at my hands, curling and uncurling in my lap. More than a month I'd been hoping for news of those two names.

"I'm sorry to say, no, they stayed down in North Carolina."

"*Stayed.* You say that in the past."

"And so would you. They're dead, the both of 'em."

"Both." I closed my hands upon my thighs. What I'd hoped for wasn't this news. I looked up at him.

He nodded. "Place in Greensboro where they took lodging burned to the ground the week past."

"You think it was Mel?" He and I had debated without resolution whether she or the sorcerer we'd never clapped eyes on had burned up the kid in Wentworthy's.

"Could be, I guess. Fella who sent word to the English Hill fire brigade said it was like no blaze he'd ever encountered. Burned like St. Elmo's fire dancing on a yardarm all blue and white, too hot to get near. Wasn't so much as a bone left arter. Six people, includin' a child."

I worked the cap on the whale oil, screwing it on and off.

Renehan asked, "You think Mel would burn up a child to get at those two?"

My fingers caressed the bottle, slid to the table. "No. She would never."

Renehan sat across from me. "James, man, I know you want this to be proof that she's still here, but this isn't her handiwork, nor was the *b'hoy*. It's our mutual enemy covering his tracks. Too many peculiar fires for it to be anything else."

"Then why didn't he do Harrison that way?" I'd long since told him

Isaac's version of events.

"Sounds to me like it was important to him to frighten your man to death. Fire's too quick—especially his kind of fire."

All the men who had taken part in murdering Mel was dead. I ought to have felt some kind of satisfaction, solace at least. Not nothing. I picked up a polishing cloth and started to work on the glass cylinder of one of the lamps. "Garvine's arm all right?" I asked. He had two fingers that would be webbed like a duck's foot forever after, and I think it had hurt far more than he ever admitted to anybody, which was ironic, seeing as he complained about everything else.

Renehan said he was almost healed, and then got up. "Anyhow," he said as he turned away, "I thought you'd want to know."

I did, though right then I couldn't say so. All the signs I had clung to of Mel beyond the grave had gone up in the smoke of that blue fire. There would be no vengeance for me.

⤐ ⫷⫷

The whole time Mr. Tyler was in Philadelphia, we turned away petitioners. Some railed at us, disbelieving us. But when the family returned, not two hours passed before they were at the front door again, as if they had been lying for him in the cold of Lafayette Park.

Jasper went on an extended holiday with his daughter's family, and Renehan, Tall George, and I took over his duties on the front door throughout the day. We had a new cook now, a heavy-set woman name of Mariama that Tyler had gotten off a neighbor back on the James River by swapping three field slaves for her. That news sent Sally into a fearful state that lasted for days, until we got news that none of the three was her son. He remained safely at Walnut Grove, where he had my duties now of answering the door.

Mariama was another Gullah woman. She and Ethel got on like a house on fire, the two of them filling the kitchen with their incomprehensible dialogues, and Zenobia, who grieved over Mel almost as much as I did, complained to me that she felt demoted and shut out.

When the *maudit* Mel had died for finally arrived, Zenobia started spending more time out of sight, doing as Mel had taught her, making new charms and placing them wherever she thought some had gone missing. While I disliked the things even more now, the making of them was Mel's legacy to Zenobia, and so I helped where I could, mostly standing guard the nights she checked the parlors along the public floor. I hoped it would shock our enemy to find out the house still wasn't open to him.

Mr. Tyler had returned from Philadelphia with some kind of secret that he, Mr. Robert, and Miss Priscilla shared between them. They wouldn't say what it was. I asked Samuel and Sally both, but neither of them knew anything beyond that Mr. Tyler had been very excited about someone he met in Philadelphia. I thought maybe it was the British diplomat, Lord Ashburton, whom Daniel Webster was waiting on even now.

The Friday following his return, I delivered the usual afternoon tea to him in his office. Outside, the waiting hall was packed like a box of cigars with petitioners, a number of whom looked, and smelled, as if they had ridden in from the countryside that morning. The air in that space stank like rancid old butter. It didn't seem to bother the petitioners—those men must have been used to themselves—but if I could have pulled Andrew Jackson's standing desk off the wall and snuck out the door behind it, through the anteroom and yellow oval library to avoid them, I would have. Down the two steps, I passed Osbert Drummond. Nothing much ever seemed to perturb him, but even he, charged with maintaining order among the petitioners, was keeping to the central hall that afternoon.

On the public floor again, I encountered one of those Locofocos who had stood by us against a mob last fall, Mr. Ingersoll of Pennsylvania, exiting the Blue Saloon. With him was a pale young man. It appeared the congressman was giving him a private, guided tour of the house. The young man had a great plume of dark hair sprouting from the right side of his head, where his hairline appeared to be in retreat, but the hair hung down on both sides of his face sort of like ears on a hound dog. His lips were pursed too, as if everything he saw caused him to cogitate. He wore a garish yellow vest under his tweeds. I confess, my first and unfavorable impression was that the congressman was escorting somebody from his home district—which is to say, a bumpkin who had over-dressed for the occasion. Surely, that wasn't the fashion somewhere.

Ingersoll hailed me. "We've come to see President Tyler as per arrangements."

This was the person Mr. Tyler had met in Philadelphia? I led them up the stairs. Drummond looked us over as we passed him, and his expression told me that he had reached a similar conclusion to mine.

Everybody in the waiting hall turned and stared. Their odor reached us as we neared.

The young man made a polite cough. Congressman Ingersoll pulled me aside before we could climb up among the petitioners.

"I don't believe you understand the situation," he said. "The young man here is none other than the celebrated author Charles Dickens, and I do not wish to do him the disservice of being pressed into that malodorous space with those Jonathans like a hunk of wadding stuffed down a muzzleloader."

I had never intended to leave them in that hall in the first place, but I stood there goggling, dumbstruck by the identity of our guest, the very man whose words I read to my sister night upon night, a man whose work testified to the unfairness of the universe, who used his voice to overturn terrible wrongs—injustices, cruelties, and the cowardice that men visited upon one another because they stood to gain by it—if only in books. He'd such capacity to see into the human heart that I had imagined he must be far older than I. Instead, he was so…so callow-seeming, a young Moses in a strange land.

Ingersoll said, "James?"

I blinked at him, surprised that he remembered my name. I nodded, said, "Yes, sir. If you gentlemen will wait here, I shall ensure that Mr. Tyler is prepared to receive you."

I left them, climbed up and entered Tyler's office without knocking, interrupting his current petitioner, who from what I could tell by the little bottles he had set on the table was a Thomsonian asking the president's endorsement of some herbal tonics. Mel would have known what they were.

Robert stood beside the man as if about to eject him anyhow as Tyler, seated, shifted his attention to me with a look of irritation.

"Sir," I said, "Mr. Charles Dickens, the author, is waiting upon you in the company of Mr. Ingersoll in the central hall outside."

Normally he would have been furious that I had intruded, but in this instance he stood up excitedly. The flummoxed Thomsonian glanced from him to me, but it was Robert who quickly said, "Thank you, Mr. Agee, please leave us samples and your calling card." He put a hand around the man's arm and turned him toward the door behind me as Agee grabbed up his bottles.

"But I wasn't—"

"Oh, but you were," Robert assured him, and directed him around me and out the door.

Mr. Tyler didn't have to say a word. I trailed Robert as he walked Mr. Agee down the two steps and past Ingersoll, who was standing alone now.

Seeing me, he hurried up into the waiting hall. To my surprise, young Mr. Dickens stood among the clustered petitioners with whom he had already struck up a conversation as if their smell didn't exist, his happy profile silhouetted against the huge half-circle fanlight window. Ingersoll clutched him, saying, "Come, sir," and drew him back to where I stood ready to open the door.

Although they had been conversing pleasantly enough, the petitioners glowered jealously after this man with the mop of hair who was allowed to circumvent their mean purgatory.

>>> -<<<

The following night's levée proved to be about as big as New Year's had been. Word of Dickens' presence had leaked out—for all I know, Miss Priscilla had ridden out and spread the word herself.

That levée was already a special occasion. Another writer, Mr. Washington Irving, was being fêted and celebrated. Mr. Tyler had made him our minister to the court of Spain and he was to set sail the following day. I had read some of his "Geoffrey Crayon" stories at William and Mary, works I had copied out in order to understand elements like syntax. I could never have said to him, but I owed a great deal of my reading and writing to Mr. Irving. That both he and Dickens were here on the same night astonished me. Yet there was nothing I could say to either man publicly. I was, in a way, like our sorcerer—in plain sight, never recognized nor acknowledged.

A military band performed in the hall outside the East Room, and filled the whole floor with brass notes that shook the chandeliers and echoed back from the high ceilings. I hoped they would drive off the spiders up in the corners too.

In the yellow Washington parlor, Mr. Tyler, Robert, and Miss Priscilla stood among various dignitaries and diplomats alongside Mr. Irving. He turned out to be a rotund man with the sleepiest eyes I think I'd ever seen, although he was nothing approaching drowsy at all.

In the State Dining Room, among the other food, Mariama had prepared a dish called *salmagundi*, which proved to be a humorous reference of some sort to Mr. Irving himself. He actually applauded when it was unveiled. He seemed to be surrounded by a group of writers, all of whom were in on the joke. At that point I would not have been surprised to find the poet Edgar Allan Poe in a parlor of the President's House. He had been writing to Robert Tyler for months, requesting a similar posting to Mr. Irving's. Mr. Robert complained about it during numerous dinners. I thought of Mr. Robert's own book of inferior and ignored poems. It was jealousy that soured him on poor Mr. Poe.

Soon after the *salamagundi*, Mr. Dickens arrived in the company of his wife. Fires blazed in both of the vestibule hearths, but for all that, it was cold as a mausoleum. They stood before the one on my left, holding out their hands for warmth. With a tilt of his head, Jasper directed me to them. He looked a bit amazed by their presence too. I hurried over, introduced myself, and then led them off to the Washington parlor where Mr. Irving had returned after the ceremonial dish, and was holding court with the Tylers and some of the other writers and hangers-on.

Mrs. Dickens was a plump woman. When I directed them through the vestibule door, I saw how, following, she looked upon her husband as if he was the lamp that guided her through the storm.

From the doorway into the parlor, Dickens spotted Irving and shot like an arrow straight for him, nearly leaving his wife behind. I stayed beside her until we caught up.

At the sight of Dickens, Irving stood up and approached. The two men shook hands energetically, Dickens saying, "Why, you are a wondrous storyteller, sir!" while Irving gushed, extolling the crowd with, "If none of you has read *Oliver Twist*, I tell you, it will stand the test of time and be read long after I am but a footnote in our century!"

"Oh, sir, really," Dickens replied, but I could see from his flush how he liked hearing it said.

Beaming, Mr. Tyler inserted himself into the discussion, introducing Robert and Miss Priscilla, and Dickens put up a hand and said, "Of course, Catherine and I must meet your wife. That's the first order of business, is it not? Please, lead the way, sir."

Mr. Tyler invited Washington Irving to come along too, and the group of them went out. I followed as far as the west stairwell, but my duties lay on the public floor, and much as I would have loved to see the expression on Miss Letitia's face when her guest's identity was revealed, I returned to the vestibule, where Jasper was just now taking the calling card from another couple. They removed their coats, which I carried into the anteroom. Then I took their card and escorted them to the East Room, announced them at the door, and stepped back to let them pass.

For the next hour perhaps there was swirls of dancing up and down the East Room, limited by what a military band could play. The emphasis fell upon waltzes.

When next I saw Mr. Dickens, he was standing in the Blue Saloon, engaged in discussion with members of both the British and French delegations. I carried a tray of filled champagne glasses, and they stood near enough to the doors that I went straight for them.

Dickens was speaking to the French ambassador, the comte de Bacourt, a short man with long gray hair, parted in the middle. "You have heard of Baron Dupotet de Sennevoy then, monsieur?" The Frenchman replied reservedly that he had. He turned to me and took one of the champagne flutes.

"Well, I have had the pleasure of his company," said Dickens. "Dr. Elliotson introduced us."

The English delegate named Cruickshank, tall and sharp-faced, replied, "That would be the Doctor Elliotson who resigned his position at St. Thomas Hospital? Sordid business, from what I heard."

Dickens sighed in exasperation. "That's how it was portrayed in certain press, yes—but I tell you, I was on hand for many of his demonstrations and saw with my own eyes how Elliotson used mesmerism to overcome fits of epilepsy in otherwise incurable patients."

"Parlor tricks," dismissed Fox.

"No, monsieur," replied the comte de Bacourt. "Not at all."

Dickens turned to thank him and snatched a glass from my tray all in one sweep. Proudly he said, "He chose to resign rather than be restricted in his researches. In Boston, I met a man, a Dr. Collyer, who is studying it. It's taken seriously here."

I wondered what the "it" could be.

Ambassador Fox shrugged. "Well, it would be, wouldn't it?" He lifted a glass of champagne from the tray. "Really, Dickens, you've been taken in by charlatans."

"No, sir. Furthermore, I'll have you know that I am myself a trained mesmeric operator."

Fox snorted at that news. He looked past Cruickshank at the other member of his party. "What do you say about this nonsense, Ettryne?"

The young lord considered his champagne, took a sip. He seemed disinclined to answer immediately. By now they all had their champagne and I should have walked away, but I could not help being curious.

He drank again. Then softly he said, "Herr Mesmer found *something*. But he was far too naive and ignorant to separate what was true from what was humbug. And like so many others, he fabricated explanations conforming to his benighted preconceptions. Magnets and fluids and other preposterous twaddle. His salons turned into orgies, as the comte de Bacourt knows full well."

"Exactly," Fox said in triumph. I still didn't know what he was triumphant about.

Mr. Dickens excused himself and walked away, red in the face.

He plunged deeper into the room, as did I with my half-emptied tray. Then one of the more lubricated gentlemen near the south portico doors—a Tennessee congressman—turned his head and attempted to spit his chaw juice out one of the doors, except that as this was February the door was not open. The men nearest him shouted and jumped, finding the drapes and themselves spattered with brown juice. The inebriate wiped sloppily at his chin and hollered back at them, as Mr. Dickens, his mouth unhinged, began to back away.

Renehan and Drummond abruptly charged past me, aimed straight for the spitter. I turned and escaped. Everyone else in the saloon paused to watch them, but I planned to stay in the cross hall until the doormen were done.

Dickens emerged right behind me. Flustered, he cast about, saw Mr. Irving in discussion with the Spanish envoy, and took a few steps toward them, but then hesitated, as if he felt he would be intruding. After all, Mr. Irving was about to set sail to Spain.

He reversed direction, and nearly crashed into me. I glimpsed Ambassador Fox looking at him from within the room just before Drummond burst out holding the drunken spitter by the collar ahead of him. Renehan emerged behind him, gave me a wink, and just watched as the drunk squirmed and kicked, trying to get purchase on the floor weaving that Drummond wasn't about to give him. They passed through the vestibule door.

"You are the butler here, are you not?" I realized that Mr. Dickens was speaking to me. "We met yesterday."

"Yes, sir," I said.

"Well, sir, my wife remains upstairs with the president's wife and daughter-in-law. They were admiring her baby. I came down here for what I thought would be a diverting conversation with my countrymen." He glared back into the saloon. "In any case, I wish to return upstairs. I was wondering if you might accompany me."

"Sir?"

"It is the family's private floor. Should I not be accompanied?"

Martin Renehan came alongside me. "Here, James, I'll have that." He took the tray and walked off into the State Dining Room.

I led Mr. Dickens away then, along the hall and into the west stairwell. To the right of the stairs, someone had opened the door that let out on top of the west colonnade. I excused myself and went and closed it. He watched me from the second stair, then said, "Your house at the moment seems more like a London gentleman's club than a home."

"That so, sir?"

"It wasn't a compliment."

"No, sir," I said.

He stared hard at me. His brown eyes were penetrating and disarming. "I am informed by Mr. John Quincy Adams that you are slaves here, and not servants."

I had not encountered John Quincy Adams this evening, but he did sometimes attend. "Yes, sir. That is so."

"Hardly the beacon of liberty, is it?" he replied, then added, "I do not mean to embarrass you in any way, Mr. Christian."

I found myself smiling, no doubt like an idiot to him. I said, "I have read all of your novels, Mr. Dickens."

"What?" Genuinely startled. "Surely not all of them, Mr. Christian."

"All of them, yes, sir. I read them aloud to Ms. Letitia."

"Really?" The news brightened his mood still further. "And you enjoy them?"

"I find much in them worth reading, yes." I recited, "'Let no man talk of murderers escaping justice, and hint that Providence must sleep.'"

Open-mouthed, he stared at me.

"*Oliver Twist*," I said.

"Oh, yes, *I* know that. You remember it verbatim?"

"It is a certain skill I have, sir."

He looked down upon me as if seeing me anew, and with an expression that did not seem able to settle anyplace. Finally, eyes as glossy as if japanned, he said, "Thank you, Mr. Christian. Now, let us go find Kate."

Miss Priscilla and Mrs. Dickens had left Miss Letitia and stood at the other end of the hall outside Miss Priscilla's chamber. Mary had been returned to her little bed and Sally's care. The two women seemed to be getting along like two old friends who had years to catch up on.

Seeing us approach, Mrs. Dickens fairly beamed. "Charles," she said, "you'll never guess what Mrs. Tyler here has told to me."

"I can't imagine. What?"

"She suffers from bouts of somnambulism."

All his focus shifted to Miss Priscilla. "You walk in your sleep?"

Flushing, she replied, "Your wife described for me the work you've been engaged in with—is it Dr. Elliotson?"

"Yes, of course she has." He grinned. His wife had made him the center of attention, which seemed to suit him. "Now, please, tell me of your experiences."

She glanced my way, uncertain. I thought she would say nothing, but Dickens had strong powers of persuasion. She was drawn back to his intense gaze.

She then described the event I knew about from Mel, although Priscilla seemed to have no memory of the figure Mel had seen, fashioned from the East Room drapes. She recollected "only a shadow which had led me into that room." Then she continued, "I thought it had stopped, to tell you the truth. I believe it did for some months. Until October. I have now come to my senses standing in other rooms, but usually the East Room, with no knowledge of how I traveled there." Again, she gave me a look—this time as if she had more to say, but she gave her head a small shake. Whatever it was, she would not speak it.

Mr. Dickens' serious expression made him look older than his thirty years. He pushed his dark hair back over his ear, kept his hand there, clutching the hair, deep in thought. "Yes," he said absently. "Yes, I am certain I can help you, Mrs. Tyler. As Kate can tell you, I am myself a trained mesmeric operator. I can place you in a trance—perfectly harmless, I assure you, it's a simple matter to bring you out of it. There are, you see, many factors—stressors—that can contribute to these episodes, and once we learn the cause, it's almost certain we will banish them from your life."

"Really?" She tried to sound hopeful.

Mrs. Dickens answered, "You will find it quite soothing, really, and awaken feeling you've slept a full night through."

There was no reason to remain here, and it troubled me to have heard Miss Priscilla's confession. I was intruding, and I started to withdraw.

Miss Priscilla reached out and said, "No, James, I would like for you to remain. This is not something Robert can know about—he would *never* understand, Mr. Dickens—but I should like to have someone I can trust with me."

Although I had always known there was understanding, even harmony, between us, her statement of trust made me proud in spite of myself. "All right, ma'am," I replied. "I'll stay."

"Where should we do this then, do you think?" she asked me.

"Might want to use the anteroom beside Mr. Tyler's office. There was a fire laid on in there earlier for Mr. Webster and some folks, but they're all downstairs now."

She agreed, and we climbed to the waiting hall. I held open the door for them.

The anteroom fire had burned to embers, but two pieces of wood and a few pokes got it burning again nicely. The small room quickly warmed. It was furnished with comfortable single and double armchairs that had been pulled into an approximate circle on the blue rug. There were two narrow bookcases, two small tables with whale oil lamps, and of course spittoons.

Miss Priscilla reached to light a lamp, but Dickens said, "No, Mrs. Tyler. Low light is preferable."

He dragged one of the chairs from the circle into the center of the room. "Please," he said, directing Miss Priscilla to the chair. She gathered her crinolines under her so that she could sit. I took the chair nearest the hearth, turned it. Mrs. Dickens fanned her own skirts and sat opposite me.

Dickens hauled one up so that he faced Miss Priscilla, so close that their knees nearly touched. The firelight flowed over his profile. His glinting eye looked peculiarly sinister.

"Now," he said, "close your eyes, Priscilla, and begin to breathe slowly, steadily. Long deep inhalation—yes, *good*—and now slow exhalation. Open yourself up. To me. To the room." He looked around. "To James. To…possibility."

Miss Priscilla's body relaxed in stages as he spoke. Like a breeze, she seemed to rise and fall. Dickens smiled. This must have been how he wanted it to go. He held out his hands, close to her face but not touching it. He started to move them in circles.

Under his breath he was humming something. I didn't think he was aware he was doing this, but the similarity to Mel's way of settling a room made me ache with remembering. I didn't want to watch this anymore.

Then Mrs. Dickens seized my attention. Her head drooped of a sudden. Seemed she'd nodded off in the warm darkness. She let out a slow sigh. Mr. Dickens was so focused on Miss Priscilla that he didn't seem to see.

Mrs. Dickens stiffened, slowly raised her head with her eyes closed. Her lips twitched like she was speaking tiny words, and her face had changed—the press of her brows, the way her lips curled, was peculiarly familiar.

I must have made some sound, because Dickens paused and stared my way, then twisted around to see his wife. She continued staring at me without opening her eyes.

She said, "James," and the hair on the back of my neck stood stiff. Miss Priscilla came to, beheld the face of Mrs. Dickens, and her fingers went to her mouth.

Our reactions didn't help Dickens. He'd no idea what was happening. No way he knew that voice I'd never thought to hear again this side of the grave.

He asked, "Kate?"

"He is here, James," said Mrs. Dickens. "Him's in this house right now."

"Oh, dear Lord," Miss Priscilla whispered. It wasn't my imagination. She knew that patois as well as I.

Dickens repeated his wife's name. She paid him no mind.

The hall door came off the latch and swung silently open. Only I saw. Priscilla's back was to it and Dickens was staring at his wife. The fire fluttered in response to the new draft.

I got up carefully and walked to the door, half-expecting to be attacked by the darkness that had struck me down here before. If he was here as Mel said, then he might be right outside. Mrs. Dickens' head turned to follow me, wearing that half-smile still.

I leaned into the hall to grab the handle of the door.

At the end of the dark waiting hall and silhouetted against the huge half-circle window, a figure stood facing me. I recognized the shape of him, his livery, realized it was dripping wet: Isaac. Why was *he* here?

Behind me, Mel's voice called, "James," drawing me back. I closed the door.

Mrs. Dickens rose from her chair as I returned. I reached the hearth and she came straight across to me; her hands slid up my neck, clutched my head. She kissed me hard, then leaned back as if looking me over through her eyelids. "Never thought I'd taste you again, James Christian." The way she cocked her head, even her scent belonged to Mel. It was the smell I'd clung to in the sheets of my bed until it had faded. I was breathing as if I'd just run from the kitchen, but every breath was like swallowing broken glass. I wanted this and I abjured this.

Both Priscilla and Dickens had stood up. He didn't seem to know whether to express amazement or outrage. He'd extended a hand but hesitated to interrupt the strange events he had set in motion.

She lay her face against mine and Mel's voice whispered in my ear. "I only got a minute with Isaac watching for me, so listen close. Him's got his claws in Miss Priscilla again. She's his other plan. Now, I want you to remember the thing happened to you when the *bokor* touched you— remember it for me. Then you got to find a bias, you hear? Find—"

She suddenly jerked away. The nails of one hand raked my cheek as she bent back. It was like watching a sapling being pulled toward the ground. She bowed so far back that she seemed to be staring at the ceiling. In a corset, that should have been impossible without snapping her ribs.

Priscilla moaned and backed away from her.

Dickens bounded to her and grabbed her by the shoulders. Something like an electrical charge flung him into the chair he'd sat in.

Mrs. Dickens drew an awful rasp of a breath. Her hand reached out and caught my forearm so hard she might have crushed it. "Him's here!" she cried. "Isaac!" Her head twisted to the side and water poured from her mouth onto the carpet. Her face gleamed with sweat, but no longer bore any trace of Mel. Her mouth worked as if whoever was operating it didn't know how to any longer.

Then she simply collapsed. Her hand pulled me with her, and I caught her. "Kate, oh Lord, *Kate!*" Dickens scrambled up and together we lowered her into her chair.

She didn't respond. Her head hung limply to the side, but she was only unconscious.

Anguished, Dickens looked up at me. "What was that? What ghost spoke through her? It *knew* you."

I didn't answer. My eyes were burning and I looked away from him. I could still taste her lips, breath.

But he would not let it go. "What did she whisper to you? Something about a bias? A bias toward what?"

I shook my head, rubbed at my eyes. "I don't know, sir. I don't know what just happened. I don't know what she meant." I felt my cheek where she'd scratched it.

Miss Priscilla, still pressed to the door, begged, "Wake her up. Please."

Dickens went down on one knee as if proposing, then began rubbing his thumbs across her eyebrows from the center out, maybe three or four times.

Her head bobbed, came up. She moaned and her eyelids fluttered open.

"Charles," she said, almost dreamily. "Did I— Oh, I did, didn't I? I went under. I can see it in your face. What happened?" She looked at me, at Miss Priscilla.

For once Mr. Dickens had no words, but could only shake his head. She brushed back his hair.

"You were asleep," Miss Priscilla said. She'd mastered her fear and came forward, around the chair, her hands out. The two women linked hands.

"I didn't mean to— You could still work your skills on Mrs. Tyler, couldn't you?" his wife asked brightly.

"No," he answered. "That's quite enough demonstration for tonight."

"Absolutely," Miss Priscilla agreed, dissembling. "Thank you for showing me its efficacy, Mr. Dickens."

"Elliotson should be delighted though, yes?" Mrs. Dickens had no notion of what had occurred, but we three could hardly look at each other, and she must have noticed. "It's my fault, isn't it? This was supposed to benefit Mrs. Tyler, and I—" Her chin quivered.

"It's nothing like that," he said. He implored Miss Priscilla with his eyes.

"No, it was an amazing demonstration, Mrs. Dickens, really," she said. "But we've been so long away from the festivities. I cannot monopolize your famous husband's time. There are so many who wish to meet him still." She glanced my way. "James," she said, stepping aside.

I took my cue and went to the door, steeling myself to open it. Even as I took hold, Mr. Robert Tyler pulled it open, flinging me into the waiting hall. Nobody stood in front of the huge fanlight window.

He smiled curiously me, but spoke to the other three. "I thought I must find you all up here. Giving the Dickenses the grand tour. You know you cannot get to Father's office through that door. There's a desk nailed across it. Did you show them little Mary?" He smiled to Mrs. Dickens. "Did she? She's learned to walk, an absolute little devil too."

We let him natter away, creating a version of events that we could all live with. Standing in the hall behind him, I had become dispensable. I bowed and quickly took my leave, down the steps and then the full length of the hall. I could feel Dickens watching me go.

Descending, I kept going past the first floor all the way to the brick hall. I didn't stop until I was in my room. By then my whole body was shaking, and I folded up on my bed, my arms wrapped around myself.

She was still here. I couldn't see her, couldn't feel her, but she was still here, and I was in Hell.

Thirty-Three

It was Samuel, Tyler's body servant, who interrupted the interminable monologue of the man named Brisbane. Daniel Webster had foolishly agreed to listen to the brown-skinned, flat-nosed Polynesian in a collar gush about his useless little island called Hawaii.

Samuel carried a silver calling card tray. Tyler reached out for it, but Samuel said, "Beggin' pardon, sir, this is for Mr. Webster."

Webster turned, took the card, and jumped to his feet. "My apologies, John, Mr. Brisbane—I'm sure that we will all be visiting your paradise *very* soon—this must be dealt with immediately." And he followed close upon Samuel's heels out into the waiting hall. The stranded petitioners all stood eagerly. "Oh, sit down," he snapped, and his stentorian voice dropped every one of them. "Samuel," he asked. "Samuel, do you know, is the Green Parlor occupied?"

"No, sir, I don't. Been up here all morning." He indicated his chair just inside the waiting hall.

"Of course you have." Webster headed for the stairs.

On the back of the card was scrawled, "Have lodged at the legation. Gathering all the Foxes, will meet you within the hour to drop the axe."

Lord Ashburton had at last arrived.

⋙ ⋘

The Green Parlor was unoccupied, as he had suspected. It contained a round table, settees, and armchairs. He found James and had four chairs carried in from the East Room while he dragged two of the armchairs away from the wall and set them up facing the other four. He wondered then if his friend would even sit during what he imagined was going to be a brief caucus.

Webster found that he could not sit either, but paced to the curtains, looked out over the south portico, turned and walked back to the armchairs. He strode this circuit a dozen times before the doors from the hall opened, and the British delegation, led by Alexander Baring, Lord Ashburton, entered the room.

Pear-shaped, leaning much of his weight on his walking stick, Ashburton swayed in through the doors, the others behind him. The layout of the furniture likely gave the four members of the negotiating team some hint of how things were going to go—Webster didn't bother to see looks on their faces. He was smiling into the gray eyes of his old friend and clapping him on the back. That turned out to be one isolated pleasant moment before Baring struck. Turning around as the foursome of Cruickshank, Featherington, Ettryne, and Fox selected seats, he said, "You needn't bother sitting, gentlemen. You will not be here long enough to warm the cushions."

Despite this admonition, Featherington, horse-faced, sank down on his seat, as if stricken. One by one, in protest perhaps, the other three sat; Fox, his eyes flicking between the two men opposite, last of all.

Ashburton continued, "It is the pleasure of Her Majesty the Queen that I enter into, which is to say, overtake the negotiations between England and Secretary of State Webster concerning…well, in truth, concerning all matters betwixt us, which you have shown no capacity to resolve in well beyond a year of discussion. Therefore, you three gentlemen are henceforth relieved of your duties. I am by no means throwing you out of the legation or the city. You may continue enjoying the social season in Washington while you wait for warmer and safer weather to make your crossing. However, you will no longer be hobnobbing at the expense of Her Majesty. That will be down to myself and Ambassador Fox. You will pay room and board at the legation hereafter. Am I clear in this?"

Featherington and Cruickshank stared from Ashburton to Fox, as though they expected at any second to be told what a great jape it had all been.

Ettryne seemed to understand perfectly. His demeanor no colder than usual, he rose up, drew his walking stick like a rapier from beneath his arm, and tapped it on the table, once, twice. His lips were pressed tight and disparagingly curled. His blue eyes smoldered. "Ashes to Ashburton then," he said. He turned and strode from the room.

The other two, not to be outdone, arose together. "I don't give a farthing for your safe weather," sneered Cruickshank. "I'll sail when I like." Featherington seemed unable to think of anything more insulting to add, and simply followed.

Fox stayed at the table. "I am still the ambassador at least?" he asked meekly.

"Of course. You simply are no longer negotiating."

Fox gave a nod, then exhaled long. He said, "You've made permanent enemies there, Baring."

Ashburton looked unimpressed. He leaned forward on the table between them. "What of it? Should they defy me, any one of them, they will find themselves recalled by the Queen and most likely posted somewhere far less appealing, say, Van Diemen's Land. Let them govern a penal colony awhile if they find this task so impassable. The same applies to you, Fox, but you are going to work with me, *aren't* you?"

Fox closed his eyes, nodded.

"Good. Daniel, we will meet at the British legation house rather than here where, from what I hear, the shabbiness of the place is too disgraceful to mention."

"This would be Dickens?"

Ashburton laughed. "The young author was quite incensed. I've brought a copy of the journal with me. I doubt your president will be very much amused to find he's dwelling in a London 'gentleman's club' full of tobacco spitters and legislative imbeciles."

"Oh." He wasn't sure he would disagree.

Ashburton said, "So then, tomorrow across the park and the square."

"You make us sound like Masons, Alexander."

Ashburton laughed.

>>> <<<

When Webster next turned up at the legation, he saw no sign of the three dismissed negotiators. According to Fox, they had moved to hotels and boarding houses—except for Ettryne, who had never resided there. He had lodged at Brown's Indian Queen Hotel from the beginning, which suited what Fox perceived as "his contrary nature."

"He would get along well with John Tyler then," Webster muttered.

Two weeks later, the three men turned up at a Saturday levée. Webster did not attend, but Robert Tyler filled him in the following day.

"Fairly corned already when they arrived, and only got more so as the night wore on, like this was sort of a frolic for them. Some women complained to my wife, in particular about that fellow Cruickshank, who seemed unable to allow any remark to pass without some crude and offensive rejoinder. The other two merely goaded him on to see how far he would go."

Webster said, "I'm surprised Fox didn't have them ejected."

"Fox weren't in attendance," Robert explained. "When the party moved on to Dolley Madison's round about eleven, they all three disappeared. I expect they got lost crossing the park without a rope to lead them from tree to tree. No one complained at their absence, I assure you."

Webster replied, "I'll mention it to Ashburton." Just then he found it all rather amusing. "I hope the fools aren't expecting to secure new positions in the diplomatic sphere after *this*."

When he did describe the events to his friend, Ashburton responded, "Cruickshank at least has a military commission awaiting him back home. Let us hope we get him out of the country before he can prove his uselessness. I knew his grandfather—naval commander in the Colonial War—I really should try to rescue him."

"And the others?"

"Featherington. So aptly named. What a simple fellow, and so easily manipulated by those of stronger will."

"You refer to Lord Ettryne."

His lips pinched tight. "You heard what Fox said about his contrariness. There are those back home who would be delighted if he were to break his neck climbing a gangplank. In fact, the reason he was part of the negotiating team is that certain powerful people wished him as far away from London as possible. Van Diemen's Land will very likely *be* his next posting."

"What did he do—get a serving girl in the family way?"

Baring shook his head slowly. "It's not like that. There is something in the lineage though, like a Habsburg jaw. Sheer inbred irritant. His father was a wretched drunk who thought he was magnificent. His uncles were no better—two vainglorious fools right up to their deaths at the siege of Fort Erie."

Webster sat back. "Fort Erie," he said. "They died here?"

"Battle of Chippewa."

"Now, wait a minute. He can't be more than twenty-five."

"Twenty-nine. His father got *him* on a serving girl—you were only off by one generation, old man. Right idea though. Sent her to the continent somewhere. Inferior bloodline naturally. He did make money, but no one knows how. Came home and settled in like the plague. I predict he'll be the last of them to go. He has ridiculous sums to waste and no incentive to appease anyone. No one wants him here and no one wants him back. If we're fortunate, he'll find some other adventure on his own to cock up." He dismissed the topic with a wave of his hand.

He leaned over the map and poked his finger at it.

"Now, Daniel, about this fort—what do you call it, *Fort Blunder?*—that your people inconveniently built on our side of the border…"

⫸— ⫷

None of the trio reappeared after that, and Webster assumed they had all departed. During a session at the legation, Fox mentioned he'd heard that Featherington at least had booked passage on a ship home.

The week following, John Tyler announced that after months of rehearsing with James, his children were going to perform a brief concert at the Saturday levée. He expected his cabinet members and their families to attend, which meant that if he went, Webster would have to tolerate the likes of Abel Upshur and Hugh Swinton Legaré; and although he cared for neither man, he turned up, hauling Fletcher with him. Soon, he thought, he would be done with all this.

He was standing in the East Room alongside his son, John and Robert Tyler, Priscilla and the two children, when Cruickshank entered. Cruickshank was by himself. His frayed appearance was shocking.

The man had surely given himself up entirely to drink. His clothes were filthy as if he had taken up lodging in a gutter; his chin unshaved, his eyes red-ringed with madness. *How in Hades had he managed to get past Jasper?*

Webster tracked him as he wandered among the clusters of people like some decrepit ghost. He engaged no one in conversation, but stared about oddly, watching the dancers as if they were creatures he had never seen before. When he spotted Ambassador Fox, he immediately retreated, crossed behind the chamber orchestra, and drew up as if to hide in back of a group of socialites dressed with their ribbons and their scalloped, tiered skirts and fluttering fans, all chattering away so intensely that they didn't notice him.

He slouched closer, then all of a sudden reached out to the woman in front of him and touched, squeezed the coils of her golden hair. Shocked, she turned and slapped him. Cruickshank pulled his arms in tightly, made an apologetic, almost simpering, smile, and cast about to see if anyone else had noticed. Drummond had and was already on his way across the room, but before he could reach the socialites, Cruickshank scurried around the women, dived between a few other groups, and fled into the hall.

Drummond followed as far as the doorway and stood there looking out a moment, but then shrugged and returned to his position between the fireplace and the interconnecting door to the Green Parlor. Cruickshank was now someone else's problem.

It was simple curiosity that led Webster to pursue. The children would be playing soon, so he didn't have long. He intended to discover whether Cruickshank had left the house and if the other two scoundrels, Ettryne and Featherington, were lurking somewhere too.

He found Cruickshank seated on a low chair in the Blue Saloon with a glass of claret and a cigar. He was watching everyone above and around him like a child who'd stumbled into his parents' party, but when he noticed Webster in the doorway, he got up and quickly walked out onto the south portico. It was raining, but half a dozen or more men stood about, shielded from the rain while they smoked and jawed out there. Webster had no doubt that if he followed, Cruickshank would run onto the lawn.

Instead, he walked on into the Washington Parlor next door. There he discovered Lord Ettryne engaged in what was clearly a flirtatious conversation with a young socialite in a green gown—Tappet, he thought her name was. Like Cruickshank, Ettryne was immediately aware of Webster's scrutiny but simply ignored it, or rather, he leaned even closer to Miss Tappet and whispered something in her ear. She laughed, wide-eyed, and rapped him with her fan. "Scandalous!" she told him. "I'm ashamed even to entertain such a suggestion." Obviously not ashamed enough to walk away, although she did blush and lower her eyes upon noticing Webster's scrutiny.

Ettryne was uncommonly handsome, certainly vital—he had to give him that. And obviously unlike Cruickshank, he hadn't let the drink take him.

Webster left them and passed into the dining room for some food before the children performed. He did not encounter Featherington. Possibly the man's ship had already sailed.

Webster returned to Tyler's company. People were dancing a Virginia reel and he was clapping along. Webster spotted Ettryne again, this time at the far end of the East Room, engaged in a lively discussion with Mrs. Cornelison, who was surely twenty years his senior but acting as coquettish as a girl. Webster had never seen her behave like that. A few minutes later, the chamber orchestra finished the reel. The dancers applauded, and he glanced over to find that Ettryne had moved on to another, Señora de la Fuente, wife of one of the Spanish representatives. Her husband had been in the Blue Saloon with the other smokers.

How many of Washington's women had the man cultivated? If that was even the right word for it. Given the schedule of their negotiations, when had he found the time? Webster began to wonder if Ettryne hadn't routinely scuttled discussions in order to rendezvous with his conquests. It would also explain why he kept to a hotel where discretion was the order of the day. Yet if he was so contrary, how did he even get along with these society women? *Charm* was not a word Webster would have applied to Ettryne—at least, not until now. The man was proving something of a puzzle, an outright rake. There was but one thing to do: speak with Dolley Madison. If there was gossip (and there must be gossip given his flitting openly from woman to woman like a hummingbird seeking nectar), she would know all of it.

With the orchestra disbanded, Tyler announced a short recital. Four of the servants and Drummond the doorman began placing chairs in rows where the dancing had been.

"Webster, come along," John Tyler called. He gestured to a chair beside him. Tazewell, in his little gray tailcoat, was already seated at the piano and looking more nervous than happy. His teacher, the educated slave James Christian, finished helping arrange chairs, and walked over to stand on the far side of him. Tazewell glanced around, and Christian nodded encouragement.

Once everyone was seated, Tyler proudly introduced his son. Then Tazewell began to play a Mozart sonata that Webster had heard him practicing at least since the beginning of the year. He could not recall having heard him get through it even once without stumbling, but tonight it was as if the music possessed him. Tazewell stared at the sheets of music so hard that he might have set them on fire with his glare, and his performance was flawless. Behind him, the expression on James Christian's face was of utter disbelief.

Well now, that's most peculiar, Webster thought.

Tazewell came to the end of the piece and then sat, seemingly stunned himself, his hands folded into his lap.

Priscilla recovered from amazement first and started the applause. Shortly the entire room was standing and applauding. No doubt they, like Webster, had expected to endure politely the sort of clumsy child's public recital that echoed in every parlor in every house at one time or another. This had been as if they'd been listening to the young Mozart himself.

Another moment the boy sat, still dazed. Then he rallied, beaming, looked around at his father, at his teacher. People came up and congratulated him, shook his little hand. Tyler walked over and shook hands with Christian, saying, "James, you've done absolute wonders. I can hardly countenance what my own ears have heard. Is Alice going to amaze us as well?"

She, standing beside him, burned bright red and cast her brother a withering look, as though she thought he had played uncannily well just to upstage her. James Christian seemed uncomfortable and confused, accepting the credit from Tyler. Everybody shortly settled down and returned to their seats. By now a much larger crowd had formed. People who had fled the room before the recital had returned, and more poured in from the Green Parlor and the hallway to stand around the perimeter, even some of the servants.

Everyone watched as Alice spread out her skirt and settled upon the bench. Like her brother, she turned to look at her teacher, and he gave her the same supportive smile, although Webster detected concern in his eyes now. Was he worried that she wouldn't measure up, or that she would?

Alice faced the piano. Her eyes shifted nervously. At that moment, he almost expected her to resign.

Then, cautiously, she started to play and almost instantly a look came over her as if all the distraction of the soirée had fallen away and the music, a Chopin mazurka, had wrapped her up in its cocoon. He recognized the same spellbound look that had settled upon Tazewell.

She sailed through the mazurka: Her fingers trilled, sped and slowed, expressed the music fluidly. Then, before anyone could draw a breath, she almost immediately began one of the composer's waltzes. Her fingers shimmered over the keys. Webster couldn't imagine anyone performing it better.

Tyler leaned toward him and whispered, "By God, Webster, I wish her mother was down here to witness this. Can you believe it?"

No, he couldn't. Nor did James Christian, who looked positively awestruck, his worried gaze fixed upon Alice's fingers.

When the waltz came to an end, the applause was immediate and accompanied by various men around the room shouting "Brava!" at Alice. Like Tazewell before her, she seemed momentarily still carried away, and then blinked and came to herself as if surprised to find that she was seated at the piano. But she had the presence of mind to rise and take her bows. Her teacher was next on the bill. He had gotten to his feet and come forward to congratulate her.

Priscilla leaned over to Robert on the other side of Tyler and said to him, "I must go check on the baby." The Tylers and Webster rose to their feet.

"Surely you don't," said her husband.

"Shall we hold off from having James play then?" Tyler asked.

"Oh, no. Please continue for the enjoyment of everyone else. James will understand." She walked past them, her husband looking mildly annoyed to have his comment ignored. He often seemed sharp with her, a trait Webster didn't care for: He expected there would be repercussions later.

While people came up and congratulated the children or queued up for the punchbowls at either end of the room, he took the time to scan the room. Ettryne had gone. So had both Mrs. Cornelison and Señora de la Fuente. Surely they couldn't both be meeting with him?

Perhaps Ettryne had gone looking for Cruickshank—but, no, *there* was Cruickshank, near the Green Parlor door. It seemed the two diplomats were having nothing to do with each other tonight; and still no sign of Featherington.

Webster finally gave up watching. It wasn't important after all. He was merely satisfying his own curiosity. But he would need to speak with Dolley Madison.

Thirty-Four

James Hambleton Christian

Mr. Tyler turned to me. "Your turn next, James," he said. "Show them your worth."

I hardly heard and didn't move. I was watching Tazewell eyeing Alice as she sat beside him. From the look she threw back, it was clear that both of them had experienced a weird rapture.

Robert stood, facing the doors. I knew he was watching for Miss Priscilla. She didn't reappear, and I grabbed onto that as my excuse to Mr. Tyler. "I wouldn't want to start without her presence, sir. Why not let folks refill their cups of punch awhile longer? Give 'em more of a chance to marvel at the children's performances."

"What? Well, yes, all right, fine idea, let them." The important portion of the recital had already happened: His children had shown themselves to be musical prodigies. In fact, I was surprised he wanted me to play at all. Maybe he knew I couldn't match what we had just seen; *I* certainly knew.

When he turned away, I went straight over to the children and knelt down. "Tell me what happened when you began to play."

Alice, round-eyed, looked away as if the subject terrified her too much, but Tazewell had recovered from his experience. "Was like I was sitting and watching somebody else play. Even though they was my hands, I didn't own 'em."

Alice looked at him from the corner of her eye. "We were possessed!" she hissed.

Yes, I thought so too, but I didn't want it eating at her, for there was nothing she could do and it was over. So I lied. "Oh, you were transported, is all. Why, every great musician sooner or later is lifted halfway to heaven by the music itself." I doubt Miss Alice believed me, but she allowed herself the comfort of pretending that she did.

Right then I half-expected the same was about to happen to me.

After fifteen minutes, when Miss Priscilla hadn't returned and everyone else who wanted to had made good their escape from the room, Mr. Tyler said, "You must play, James, or I will be the one who looks bad."

"Yes, sir."

Mr. Robert was still watching for his wife, but I walked over to the piano. I wanted to tell Mr. Tyler that he ought to want to prevent me from playing right now, but I just obeyed, sat on the bench, found my music sheets and set them before me. Glanced around the room once more. About half the chairs were empty and hardly anyone standing seemed to be paying me any attention; but I was convinced that Mel's sorcerer must be among them. He'd had his amusement, making his puppets play.

There was Webster, looking stern and troubled; Upshur, the man who'd referred to Renehan as a *mudsill*; Fox, the sneering little ambassador; there came Deborah though the door from the Green Parlor, holding a tray with a few glasses of wine on it; beside her, the Spanish delegate, de la Fuente, engaged in some heated argument with his wife; and beyond them, the Englishman Cruickshank, looking wholly wretched like somebody'd given him Jesse by dragging him down Pennsylvania Avenue—people in all sorts of states, but of all of them, only Cruickshank was staring my way. Straight at me.

With one eye on him, I started to play. When I wasn't seized by some unaccountable force, I stumbled. Had to stop, apologize for my nervousness, and begin again.

That was when Cruickshank shouted, "Don't you let him play!" and came charging at me through the crowd, everybody turning, twisting around. The first person he shoved was Deborah. She tumbled out of sight behind the rows of chairs. Furiously, he yanked empty chairs aside, shoved men and women out of his path, clambered almost to where Daniel and Fletcher Webster sat. Fletcher stood up pugnaciously.

Drummond was hauling after the man now, and Renehan burst in from the Green Parlor door, took one look at Deborah getting to her feet, and bolted after his brother. People shouted, shrieked. Fox screamed, "Cruickshank, stop!"

Cruickshank dodged a swing from Fletcher Webster and, wheeling around him, cuffed Tazewell to the floor. Robert Tyler grabbed for him, got a handful of jacket and pulled, tearing it, throwing Cruickshank off-balance before he could reach Mr. Tyler, who now seemed to be his objective. He fell against the back of the piano hard enough that it rocked. His crazy eyes met mine over the top of it—eyes holding, pleading. Then he pushed off and ran.

Drummond, scant inches behind, brushed past the piano, swiping at the air. Cruickshank made it to the drapes, threw open the balcony door, and sprang onto the promenade roof of the east colonnade.

Martin Renehan shot past, and that was too much. I took off after him, piano recital be damned.

It was raining good and steady outside. I jumped to the roof in time to watch Cruickshank run straight to the end of it. He never slowed, never looked back, but raced right off the end as if he expected to fly away.

I heard the soft thump of his body hitting the ground before I'd caught up with the two doormen. We walked to the edge.

Below, Cruickshank lay in darkness, an ill-formed shape. He might have been alive. It wasn't that far a drop.

Renehan asked, "Will someone tell me what in feckin' hell that was about?"

"Man didn't want James to play," Drummond said. "He was crazy, Martin."

"Was he?" He was asking me.

"I don't know. He looked scared, like he couldn't help himself."

We headed back inside. Behind us the night seemed to flicker with blue lightning. The room was still in some chaos. Robert and the Websters, and now Samuel, stood around Mr. Tyler and the children. "Good thing Priscilla wasn't here," Mr. Tyler was telling his son. "She'd have been right in his path." He turned to the doormen and me. "James. Gentlemen." He seemed nonplussed that we didn't have Cruickshank in custody.

"Excuse us, Mr. Tyler," I said. "Cruickshank ran off the end of the colonnade."

As I spoke, I glimpsed Robert Tyler, his back to us all, watching the doors. Miss Priscilla stood there. She seemed as dazed as the children after they had performed. The *children!*

They sat together. Tazewell was all right. Alice appeared shaken and exhausted, flustered but fine.

Renehan said, "Osbert, you stay here, guard Mr. Tyler. James." He and I ran for the Green Parlor.

At that end of the room, Deborah was picking up broken wine glasses and setting them on her tray. To my surprise, a few of the ladies were doing their best to help her, though they couldn't bend over far enough to pick anything up.

The Green Parlor had one door letting onto the south portico, disguised as a window, same as in the Washington Parlor. We ran out and down the steps, then quickly across the wet lawn. I wished I'd brought a lantern.

By the time we reached the end of the colonnade we could see just well enough to make him out. It looked as if he'd tried to crawl a ways. Steam rose off him in the rain. A lot of steam.

Renehan threw an arm out and stopped me. "Ya smell it?"

I did: The terrible stink of the hanged man from when I was nine. I backed instinctively away. "But what's burned," I asked. "It's been raining out for hours."

Renehan turned away from the body, saying nothing. I gave it a last look— just a stretched-out lump on the grass.

Back inside, people shied from us as we passed among them. We were wet, scared, and angry. It must have radiated off us.

In the East Room, some guests still stood around the punchbowls and chatted as if the events of this evening had been staged for their entertainment. I expected if Mr. Tyler had been murdered in front of them, they would have been discussing it the same way.

Samuel stood with Mr. Tyler, but Mr. Robert, Priscilla, and the children were gone. So was Drummond. "I sent him along to guard Robert and the children, to be safe," Mr. Tyler explained. "I believe Daniel and I were his intended targets. Daniel was concerned that Lord Ashburton might be included, a plot, and has gone to make sure he's safe. What did you find?"

We reported that Cruickshank was dead on the lawn.

"Indeed," said Mr. Tyler. "We had a madman in our midst, one who had fallen on drink and probably laudanum for his courage from the look of him."

Renehan and I said nothing.

⟫⟫- ⟪⟪⟪

Tyler sent us back out to place the body under the east promenade for the night, but the body was gone and there was no sign of him. "He can't have been alive," Renehan said. In the morning, he, Garvine, and Drummond roamed all over the south lawn and carriage paths, and all the way to the Treasury Building. There wasn't a sign of him.

I asked each of the children to attempt their performances of the previous night. Tazewell in particular was scared even to sit before the piano. His sister screwed up her courage, though, plunked down on the bench and began to play. Nothing took hold of her. She performed well, if a little trepidatiously, which is to say, about how she played the Chopin piece any other time. Then Tazewell sat beside her. She drew back her hands and he started in on the Mozart, his left fingers not quite executing the Alberti bass.

"It didn't come back," said Alice. Tazewell stopped playing.

"I would have been surprised if it did. It's a rare experience. Trouble is, your father's like to have you play something at every levée from now on."

"Oh no," Alice despaired.

"What do we do, James?" asked Tazewell.

"Best thing I can think of is tell him you got to learn a new piece. Going to take months."

Alice brightened. "Might take till Christmas."

"I expect it might, indeed." I gave her a wink. We were conspirators against the rest of the family, as we'd been now and again back at Walnut Grove.

That night it rained again. Mr. Tyler asked for a bottle of sauterne to accompany the dinner of quail on a bed of sweet potato mash. Tall George retrieved it from the cellar for him.

After everyone had eaten and turned in, and after I'd finished blacking his and Mr. Robert's boots in the mess, I retreated to my chamber, perched in my rocking chair, and contemplated the last third of that same bottle that George had opened. It was an old and dusty one. I noticed as I sipped the sweet wine that the bottle had been scratched with a nail or something. I made out "T:J" on the side and had to wonder if it had belonged to old Thomas Jefferson, bless him. His wine was a blissful, golden nectar.

As I stared at the rippling blue glass, something moved within it—a shadow-shape. I lowered the bottle quick.

Zenobia stood in my doorway. She was shifting from leg to leg, her expression like she had something huge to tell that she couldn't find the start of.

"Here," I said, offering the bottle. She didn't come nearer. "Just say it, girl." I had to chuckle. I sounded to myself like Renehan.

"*Ouangas* is gone," she said. "A lot of 'em."

Hadn't Mel stood right there and said almost the same thing? It was all beginning again. "What's a lot of them?"

"Come on 'n' I'll show you." She didn't move, waiting for some sign from me.

"All right." I shook my head, set the bottle aside, then got out of the rocker, feeling old-man stiff. When I looked up, it was Mel in the doorway, not Zenobia, waiting on me like all the other times when she was agitated, and I gasped and stumbled back against my chair, sent it rocking. It clipped me hard in the back of the leg and I had to catch myself so as not to fall.

"What's wrong, James?" she asked, but she was Zenobia again and nobody else.

I put my hands to my face and rubbed myself awake. There was no ghost here, I told myself. Didn't need to be. My thoughts were all possessed with her. Dickens and his wife had brought her back, let me hear her, smell her, even taste her, and I had been clinging to that shiver of her. It was fading, no matter how I worked to keep it there. The more it faded, the more I sought her in every shadow's line, every glint of light. I was stamping her on every surface with all my will, and even so, she was almost gone.

I snapped at Zenobia. "Nothing's wrong. Just banged my leg on the damn chair is all. Let's get us a lamp and you show me what you're talking about."

Instead of going upstairs she led me along the brick hall to the east door. The raindrops pattered against the door like a hundred little fingertips drumming for us to open up and let them in.

"You don't mean to say we're going out in *that*?"

She reached for the candle lamp I'd swiped from the kitchen. I gave it to her and she flung open the door, then led the way quickly under the open roof section of the colonnade. The rain didn't reach us there. It was a warm evening, but our breaths steamed in the candlelight.

A few steps along, she stopped and lowered the lantern. On the ground in front of her lay shreds of something—scraps of burlap and colored cloth, bits of animal bones, teeth, but mostly a dark, smeary mass that seemed resistant to the rain.

I crouched over it, but she tugged on me. "James, don't touch it. He maybe cursed it for the likes of us." Looking around—out the end of the colonnade, into the empty rainy night—I could see nothing. Of course, our light blinded us to the darkness farther out.

Zenobia started singing a *priyè*, her voice shaky, scared. From the shreds of cloth, I guessed I was looking at maybe three or four different pouches and their contents. Zenobia finally stopped singing.

"Where these come from?" I asked.

"I don't know. Can't tell 'em apart. I been using the same cloth what Mel did. Might be more blown off 'cross the lawn too."

"When did they turn up?"

"I think after the levée."

"What—last night's levée?"

She nodded. "Cain't be for sure, but I check every few days on account of Mel, she always said to be vigilant, else that thing git loose in here again."

That thing. "How'd you know to look for them here?"

"Didn't. Ethel and Mariama found they some bits of calico 'smorning on the way to the privy. Skeered Mariama half outen her wits. That poor Gullah woman's sure they's a *haant* livin' here, come all the way from Charleston to suck out her marrow."

"More'n one." I didn't realize I'd said it out loud until she was staring around at me with her wide eyes. I didn't want to discuss any of that, so I said, "Got to be from someplace."

She agreed. "I looked in the dining room. Two of the *ouangas* ain't there no more."

"But the rooms were full of people. How's he doing it?" I was asking myself more than her. How was the sorcerer rummaging through rooms where people were milling about all the time? He would need to distract everyone, divert them... And suddenly there was the explanation for what had happened last night. "You were down in the kitchen all night, weren't you? You didn't see how the children's performances drew everybody out of the rooms up and down the hall. I mean *everybody*, Zenobia. Between them and that man, Cruickshank, attacking Tazewell."

"How could he search the rooms that fast?"

"I don't know. But that has to be it. He's got to be confused now. Thought he put an end to all this."

"I don't got her skill, James. I'm only a *hounsi*. She wasn't but started teaching me. Takes years to get powerful and call down the *lwa* like Mel could."

"But just now you was singing same as her. I know that *priyè* even if I don't understand what it does. And if some of the charms are gone, you make more. I know she taught you that."

"We don't got enough *maudit* but for a handful. We's almost used what come after that last time I went with her to the market."

That memory stayed shut and I wasn't going to let it open. "So get more," I said.

She pushed out her lip. "I can try. Know who she talked to at the market. I can ask."

"Good. Tomorrow, right away, but you don't go alone, you hear? You go with me or Cyrus, or even one of the doormen. From now on, you don't leave here by yourself for any cause, even if somebody is sick and dying and they send for you by name—*especially* if they send for you by name."

She stared scrunched up at me at first as though I was talking nonsense. Then her expression melted to comprehension. "Oh," she said.

I took the candle lamp back from her. "We need to go assess the damage."

⟫⟫⟫ ⟪⟪⟪

We climbed the service stairs to the first floor. Keeping the lamp inside the tight space, I looked out.

The cross hall chandeliers had been doused and all the rooms lay silent and dark. Tyler could have been working in his office upstairs, but I expected he, too, had turned in.

We strode quick across the hall and around the heat-retaining screens still set up outside the State Dining Room. Once inside it, I closed the doors behind me. I took a table candlestick from one sideboard and lit it off the lamp, handed it to Zenobia.

We went hunting. "Four charms in this room," she said. One was a feathered *pakét kongo* of Mel's making. It lay inside the furnace vent, nearly invisible and impossible to reach without taking off the vent cover. While she looked for that, I sought the ones she had pressed deep in the backs of the sideboards. Three of them, all were missing. Might have been the shreds we'd found outside.

"Someone thinks he unprotected this room. Or maybe couldn't reach the *pakét kongo* nohow. Not with folks coming and going all the time, so it's still there." She drew a long breath. "This be the only room, I got enough to fix it."

"Fix what?" asked a voice from the other end, and we both jumped. It was Jasper. He hadn't made a sound opening the doors. Our candles barely illuminated him there. He didn't have a light of his own. "I saw your light through the glass of the vestibule wall."

"Fix the curtains," Zenobia answered him. "Some of these is torn from sun rot, need stitching and maybe new cloth." It wasn't a lie. Half the long curtains in this room needed patching or replacing. The question was how much of the rest of our conversation Jasper had heard.

"Why you looking at 'em this time of night?" he asked.

I said the first thing that came to mind. "Didn't want to disturb the family with it."

He stood a moment as if considering that absurdity. "Mmmm," he said. "Well, I'm after turning in. Don't you two frisk in them curtains so much you pull 'em down while you're *fixing* 'em." He shut the door.

"'Night, Mr. Jasper," Zenobia called. We stayed exactly where we were until it seemed certain he had retreated to his room. "That man thinks—"

"Yes, I gleaned what he thinks. Better than what I came up with."

"Mel for awhile, she thought it might be him on account of he can come and go as he pleases in here."

"He can," I agreed. "Which is why it isn't him. That charm in the vent wouldn't be there anymore. He could get tools, come in here just like now, pull that cover off any night he liked."

"*Pakét* would burn him good if he touched it."

I walked over to her. "Come on. We have more rooms to search."

Our sorcerer had been busy. The charm behind the portrait of George Washington was gone, as were a half-dozen hidden throughout the Blue Saloon—only one, fitted up into the bottom of one settee, had been overlooked.

A chandelier hung in the middle of the Green Parlor with a small marble-topped table beneath it. The table had a couple little drawers in it, which I'd never much noticed. Zenobia pulled one of them out, knelt, and reached in behind it. "Gone," she said. She slid the drawer back in.

Another charm had been hidden behind the overmantel mirror above the fireplace, but that, too, was missing.

"No protection at all in this room now."

Rain tapped at the leftmost window in a sudden barrage. The south portico didn't shield it. The ceiling creaked then as if someone was awake and walking around above us. I found myself turning in place, looking first at the window, then up into that darkness, and finally at the reflection of our lights in that unprotected mirror. I whispered, "Where is the hateful shadow then?"

"I don't know. Mel, she trapped that *tebo* up in the attic. Said she'd kept it from finding its body." Wan lightning flickered outside.

"Body? I know she called it the *vessel*."

She nodded. "*Tebo's* made out of something that was alive. So the vessel is like a body."

"How the Sam Hill does anyone hide a body in this house?"

She frowned. "I don't know," she murmured. "Mel never said."

Right then was when one of the narrow doors from the East Room started to swing open behind her.

"Zenobia," I hissed, "come over here right now." Stretched out my hand, but I couldn't help that I glanced past her, and she couldn't help looking there too. She practically jumped the distance to me.

The door pulled back, and a shadow moved into the recess. I thought, *Well, I asked for it, didn't I, and here it was*. I wasn't close enough to the fireplace even to grab a poker in defense.

Then the shape moved to where my lamplight fell upon it, and became Martin Renehan, himself about as bug-eyed as I felt. He recognized us in the same instant. "Great snakes, you two are as quiet going about as a coach-and-four."

"What are you doing in the East Room?" I asked, and when he didn't answer right off, God forgive me, I thought sure it was him we were hunting: He'd come out of the world of the plug-uglies at a convenient time, could have known, even hired, the men who killed Mel. He'd said he and his companions were sent for by Mayor Seaton, but had anybody ever checked it? Had Tyler or Webster even inquired, after the mobs convinced us how much we needed them? What did any of us know about Martin Renehan that he hadn't told us himself? In two seconds I had all but indicted him.

Then, quietly, he replied, "I'm waiting."

"What for?" Zenobia asked.

Renehan pressed his palm against his forehead and smoothed it over his hair. "Well, there's no keepin' it now, is there? Best if you see for yourselves. Come on. Bring your candle. Just the one if you don't mind."

I had Zenobia blow out hers and leave it on the round table.

The doorway into the empty East Room echoed with creaking floorboards. Then we'd reached the immense carpet and went silently. The rain spattered across the windows in sweeps. Lightning flashed brighter now, throwing shadows, glittering off the three enormous chandeliers like to set them ablaze. Thunder rumbled sometime after. The rain had become a thunderstorm.

Most of the chairs, couches, and divans were still pushed near the walls as if the levée had just broken up. The chair Mr. Tyler had sat in watching Tazewell and Alice had been pulled farther into the room and turned to face the double doors from the hall. Renehan went straight to it and sat. I had the impression it was where he'd been when he heard us next door.

He gestured us over. Zenobia eyed him, then me. I shook my head indecisively, didn't know what to think. She walked over to him and sat on the piano bench.

I could stay here or follow. I followed. Set the lamp on top of the piano and sat beside her. We all three faced the main doorway.

"Martin, what is it we're waiting for?" I asked.

"If things run true to form, you'll know soon enough. Just don't move from there no matter what."

I had to figure it wouldn't be a visitation. Renehan would have been as scared as any of us if ghosts were passing through here. He didn't seem scared. Grim, more like.

It wasn't long before half of the doorway into the hall grew darker: One of the doors had opened. Zenobia sucked in her breath and grabbed onto my hand.

A filmy shape flowed into the room, then came straight toward us as if drawn to the light on the piano. She passed directly before us, never hesitating, never glancing our way. Straight to the center, the door that let out onto the colonnade roof.

Miss Priscilla. Her eyelids were closed, as if her soul was still asleep upstairs. Eyes just like Mrs. Dickens. It chilled my blood to see it.

"Look," Zenobia said.

In her hands, the way she might have held a baby chick, Priscilla carried a burlap pouch stitched roughly with appendages like a four-armed starfish.

One of Mel's *ouangas*.

She reached the balcony door and drew it open. Wind whipped in, billowed the curtains out so far that the sashes came loose and the drapes flapped like batwings around her. Our candle blew out.

Zenobia sprang from the piano bench. Even as Renehan hissed for her to stop and got to his feet, she snatched the burlap pouch out of Miss Priscilla's hands and backed aside. Priscilla didn't seem to notice. She started out, oblivious of the rain spraying across her.

Renehan ran to her. "James, help me," he called.

We took her by the arms, guided her back inside. Renehan pulled the door shut after her. She was dripping wet, her hair stuck to her face and her soaked nightgown pressed to her body. Her bare feet squeaked on the floor. Her mouth was moving as if she was speaking to us in her sleep, but I couldn't hear a word. Despite our holding her upper arms, her fingers kept working as if she was tearing something apart. Then one hand flipped into the air, flinging something.

Once she'd accomplished that, her head rolled back, and if we hadn't been holding her, she would have collapsed. Renehan directed us to where we laid her down on a divan. Outside, lightning cracked. She jerked, made a moan as if it had stung her.

"You knew it would be Miss Priscilla," I said.

"Third night after a levée I've encountered her," Renehan said. "Every time she's got them things in her hands, goes out to that little balcony and rips 'em to bits."

"Why didn't you tell us?"

The light from the lamp caught the flint in Renehan's eye. "Tell you *what*, exactly? What is it I'm looking at here then? You two know?"

"It's her's been scattering them," Zenobia said. "All them bits down below."

All the anger seemed to leak out of Renehan. He sat on the edge of the divan, watching her. "First time, I was making late rounds," he said, "and here she come down the stairs. I thought, well, and she knows I'm down here on duty and has come to see *me*, on account of I'd expressed my, ah, opinion that there might be something between us if she allowed it. I mean, Christ, man, the way her husband treats her, neglects her, with all his politics and running off to Philadelphia and New York for his business. She's tending a babe, this house, and every week the dinners, the parties… And she does it like it's nothin'. So I had this fool idea of what was what. Only, she come down the stairs and didn't even see me. Eyes closed as a corpse." He pointed to Zenobia. "Had one of them cloth things in her hands—"

"*Ouanga*," Zenobia said.

"She walked right out there and tore it up, tossed it off the promenade, and like that she whipped right around and swooned to the floor there. I thought she was walking in her sleep. I shook her, tried to wake her. That stuff on her hands stank like swamp mud and shite, but she wouldn't wake. Then her eyes opened, and I started to say something, but they weren't her eyes, you know. Was like somebody else was lookin' through them." His voice went tight. "And familiar, like I must have *seen* that person before. She got right up and walked back to her room. I chased her up the staircase, watched the door close after her.

"The next night I waited and she didn't come. Then a week ago she comes floating down the stairs and through the doors with a handful of them things, repeats everything exactly as before, only this time I don't so much as touch her, ya know? She collapses, and I just wait. You watch now."

As if his words were a cue, Miss Priscilla sat up on the divan. It was clear she had no awareness of us nor of her own storm-soaked state. She came straight at us. The dim hall light revealed her expression, and it was all wrong. It wasn't just her eyes, more like a change in the the way her face pulled itself.

We got out of her way, and she walked stiffly out of the room, leaving a trail of wet footprints. Not one of us moved for some time after.

"Tell me, what sort of sleepwalking would you call that exactly?" Renehan asked.

I looked up past the nearest chandelier into the blackness of a ceiling twenty feet overhead, smeared with lamp smoke and covered in cobwebs. All the demons of Hell could have hid up there, listening to us. I hated this room, from the first time I'd entered it.

"I got some wine downstairs," I said. "Not enough, but it'll get us started."

We sat at the mess table. Renehan left and returned with a jar from his room, a clear brew he called *poteen* that made my eyes water. Recovering from my first, and last, sip, I said, "You could start fires with this."

"Oh, you could burn down the city," he agreed, and took another pull off the jar like it was nothing at all.

Seated around the table there we told what we knew. I went first because my story came first. Told them of Isaac and General Harrison, of the room nobody could find, and the lamplighter. I couldn't recall whether Zenobia had heard any of this.

The look on Renehan's face likely mirrored mine the day Isaac had told me his story up in the stables. Then I explained how he had drowned, and where Mel had seen his ghost on the bench beside us. They both gave that bench a look like it had already jumped at them. Renehan crossed himself and then flicked a tiny bit of his *poteen* in its direction—"libation for Isaac, hey?" he said.

When I got to the part where Mel wouldn't let anybody set foot in here till she had spread cornmeal everywhere, I let Zenobia take over the telling. *She* could explain *veves* and *ouangas* and *pakét kongos*, and how Mel used all those *vodou* things against the *tebo* haunting this house. Renehan held up a hand.

"I've no idea what you're talkin' about, all these things."

Zenobia considered awhile. "Think of a *tebo* like a mob you can't see and what can slide out of any mirror or glass or any other thing that's like to shine. Gets its life from the one who creates it, the *bokor*."

"And what the hell's a *bokor* when it's home?"

"The one who controls that mob," I said.

"A sorcerer," Zenobia told him.

I went on, "We been trying for almost a year to figure who it is. Mel had us looking for someone who watched everybody else, but we've never been able to find him anymore than we could figure how he reached the private floor, the attic. Now we know that, thanks to you. I'm sure it sounds like superstitious balderdash."

"It does, just a mite."

"That's what I thought at the beginning, and I'm not sure I believe half of it even now."

"Oh, I don't mean to say I'm not believing it." He took another pull from his jar and offered it to us. We both respectfully declined. He set it down and then crossed his arms with a look on his face of casting his thoughts someplace. "When I was a lad," he said, "my gran back in Armagh told me about this thing she called a *fetch*, supposed to be an agent of the devil. 'Course, to gran, everything peculiar was the devil, so I wasn't much impressed when she said it.

"A fetch, see, was like a double, like a person you knew, only it was never them at all, but some evil thing that made itself appear like them. She claimed she'd met a fetch herself on the cathedral road—looked like a midwife she knew until she come near and saw how the woman's face was pulled all wrong, where her skin didn't fit and her eyes was black and dead. Was like someone else wearing that midwife's skin. Startled gran so much she got herself off the road and hid in the field next to it. She watched the fetch stride up into a house where a new baby'd been born some few days earlier. The real midwife—the one the fetch was imitating—had delivered it. Quick as you like, the fetch plucked that babe's life like a flower and come right back out again and headed down the road before the family knew what had happened. Was my gran saved the poor midwife in the end, because she'd seen it all. They never found the fetch—leastways not looking like that woman. They came upon a lump o' something sticky and black like had crawled out of a bog. That was all that was left of it. No saving the baby though. Was too late for that."

I sat up straight. "The lump in the road, did it stink to blazes?"

"It did indeed. And how would you be knowin' that?"

So I told them both the story of Alice's encounter with black funeral crepe in the East Room. "But surely that's not what we saw this night. Miss Priscilla was herself, not something pretending to be her."

He shook his head. "All I know," he answered, "is what I told yas—three different times now she comes down the stairs with whatever you call 'em, and afterwards goes back up, eyes wide open now but sound asleep."

"It's been more than three times," I said, then had to explain how, after the very first levée, Mel had encountered Miss Priscilla sleepwalking in the East Room.

"What, she was tearing up them things even then?" Renehan guessed.

"No. It was… Mel said it was like Miss Priscilla had come down there to meet somebody. Only, same as with Alice, when Mel pulled aside the drapes where he hid, there was nothing, nobody."

Renehan didn't like the sound of that, and banged the jar down on the table. Zenobia jumped.

I said, "We hadn't been here but two months and the sorcerer'd already gained access to Miss Priscilla."

Softly, Zenobia added, "He needed her to go where he can't git at. All this time, hasn't been him removing the *ouangas*. Been Miss Priscilla."

"All right. But how could he know he would need her? Mel had only just made up a few charms that night." Even as I asked, I heard Mel's words explaining: *Wants to harm everyone. This is punishment.* He wasn't going after Priscilla for the charms. He was going after her because he could. It was revenge on the Tylers.

"What difference does it make?" Renehan charged. "Goddamit, he's got his claws in her!"

The phrase startled me, sent me tumbling down into a well of memory: Close by me, Mrs. Dickens said the same words: *Got his claws in Miss Priscilla.*

In a kind of dream, I recited, "None of us can keep him out. She's his other plan alongside the *tebo*."

Remember the thing that happened to you… Remember it for me.

I wasn't in the mess anymore. I was standing in the waiting hall as a wave of blackness struck me down. I cringed at a sting to my hand, looked down, saw the white glove beside it, the fingers gripping the shining knob of a walking stick. Right there beneath the silver ferrule a needle protruded, a drop of my blood on its tip. Confused and already losing consciousness, I tried to see him, my poisoner. The memory swirled, started to sink, dragged down. Then Mel's voice: *Remember it.*

I had interrupted him in his hunt for the charms harming and limiting his *fetch*, his *tebo*, whatever name we called it. I'd very nearly caught him outright where he didn't belong. He hadn't killed me, but only because he hadn't been prepared. It was a mistake he would never make twice.

Mel had said we should be on the lookout for a man watching everyone. But we were wasting our time, because he didn't have to watch everyone. He had Miss Priscilla and who knew how many other surrogates wandering through the parlors, the house, searching for the charms. *"The man who watches everyone,"* Mel had said, and I recalled noticing how last night during the recital Webster had kept staring off into the crowd. Somehow the Great God Daniel had gotten the scent too. *Lucky,* I thought, *that you didn't find him, Mr. Webster, or you'd be wherever Cruickshank is tonight, and I'll wager he ain't enjoying the location.*

The children's performance had been a jape, misdirection. He was laughing at us in our hopeless ignorance, teasing with his powers.

I focused hard upon the black and deadly stick where it joined the white glove, followed up the curve of his arm, to the sharp and handsome face and those eyes, blue and cold as snow in the moonlight, that withdrew into the blackness that cloaked him—

"*James.*" Renehan was on his feet and snapping his fingers in front of me.

I blinked at him, at Zenobia. It took me a moment to realize where I was.

Tentatively, Renehan held out that jar of liquid fire of his.

This time I took a pull that made my eyes water. I hissed and just kept from choking. "I saw him," I wheezed. "I saw the *bokor.* Zenobia, I know who he is."

Thirty-Five

Today Tazewell Tyler was Major Ridge, a famous Cherokee warrior, and as such he prowled the house, unseen and silent. He had sneaked the length of the first floor, eluding Robert and the doorman Jasper and whoever it was Jasper had delivered to Robert in the Green Parlor. He had made his way to the west stairs and now crawled from the top step to the stairwell doorway to take the lay of the land up here in the "mountains."

At the moment, the changing of his mother's linens was in progress. Three chambermaids entered the small room, and a moment later she emerged out the doorway in a deep blue dressing gown, carried by two of them and Devonee. They would be taking her down to the outdoor privy, or maybe to the Blue Saloon. Days when the house was quiet, she liked to sit an hour in there before supper and look out across the south portico at the carriages and horses that passed.

After she was gone, Sally came out of the room alone, carrying the covered chamberpot and a bundle of bedding, and heading straight at him.

Tazewell pressed back against the wall, lying flat. Late afternoon sun poured through the enormous fanlight window behind him. Sally, shielding her eyes against the light, walked right past him and down the stairs. The stink of the chamberpot wafted briefly behind her. The floor lay silent. The enemy was gone.

Tazewell, brave Cherokee, got up and ran for his mother's empty room. As proof of his skill, he would get in there, make off with some trinket or other, and then present it to his mother later like an elaborate magic trick. She was always amazed, always wanted to know how he had done it; but, of course, he could not tell her.

Once in the room he didn't expect to be interrupted, but the sound of approaching footsteps made him dive for cover under Devonee's cot. The schrank hid most of it, and so he dared to stick his head out a ways. His sister-in-law came into the room.

Tazewell hadn't realized that Priscilla was returned from her afternoon of paying calls upon the society people who had left their cards. She had taken him along once because he'd begged to go, and they'd visited some old Methodist woman who wanted to meet the president's children and had repeatedly pinched his cheeks. She had smelled like horehound drops, which she kept offering him the whole time he was there. He'd never asked to go calling on people again.

He thought maybe he would spring out and scare Priscilla. He peered around the schrank.

She'd paused just inside the door. There was something wrong about the way she stood there—her arms bent, hands raised in front of her. She turned in a slow circle, and he noticed that her eyelids were drawn low, her eyes showing only a slit of white. He'd always thought Priscilla was the most beautiful woman he had ever seen, but now she was unsettling, strange. Her head tilted as if she was listening for some sound so faint that Tazewell couldn't hear it, though he was compelled to strain for it too.

She began then walking a slow circuit of the room, and he drew all the way back against the wall. He still wanted to surprise her, but for the first time in his life he found her frightening.

The doors of the schrank opened, shelves slid in and out, and then the doors closed again. Her feet came to the side of the cot. Stopped. Turned, pointed toward his mother's bed.

Then all at once her head appeared, upside down, between her ankles. He almost screamed. Her eyes remained slitted, blank, but otherwise looked straight at him. It was impossible—despite her corset she had to be folded in half at the waist like someone in a carnival.

She grinned. Then her head withdrew. He expected her to reach under and grab him. She surely had seen him, how could she not? But she moved on, over to the mirror.

The base of the mirror leaned forward a moment, then rocked back, flat on the floor. It had taken two men just to move that mirror across the room so that his mother didn't have to look at it. Priscilla had pushed it as if it weighed nothing.

He wanted to bolt, scramble out and run; but he would never escape before she caught him.

Across the room now, she stood beside his mother's bed. He elbow-walked himself to where he could see her again.

With one hand she reached down and lifted the stripped mattress up until it stood on edge. Then she leaned forward and snatched something off the slats. He couldn't see it, but he could see a brown stain on bottom of the mattress, a shape kind of like that of an onion bulb.

Priscilla dropped the mattress. Her hand, clutching the object tightly, began trembling. She made an odd moan, lowered her head as though struck by pain, then took a step and nearly fell. She caught herself against the schrank. Pushed off to the door. Her steps were hesitant, like somebody drunk. She pressed around the jamb and out of sight.

Tazewell crawled quickly from under the cot, crept to the doorway in time to see Priscilla launch herself straight across the hall.

As she stumbled beneath the hall chandelier, it began to swing on its stem as if a hard wind accompanied her.

She reached the empty guest room directly opposite on the north side of the hall, opened the door, and flung the thing she held inside. Closing the door again, she leaned awhile against the wall, long enough that he saw blood dripping from her fingertips. She turned, facing him, and he lurched out of sight until he heard her retreat down the hall. He dared another look around the jamb. She plodded with increasing steadiness, cupping her wounded hand in the other.

When she had gone into her own room, Tazewell sneaked into the hall. He stared after her, trying for the life of him to understand the impossible things that had just occurred, wiping at his eyes.

He crept across the hall to the guest room door, but backed away from the blood on the knob and fled into the stairwell, down the stairs, Major Ridge and all the Cherokee nation forgotten.

>>> ‑ <<<

It was done!

Webster could have danced a jig. Together, he and Lord Ashburton had sat down in the Department of State Building and signed the treaty he'd all but given up any hope of achieving. Now the northern boundary was defined all the way to the Rocky Mountains, and slaving had been abolished—which would infuriate Tyler but was, in reality, more a victory on paper for Baring than in practice. Slaves would simply be run to some Caribbean isle and brought over clandestinely, a matter of concern to someone, but not him. It was *signed*. And as he climbed the steps to Dolley Madison's house, he could feel the office of secretary of state sloughing away like a shed skin.

He had brought along a celebratory bottle of wine so that she would not have to expend her own limited supplies. Though she remained close friends with Letitia, she was the first person he thought of not connected to Tyler's government nor the pestering Whig Party who would toast the treaty with him.

Indeed, they sat in her parlor and chatted like the old friends they were. Ashburton was making arrangements to sail home. Fox would get his legation back. Featherington had sailed weeks and weeks ago. The less said about the madness of Cruickshank the better. But then Webster recalled the behavior he'd observed in Lord Ettryne. He had meant to ask her long before this about the young rake—if indeed that term fit him.

Dolley's rounded eyes and laugh told him he must be the only person in Washington unaware of the young lord's reputation. "Heavens, he has been quite the dandy practically since he stepped off a ship, Daniel. The women in our little society who have confided in me about the delirious effects of being with Lord Ettryne—why, they're mooncalves after being in his company.

"I have beheld it over and over at my own little parties. You would know it if you didn't eschew them. The man winds women around his fingers with no effort at all. That Spanish diplomat's wife—

"Señora de la Fuente?"

"Yes, the señora has sailed home herself, though whether banished by him or under her own steam, I can't say, as her husband has put it about that she is ill and traveling home for her health."

He nodded, recalling the night of Cruickshank's death.

"The most shocking thing about it," said Dolley, "is that at the same time he captures them, they swear he rebuffs every single one of them. Does not lay a glove upon them, which has the effect of making them madder for him still. The women I've spoken to—you know Mrs. Cornelison, of course—they are unable to give any account that makes sense. Hours pass in his company. The next thing they know, they're back in their coaches and he's bidding them goodnight. It's as if they've dreamt the whole affair." She leaned forward and put her hand on his arm. "Oh, Daniel, do tell me you know someone who has at last penetrated his armor."

He sighed with laughter. "No," he replied to her. "Nothing of the sort. I have, however, witnessed that delirious effect you speak of. Frankly, it had me thinking he had been derailing negotiations all along just to give him more time with his conquests. Now you seem to be saying there *are* no conquests."

Dolley looked him in the eye and laughed as if it was all the most whimsical entertainment.

"In any case," he said, "I expect now that this matter is resolved, he'll go quietly away with his arrogant tail between his legs. And if he doesn't, it will be someone else's problem, not mine, for I shall be quit of the cabinet." He raised his glass.

>>> <<<

She woke with a start.

Awhile she listened to the silent house, the breeze flapping the curtains of the open window. Without even thinking, she reached for her prayer book, making sure it still lay beside her.

Moonlight poured through the open window while a warm breeze circulated. The shadows of the curtains rippled and fluttered. Moonlight fell across Devonee's large feet where they stuck out from behind the schrank.

The mirror stood in the corner beside the window, out of Letitia Tyler's line of sight. It had been safe there, protected. But it wasn't protected anymore. Even from her bed, she could sense the thing that had lurked in the mirror last summer, that Mary Elena had banished.

How was it returned suddenly now? She couldn't even explain how she knew that it was watching her.

Letitia patted around in the covers. She dragged her Bible up onto her bosom, held it tightly to herself, then began to recite her memorized prayers.

I commend my soul to the Lord God. Be sober, be watchful. My adversary the devil prowls like a lion, seeking someone to devour. I resist him and hold firm in my faith. Thanks be to God. Christ have mercy! Lord have—

A flash lit the room.

She wondered at first if it was inside or outside her head. She had experienced "mind lightning," as she called it, in the midst of her strokes. It had acted as a warning that she must sit or lie down right away. Mind lightning usually preceded fits; but no paroxysm followed. Moonlight still flooded the room, so it couldn't have been real lightning either.

Maybe, oh maybe it was God answering her prayer, sending an angel to rescue her! She'd prayed for so long for salvation as her body failed her. Mr. Tyler would never have said it, but she knew she was a burden to him. It was why she made so little fuss. Her daily prayers were always for her family, their comfort, their joy. Now she pinned her hope upon an angel in the flash of light, the fluttering she could hear.

The shadows of the curtains billowed wide then, like wings to either side of something glowing brighter than moonlight. Look how the curtains curved, mirroring each other, shaping it between them. It must have been as tall as the window. Another moment and it would speak to her. Another moment— But instead a liquid blackness seemed to drip down from above the window and slowly suffocate the light, the hope of her angel. Darkness wormed across the floor. It flowed up the cot and over Devonee's feet. The room itself seemed to be disappearing, Devonee swallowed up, the cot gone.

Long black fingers slid and reached around the schrank. Their touch set it to life. Pulled both of the elaborately carved doors open. More darkness emerged from behind the hinges, the deeper interior of the cabinet. It poured out and down. Like a flood, it spilled onto the floor and flowed toward her bed.

Letitia's lips opened wide to yell, but only a mewl of terror escaped. She grabbed madly for the slate, for the chalk now. If she could rap the chalk, wake Devonee. Her fingers found the edge of the slate but it seemed to wriggle loose from her grasp. Something skittered from under it onto her hand, and then twenty more before she could even react, blackness with legs prickling up her forearm. She dropped the tablet and flapped her hand about, waving furiously, slapping the bed again and again. Her knuckles struck the chalk, and she gripped it, but the slate, as if alive, danced away. Her eyes rounded like those of a terrified horse.

The mass of writhing blackness from the schrank scuttled up the bed sheets in a wave that seemed to crack apart into a thousand splinters that came scurrying from the sheet to her nightgown. Her body shivered, she tried so hard to move, to arch her back, and her tongue pushed out her open mouth, again to scream her near-silent scream.

And as if they'd been waiting for this moment, the inky spiders scuttered up her chin and tumbled over her lips, fought their way down her gullet. She squirmed and juddered as they filled her, more and more coming. Her hands spastically clawed and beat at the covers. She couldn't breathe enough to spit them out, but with every clogged inhalation only sucked down more of them. They beetled their way into every crevice inside her—her lungs, her belly, the chambers of her heart.

She shook so violently that the Bible flew off her. It slammed against the wardrobe with a report like a gunshot, its echo reverberating through a long, dark tunnel.

>>>> ◀◀◀◀

Devonee woke straight up. She'd dreamed that somebody had fired a musket at her; and in that pitch darkness, for a moment she had no idea where she was.

Upright, bleary, Devonee pressed against what felt like threads or bony fingers, and she cried out and windmilled her arms. As a small girl, she'd been locked in a root cellar for having dared to look her owner in the eye. The place had been pitch dark and the jabbing roots had dangled in the air like ghost fingers. They snagged her hair, grabbed at her clothes. After being let out, she'd never made the mistake of looking him in the eye again.

The back of her hand struck the side of the schrank, and she yowled. The noise and pain brought her full awake on the cot. She clutched her hand, and called out, "Miss Letitia?"

Leaning forward until she could see around the schrank, she spied the Bible lying open in a strip of moonlight on the floor. It had fallen off the bed. No doubt Miss Letitia had let go of it in her sleep. The Bible and her prayer book meant everything to Letitia, and Devonee knew that her mistress would be in a panic if she woke and found either one missing. Prayer was all she had.

Devonee swung her big legs off the cot, and with a groan she picked up the volume. She leaned against the schrank to get upright, noticing then that the doors had swung open at some point. She couldn't recollect if she'd latched it proper. It was the sort of thing she did without thinking anymore. No matter. She pushed the doors closed, then leaned over her mistress, whispering, "Here you are, Miss Letitia. It done got away from you agi—"

The hairs suddenly stood up on her arms and on the back of her neck. In the dark, even before she'd touched Letitia's outflung hand, the great stillness of the room told her: Not even the rustle of a sheet, nor the tiniest whisper of a breath escaping.

Letitia's skin was still warm, but clammy. Something crawled up over Devonee's thumb. She yelped and snatched back her hand so hard she rapped her knuckles on the wardrobe again. Light, she needed light right this instant, but the candle was out, and there was no means in that room to light it. Miss Letitia refused to allow those things called *lucifers* in the room.

Devonee hooked her finger through the ring of the chamberstick on the small night table and tottered fast out into the hall.

On the table beside the main stairs, a night candle cast a feeble flame. Hurrying to it on aching legs, she lit her own candle, and then hurried back into the room to confirm what she knew.

Letitia Tyler lay dead on her back, her eyes wide and her mouth open in a most awful final and eternal howl, as if she'd spied the devil in the darkness above.

Then, impossibly, her lips moved again, and a small black spider thrust itself out of her mouth. It skittered across her cheek and fell into the bedclothes. Devonee lifted the Bible and slammed it down like the wrath of God.

She was whimpering in fearful grief, but she leaned over and made herself take Miss Letitia's face in her hands, closed first her mouth, and next her eyes.

She clutched herself round the middle and started to bawl for real then. Lifted the candle and hurried off, shouting to wake the household.

Shortly, more wails joined hers. A miserable chorus poured from the rooms and down the hall.

In the tall corner mirror, dark-red shadows swirled, until the curtains, billowing upon the breeze, swept across the surface and wiped the shadows away.

Part V:
It Will Have Blood, They Say

Thirty-Six
James Hambleton Christian

"A tragic, fatal stroke" was the doctor's verdict. Of course, he hadn't heard what Devonee had to say, nor what Renehan, Zenobia, and I knew. Our enemy had pounced before we could do anything about it.

We sat at the mess table, while upstairs the East Room had been made over once more into a room for a viewing and eulogy, hung in black crepe; and people like Dolley Madison and Mayor Seaton, and even Henry Clay, were filing past her coffin before taking their seats.

"But yer man wasn't even in the house," Renehan argued.

"Didn't have to be," Zenobia explained, "long as his *tebo* free to act. Miss Priscilla musta cleared a path, is all I can think."

"Then we have to find this *tebo* thing or there's no stopping him!"

She clucked her tongue at me. "Mel never found it, all the times she looked. What you think our chances are?"

"What I don't understand is, Mel insisted the room had protection and nobody could get at my sister…" My throat caught. I shook my head. I hadn't expected the sudden crush of grief. "She was supposed to be safe in there."

Renehan said, "You keep callin' her yer sister. I'd thought it was maybe some Christian way of speaking of her, but… What's so funny?"

Wiping my eyes, I couldn't help smiling at his unintentional joke. "It *is* a Christian way of speaking, Martin, if you're referring to Colonel Robert Christian." All humor left me, saying his name. "He was our father, mine and Letitia's, the upstanding master of Cedar Grove Plantation, who just liked himself a little black beauty on the side now and again. You understand? My sister was a few years older, but we played sometimes as children, and she was always decent to me." I scraped a thumbnail at something on the table, then made myself pull my hand into my lap. "Later I was handed off to tote for her brother when he went to college, but before I'd returned, Colonel Christian had found himself another girl to use—got tired of seeing my mother around, so he rid himself of her. Even though Miss Letitia asked about her for me, he never would say where he'd sold her to." I gave him a hard stare. "That *Christian* enough for you?"

"Jesus, man, I'm sorry. But you ought to be traveling home with the body, you as much as anyone should be."

I let out a frustrated sigh. Renehan, forthright as he was, did not understand how things stood between my *new* owner and me. "Mr. Tyler already declared otherwise. See, I'm part of Miss Letitia's dowry. It's like he's won himself a horse he didn't want in a poker game, and despite how he praises me sometimes for educatin' his children or running his household, truth is, he never has liked having me around. If he sees clear that this house can be run without me, he'll waste no time getting me gone. And if he don't, well, come 1844 I'm sure to find myself standing at auction somewhere with somebody's fat pink fingers pulling at my jaw for to get a look at my teeth. So either I got maybe a week or so here or a couple years at most. You can depend on that."

Renehan made a face of disgust. Here in Washington, there weren't any auction blocks, so he never had to look at it. Buying and selling people was something happening somewhere else.

"Maybe you can help with that, Martin. I've no cause to stay here and be sold. Mel's dead and my sister's dead. Mel argued the *bokor* didn't kill Harrison right off because he wanted to kill Harrison's wife first, his family, only they didn't turn up. Ettryne will want the children now, and I'm in his way too. I ought to get out while they're all gone."

"You can't mean it," he argued. "You'd never abandon those children— they're *hers*. However rotten the way you got bound to them, your blood's their blood."

"Tyler—"

"To hell wit' him, man. You stay for them children. I'm staying in for Priscilla!"

Zenobia watched us back and forth, her bottom lip held in her teeth like she was about to scream.

I couldn't help laughing. "Priscilla, who's destroyed all the protections Mel put in place. Can't help herself." I stared him down. "You know you can't ever win her."

His expression twisted up. "Oh, I know. I'm not dense. But that's not why we're here, the three of us, is it?"

How long I had done for my sister. I recalled how small Tazewell was his first time at the piano in Virginia, his fingers like stubs on the keys, his bare feet swinging under the bench. Alice dominated by Elizabeth into being the quiet and shy one. The sweet one too. I knew how special to her mother she was. Mel knew it, and her voice in my head told me, *You can't throw them to this monster, James Christian. You all they got.*

"All right, I won't," I answered, then realized I'd spoken it aloud, and quickly clarified. "I won't let him have them."

➤➤➤ ◄◄◄

Even before I'd entered the East Room, I could hear Reverend Addison's voice proclaiming, "When we leave this world, it is with, we hope, a clear sense that we have accomplished all of those tasks set before us." His voice rang off the high ceiling, returning in echoes of a prophet declaiming as if in a vaulted church.

Everyone's back was to me, save for Addison himself, and Drummond and Garvine, who stood at their posts beside this door and the one into the Green Parlor respectively; and they barely noticed me. Renehan entered from the Green Parlor about then, but remained beside Garvine rather than calling attention to himself.

Despite the warmth of the day, the family sat close together at the front. Miss Letitia's body lay in state off to the right on the same bier that had supported General Harrison. It was like the world had run full circle and would keep on orbiting from one body to the next in here until the sorcerer had them all. At least he was not so bold as to have put in an appearance.

Miss Priscilla sat between Mr. Tyler and Robert on the right, wife and surrogate to the two men. I'd thought she might have the baby with her, but Mary was upstairs in Sally's care.

Tazewell and Alice sat on the left side of Mr. Tyler, between him and Dolley Madison, who was dabbing at her eyes as Addison went on about the family's "privilege of caring for Letitia." I could not help finding the arrangement unusual. Priscilla and the children almost always sat together, at dinner, at services, at parties. Tazewell was about as in love with her as a boy could be—in some ways more so than Robert. Robert, despite his tears, seemed only more ill-tempered than before.

Not one of the household slaves was here, not even Samuel nor Devonee. She was downstairs right now weeping in the room where she would hereafter be consigned to sleep with the other women, assuming Mr. Tyler didn't hold her responsible in some way and send her home.

Reverend Addison closed by assuring us all that Letitia Tyler "has only moved from this President's Mansion into that great and welcoming House of God to dwell for all of her days. One day we shall all find her there."

A woman I didn't recognize got up and sat at the piano. She played the opening chords of a hymn by Charlotte Elliot. It was only seven years old, and so everyone held up small sheets of paper with it written out, and began to sing:

"Just as I am, without one plea,
But that Thy blood was shed for me,
And that Thou bidst me come to Thee,
O Lamb of God, I come, I come."

I remembered it without the paper and sang quietly along. It had six verses but only three had been written out for today. The reverend said the

Lord's Prayer and stepped down.

The mourners arose, some of them slowly, Miss Priscilla visibly shaken and clinging to Robert for support. He scowled at her weakness. I glimpsed her hands. They looked red as if she had been tearing at nettles throughout the eulogy. Mr. Tyler stepped aside and she reached out to Tazewell, but he jumped away from her and gave her a look of such reproach I was shocked. Alice, too, shied from her. The children worked their way into the mass of adults, putting Dolley and Tyler between them and Priscilla. She was weeping openly, one hand to her face now, and I feared she might tear her own hair out. Mr. Robert sat her down and sternly said something to her. She buried her face in her hands and he stiffened. The depth of her grief seemed to embarrass him. It certainly looked deeper than his own. One of the cabinet members approached him, and he made a smile and the two men shook hands and spoke, as if she wasn't even there. I wanted to approach her but could not find a way to do so.

The coffin now had been closed and the lid set in place. In a few moments they would carry Letitia outside for the last time and place her in the wagon I knew Cyrus had waiting in the carriage lane. They would nail the lid shut and he would drive her to the train depot. The family was going home with her, back to Cedar Grove, her father's plantation. It had been her wish, to which Mr. Tyler acquiesced.

Surreptitiously, from the Green Parlor door, I watched them with the coffin. From behind, someone tugged at my sleeve. I found Alice and Tazewell standing there. They had gone into the hall, but come in here. Alice glanced back at her brother. "He needs to tell you something. Before we go."

The cross hall was thick with a funeral crowd. The family would now make their way to the vestibule through this gauntlet of sympathy.

"The Yellow Library. I'll meet you up there in two minutes." They went out. I crossed through the parlors as I had so many nights with Mel, then went down the west stairs. I wanted Zenobia with me.

⟫⟫⟫- -⟪⟪⟪

"Something is wrong with her," said Alice.

"How do you mean?"

Alice glanced at her brother. "Tell them," she insisted. When he hesitated, she waded in on her own. "She took things from Mother's room."

Zenobia peered at her. "What did she take, Miss Alice?" The way she asked was commanding. I'd never seen Zenobia act like that.

Instead, it was Tazewell, seeming scared of his own answer, who replied. "Was a thing she cupped in her hands. Had a bunch of feathers stuck in it."

Zenobia said, "Had to be," as if she'd expected it.

"Probably shredded and blown across the lawn," I guessed, but Tazewell shook his head.

"No, she threw it in the room across the hall, the empty one. Her hands were all red like the thing cut her. It was real powerful—it set the hall chandelier to rocking above her when she crossed."

"Wasn't no *pakét kongo* did that," Zenobia said. "Was *him*—his holding power over her while she had it. Like a big ol' wind circlin' her."

"What's she mean?" Alice asked me.

"Miss Priscilla's not responsible like you think. She can't help it. You're both angry with her, but you shouldn't be."

"Give her your love instead," Zenobia added. "She knows, at least some, that she's doin' it. Bein' forced to do it."

"She killed my mother," Tazewell stated flatly.

"You *saw* the chandelier," I said. "You think Miss Priscilla caused that?" I went to one knee between them. "This is happening *to* her the same as to you. Think of how much she loved Miss Letitia."

"What is it that's happening to us?" Alice asked.

Before either of us could answer, Robert Tyler's voice boomed through the hall. "Alice. Tazewell! We're leaving shortly, you need to come along."

I quickly led them into their mother's room. "Go out from here," I said. "He'll understand you needing to spend time in this room."

Alice gave me a look that said she had many more questions, but she hurried through as Mr. Robert called out sharply. Tazewell gave me a final glance over his shoulder. "She really can't?" he asked.

"Could you stop playing at your recital?" He seemed to grasp it then. "She's heartsick, Tazewell. I know you can see *that*."

He gave a final nod.

Zenobia and I remained where we was, making not a sound in the haunted room.

Their luggage was already packed and on the wagon. Right now, Mr. Tyler would be looking for me, to deliver his final instructions before departing.

All at once Zenobia lifted my sister's bedding, and with effort shoved it upright against the wall. On the mattress bottom and the wood slats nearest the wall were two corresponding greasy smudges the shape of a parsnip.

"Should have been safe there. Nobody knowed or ever seen it," Zenobia said.

"Priscilla couldn't have known about it, could she?" I walked out into the hallway. "Stay here. I've got to go down, but I'll be back soon as they've gone."

I crossed to the service stairs and hurried down, emerging in the tiny space next to the vestibule. I circled around the cross hall. Down in the East

Room, people were still sitting and standing around as if the funeral had merely been a prelude to another party.

Jasper stood at the front door.

"Is he—" I gestured at the door.

"At the wagon, and 'e was askin' after ya. They're waiting on Miss Priscilla to come down with the baby now. Guess Mary's givin' her an 'ard time."

As good a pretext as any, I figured.

Mr. Tyler stood on the portico just above the carriage, with Drummond nearby and looking out into the park, his hands in his pockets like he hadn't a care in the world.

Tazewell, Alice, and Robert were aboard the carriage already with a space left for Miss Priscilla. Behind the carriage, the buckboard held the coffin, and Samuel and Devonee. She was bawling and clutching herself against her mistress's coffin. Samuel looked to have tired of trying to comfort her and had moved away to sit atop some luggage. Our eyes met across the distance. I couldn't say if he was smirking at some notion of how this event and his inclusion in it placed him above me. I did not care anymore. He could have the President's Castle.

Tyler said, "Ah, James. Good," and gestured me to him. Already there was something different in his manner toward me. No one else might have noticed, but shifting from Samuel to him, I no longer doubted how my future would fall out.

"You have everything well in hand, I expect?"

"Yes, sir." He probably anticipated the more detailed report he usually heard from me, but I chose to disappoint him, and just stood there stiffly, having answered his question.

Finally, he realized I intended to say nothing further. "We may be some days," he said. "You will look after things in my absence."

"Of course, sir, Mr. Tyler."

"Fine. Fine." He leaned past me. "What can be keeping Priscilla?"

I didn't know who he was asking, but Robert started to climb out of the carriage.

"I'll attend to her for you, sir," I said, and strode fast back inside.

There was something entirely wrong in Tyler's mood, and not merely as he regarded me. I couldn't figure it, but he seemed too even-keeled for the man who had been sobbing all the day before; it was like he was reconciled and looking far ahead at better times. I wondered if Ettryne hadn't got at him again.

Miss Priscilla entered the vestibule about the same time I did. The baby was awake and restless in her arms, burbling and twisting to look about.

Priscilla's face was drawn, lined, the puffy skin around her eyes darkened with grief and lack of sleep. She stopped me before I could have Jasper open the door for her.

"Why are you not coming with us, James?" she asked, and placed her free hand on my arm. She wore her traveling gloves now, hiding the redness of her hands. "I asked but Robert would not even hear me out, and Mr. Tyler is adamant. I fear—"

I gently took her gloved hand.

Mary had turned around to consider me. She smiled and babbled incomprehensibly.

"Don't now," I said, but it was as if her touch poured her grief into me, and I had to fight to keep my voice steady. "You and I were her two reliable partners. She knows that whatever happens hereafter, we did our best for her, you and I."

Her eyes teared up as I spoke, chin quivering. She shook her head. "No, I did an awful, terrible deed—the enormity of it will never quit me."

I bent my head until she had to look into my own wet eyes. "Wasn't you. And I know it wasn't because I know who it was, same as you do—his tricks and his deceits are coming to light."

That seemed to stun her so much that she gaped at me.

Then the door opened at my back, and Robert Tyler stormed in. "We will miss our train on account of you!" he snarled. He might well have been furious at both of us. He took her hard by the arm and hauled her past me with an, "Excuse me, James," shooting me a look that might have cut me dead, as though he thought I would try to interfere, as if he wanted me to. The door closed and they were gone.

Jasper said, "I never seen the like, and after that poor woman's funeral no less."

"That poor woman," I agreed. I had to hold off my own grieving for her now. There was no time. The Tylers would only be in Virginia a few days.

I left Jasper and went back to the private floor.

Zenobia stood in the doorway of Miss Letitia's room, but I walked to the empty guest room Tazewell had indicated.

The handle on the door was stained with what I supposed was Priscilla's dried blood. Muggy air hit me when I opened the door. The windows were closed in there, but bright light filtered in from behind the blue curtains sashed either side of the big window. It took only a moment to locate the flattened charm on the floor. She must have just tossed it in. I crossed the room, past the bed, and was standing over it when Zenobia reached the room. Renehan had rejoined us too. He followed her.

"She didn't tear it up," I said.

"Didn't need to," Zenobia replied. "Couldn't do Miss Letitia no good here, and she wouldn't have known it was missing."

The cloth had turned dark, like something soaked in coal tar. When I picked it up, my hands tingled. The charm smelled musky, like fresh dirt and some rutting animal. Most of the feathers sprouting from it were snapped in half. The stitched *veve* was almost invisible. "Here," I said, and carried it to Zenobia before my hands burned any worse.

She took it by the feathers and I shook my hands to get rid of the sensation. It was like I'd cut up a hot pepper. "At least it ain't tore up," she said. "Still plenty powerful by the look of your reaction. That's one we don't need to make. I'm gonna put it down in Tazewell's room. But we gonna need a lot more *maudit* to make new ones. That *bokor*'s had Miss Priscilla carry off everything he couldn't git to. I expect most of the rooms in this house is open again. He'll be ready when they come back, and he ain't gon' wait this time."

"No," I agreed. "But neither are we."

Renehan asked, "What *are* we doin' then?"

"We are going to catawamptiously chew the bastard up."

Martin Renehan showed his teeth, somewhere between a grin and a snarl. He wanted nothing more in the whole world.

Thirty-Seven

Martin Renehan answered the knock at the front door. The colored servant outside said, "Note for Mr. James Christian from Mr. Paul Jennings across the park."

Renehan took the note, pressed a coin into his hand. "Thank you, I'll see it's delivered." He closed the door and unfolded the note.

Three words: *He is risen.*

Renehan refolded the note, tucked it into his vest pocket, and hurried across the oilcloth-covered floor. He and James had convinced Jasper to take some extra time with his daughter—after all, with the family away, no one would be the wiser and they were happy to cover for him. Gratefully, he had accepted.

James had enlisted Jennings' help, knowing that Webster often loaned him out to his former employer for her parties. The note was their cue: Lord Ettryne had turned up at Dolley Madison's soirée, which had begun early as no event at the President's House preceded it.

If they'd allowed him his way, Renehan would have walked straight across the park to the soirée and shot the man dead. He had argued for it, but James and Zenobia both had talked him out of it. No one would have believed anything they could say to justify his actions. He would assuredly have been hanged here or in England.

"Beside," Zenobia had said, "you kill him without you find the demon he got hid in this house, you ain't gon' stop things."

He crossed the hall to the State Dining Room first. At the far end of the table, Eli Garvine sat with his boots up on the polished table like the lord of the manor. He puffed on a cigar. A half-drained bottle of sherry sat on the table, left over from the funeral after they'd kicked all the grubbing well-wishers out.

Garvine stared him down, took the cigar from his mouth with his scarred hand and pleasurably tapped the long ash off it onto the floor. "So, your message come, did it?"

"Time for me to go, yeah. You're on door duty now, Eli. Don't let nobody in, and stay out of the parlors."

"You worried I'll drop my cigar or somethin' while yuz off with your darkie friends?"

"Maybe I'm concerned that you'll run into that blue fire again, what wants to make your hands match."

Garvine lowered his feet and sat upright. "You don't really think that."

"I *really* think I don't know, Eli, save that it's better not to go asking for it." He turned to leave, but paused to add, "And don't steal the silver while I'm gone."

Garvine barked a laugh, hauled himself to his feet, snatched the sherry bottle, and headed for the vestibule.

Renehan took the tiny service stairs. He found his brother seated in the mess along with James, Deborah, Marcellus, and Zenobia. They had bowls in front of them. Around the table sat other ones, empty. Everybody had eaten. Drummond was munching on fresh cornbread out of a skillet. He looked up with big cow eyes. Renehan took a square of the buttered cornbread for himself.

"It's time, Osbert." He fished the note out of his vest pocket and set it in front of James Christian. "You need to go get the wagon from the stables, run it up to the south side here. We'll meet yas."

James opened the crumpled note. "Marcellus, if we aren't back by dark, you take care of dousing the lights, all right?"

Deborah, the half-blood Cherokee, astonished Renehan then: She spoke. "If anyone asks, we say James is already turned in and studying on his Bible, so is not to be disturbed." She had a funny glint in her eye. She was excited to be a part of this plot. She cast James a look that he didn't see, and Renehan wondered if his friend had any idea within his mantle of grief that this woman was in love with him.

»»» «««

They took Jefferson's carriage paths toward the canal, then loped up toward Canterbury Theatre and Centre Market, where Drummond slowed to let Zenobia down. Though it was late in the day, she swore that the particular stall she needed would be open. She knew where to find them afterward.

The three men rolled on down 8th Street back to canalside, entering the lane not one hundred yards from where Mel had been murdered. Renehan kept an eye on James, who, to his knowledge, hadn't revisited this spot since that frigid day months ago; but James stared straight ahead, never even gave it a glance. Osbert reined in below the hotel.

Renehan jumped down. He wore a lightweight frock coat of dark brown, and tan fly-front trousers. The Osbaldeston tie was all the rage, and he wore one to secure his image of someone who belonged in the Indian Queen. James was dressed as for serving at one of Priscilla's parties, but he was going in a different way, infiltrating the staff.

They climbed up to the hotel. At the rear, James wished him luck and veered off to the "Servants and Coloreds" entrance. Renehan walked on around and through the front doors.

The hotel was quiet. A sprinkle of people decorated the wide lobby. As he gazed around, he spied a face familiar to him and immediately turned away before his own was recognized.

He walked up to the desk. The mustachioed man there welcomed him.

"I've a note here." He drew it out of his coat and let the man glimpse the presidential seal on the envelope. That it was an old envelope belonging to Martin Van Buren didn't really matter—the eagle, shield, and motto of "Out of the Many, One" were sufficient. "It's to be delivered to a Lord Ettryne?"

The man blanched visibly, but he reached for the envelope. Renehan snatched it back.

"I'm sorry, but I'm to deliver it to him directly, or at least to his room."

"Well, *I'm* sorry," said the clerk, "but Lord Ettryne has gone out for the evening. I called his carriage myself. So if you'll leave it with me…"

Now came the tricky part. He couldn't read which way the man would go, but they weren't exactly hitting it off so far. Nevertheless, Renehan surreptitiously slid a gold Coronet Head $10 piece across the counter. "Are you sure you couldn't see your way to telling me his room number and allowing me to deliver this meself?"

The mustachioed man saw the coin and his eyes widened.

At that point, a hand the size of a porterhouse steak dropped upon Renehan's shoulder. "He's sure," said a deep voice.

Renehan turned slowly about. "Why, Torrance, me old fella. How are you?"

"I saw you come in, and I saw you try and duck."

"Oh, I wasn't ducking at all. I have business with a feller lives here. Tell me, how's things in the Northern Liberties company?"

"Well, I wouldn't know. I work here now, not in a fire brigade. Know what my job is? Keepin' riffraff like you out."

"Torrance, man, I have to deliver this letter." He tried to show him the seal on it.

"Well, you do that right now, and then I'm gwin help you find your way through the door."

The desk clerk reached, but Renehan slid the gold coin back into his pocket. "Sorry," he said. "Not how I can leave it."

The meaty fist slid up and grabbed the back of his collar, and the other fist pressed against his spine. He had no choice but to exit as Torrance directed. At least, he thought, he hadn't lost the $10 in the bargain.

>>>- -<<<

Outside, he straightened his clothes and kept walking. He could feel Torrance watching from the front door. He turned at the corner.

Zenobia was approaching the wagon from the direction of the market. She looked as dejected as he felt. A couple young boys walked around by the rail where his brother had pulled in.

By the time he reached the wagon, she had climbed up beside Drummond. Renehan asked how she had made out.

"Some *maudit*, hardly enough. Goin' send for more, but I don't think we gots time to wait."

He nodded, glanced around. "No sign of James then?"

"Not so far," his brother said.

"Maybe he's had some luck. What say we go in after him, Zenobia?"

"Martin?" said his brother.

"Osbert, ya gotta stay with the wagon."

"That's just it. I don't. See them boys? For a price they watch your horse or carriage."

"Yeah, I bet they do."

"I was going to give them a dollar. And another when we come back."

"Dollar's probably more'n they make off a *dozen* wagons."

"That was my thought too." Osbert smiled.

Renehan guffawed. "Sometimes, Osbert, you astonish me. All right. Come on then. Go pay your boy and let's find James before the hotel eats him. Ain't none of us goin' through the front door in any case."

Together the trio walked up to the entrance for "Servants and Coloreds." Renehan almost hoped Torrance was watching from upstairs. Osbert would knock him into Virginia.

Thirty-Eight

James Hambleton Christian

The hallway was dusty and dim with half a dozen rooms off it, storage first, kegs and crates in one room, another that was nothing but shelves and cupboard drawers on the long wall filled with hotel stationery and envelopes and the like. A couple old boxes tossed in one corner and it looked like mice was living in them. This close to the river you could probably add water rats as well, although I'd never seen any during the time Mr. Tyler and I stayed here.

The smell of cooking wafted from the kitchen into the hall, and under it the sweat of people at work.

I passed the laundry room full of washtubs and boards. Linens were drying on a line. Four women was working there. The nearest, bent over a tub, saw me and stood up, putting her hands on her hips and stretching her back—a round-cheeked woman with her hair tied in a rag. I didn't recognize her. "Oh," she said, taking in my outfit, "you work for someone? Well, you passed the back stairs behind you there where you come in. They's two others, down either end of the big hall. But you go on along by the kitchens, git yourself something to eat if'n you like, if your mister don't need you right away." She gestured me on with one elbow. Behind her the other women had stopped to consider me.

I thanked her for her kindness and continued on along the hall.

Two overhead oil lamps lit this hall. I ducked to pass them, and walked in stretches of dimness between the lights.

The hall soon intersected the longer corridor that ran from one side of the hotel to the other—their cross hall. I hadn't been here in over a year but it was still familiar.

Like the President's House, they had their own dining facilities down here, considerably larger than ours. Of course, the hotel employed ten times the number of people. They had to eat in shifts—I remembered that—bringing their food down the backstairs from the kitchen. This particular dining room was for colored staff only.

I paused in the doorway. The nearest folks looked up right away. I nodded to them, but I'd already recognized a very dark face down the way, and walked along behind them.

He was meditating on a crisp chicken thigh, and when I plunked down across from him, he looked up, then away, then back again in surprise. He broke into a smile revealing his missing tooth. "Why, Mr. Christian," he said. "What you doin' here? Don't tell me they done kicked you out and you lookin' for a job."

I glanced around me, nodding, saw that off to my left another of them was Harrison's former cook, Hannah Weems. I'd passed right by her.

"Mr. Bibb," I said with some delight, then twisted around. "Mrs. Weems. Delighted."

Bibb offered his slender hand, and I shook it. It was greasy.

"Oh, forgive me," he said, drawing it back, offering me his white napkin. "I'm on my dinner break, and it ain't all that long. 'Nuther five minutes you wouldn't a seen me here."

"That's all right. You eat up. Don't you let me slow you down now. I'm interested in a man what's staying in this hotel, and I think you might know more than most about him, you and Mrs. Weems. You would have seen him in the President's House."

He chewed his chicken, nodding, then asked, "How'd you know *we* was here?"

"I didn't." I glanced over my shoulder again. She looked worried, as if she'd already sussed out my reason for being here. "But I admit I am relieved to have found somebody from the general's staff."

He finger-scraped a piece of chicken meat out of his teeth, nodding. "This here's where I worked 'fore Harrison took me on an' I thought I had it purdy good. But we know how that resolved, don' we? 'Least they didn't dun me for it—mostly 'cause I brought 'em Mrs. Weems when I come back. She a hell of a pastry cook and Glory knows the people upstairs they likes they's pies." He set down the bone he'd finished gnawing on. "So who is it you wantin' to know about?"

I said, "Oh, you'd recollect. Member of the British delegation name of Lord Ettryne."

I never felt a room go so still so fast. Everybody had been listening of course, and now it was as if every heart in the room had stopped beating at the same moment.

In that pocket of silence, footsteps came striding past, skidded to a halt, and backed up. It was Renehan, looking nonplussed, and behind him Zenobia and Drummond.

"What the devil?" he asked. "You stopped in for more supper?"

All the others marked his intrusion.

"Martin," I said. "Zenobia, Osbert. This here is Mr. Bibb who worked in the President's House under General Harrison. You might want to come in and sit a spell."

They hesitated in the doorway—understandable what with everybody in the room staring at them.

I half-hoped the three of them would sense the strangeness of the situation and withdraw, but they didn't. "How'd you fare at the front desk?" I asked Renehan.

"They refused to take any note from me to Ettryne. Threw me out in fact for asking. Hell, the desk man wouldn't even take a bribe."

Bibb asked me, "These white gentlemen with you on this?"

"All four of us got a personal stake in this, Mr. Bibb."

"Hmm. Personal, you say. All right." He'd set down his chicken, as if his appetite had deserted him.

A woman seated at a table behind me asked, "What might your reasons be, mister?"

I swiveled around. They all sat watching us, waiting. They had no intention of helping us out. It was one thing to say we had cause, quite another to say we wanted their help against a man with the power to set people ablaze and take possession of their souls as he pleased. That was sure to lose us any allies. Finally, I had to give them an answer.

"He killed somebody matters to me—two people now. My sister." My jaw tightened but I went on. "And a woman I loved. Would have married." *There, Mel. I said it.*

Renehan interjected, "And the man's goin' to kill a lot more if he has the opportunity, which will include us for certain and some children besides."

The people around us eyed one another, not sure how close they wanted to get to people who knew already they was on some list to die, but the silence stretched on. They weren't going to say anything, and I was regretting again that Renehan and the others had turned up.

Mrs. Weems gave me a stern look that all but told me to go away. Instead, I said, "Annabelle Costin."

A pretty girl sitting beside Mrs. Weems gasped.

"That's you?"

The look of betrayal she shot Mrs. Weems said everything. She got up and hurried out, pushing around Renehan and Drummond. They had no idea what was going on.

Zenobia faced me. "Mel spoke that name once."

"I'm sorry," I said to Mrs. Weems. "I didn't even know she worked here. I was just remembering the story you told me about her, about the bites on her shoulders and back."

I could have closed my hands on the fear in that room then, it was so thick. The hotel people got up, first a couple, then most of them. They took their plates and serviettes, and walked out. Shortly only Hannah Weems, Bibb, and the four of us remained.

Bibb stared down at his plate and quietly seemed to speak to the chicken bones on it. "Whatever you think, nobody here likes that man, not one bit.

Scared to death by him is what they is."

Mrs. Weems stood and hurried out. Her footsteps clattered down the hall.

Bibb let out a sigh, as if the last of the forces restraining him had left. "Gots a whole suite to hisself," he said. "Pays for two rooms side by side. One of them nobody's ever seen the inside of, not since the day he arrived. Been very *clear* on his privacy. Oh, he's all friendly like on the surface, but it don't run any too deep, as you have no doubt learned for yourselves. He tips good, so he's bought him plenty of compliance. And my goodness he's had maybe every woman in Washington society up there in his suite. They have their tea and they do laugh, and they stay awhile after. Gits real quiet then. Me, even if I was *invited*, I wouldn't go in those rooms."

"Well, *I'm* goin' in," Renehan snarled, "as yer man isn't at home this evening to stop me. All I need is someone to show or tell me where in hell the rooms are." He leaned back as if to see down the hall. Those people weren't coming back.

Bibb stared down at his plate as he said, "Tell me some'n, James. He done for Isaac, didn't he?"

I nodded. "Isaac and Harrison both."

"And he weren't even at the house when they happened."

"The night you told me about—the East Room doors inviting you in—"

Although he kept his head bowed, he looked up at me. "The shadows what danced on the walls," he said. "I know."

"What you don't know is, he's killed Mrs. Tyler, the president's wife. And he is just getting started. Didn't stop with General Harrison."

His eyes closed and he shook his head. "Sweet Jesus have mercy. They gone have to burn that house to the groun', get rid of what's in it. Ya cain't see it. Cain't git away from it, like Annabelle. And here she is, workin' in the hotel with him. Myself have stayed far from him since I come back to work here, so's he won't take no notice of me. I know he recognizes who was there when the gen'ral died. Seen him look at Annabelle like he'd pick his teeth with her bones."

As he said this, he patted himself down and poked through his pockets, and finally placed his large, long hands against the table, making ready to stand. "Afraid I gotta go back to work, James," he said, "afore the others think I've spent too long wit' you." He rose up. "You know, they give me a key opens all the doors in this hotel. Yessir, entrusted it to me in case there should be an emergency some night. We clean 306 all the time, but to tell the truth, I have never yet tried it on Room 308." He picked up his plate and cup. "Perhaps we'll chance across one another if you get up that way. If not, it's been a pleasure seein' you agin, Mr. Christian." He nodded solemnly to Zenobia, and then sauntered off.

On the table where he'd eaten his chicken lay a slender brass key. It had an odd-shaped bit at the end of the shank. The plate attached to it was inscribed with a "0."

"308," Renehan said, and grinned as if he couldn't believe it.

"Time to go borrow some stationery." I slid the key to myself and put it in my vest pocket.

"Stationery? What the hell you want that for? Why not go up right now?"

"We just been told nobody's opened the door to that room since Ettryne moved in," I explained to him. "Right from the start this has all been about thresholds and doorways. Assuming she knows how, Zenobia needs to draw a whole sheaf of *veves* before we go up there. Unless, of course, you prefer bursting into blue flames the instant you turn that key."

He gave me a black look. "I prefer ta keep the blue flames for Garvine."

>>>— <<<

In the room with all the shelves of paper and envelopes, I peeled off a dozen sheets of rag paper with the hotel's crest. Drummond pulled a pencil stub from his jacket and offered it to Zenobia. She stood over the sheets of hotel stationery and shook her head at me. "I only know a few of the *Mystères*," she said. "Ones Mel used on the kitchen level."

"Kept him away from us, didn't they?" I asked. "Go ahead. We haven't any choice now."

She drew four different *veves*, since she didn't know which one might work, then made four sets of each so that we all carried them. Drummond tried to figure out what to do with them, finally crumpled his up and stuffed them inside his jacket. Zenobia folded hers, tucking them in on both sides of her shirt. Renehan and I did the same. We were all sweating, kitchen heat and fear combined.

Just inside the rear entrance stood a door to the back staircase of the Indian Queen. We went up, Renehan leading the charge, me and Zenobia in the middle. Passed the kitchen door. Mrs. Weems pretended not to notice us go by.

On the third floor, I opened the door, looked out. I saw no sign of Bibb nor anyone else. Made me wonder if he'd warned everybody off. From their standpoint it could be useful to say they hadn't borne witness to anything that happened. If we did burn to a crisp, no one would be coming to our aid. And for all we knew, just opening that door would do it.

308 faced the rear of the hotel. Were Ettryne in his room, our tying the wagon up down back was a waste of time. It also meant he had watched as his toughs killed Mel.

We clustered around the door. In my pocket, I fingered the shape of the key. My mouth went dry and a knot twisted in my belly. I could see that the others were suffering the same—in that moment we all favored skedaddling and had to fight the urge. Just being near that door was twisting us. Drummond's face was a sheen of fearful sweat, and he made a noise low in his throat, took two steps back like he might run. No wonder nobody had ever gone inside here.

Renehan, head lowered, his teeth gritted against the repulsion, leaned past me and pounded on the door. Nobody answered, but the steep of dread withdrew as if the noise or his touch had shoved it away.

I wiped at my forehead. Down the hall, half a face peered out a doorway—Bibb, watching to see how things went. I imagine, if they went badly, he was going to want to pluck his key back from whatever remained of us.

I fitted it in the lock. Immediately there came a sharp sound like water hitting a hot griddle, and my fingertips stung. I snatched back my hand, shook it, and rubbed my fingers together. The sizzling faded.

Zenobia reached out and with one finger pushed against the door. It unlatched and swung back a sliver.

Despite the sun still being above the horizon, everything behind the door lay in darkness, and heat like from an oven rolled over us. I stuck the key back into my vest pocket against one of the folded *veves*. Renehan reached into the side pocket of his coat and drew a pistol—one of those small guns with three rotating barrels. Might have been Mr. Robert Tyler's Allen Pepperbox, or else its cousin. He held it up, while thumbing back the percussion hammer. "Open it up," he said.

With my foot I nudged the door wider.

The intense reddish darkness was due to heavy curtains being drawn tightly closed over the two windows, which explained the stifling heat too. In the strip of brightness from the hall I made out the cane-backed edge of a daybed, and beyond it a chair to the right of the window straight ahead, and a round tea table with a lamp on it. There was something sticking up in the middle of the room like a small tree.

I couldn't imagine how anyone could tolerate that airless heat or the coital, musky reek of the room.

Renehan, bolder than the rest of us, walked through the open doorway. Something flashed all around him, which made him jump, and I feared he would drop the hammer on that pistol he held, but he shook off whatever pain he felt, and passed on inside. Steeled for it, I followed him, but there came no second flash. I guessed that Zenobia's *veves* had protected him and broken whatever spell had been set. She closed the door behind us.

We four stood shoulder to shoulder in the dimness to let our eyes accustom to the darkness, but I'm sure each of us was ready to jump for our lives. The "tree" in the middle of the room resolved into a pedestal stand you might have in a foyer to support a bust of some famous man. There were markings and images all over the wood floor too, like a strange carpet, though I couldn't really make out the design yet.

Drummond marched over to the window and tried to throw open the curtains, but they'd been stitched together down the middle. "Ozzie," Renehan warned. Drummond dragged the drapes to one side. Behind them, the window was in fact open, but the shutters outside hung closed and latched like for winter. It was crazy.

"Hang on now," Renehan said, but too late. Drummond shoved wide the shutters.

Golden light off the sunset flared through the room, nearly blinding us where we stood: The walls at both ends had been hung with dozens, maybe hundreds of mirrors of every size and shape. Wherever we squinted from behind hands or arms, we beheld mirrors nailed to the walls from floor to ceiling, mirrors leaned along the mantel over the small hearth.

All around us, from the plaster overhead, all manner of faceted crystal objects dangled on threads. The crystalline baubles threw off more light; rainbows and sun dogs that encompassed us. Mirrors in back of us caught and threw the light into the mirrors before us so that glistening, dust-mote-filled lines crisscrossed the air. We stood snared in a web of light, an infinity of our images bouncing between walls of glass. Each movement we made cut off or released beams, threw our shadows like nearly solid objects ahead of us. Beside and behind the door we'd entered, mirrors adorned a large armoire.

All of these twining beams and reflections intersected above a six-foot-long Directoire daybed. I imagined Ettryne seated there, cross-legged, the beams and globes burning into his skull, his torso. Or for all I knew, maybe he could push them about.

I squinted between my fingers. The tables—there must have been four or five pressed against the walls—all had oil lamps of some sort on them.

The strange "carpet" was more clearly visible now. A great hand-drawn map of much of the world had been drawn across the floor, and odd writing surrounded it on each of the four sides, though it was no writing I had ever seen before. The pedestal, of dark marble and bearing a glass dome, stood right atop where the city of Washington would have been.

In the shadowy corners and spaces between wall mirrors hung all sorts of fetishes, mostly animal faces and figures, but none of them real. Those I could identify proved repulsive, with impossible glass eyes, snouts, fangs.

My eyes adjusted to the variable light and dark, or maybe the sun shifted outside, sinking lower. That was when I noticed that the walls of the room were covered in a red-flocked paper of repeating fleur-de-lis pattern.

Isaac hadn't been wrong about that room that devoured Harrison. We had found it.

The air seemed to vibrate with that light, a sensation as if someone had slapped my head. I was about to tell Drummond to draw the curtains again, but my attention, like so many of the threads of light, was pulled to the dome on top of that waist-high pedestal. Writing was etched in the glass, more letters and symbols I could not decipher. Something solid lay inside it too. Something reddish brown and glistening.

My first thought was that it was some kind of sacrifice, a lump of cow heart or liver or something. It had caught Zenobia's attention ahead of mine, and she walked past me for a better look. She hunkered over the pedestal. I came up behind her.

It was a dolly lying under that dome. Like the poppet Mel had nailed up, except much bigger, thicker, and fashioned of oily wet leather stripped right off some animal in pieces and stitched together with thick black thread. It was like something made out of fatback. Lines of black thread stitched into it represented eyes and mouth. Raven feathers stuck out of it, or maybe it was lying on top of some. A string of bear claws lay draped across its thick neck.

Renehan came to see, jostled between us, and accidentally nudged Zenobia off balance. She put a hand out against the dome to steady herself.

The instant she touched the glass, the doll that had been lying inert slammed itself upright against the dome right under her hand. She shrieked and fell back against me, her hand snatched away and raised high as if she was testifying.

The doll dropped back, but it was sitting up now. The stitched-thread eyes had parted. Opened. They stared at us, round and lidless, red as blood with tiny black pupils. Alive. Alive and filled with pure hate.

Renehan cursed under his breath, raised the pistol beside me.

Those awful eyes shifted to him. The stitched mouth opened, an empty hole, and it let loose a screech so fearsome we all clutched at our ears; but the screaming was inside our heads, blasting through us, out through the walls and into the world.

The beams of light rolled through the air as if attracted to the sound that was no sound, until they criss-crossed the dome—a spider's web relocating its center to that pedestal.

The mirrors pulsed a dull red as though their surfaces were copper.

"What is it?" asked a voice. It sounded bored, at once familiar and strange.

The latticework of rays rolled again. One flashed straight into my eyes. Squinting, I turned my face away. The same had happened to the other three, lines all leading back to the poppet in the dome. It stood upright in the center, its beady red eyes looking from one to the other of us.

"Ah, I should have expected this. And another *mamaissi* in your midst—where do you find them, Mr. Christian? You will need a ready supply, I promise you."

His voice, not angry but thick with disdain, seemed to drop like rain out of the air. He was everyplace in that room.

"Have you informed her yet how she will die in this capacity? Hmm? No? She will. You all will. I shall peel John Tyler's family from him like layers of skin, flay him down to the bone, and then take his chattel. Break his heart, his mind, his soul, and yours defending him."

Renehan was turning and turning, the Pepperbox raised, as though he might glimpse the true Ettryne somewhere and shoot him. The voice made him seem to be in the room with us.

"Oh, the whirling lovesick mick. You have my pity. But then, I've *had* your beautiful Priscilla."

Renehan fired his pistol and one of the large mirrors shattered.

"You'll be sorry you did that," Ettryne said patiently, like a parent to a naughty child. "Later, however. I've a party to return to."

Renehan, in a fine pucker, shot the next mirror along, but the voice had left us. The light was wheeling around again. The rays no longer met upon the dome.

Something jangled and plinked. Shards of the mirror sprinkled upon the carpet shivered, shifting. They lined up on Renehan.

Drummond must have seen it, too, and guessed what was coming. He launched himself at his brother even as the shards shot like bolts, struck and bounced off, most of them. But half a dozen embedded in Drummond's back. The two men fell, Drummond on top and roaring in pain for all he was worth.

The doll slammed up against the dome again, screeching and chittering until my head felt it would burst.

"Zenobia, we have to get out of here!" I yelled, grabbed one of Drummond's arms and hauled him halfway off Renehan. She hurried to grab his other and help me pull him up. He bellowed like a bear.

More mirror shards shot at us. One slashed my cheek, and I ducked my head. Others struck me in the side but bounced or shattered. It had to be the paper *veves* protecting us.

We dragged Drummond through the doorway. Renehan, right behind us, slammed the door on that hideous red room. The sound of more smashing glass thundered against it like rain on a cabin roof. Drummond, on his knees, hissed and groaned and tried to wrestle from our grasp to reach around to his back.

Renehan leaned against the door and let out a moan. A dagger of mirror jutted from his thigh. He cursed and sucked air through his teeth, then with a yell pulled out the glass and flung it down the hall. At his back, the door flexed as if it might explode outward. Zenobia stepped back. When she moved, I saw, halfway down the hall, a horrified Bibb watching us. I fished the key from my pocket, held it up, then threw it his way. He didn't move, just looked at where the key came to a stop.

The three of us pulled Drummond onto his feet again. Renehan said, "Brace yourself," and plucked one shard after another from his brother's back. Drummond's own hands were bleeding. They jerked with each dagger pulled out of him, but he didn't make another sound. "That's all of 'em, Osbert, all right?" Drummond nodded, his face gray and shiny.

Renehan and I draped his arms around our necks and hauled him clumsily along the hall. A few doors cracked open as we went by. Maybe they'd heard the gunshots. The doors closed as we staggered past.

On the stairs Drummond tugged free of us and managed to make his way down on his own by clinging to the banister, grunting. A dozen dark splotches decorated his back. The *veves* had saved him from the worst of it—had saved us all. Without them, we'd have been pincushions.

I wiped at the blood on my cheek. Renehan was limping, his hand pressed to the wound in his thigh. "My good trousers, no less," he muttered. He had tucked his pistol out of sight.

Making for our wagon, we tried to look as normal and respectable as possible, although I doubt the bleeding, limping group of us fooled the dungareed boy Drummond had given a coin. Drummond and Renehan got in the back. I took the reins, and Zenobia climbed up beside me. I drove us back down toward the canal as fast as I could get the horses to go. The sun lay on the horizon now.

Zenobia sat hunched beside me, arms wrapped around herself as if she was freezing in the heat.

"How'd you make out at the market?" I asked.

"Hadn't enough to do us more'n a few rooms. After this, we got no choice. He goin' to come after us, ain't he?" She looked over at me.

"He knew you'd trained with Mel, just by looking at you."

She sat as we drove on, then out of the blue asked me, "How far's the place called Chesapeake?"

"I don't know. Forty miles give or take. Why?"

"The *maudit* root—the old woman in the market stall say it comes from an old *houngan* out on the Chesapeake."

"You're as bad as those Gullah women, Zenobia, talking your own language," I teased, trying to make us both forget the voice that had promised our deaths. "What's a *houngan*?"

"He's like Mel was, only more powerful even. Market woman, she made me a map to get there. We were to go right away, we could get to this old Abias and back and nobody'll even notice we been gone."

I pulled up on the reins.

Renehan yelled, "What in hell?" I didn't pay him any attention.

I grabbed her shoulders. "Old *what?*"

Confused, afraid, she replied, "Abias. The *houngan's* called Abias. All Mel's *maudit* come from him."

"You got to find Abias." Mel's face—Mrs. Dickens' face—pressed against mine, her lips whispering in my ear.

Not "a bias" as Mr. Dickens and I had thought. She was directing me to someone powerful, someone who might help. We hadn't understood.

I looked over at Zenobia; at Renehan behind her, still glowering at me for the rough and unexpected stop; at Drummond, lying on the boards darkened with his blood now as well as Mel's. I closed my eyes, banishing that memory.

Our enemy had fixed on all of us. Now I wished that Renehan *had* shot that damned shrieking dolly. I couldn't even begin to figure what it was. The mysterious *tebo?* If so, then it wasn't even in the house, and that made no sense.

What in all hell *was* Lord Ettryne?

I flicked the reins and turned the horses for home. If we intended going to the Chesapeake and back, we needed to leave as soon as possible.

Thirty-Nine

"Swear you don't bear me a grudge for this," Martin Renehan said as he clapped the manacles around James Christian's wrists. The manacles, separated by a flat iron bar, held his wrists side by side. An iron pin through the lock hole held the two manacle halves together without actually locking them. "It looks legitimate. Anyone eyes ya up close, just keep your hands low. Shake the pin out anytime you want 'em off, but it's gonna take the two of ya to fit 'em back on."

The chain from them wrapped around the rail of the wagon behind the bench seat and ended in a second set of manacles already worn by Zenobia. Barefoot, she sat against the wagon side, straight-legged, staring down at the dark smear of Osbert Drummond's blood in the wood. She had on her real apron over a thick dirty-white skirt, an old checked shirt worn near to gauze at the elbows, and a bandana around her head, tied as Mel had done. James had exchanged his proper clothing for a linen shirt and the osnaburg trousers that Samuel had worn coming north from James River. Like Zenobia, he was barefoot.

It was Absalom Lee who'd insisted they couldn't drive out of the city any other way. He knew too many stories about members of the free black community who'd been taken on the road by slave hunters. "Lot of 'em don't care if you can show proof of identity. Once they git you south, it don't hardly matter. Either you two gen'men gotta dress like their massas or else you gotta be shown to be transportin' 'em." They'd settled on the latter plan.

James worked his wrists in the black iron, staring at his hands as if they were someone else's. "I don't bear you a grudge, Martin, Absalom was surely right. Thing is, I never wore chains in my life. Seen plenty who have. Zenobia for one. Tyler bought her at auction when she was ten." He asked, "You ever witness an auction? They bring the children up on the platform naked, children and maybe half the adults, the women especially."

Renehan tried to meet Zenobia's gaze but she continued to stare, shame-faced, at the wagon bed. "Hell," he muttered.

From the bench, Eli Garvine clicked his tongue against his teeth and called back, "Well, maybe we'd best strip her for the trip—"

"Shut it, Eli."

Garvine only chuckled, happy to have galled him.

Renehan would rather have brought Osbert along, but his brother had enough wounds in his back at the moment that a long ride in a buckboard was out of the question. "Here, James," he said, and slid a narrow wooden box into the back of the wagon. "I got this out of Robert's little office when I went up for the stationery."

With effort, James Christian leaned to the side and lifted the polished lid. The .34 caliber Paterson with octagon barrel lay packed with a cleaning kit and a spare cylinder.

Renehan watched him close the lid again. "It's a five-shot, too big for me to stick in my trousers if I'm driving. No one's going to expect you to be armed in any case."

James looked up. "You do have the papers?" Renehan patted his vest.

Using the presidential stationery, James had written false papers of ownership documenting that the two auctioned slaves on board were being taken to their new owner, a Mr. Tazewell of Federalsburg. One of the signatures was Renehan's own, but he didn't think a slave hunter would know real papers from pulp in any case, nor care, as Absalom had said. He'd encountered a few of their ilk—in his opinion, too thick to be firemen.

⋙ ⋘

They rolled out of the city along Pennsylvania Avenue, and long after the city had vanished behind them that was still the name of the dirt track according to a small wooden marker they passed.

Zenobia's map put their destination as Tilghman Island on the Chesapeake Bay. Renehan had stopped in Tyler's office long enough to familiarize himself with a real map that showed it. The old geezer Zenobia called "the *houngan*" lived there. It was just one more weird word among the rest: *bokor*, for a sorcerer; and *tebo*, for whatever had done for Letitia Tyler; and never mind all the different manky little calico packages.

So far as he was concerned, the world of magicking couldn't crawl off and die soon enough. Leave him the human fiends. Unfortunately that no longer seemed to include Lord Ettryne, who was as good as the righthand man of the devil. Renehan couldn't help wanting to kill the bastard, even though Zenobia said it was going to take some powerful force of goodness to counter him, and Renehan knew that didn't describe him. Had been a lot of things in his twenty-nine years, but only a *gobdaw* could have called him *a force for goodness*.

Perhaps an hour out they found their way blocked by a pole laid across two low pylons, like a station on a turnpike road, only this one was simple, and portable. Three men with torches stood before the pole. Two wore slouch hats, their faces obscure in brim shadows. The third was bald and had a livid scar that ran from his forehead to his chin, as if he'd walked into an ax. A fourth worked the pole, pushing it up to let wagons pass. Or not.

Heavyset, he had the crossed eyes and countenance of an idiot.

Renehan focused on scarface as he drew up. Garvine laid the musket across his lap. The slouch hats walked around to look over the sides of the wagon. Each held a sheaf of papers.

Slave hunters, all right, maybe even legitimate ones. Renehan hoped so, as it would mean they would fail to find who they were looking for.

He remained seated, holding his own documents as if ready to present them. Garvine unobtrusively swiveled his gun so that it pointed over the horses at scarface, who took note of this and stayed where he was.

The slouch hats came back to the front, shaking their heads that no, nobody here matched their warrants. Scarface scowled.

No one asked to see the paper Renehan held. Scarface slapped the pole, and the *gombeen* threw his weight onto the end to swivel it up out of their way.

Nobody spoke a word.

As Renehan flicked the reins, Garvine lifted the musket upright and turned to watch the slavers recede into the night. Renehan glanced back at James, whose hands rested upon the Colt box, and Zenobia, who was looking at the box too.

Garvine said, "Now, that could have been lots more fun."

"*Your* sort of fun, Eli," Renehan said, "tends to get folk killed. We'll be taking a different road back and that's for certain, so start figurin' how we're going to avoid them boys and cross the Patuxent come tomorrow."

"I won't mind meetin' them again." They watched each other until James interrupted.

"Mr. Garvine, I know already that you hate coloreds same as you hate everyone else, so tell me, why you here at the risk of your own neck? Besides, that is, that you just enjoy stirring up trouble."

Garvine glanced over his shoulder. "I'm gone all soft on you niggers suddenly—that what you thinkin'?" He raised his left forearm into the air and tried to spread his fingers apart. Scar tissue now permanently joined half of 'em as if he was part frog. "Fact is, got nothin' to do with you, 'cept as how stickin' to you's gon' lead me to the son of a bitch did this to me. When I meet up with him, I'm personally carvin' his eyeballs out with this hand."

The rest of the drive east proved uneventful. They encountered no one else on the road before reaching Herring Bay, which was where Zenobia's market map directed them.

Two boxes representing houses were drawn on the map, and the shapes of two houses stood out along the point, just visible and separated by a quarter-mile of sparse trees and thick growths of grasses. There was no lighthouse, nothing to indicate that they had arrived at the Chesapeake but the smell. Their destination could not be seen in the darkness across the water. The air was warm and moist, and brackish enough he could taste it.

After he pulled up, Renehan climbed into the back. "Here," he said, and pulled the pin from Zenobia's manacles. She shook her wrists, but continued to stare, as if ashamed, at the wagonbed.

Renehan asked, "Zenobia, girl, how on earth did Mel get to this *houngan* fella?"

She raised her head then. Her eyes glistened in the moonlight. "Oh, Mel never come here," she said. "Got word to him through people at the market. He got a big reputation wit' folks. Provided Mel all the things she needed."

"That's fine for your supplies, but how are we getting across to the island?"

"Woman who give me the map said they's some oystermen here in them houses what'll ferry you over an' back for coin."

"Mebbe so, but I'm not inclined to try creeping up to some oysterman's shack before daylight. Probably watching us right now."

"Well, won't be too many hours," James said. "We're not turning around after coming all this far, unless you have some interest in driving the two of us north, say, a hundred and fifty miles?"

Garvine barked a laugh. "He's inviting you to join that railroad smuggles slaves, Martin."

Renehan ignored him. He knew what James was saying. "Just remind me how your man's going to help us with Ettryne once we *get* to his island."

Zenobia had no answer for him, nor did James. It was the Chesapeake and Abias, and all of it predicated upon the urgings of a ghost.

Garvine laid his rifle down and folded his arms. It wasn't long before he began snoring.

Martin Renehan, sighing, got down from the wagon. James and Zenobia huddled together in the back. He left them and walked off into the high grass. At a level spot, he stomped some of the grass flat, then like a deer lay down on it. He looked up at the stars, thankful that at least it wasn't raining. How in hell had he gone from uncomplicated fireman to this? And what was *this*? Words like *doorman* and *bodyguard* no longer even came close. He was still turning it all over in his mind when he fell asleep.

The scrape of chains woke him and he sat upright, alert for trouble; but it was only James getting down from the wagon, heading toward a nearby thicket.

Like a rabbit, Renehan knelt in the grass and peered around in the sunrise light. A man was standing outside the nearest house. He didn't move, and appeared to be watching them. Most of him was steeped in the house's shadow. A wide woven hat covered his head. Renehan thought he was a colored, but a moment later the man wasn't there anymore, though just where he went was perplexing, as if the shadows had absorbed him.

Renehan got to his feet, pushed at his back, then walked off into the deeper grass to relieve himself. When he returned to the wagon, Zenobia was just returning from the nearby stand of trees.

He tipped his head at the house. "House is awake, been watching us."

Garvine peered toward the water but shook his head. He climbed down, leaving his rifle beneath the board he'd been sitting on, and wandered off, stretching himself and groaning, toward the same trees.

Renehan said, "No point in waiting now."

They set off toward the house. Garvine cut from the trees straight for them, glancing back at the wagon. Renehan could imagine his anxiety at leaving his gun behind.

It was more shack than house, with open holes for windows, and nets, spears, oars, and assorted odd objects leaning against or hanging off the walls. Renehan thought it had to have been made from some ship that had been sectioned and dragged up here.

A path ran down from the far side of the shack to a narrow reed-and-sand beach. An overturned skiff lay directly below. The man in the straw hat was down there walking lazily among dozens of large black rocks that cluttered the beach. Out across the bay lay the outline of what might have been Tilghman Island. It looked far away.

Renehan had reached the top of the path when the "rocks" began moving. They glided along after the man like a herd of sheep. Horseshoe crabs.

The man came to where the bank above him jutted out like a promontory. He turned about and tilted his head up to see his guests, finally giving them a better look at him. He was a very dark man, his woolly beard like a hunk of gray cloud hovering under his nose. He wore an old red shirt that just barely contained his belly, which drooped over his worn brown pants. Patched, they ended in shreds around the ankles, and he was barefoot.

The crabs crawled on past him and into the water. He waited until they had all gone before he strolled back toward his overturned boat.

As he neared the path, he called out, "Yah gwine come down or no?"

He sounded just like their incomprehensible cook, and James muttered, "Gullah," with something less than enthusiasm.

"Yeah, but we still have to get across, even if we have to draw him a picture to do it."

James called out, "Was hoping to use your services to ferry me and my folk across to Tilghman Island."

The man looked across the water, scratching unconsciously at his beard, then crouched down and with a stick began drawing a spiral in the sand. He looked up at them again. "Wuffa you wantugo obah dey, huh?"

"There's a man over there. We need to speak to him. I was led to understand you could take us there in return for payment, as you might have some acquaintance with him."

The old man raised one foot, dusted the sole, seemingly absorbed. "Whudee called?" he asked.

"Abias. So we been told."

He planted both feet and eyed them critically. "So, you did come aft'all."

They just stood together for a moment. Then Renehan laughed as the implication became clear to him. About the same time, Zenobia said, *"You're* Abias?"

The old man climbed back along the path. Close up, he had an etched face with wide prominent cheeks above his beard. He laid one rough dry hand on Zenobia's shoulder and another on James'. "All of you's in terrible trouble."

Forty

James Hambleton Christian

The wagon rumbled along a rutted track. We had driven north rather than encounter the slave hunters again, before turning toward Washington on this rougher path. Renehan kept staring at me over his shoulder, and Zenobia eyed me from where she sat opposite, both of us fake-chained again. It soon enough became intolerable.

"How do I make myself any clearer?" I yelled. "I don't care what that old man said. I-will-not-*do*-it!"

They traded a look, then went back to keeping their own counsel.

Ahead of us, the sun was on the verge of setting, and a peach-colored sky held the light. We had been almost the whole day in Abias' shack. Everything he had to say, everything he had stirred up in us, everything he expected us to do culminated in a ritual that he insisted we must carry out if we had any hope of defeating Lord Ettryne and his magic.

It was a ritual whereby I was required to die.

>>> ‒ <<<

Inside, the shack had been like a cabin, and either it was constructed from pieces of a ship or else Abias had started out to build one and abandoned the notion after laying in the timbers and planking, and the line of scuttles between the upright ribs to let the light in. There was just the one chair, one bed, whale-oil lamps on bench boards that ran around the sides, and a cast-iron stove so small it reminded me of the model Renehan attacked the day the doormen arrived.

The uprights and the beams overhead were festooned with drying plants and animal skins, leaves, seed pods, things I couldn't identify. Scooped-out horseshoe crab shells lay under the benches. They were filled with still more stuff, everything from eel skins to what looked like plain old dirt. Maybe it was the combined aromas in that small space, but after awhile it started to seem like the world had been freshly painted in brighter colors and nothing was any too solid.

Abias had us tell him our separate versions of things, what we'd seen, what we thought—everything from the death of Harrison to the details of Ettryne's private hotel room. After hearing all of it, he looked at me and said, "You didn't believe in Mary Elena's magic at first, did you, James?" His thick

Gullah speech had just up and vanished once we'd identified ourselves.

Wasn't any point in lying. "No, I didn't," I said. "Got everybody to do their work and I left it alone." He nodded, not judgmental, more like satisfied by my answer.

Then he turned to Zenobia, crossed to where she sat on the floor, knelt and whispered to her. His hand passed across her face, fingertips touched her eyelids. He got up and shuffled away, telling her to go ahead and speak.

When she started to talk, we all stared at her. Her voice had gone flat. Even the way she shaped the words belonged to someone we didn't know.

She spoke of Letitia insisting to Tyler that I accompany him to the President's House, about Mel making her charms in among the furnace coal and hiding them in the public rooms at night, then how Letitia became a target and Mel had fashioned a special charm to seal her room from both the malevolence and Lord Ettryne himself, though she didn't know his identity or even how his magic operated. I could not recall having ever seen him anywhere near her room.

Then all of a sudden Zenobia was describing my feelings for Mel and hers for me. "Loved each other," she said, "more than either of you ever let on, protecting yourselves against the day one of you would be sold. Never expected death would be the thing to separate you. Despite all that, you believed Letitia had the power to grant your freedom."

I knew then it never would have happened.

Zenobia could not possibly have known it. My face was hot and my guts churned up at being laid bare; the sharp truth I'd kept at bay now dragged out so I had to look at it, feel it, admit it.

She paused, then just announced that Deborah had feelings for me too, but would never express them out of respect for Mel.

Hardly had I wrapped my mind around *that* than Zenobia started in on Renehan the same way. He was in love with Miss Priscilla, and while she had feelings for him, she loved her husband in spite of his harsh and judgmental nature and would never be persuaded to throw him over. She could not reciprocate what Renehan felt, and would deny any deeper connection, the way she hid from herself what she'd done with Ettryne, or rather what he had done with her. "Where the truth of it is," she said, "he can make her do *anything*." The weight of that last word made it obscene.

Renehan's jaw worked like he was grinding the grit of twenty curses between his teeth.

"It came about because of Miss Priscilla's duty to visit anyone who called upon her, as Dolley Madison instructed."

Ettryne had left his calling card and she had been obliged as Tyler's hostess to visit. She wasn't alone either, Zenobia said. Ettryne had called upon and taken possession of at least a dozen of Washington's socialites, turning them however he liked. These women had all done his bidding. In the President's House, he had sent them looking for every charm Mel had hidden. Sometimes they would take them; most of the time just reported where the charms had been hidden, and he would have Miss Priscilla steal and destroy them later, or he would do it himself while Daniel Webster wrassled fruitlessly with Ambassador Fox.

Renehan's hands kept balling into fists. I expected him to punch a wall plank pretty soon.

I interjected. "Am I allowed to ask her something?"

"Certainly," Abias replied. "Anything. The oracle mus' ansuh."

I let that pass. "All right. How come if he had all these women hunting down everything Mel did, he didn't act sooner? Took him till winter to...to murder her." I breathed, closed my eyes. "More'n a year to kill my sister. Why?"

"What he wants is nothing less than the destruction of the nation that slew his brother," she answered in that hollow voice.

General Harrison had no clear successor. Ettryne had hoped the country would crack apart as factions fought over who should be the new president; only, Tyler had acted so quickly that it had come to nothing. Then for a long time after we moved in he had no idea his creature was being obstructed. He was letting us settle in. In Harrison's household, nobody had even comprehended what was going on. The *bokor* thought he had all the time in the world to peel us apart slowly. But when he discovered the poppet, he knew he had an enemy in the house. He thought her simply an ignorant slave—the dolly a pathetic attempt to keep him out. "Isn't the same as his magic, but it made him aware of barriers being erected. The day he attacked you in the waiting hall, he was seeking the hidden talismans. He thought he could handle everything simply by himself."

Then his own nation was threatening war with us, rattling sabers, and he sat back to watch the show, expecting the man McLeod would be hanged and England declare war. With their superior navy, they would have destroyed most of our coastal cities. They would have taken Washington all over again and burned the house to the ground this time. He was prepared to lead the charge. He worked tirelessly to make it a reality. But each conflict collapsed. Weak men—weak in his eyes—failed to carry out any of their threats.

The politicians all failed him. Ettryne charged the *tebo* to begin killing again. The children first. One child after another and then Tyler's wife. That's when Ettryne discovered that Mel had all but imprisoned his shadow demon, way up on the attic floor of the house, far from its body. He comprehended finally just how powerful she was.

"And so she had to die."

The words hung in the air like a chill.

Garvine, who'd uttered not a word, finally piped up. "We gotta kill us this bastard right now, today."

Abias closed his eyes and nodded. "You do," he said. "But it ain't no easy chore. You cain't take that rifle o' yourn and jis' shoot him."

"Why in hell not?" Garvine asked.

"On account of, he ain't people any longer."

Garvine sneered, then laughed with the sound of somebody rigid in his beliefs of what's possible. I knew I'd responded to Mel with a similar noise many times over the years.

Abias said, "He made him some terrible sacrifice long ago for this power. An' he found someone wit' so much hate in 'em that he could take hold of it and shape it into something. The *tebo* got two faces. You seen one of 'em in his room. Its twin is somewhere in that house. Your Mary Elena, she never found it, though I'm sure she was lookin' hard." He glanced at Zenobia, but she, or the oracle, remained still, as if asleep. "It lured the general to his death," he said. "That Isaac, he saw the room, didn't he? Saw it all shining."

I said, "He saw Ettryne's room. The demon walked Harrison right into Ettryne's lair."

Zenobia nodded at that.

"Now, how in hell is that possible?" Renehan asked. He was in a fine pucker, weary like Garvine of all the magic, just wanting revenge.

"Twisted the world up," Abias said. He grabbed a length of rope off the floor, made a loop at one end. "Open the door"—he passed the other end of the rope through it—"and you ain't where you think."

"That's bloody mad."

"'Tis. An' it cost him plenty to do it, why I say this is all about hatin' somethin' or someone so much that you don't care the cost to you or anyone else. It kills you, you're still gonna do it."

"Come not between the dragon and his wrath," I quoted.

The doormen both turned and gave me a look. Zenobia, the oracle, faced me too.

Quietly, I said, "I accept he can bend the world this way. Mel said his magic was like nothing she'd ever encountered. She never did comprehend the full shape of it. How are *we* going to do what she couldn't?"

Abias answered, looking carefully at each of us in turn as he spoke. "He made a sacrifice. You gotta do the same. Blood of the family, the life what runs in the children, has got to be the source of it."

I balked. "You expect us to sacrifice one of the children to stop this? Hang 'em up like a pig and slit their throat?"

Abias said nothing, but Zenobia, her eyes closed, suddenly sat more erect as if staring straight at me. Garvine and Renehan caught it, and they looked from her to me, and then to Abias. He looked at me too.

"Oh. I see," I said. "It's my life that's forfeit." Why not Tyler's? Why was *he* exempt? They were his children, his blood. Was his damn *nation*.

Abias had pulled at his thick beard and then shaken his head solemnly. "This Ettryne," he said, "he's hunting the father's side, but he killed the mother. Made him a significant mistake there."

He stared into my eyes.

"He don't know 'bout you at all."

⫸⫷

By the time we reached the outskirts of Washington again, it was pitch dark and we had argued everything to a standstill. If we believed Abias, my blood had to flow, my body had to die. Then if we didn't leave me dead for too long, and Zenobia executed everything just right, I could be revived. Maybe.

Garvine found my objections both amusing and a means of twisting me up. "It ain't permanent dead, right?" he argued. "An' if it is, well, we promise to honor your memory, don't we, Martin?" He grinned around the words at me.

"Well, thank you ever so much for your kind offer, Mr. Garvine," I replied. "An' you can go to Hell."

Garvine made a face of mock offense then started to laugh. A moment later I surprised myself by laughing with him. After all the time we'd spent in each other's company, maybe we'd finally got the measure of each other. Renehan shook his head and then was laughing at us both. Zenobia, sitting in the wagon bed beside a big tied flour sack that Abias had entrusted to her keeping, remained as bemused as if she'd just discovered that all of her companions were lunatics. She had no memory of what she had spoken while Abias' oracle—who and whatever that was—had possessed her. Everything she knew, she was getting from us, second-hand and crazy.

Most of what the sack contained, though, she alone knew. I'd placed only one object in it, which Abias had been insistent I handle.

She and Abias had spent hours grinding up things, cooking stuff in a pot on his iron stove, and stuffing burlap pouches he'd fashioned, different from Mel's. They smelled of sulphur and tobacco, and he had rolled the contents of each in grayish-red clay dirt before filling up the burlap. They was a hundred times more potent than the charms Mel had strewn throughout the house. Even with all her learning, Mel hadn't the skill to make them.

"These," Zenobia said, "pull upon the *guédé*, spirits of life and death, *Nimbo* and *Samedi*."

I had some vague recollection of *Samedi*. Mel had called on him before. I thought his was one of the *veves*. But all I could think about right then was me dying.

We came into the city down Maryland Avenue from the northeast. There should have been no way for anyone to know our route, much less prepare us a welcome.

Dark as it was, there was a moon, showing us that while we'd passed a sign for the city limits, we continued rolling along a nearly uninhabited dirt track. In the distance ahead, fringe lights burned. My thoughts turned to Mel, to how much I wanted this to be over with, and maybe how I didn't really care whether I died so long as she was waiting for me when I got to the other side. Everything Zenobia had said about us was true. Sure, I told myself, what reason did I have to care anymore?

And then they struck.

Six men charged at us out of the darkness, three on each side of the road. One fired a musket, which missed everyone, and the ball bit into the wood of the seatback between Renehan and Garvine. I yelped and rolled away from it on instinct, which knocked Zenobia flat on top of her flour sack. My fingers worked on the manacle pin. As I pulled it free, I watched a man leap onto the side of the wagon and Garvine, with the rifle still laid across his lap, raise the barrel and shoot him in the neck. He snatched that man's gun, and shouting, "Yaha!" shot at a second man running alongside, but I don't know if he hit him because somebody else fired from across the two horses and it struck Garvine in the left side of his head. Kicked him sideways and he and the rifle both pitched from the wagon. Renehan screamed, "Eli!"

Another man, bearded and naked to the waist, charged from behind us and caught up to the back. He wielded a rough bat, and seeing it, for one split second I relived Mel's death.

He swung it at Zenobia but she rolled toward me and the bat slammed against the wagon bed. The man stumbled and flung himself on board. He grabbed for purchase, caught Zenobia's apron, and tugged. The apron tore. As he rose to his knees, I took the chain between my hands, caught him around the throat, crossed my arms over his head and then snapped them apart hard as I could. Mouth wide, he made a crackling in his throat. He struck at me with the bat and I saw sparks, but he was clumsy and blind. It raked once against my face, and then he dropped it. His other hand waved the shreds of apron as if saying goodbye to someone out in the night. His heels kicked out at nothing. I yanked tighter, hard as I could.

A shot from behind me clipped his ear, spattered me with his blood, and I twisted about. Renehan on his feet fired his pistol into somebody's face. They tumbled away, feet coming up into the air. He shouted my name without looking. I flung loose the dead man, and he bounced on his chin on the wagon bed and rolled off into the dark.

Men jumped on board on both sides of Renehan. I grabbed for the bat rolling around. Zenobia had reached into the wood box and drawn the Paterson. She just pointed and squeezed the open trigger. The gun fired, the barrel swung up, about hit her in the face, but one of those men flew backwards from the wagon.

Renehan lunged and grabbed one hurtling up on Garvine's side, got him off-balance and hauled him against the ruffian coming up on him directly; but that one had a knife and he shoved it. I was sure it sank into Renehan. The knife raised up high, dark with blood, and I whipped that bat across the villain's wrist. The man screamed, but the blade flew under the horses. He dove against Renehan, now trapped between the two men.

I snatched the gun from Zenobia and fired, but we were lurching every which way and I must have missed.

Renehan shouted, "Get out of here, James!" Then, gripping the suspenders of the one I'd struck, he kicked hard against the footboard, and both he and the attackers lurched off the side to be lost in the darkness behind us.

How I grabbed the reins I don't know, but I caught them and, standing up, drove full chisel with the revolver and reins clutched together. A gun fired way behind us in the night. I didn't hear the whizz of a ball or anything near. I called for Zenobia, to make sure it hadn't struck her.

"I'm here, James! I'm all right!" she yelled back. She was still attached to that miserable God-damned chain, but she'd shot one of the attackers and hung onto Abias' flour sack.

I climbed over onto the bench, then snapped the reins some more. In moments we were on more populated streets where one or two folks, shouting curses, had to dive out of my way. Ahead, the Capitol loomed against the sky. Last thing I needed right now was to be stopped while dressed in slave clothes and with a woman chained up behind me.

How was I going to tell Drummond his brother was dead? I focused on that unanswerable miserable question. He'd become a friend. And even Garvine. Even that foul bastard.

What Zenobia and Abias expected of me didn't much matter any longer. Our enemy wouldn't let any of us live after this.

Forty-One

No one was on hand to greet her. Priscilla Cooper Tyler arrived at the President's House shepherding Tazewell, Alice, a five-months-pregnant Elizabeth, and her own baby; and nobody she wanted—no one she needed—was on hand.

Mr. Jasper on the door had been visiting his daughter while the family was away and had himself only returned a few hours earlier to find Osbert Drummond manning it and unable to explain where his brother or James Christian might be. All he could think to say was, "They's 'round somewhere."

Jasper told her, "'E's lying too, I'll have you know. I walked down to the kitchen to grab me a meal, an' there's no sign of 'em. Everybody else's having a light supper, but not those two nor Garvine nor the girl, Zenobia. They're nowhere about."

While he predicted they would turn up, Priscilla leapt to the conclusion that the doormen were helping them escape north. James was no fool. He knew what was likely waiting for him when Tyler returned. She knew it, too, from Robert and her father-in-law's discussions on the train and after the funeral—discussions that ceased whenever they noticed her eavesdropping.

Robert, she was sure, recognized her as sympathetic to James. But it was worse than that. The night after the funeral, he had gone further, intimating privately, scornfully, that she had consorted with Martin Renehan.

"I know you leave at night," he'd said. "Oh, you're quiet about it, but I've watched you float downstairs for your assignations. I've seen how he looks at you. Rest assured, my dear, there are going to be *many* changes when we come back from finding father his new place."

When she protested her innocence, he'd whipped around, his hand raised halfway as if to strike her. But he fought down that impulse, shoved the hand into his coat, and stormed out. They hadn't spoken since. Samuel had driven her and the children to the northbound train. Even he knew something was wrong.

His new place. Her father-in-law had determined to delay his return in order to acquire a new plantation for himself. It seemed that he had already met someone—a much younger woman who had danced with him at one of the last levées, a Miss Julia Gardiner. Priscilla could barely recall her except as a pretty young thing, but she had beguiled John Tyler, and now he had only to wait a respectful period of time before openly courting her.

So here was her father-in-law invested in another woman while her own husband all but outright accused her of infidelity with an Irish tough who, she knew, believed himself to be in love with her.

Oh, if only that were the truth of it. *That* iniquity she might bear rather than the shadowy obscenity she suspected: that she was a murderess, a cat's paw in the control of a fiend who had done everything Robert imagined of Renehan and far more.

Memories from that tenebrous life had begun to leak into her consciousness like bits of daylight through cracked mortar: of being ravished while tangled in the drapes of the East Room and in the bedclothes of some unknown daybed; of being directed to carry off odd objects secreted about the house, tearing at them like a fox at a chicken.

She stared at her gloves. Beneath them her hands, as red and raw as if they'd been plunged into lye, proved to her that the lurid, fractured, somnambulant existence was too horribly real.

Robert could not match her self-loathing. Somehow, she had slain Letitia, stealing the one thing that had protected her.

Now, even though she could not say how she knew it, the fiend and his dark deformed Caliban were coming for the children. Tazewell in his room, Elizabeth and Alice sleeping together as they had for so many years, even her own little one, Mary—all were at risk. From it.

From her.

The villainous lord would bind her to his will again, even fit her hands around their throats. Without someone to stop her, he would triumph. It was only a matter of time before he became aware of her return. No one here could help.

In her nightgown she curled up on her bed, drew her knees up to try to make herself small and insignificant, and prayed that, with no champion anywhere, she might escape notice a while longer.

Please, James. Martin. Don't abandon me now!

And as if that plea were a beacon, the darkness flowed out of the corners and into her again to rob her of sight, sense, and hope.

Forty-Two

James Hambleton Christian

Cyrus and Absalom Lee came out of the stables at the rackety noise of our approach across the south lawn. Absalom carried a lantern; Cyrus grabbed the lathered team by the harness to bring them to a stop. Both of them looked at us peculiar.

Absalom lifted his lamp as he helped Zenobia climb down, and his eyes shifted, lighted on the dark smears on the bench, the gouged footboard, and the spatters of blood on the off-white osnaburg I was dressed in. Probably there was more on my face. He asked, "Mistah Christian, you hurt? Either 'n you?"

"No," Zenobia said.

Cyrus asked, "Doormen?"

"Dead."

"Sweet Jesus," replied Absalom. "How we gon' explain that to Miss Priscilla?"

I had just picked up the Paterson case. Bent over, I stopped, asked fearfully, "They back already?"

"Not ever'one. Her and the chillun includin' Miss Elizabeth, who looks 'bout six month gone."

"But not Tyler."

"No," said Cyrus, "nor Mr. Robert or the young Mr. Waller. They all remained back on the James River to look at some plantation of his cousin's he's of a sudden fired up to buy for hisself."

What had prompted that? I wondered. Maybe Jesus was looking out for us after all. Or maybe some *lwa* of Mel's. Right then I would have strung my faith to anything that promised to deliver me out of this. Still left me having to tell Drummond and Miss Priscilla how neither Renehan nor Garvine would be back ever.

Marcellus came running down from the house and swept Zenobia up in his arms. She dropped the sack Abias had given her. Marcellus was so tall, she was like a little girl in his arms. He hung onto her and accompanied us across the lawn and inside.

The ground floor smelled of onion and pork fat, and my stomach rumbled with hunger. I hoped that Gullah woman, Mariama, had cooked too much food and left something out, even drippings in a pan.

Zenobia and Marcellus were behind me one second, and then they were gone. I retraced my steps. In the dark of the scullery, the two of them clung to each other. It hurt to see their shapes, because all I saw was me and Mel, the times we'd snuck off like that.

Zenobia looked my way over Marcellus' shoulder. I gave her a nod and went into the kitchen. A candle burned on the sideboard. There was a heel of bread beside it. The ranger was pumping out its heat, and as I'd hoped, Mariama had mixed some bacon drippings and butter in a skillet, warmed by the stove. I dipped the bread and ate, stood there sweating while I tried to collect my thoughts. I heard a rumble behind me that sounded like the furnace, but it must have been thunder from heat lightning. The furnace couldn't possibly be lit now, but after all that had happened I wouldn't have been surprised had it risen up and burst into the hall. I stared that direction for a moment before turning away.

The lamps had been doused. I lit a candlestick from the sideboard candle. Before I could carry it off, Zenobia and Marcellus came in. He looked a little sheepish, and I couldn't help but smile at him: *We aren't going to lose her*, I wanted to say. *It's me whose time is short. But you hang onto her all the same.*

Zenobia had the sack with her, but it was clear she had removed most of what was in it. She said, "We need to git hold of Miss Priscilla soon as we can."

"They all gone to bed awhile ago," Marcellus said. "Everybody, 'cept that doorman."

"He upstairs? I'll have to go tell him about his brother." I was lifting the candlestick by its ring as I spoke, but Zenobia placed a hand on my wrist to stop me and held out the flour sack.

"In case you come on Miss Priscilla," she said, "an' he's got her already."

"You think already?"

She shrugged. "He'll be comin' once he knows they all here for the plucking."

She continued to hold the sack out. I wanted more time, to think, to decide, mostly to find some other way to do things than what Abias had described. Finally, I took the sack from her. It hardly weighed anything. Only one object remained in it—the snakeskin for Miss Priscilla if I found her.

Zenobia backed away, up against Marcellus. He closed over her like moonlight, and once again I didn't want to see all that affection. To hell with thinking and deciding.

I went up the serving stairs. As I neared the first floor I heard a peculiar little whistling noise and stopped. It was the tiniest chirr. It was inside this confining stairwell. I hesitated. Maybe I'd crushed a mouse underfoot. But as I waited, listening, the soft whistling repeated. It came from inside the sack. I raised it up into the candlelight, and the sack shifted and bulged. I knew that snakeskin wasn't alive. I'd handled it, put it in the bag myself. But I shoved that bag ahead of me as far away I could and ran up the last few stairs, out of that narrow space and into the cross hall.

⋙ ⋘

Beside the glass wall of the vestibule, Drummond was seated on one chair with his feet propped on another that had the stuffing poking out one side. Only a single candle sconce beside him remained lit, but he didn't notice. He was asleep.

I shook him gently awake. "Jaaames," he yawned, stretched his arms and beamed at me like a happy child, rubbed his eyes.

"What are you doing out here in the hall?" I asked.

"Oh." He groaned, lowering his feet off the other chair, sitting upright. He cracked his neck. "On account of Martin told me, if Priscilla come back, he wanted me to watch out, make sure she didn't go roaming through the house. I'm supposed to go wake her if she does."

"But *you* was asleep."

His face went red. "Uh. I kinda made a fist of it I guess, huh? I only been asleep a few minutes, I'm mostly sure. You won't tell Martin, will ya?"

I slid onto the chair where his feet had been, set down the sack. "Osbert," I said, "I need to talk with you about Martin."

He got wary then—slow he might have been, but he couldn't help noticing that I was alone. He sat upright.

I couldn't think of a good way to ease into it, so I just came out and told him how we'd been attacked on our return by men hired by Ettryne, and what had happened. When I finished, he pondered and then hopefully put forward, "Maybe he's not dead."

"Well, sure, that might be. We all hope that. But... I don't know, Os—"

"Martin's tough, you know. He's small but he's really really hard. Seen him swing a sockdollager many times that laid bigger scallawags out good."

"Yes, he surely is tough," I answered. I couldn't look at his face, burning childlike in its hope. My attention was caught by spots on the floor farther along the hall. The matting gleamed, reflecting the candles overhead. Candlewax dripped from the chandeliers maybe, I thought. Might have been Osbert who spilled it, though he didn't have a cup with him. I said, "He's a good man, Osbert. Saved my life tonight. Zenobia's too." While I spoke, I stood and walked slowly away from him, drawn to the spots. Not wax, they looked like drips of wet white paint leading into the Washington Parlor.

"He did?" Drummond asked me.

And there, at its door, one smeary half-footprint. There were going to be more inside the room. "Osbert," I said, "*have* you seen her?" I turned back to him.

"Who?" he replied, having already lost that thread of the conversation.

I reached to open the Washington Parlor doors, but at the end of the hall the East Room doors opened and out of the darkness drifted Miss Priscilla, so ghostly that Drummond gasped and knocked over his chair.

Dressed in a starched nightgown, she was barefoot. The sleeves on that gown ended in pink ribbons tied just at her elbows. She'd always had pale skin, but her hands at her sides looked the same color as the cotton gown. The same as the drops on the floor—a whiteness that ended irregularly above her wrists.

She came toward us, but then turned abruptly and disappeared into the east stairwell, heading for the ground floor.

"You know, Osbert, I don't think you had any choice about falling asleep," I said, and picked up the flour sack.

The two of us bolted for the stairs.

>>> -<<<

Last I'd seen it, the bucket of limewash sat in the storage space next to the privy under the east colonnade, tucked out of the way and protected from the elements. That had been months ago.

The brick floor between the stairs and east door was speckled with more of the thick wash, and with white footprints where Miss Priscilla had tracked it outside with her just now.

As I passed by, leading Osbert, Sally, holding a candle lamp, and Deborah looked out from the women's quarters. They both had put on nightgowns. With what I'd heard from Abias' oracle, I couldn't help looking at Deborah differently now, so I focused instead on Sally. Seeing the sack, she got big eyes, and I could feel its contents writhing.

I said, "Y'all stay here," and then went out the door.

There was a breeze in the moonlight and my candle immediately went out, but I could see the pale form already down along the colonnade, kneeling. I knew she was at the bucket. Reaching deep into it where the thick wash had settled out, and when she rose up again, her fingers were curled to cup the wet paste. It dripped off her.

Behind me, Drummond said, "What in God's name?" He'd followed me anyway.

It suddenly grew lighter and his shadow fell past me. Deborah had also ignored my instruction and come out with the candle lamp. She came up beside him. The reflector in back of the candle threw enough light along the tunnel of the colonnade to reveal Miss Priscilla's approach. Her face glistened with sweat. Her eyes were rolled back in her head, her features constricted as if she was struggling to break free of Ettryne's control; or maybe she was suffering from the excruciating burn of that lime. Either way, it was time to stop her, though I feared we were too late to keep any of the public floor *veves* from being wiped away.

As she approached me I eased aside, handed the dead candlestick to Osbert, and reached into the sack. The copperhead skin was filled with God knew what, bulging and stitched up and headless. But it rippled and wriggled back and forth in my hand as if none of that mattered.

Miss Priscilla was close now. I raised the snakeskin away from me, but I can't say whether I flung it or it jumped out of my grip and curled itself twice around her throat.

Thick as a winter scarf, the skin glittered like a choker necklace of gold set with brown jewels. The change in Miss Priscilla occurred instantly: She stopped walking and stood stiff, rising up on her toes as if she expected to leave the ground; then her heels sank and her head fell back, her dark hair hanging down, and her fingers uncurled. The limewash ran like blood from the tips, spattering her feet and nightgown as well as the stone.

A sound rose and emerged from her open mouth, horrible as a shrieking demon being torn from her belly and cast out. It stopped as quick as it had begun, and her legs gave, and she pitched forward. Drummond caught her. He didn't even have to move, just extended his big arm with the candlestick and she folded over it.

I said, "Quick, go fill a bucket from the kitchen spigot, bring it out here." Deborah ran inside, passing the lamp to Sally. "Set her down, Osbert."

He did, as carefully as if she was made of glass and might shatter.

Deborah came back with the bucket of icy water and knelt beside me in her gown. I couldn't help inhaling her smell so close. It was a nice smell and I did everything I could to ignore it.

I took Priscilla's hands in mine and shoved them into the bucket, which was almost full.

Deborah took one of her hands and we carefully worked the lime off. Sally stood behind her, providing all the light. I said, "I expect she's been to that bucket of lime a few times tonight. She's going to need salve and bandages."

"Where's that snake got to?" Sally asked.

I hadn't noticed, but it had disappeared from her throat. Sally was looking fearfully around at the ground. It was gone as if it had just melted into Miss Priscilla. I wasn't sure it hadn't.

Deborah said, "'Scorched the snake, not killed it.'"

I stared at her. Where had she learned Shakespeare? I wanted to know, but this wasn't the time.

"It was just a skin," I said, "didn't have a head."

"But it was alive!" Sally argued.

I didn't have any answer for that.

Looking up, I saw Zenobia and Marcellus in the hall. I took the candlestick from Osbert and went back inside, and, lighting my candle from their lamp, told them what had happened. "I expect she's opened every doorway Mel sealed with a *veve*," I told Zenobia.

"We made the potion, James, like Abias say to do," Zenobia said. She looked beside me instead of at me. "It's ready for your blood."

Only then did I appreciate she was holding a small stone bowl. For a long moment we all stood there. Then I rolled back my sleeve and held out my left arm. She took her small boning knife and cut across my forearm. I hissed. Blood dripped, then ran into the bowl. I watched it, found myself reciting, "'Blood will have blood.'" Zenobia stared me uncertainly in the eye.

It seemed like we stood there a long time, but I know it was only a minute. "All right," she said finally, setting the bowl aside and pushing my arm up. She used the little knife to slice into that osnaburg cloth, dirty from the journey and the wagon, and tore a strip off it to tie around the cut. She reached for the bowl.

"Not yet," I said. "We have to take care of Miss Priscilla first. Her hands are burned from the lime. And I need to see what she's done."

She nodded, so I turned away.

I took the stairs two at a time to the first floor. The drips of limewash in the Washington Parlor led straight to the south portico door. I pulled the drapery aside and knelt at the south portico door, held the candle close, but I could see it already. Mel's *veve* had been smeared out of existence. I went on into the Blue Saloon. The same had been done there, the *veves* obliterated.

As I got up, Marcellus opened the door from the hall.

"Zenobia's seein' to Miss Priscilla," he said. "Her hands are as raw as if they'd been peeled—"

"Yes, I know." I led the way into the Green Parlor, feeling a million years tired now. "Fill all my bones with aches," I muttered. The worst hadn't even begun. *Ready for your blood.* I pushed those words out of my thoughts.

"What about the East Room?" Marcellus asked.

"No need. That's where Osbert and I saw her come out. It's done already. Doesn't matter."

"Maybe," he suggested, "Zenobia can paint some new ones?"

"It's not so simple, there's a whole rite been reversed by what she's done. I can't even begin to know what we'd have to do. And anyway, he's had Miss Priscilla carrying off all the charms and destroying them. These rooms are all open to him, to his demon. Zenobia wants blood, and I think it's the only way." He squinched up his face. He didn't really understand just what the woman he loved was capable of. I knew exactly how he felt. I patted his shoulder, turned him around, and we went back down to the kitchen.

Zenobia and Deborah had Miss Priscilla laid out in her nightgown on the mess table. Her eyes were open but she didn't seem to be aware of her surroundings, of anything.

I hung back, half-wanting to evaporate like Isaac had. Glanced at the bench, seeking a puddle on the floor, a sign of continuance, but there was nothing.

Marcellus told Zenobia what we'd found upstairs. She faced him, but she was looking at me as she answered. "James is right. He's opened us up."

That was the moment when a scream tore through the house and the bell from Alice's room on the bell panel began to ring and ring and ring.

Forty-Three

Seated comfortably on his daybed, Lord Ettryne in his long bedshirt and stockings faced a wall of many mirrors, all black as if reflecting eternity. His blue eyes saw nothing, his entire being stretched beyond his physical self, through those portals and draped like a shroud over Priscilla Cooper Tyler.

He compelled her through rooms and hallways, drove her up and down stairs. He was a sheen of sweat upon her body, more intimate than her nightgown, caressing her breasts, her belly, her sex, conquering her with sensations she could not escape.

Still, she fought hard this time, more aware than ever of being engulfed, although her own will, boxed and silent, could only scream like a madwoman in an asylum. Indeed, after tonight's slaughter, he expected she would repossess herself in a state of utter derangement, fully aware after this of all she had done. She would take her own life or be found in a corner bashing her brains against the wall. Let complicity devour her. That suited him perfectly.

These lesser creatures all fell apart in the end, their constitutions unsuitable for his repeated pervasions. Had anybody bothered to inquire after Mrs. Cornelison yet? He had been using her at nearly every soirée, even when he was in attendance, sending her to prowl the parlors, casting every man she saw into a state of such depravity that even Hogarth couldn't have sketched them—she was such a prude at heart, he couldn't help himself. He wondered if she was even this night locked away, helplessly mad in her big empty house.

Priscilla, now—*she* was remarkable. He had enjoyed her more than any female since… Well, at least since that Mongol courtesan, Subotai, on whom he had first practiced remote manipulation over twenty years ago. Goodness, how time did fly. He'd revelled in Subotai's coarse beauty, her animal stink, so much more honest a smell than that of this perfumed society of women who thought their daubed scents elevated them above their own base nature. Granted, such self-deception made his work easy. Even Subotai, though, had been driven mad by having him inside her; had finally taken her life. How long before the dark-curled Priscilla—

His hands dropped. Head tilted, he stared hard at the mirrors.

They reflected the hotel room. Priscilla Tyler had vanished.

Ettryne sat forward on the rumpled bed. That wasn't possible—she couldn't so much as relieve herself without his allowance.

In its dome on the pedestal, the *baka* jumped and squealed, echoing his dismay.

His attention flicked to it. "What does your other half tell you? What's happened in that house, hmm?"

A vein throbbed in his head as he strained to find her. She was nowhere.

"Oh, oh, oh. Have you died, Priscilla Tyler? Cut your own throat with a carving knife left lying out in the kitchen while I was distracted?" He scowled. "Selfish woman, you left too soon, with much unfinished chaos to deliver." He focused on the leathery *baka* again. "Well, my little devil doll. Just what *is* your halfling up to? This isn't you interfering, is it? I don't have to remind you of our pact, do I?"

His right hand closed into a fist and the *baka* toppled. It rocked in agony, the raven feathers in its back snapping it onto its side again. The bear claws clacked around its throat. He opened his hand and the demon doll lay quivering.

"No, you didn't," he said, getting up from the daybed. "But you have the children in view, good. We've lost her but she's opened the whole house. Time for you to strike. But I want to be there. I want to watch this one unfold."

He got up and began to dress. Tonight would be his penultimate triumph, splitting open John Tyler by taking everything from him.

Ettryne wished to be on hand when the girl, the *mamaisi*, fell. How hard she would go down, trying with her inferior magic to stop *him*. If she was still alive. He considered it more likely that his paid assassins had killed her.

He walked over to the wall of mirrors as he tied his cravat, stood before a small, unexceptional one in the center of the array, its surface so tarnished and dull that it hardly reflected anything, just the contours of his face in silhouette. He placed his left hand over his right, almost as if in prayer.

"Last rites," he said.

Crossing the room again, he laid his right hand upon the dome. "And after, I'll reunite you with your halfling and release you. Our pact is close to complete."

The *baka* opened its stitched gash of a mouth as if it wanted more than anything to clamp its jaws around that gloved hand. Once dressed in his knee-length coat with wide collar and revers, his silk cravat, and leather boots, Lord Ettryne retrieved his blackthorn walking stick, gave the dull mirrors a final glance to confirm there was still no hint of Priscilla in them, then turned down the wick on his oil lamp and blew out the various candles. He strode to the door, unlocked and opened it.

Outside, Martin Renehan leaned against the jamb, his face shining with sweat. "Christ, I thought you was never comin' out," he said, stuck his pistol against Ettryne's chest, and pulled the trigger. The pistol erupted.

The flash scorched Ettryne's blue vest and he stumbled backward twice, then fell onto his back in the room. The walking stick flew into the tangle of bedclothes.

Powder smoke filled the doorway. Renehan waited for it to disperse before he stepped heavily inside, kicking the door shut behind him. He kept the pistol trained on the body, where the vest sported a brief flame around the bullet hole. His other hand, wet and red, pressed to the leaking wound in his side.

His eyes adjusted to the dimness just like the last time he'd been in here. He exhaled, exhausted, in agony. The turned-down lamp stood on the table past the daybed. A chair stood beside it. More than anything, he wanted to sit, to rest.

As he stepped around Ettryne, he prodded the body. It was loose, lifeless. He moved on unevenly, like a sailor on a rocking deck.

To his left, the little leathery monster hissed and slammed itself against the pedestal dome, its bear-claw necklace clattered against the glass. Renehan waved his pistol at it. "You're a ferocious little bag of snot, aren't ya?" The squat creature paused as if considering this opinion.

He made it to the chair, turned, and sat with a groan both of pain and pleasure. He reached with his bloody hand and fiddled the wheel on the lamp until the wick burned bright. Light spangled off the mirrors at both ends of the room. His blood dribbled onto the table.

Renehan gazed wearily upon the corpse. "Fixed your flint, didn't I, ya bastard," he told it.

As if in response, the corpse moaned and then miraculously sat upright, facing the door. Renehan leaned forward and pressed the barrel of the Pepperbox against the back of Ettryne's head. "What you suppose the odds are you'll survive *this* shot?"

Ettryne sagged forward, away from the pistol, like a limp doll.

Renehan couldn't lean forward any farther without tipping out of the chair. "Right," he said, "you're not human anymore, are you? Still, I wager one in the back of the head will be difficult to shrug off, what d'ya think? Your brains just crawl back together, will they? Let's find out." He paused to wipe sweat from his eyes, which only smeared him with blood.

Slowly, heavily, Lord Ettryne twisted about. He held up one gloved hand in surrender. "Tell me what you want, doorman. Power? Money? Life of an aristocrat? Name it, I'll grant it. Only allow me to finish what I've begun." He lowered his head as if that much talk had been an effort. His breath sounded raspy.

"Finish what you begun? That include raping Priscilla? Hey?"

Ettryne shook his head. "Only said that to taunt you." He wheezed, sat straighter. "This—this isn't your country any more than it's mine. You owe them nothing, man. They treat you like dirt. Call you a *mudsill*, don't they."

"Sure, and while the English have been so *generous*. What I want, you said." He hissed. "What I want is answers to the more burnin' questions of the day."

Ettryne barked one laugh that ended in a choke of pain. He coughed, took a moment, then muttered, "You seem a saint when most I play the devil." He flicked his gloved fingers over his head in an invitation. "Ask."

"How'd you find us? On the road."

"*That's* all you want to know? Pah. The girl handled a fetish that my...that Priscilla had carried off." He shook his head. "Let us simplify: The girl handled it. Wiped her hands on her apron, same one she wore in the wagon. Thus, where she traveled, I had her measure and yours. My good fortune, your loss. All the way to the coast and back I knew where you were. Inferred your return route. Piffling, really. I lost her there. I'm assuming they killed her, yes? At the same time as they wounded you?" He looked up, around. The piercing blue eyes held not a trace of fear. "May I sit?"

"Fine," said Renehan. He didn't like how Ettryne seemed to be getting stronger. "Far end of your bed if you would, your lordship." He kept the pistol steady. "There are two shots left in this. You move, you get 'em both in the face."

Ettryne slid up onto the bed. He held one hand over the wound in his chest as if discomforted by indigestion. "You have a good deal more stamina than I would ever have imagined, doorman."

"Yeah. Well, seems to me so far you've underestimated about everything smarter than paint."

Ettryne's gaze narrowed and his mouth went tight for a second. Then he recovered and smirked. "I have the power to heal you, you know. Close up that terrible wound as though it never was."

Keeping the gun on him, Renehan pointed across at the *baka*. "Next question. What's your little devil doll there?"

Ettryne considered for a moment. Then he asked, "Are you familiar with the American war that lasted from 1812 to 1815?"

Renehan shook his head. "Before my time. And yours, I should think."

Ettryne simpered. "Not really. My brother's business was war, soldiering. Andrew was so *noble*, so *decent*. I was off across the world on a different quest altogether—self-destruction was my goal. Oh, I dabbled in thaumaturgy here and there, picked up some little knowledge. I reveled in the many methods of altering one's perceptions. I was deemed a wastrel if you want to know. The family nearly cut me off—the second son, the one who inherits nothing but ill will—except for my brother, who refused to reject me. Shall I tell you how much of my youth I wasted on the nonsense of alchemy alone?"

"Sorry, you've lost me there. A drunkard and a lout—that I understand. My hat's off to ya. Likely it's me own epitaph as well. But you're not exactly answering my question, *m'lord*." He bared his teeth.

"No, I suppose not. I've had no one to gloat to before you." He studied the blackened but bloodless hole in his vest. Renehan's shirt by comparison was so soaked now he could have wrung it out and blood would have pattered on the carpet.

Casually, as he continued to speak, Ettryne let his right hand slither beneath the heaped bedclothes beside him. "There was an early conflict in the war, before the rest officially began. They called it Tecumseh's War, named for a Shawnee who wanted some independence for his people which this rapacious nation was disinclined to allow him. England, which is to say my brother Andrew, sided with the Shawnee."

"Still not my answer."

"This Shawnee had a brother too. Tenskatawa, a shaman—a *sorcerer*."

"We seem to have hit the mother lode of them lately." Renehan wiped his bloody hand across his face.

"The two brothers fell out over how to deal with the Americans. Tecumseh and his people were slaughtered by soldiers led by General William Henry Harrison. Two sets of two brothers against Harrison, do you see? My brother died at Harrison's hand, defending the other two.

"Oh, I knew nothing of it, not for years, not until the next time I wrote home for money, and they learned where I was. My father wrote back that I was now the surviving heir, and implored me to come home. He sent me a last letter my brother had written to me. I won't bore you with how it affected me. But the news of Andrew's death gave me a direction, a course. I had been seeking out death. Now I wanted to mete it out instead. I was already by then halfway to the darkest of arts. I knew whom to ask to go deeper. I had a purpose, and courtesy of our empire, I went everywhere, studied every system of arcane knowledge, stripped away the fakery, combined the methodologies that worked. I became a synthesist." He raised his left arm for a moment as if to admire his glove. "It all cost me quite dearly, but then great power comes at a price."

"I wouldn't know, nor care."

Ettryne nodded. He lowered the left hand into the bedclothes, alongside his right. "Of course not, you want a different story. Suffice to say, by the time I returned home, I could retard my own aging—so successfully that I became my own son. I'd the papers to prove it. Almost no one remained who knew me. My father had drunk himself to death. One or two uncles did remark how like *my own father* I was. It was sublime. I charted my course, learning all I could about my brother's death. You have a brother also, don't you, Renehan—that slow-witted brute—"

Renehan was tired of the jabbering. He cocked the pistol.

Ettryne leaned away. "Yes, all right. Let's speak of Tenskatawa then, hmm? I could feel that old shaman waiting for me. Our purposes were entirely aligned, you see. Revenge on that murdering swine, Harrison.

"I went hunting for Tenskatawa. He and the surviving Shawnee had been banished by the victors to a dusty hellhole in the Kansas territory. I found a withered old man, his magic almost exhausted, as was his hope of ever taking revenge upon the man who'd slaughtered his people and slain his brother.

"I offered him a way to see justice delivered. A magic greater than anything he knew. Of course he accepted. His rage had burned as long as mine. He freely gave me his life. All that wrath." He grinned at the memory. "It was actually difficult to contain."

"Contain? Contain how?" Renehan heard himself slur. He winced and shook his head hard to stay alert, throwing off sweat. He was getting his answer. Another minute and he would shoot this bastard and be done with it all.

"Why, in a vessel—well, two vessels really, the *ba* and the *ka*. High and low souls, the Egyptians would have said. And what better vessels for one's seething anger than something made of one's own skin?"

The meaning of that amassed in his blurring mind. Renehan shot a glance at the little red-eyed demon. It was pressed to the glass as if listening to the story. "*That's* what the doll is? You skinned the poor sod?"

"He barely noticed. He was no more aware than…you are now."

On those words, Ettryne swung his walking stick out of the bedclothes with both hands and slapped Renehan's arm aside before he could fire.

Renehan grabbed the stick in his blood-soaked fist and yanked it so hard that his chair tipped back onto two legs and thudded down again.

He found himself gripping the shaft of the walking stick. At the other end of it, Ettryne's left hand dangled like some unnatural fruit. In his right hand, he now held the hilt of the rapier that had been encased within it. He lunged, stabbing through Renehan's chest until the hilt thumped against his breastbone. The empty sleeve of his left arm pressed hard against Renehan's windpipe.

Close up, Ettryne sneered. "A high price, as I said. Now die, you cur." His right hand slid down Renehan's arm to keep the pistol pointed away.

Sparkling motes crowded Renehan's sight. He knew he was dying. He'd failed, lulled by Ettryne's long and convoluted speech.

The demon clattered eagerly against the dome, and Renehan thought maybe he saw a way he could still exact some vengeance.

He wheezed, "High price it is then, m'lord," and fired his pistol at the dome.

It took all his energy to hang onto it. He knew he couldn't cock it again. Death was turning down the lamp. But he fell into the darkness to the sound of Ettryne's scream of rage, which knelled like the most wonderful music in the world.

Forty-Four

James Hambleton Christian

It was Elizabeth screaming upstairs.

I yelled, "Stay here!" to Zenobia, Marcellus, and Deborah, and took off running across to the west stairs. Priscilla remained unconscious on the mess table.

Zenobia called after me, "James, the potion!" but I wasn't about to stop and drink down what she wanted now.

Jasper was running from the vestibule, pulling up his braces with one hand, holding his oil lamp in the other, when I reached the first floor. "Wot in 'ell's that?" he asked. I remembered when we'd suspected him of Ettryne's role. Ridiculous now to think how far we'd stretched ourselves.

I didn't answer, but swung around the newel post. He followed, and together we got about three steps up before something large came thundering down to meet us, and we jumped back down. Jasper wheeled all the way to the promenade door, ready to bolt across the colonnade roof if need be.

The shape tumbled into view, flinging off blood, limbs flailing like a broken dead pinwheel, and finally flopped down at the base of the stairs.

"Ah, God, no," I said. Jasper inched up behind me.

It was Devonee. Sent back with the children, probably to get her out of Mr. Tyler's sight.

Her head was half-squashed and twisted almost backwards. Blood was leaking out beneath her as if she'd been stabbed all over. Whatever her wide eyes stared at now, it dwelled on the far side of the veil. I reached down to close her eyes, and the moment I touched her, a spark jumped between us. I snatched my hand back, bumped against Jasper, shook and blew on my stung palm. Jasper, peering around me, sucked in a gasp through his front teeth.

There was nothing to be done for her, but neither one of us wanted to use those stairs now. We turned and ran for the cramped servants' staircase, hoping they would prove safe.

We bolted into the second-floor hall. The baby was crying from the girls' room, but Elizabeth, on her knees, peered at us from beside the narrow transverse corridor where Tyler had watched the mobs almost a year earlier. She wailed and threw her hands out to me. I went down on one knee and held her. She was sobbing, and terror had given her the hiccoughs. She clutched her belly as if her baby was kicking.

"It took—took Alice! And Tazewell, I think. I—I don't *know*." This last word bawled out.

Jasper pressed the lamp ahead of him into the room, followed it. I stood.

"Baby's all right," he called. "Didn't touch 'er, looks like."

I pulled Elizabeth to her feet. Pregnant as she was, she had some difficulty.

"Came in," she started, then began again. "It came in or it *was* in, I can't—can't be sure. We'd a candle lit, but I was asleep—when Alice screamed. Then it was already there, like oil crawling up the bed and hanging over the bassinet. Devonee was on the cot beside Mary. She went—went straight for it. Protected her." Her chin quivered. "Tazewell ran in."

But she had been fleeing the other way and didn't know for sure if it got him. I looked at Jasper's light moving around the room. I didn't hear Tazewell.

"It was—was like a vulture. Folded its wings around Devonee and she was gone. It poured into the hall. I could hear what it was doing to her." She drew down her head, covered her ears with both arms.

"Alice, what about Alice?"

She refused to look up as she spoke. "Must have taken her, same time. She just wasn't there. It—gushed right past me." She looked up. "It had *eyes*—red horrible eyes."

I left her leaning against the wall, sobbing. She didn't know that she was describing eyes I'd seen.

Jasper was holding the baby and cooing to her, pulling faces. Would have scared me, but it quieted Mary. I asked, "Tazewell?" and Jasper shook his head. I got down and looked under the beds, but there was nobody. Close to the door there was blood, but it was probably Devonee's. I hoped so.

"Jasper," I said, "please take Mary down to the mess room. Make Miss Elizabeth go with you."

"But the *children*," she said.

"I'll find them. That thing wants you too, and it'll come back for you, you stay up here."

That shook her. Jasper handed her the baby, then led the way down the east stairs and she followed.

I looked up into the waiting hall, where Ettryne had stung me with his blackthorn stick. No, the *tebo* hadn't gone there. The thing had tossed Devonee down the west stairs. I was certain it had gone back to its favorite room.

My sister's room.

The door was closed and immovable, the way it had been for Isaac the night the thing snatched away Harrison. I put my shoulder to it once, twice.

It wouldn't budge, and my cut left arm seeped some blood.

I was standing, helpless at the door, when Osbert Drummond came thundering up the stairs. If I'd wanted proof the *tebo* hadn't gone down there, I guess he was it.

He said, "Stuck?" as he came up beside me. Then like a bear on its hind legs, he put his shoulder to the door, and I joined him, and we threw ourselves against it twice more before it cracked open and swung wide.

It was pitch dark, darker than it should have been. Jasper had taken the lamp though, so I ran for a night candle across the hall and brought it over, then held it ahead of us as we went inside. The room was thick with bluish-gray webs, strung from the wardrobe, the bed, everywhere. They seemed to be the creature's calling card. Or else Ettryne's brand of magic attracted them. The room was cold, like a cave underground.

Where the flame touched them, the webs hissed. Spiders skittered off in retreat. We crossed to the mirror in the corner. It was murky, tarnished, but I remembered Isaac's story and pressed my hand to it.

The glass was solid.

"Alice!" I yelled at it. "Can you hear me, Alice? Tazewell?"

I swore I heard her call my name, but it was so faint I doubted myself until Drummond whispered excitedly, "Think I heard her."

"It hasn't killed her then. Why though?"

Behind us, Zenobia said, "Something's happened, is why."

We turned around. She stood in the doorway with Marcellus. She was holding the stone bowl. I knew then I wasn't going to be leaving this room.

"Miss Priscilla's awake now. She say something went wrong on Ettryne's end of things. She don't know what but she heard him shouting, plenty mad. Say he's comin' here." She strode into the room. Marcellus remained in the hall. "Mr. Drummond gotta go downstairs now. We all protected downstairs, and anyway, y'all can't be here for this."

Drummond wasn't going to obey her. The poor man had lost his brother and I don't think he cared much now about being protected. I told him, "She's right. You have to go. If he does arrive… Well, you'll know when to come up again." I patted his shoulder. "Protect them."

Zenobia lit the bedside candle from the candle I carried, then gave it to Drummond. "Go on." He tromped out with as much reluctance as Marcellus.

Zenobia set down the bowl. "You know you gotta do this. *Tebo* got Alice. Miss Elizabeth says Tazewell too, but I don't know. That charm what protected Miss Letitia? I put that in his room. Should have kept everything out of there."

I sat on the bed. "You and I, we ought to have run north when we had the chance. We could have coaxed Martin to do it."

She sat beside me. "You know you never woulda. That's a thing Mel loved about you—how you take care of your people. Even if like Samuel they's ungrateful for it. Even if they'd sell you off."

I shook my head. "Don't think I'm quite *that* nice."

She smiled lopsided. She was going to say something else, but the candle flame suddenly dimmed. The surface of the mirror seemed to roil like a storm cloud. "It's coming again," she warned.

There sat the bowl, a thick dark brown mixture shining inside it, full of my blood. "Now, huh?"

"Got no choice, James. All the evil's comin' here."

I stood, feeling as old as time. I picked up the bowl. "You...take care of them all for me, yeah?"

Tears welled in her eyes. "You're gon' come back," she insisted. I don't think either of us believed her, but I nodded. Then, before I could think of some other way to stall, I drank the contents down.

It was bitter, sour, and sharp as swallowing pins. I clutched myself around the middle and, half-doubled over, shoved the bowl back onto the small table. Closed my eyes until the torment stopped.

The candlelight shrank to almost nothing. I could hardly make out Zenobia. Darkness was pouring like a thick fog out of that mirror to fill the room.

I took a step, feeling more steady, pushed out my hand. This time it passed through the mirror's surface. My fingers touched something wet and alive. I gave a final glance back. But Zenobia was on her knees. She was kneeling beside my body, stretched out on the floor.

Jesus, take me, I thought.

Instead, whatever I had hold of took off at full chisel and snatched me into the mirror.

Forty-Five

Devonee had got between the darkness and the baby, and it swarmed over her like a nest of hornets.

With it thus distracted, Tazewell thought he could save Alice, and he jumped onto the nearest bed, where Elizabeth had been sleeping. Alice reached for him. He grabbed her hands, but even as he did, the void enveloped them. Tazewell stepped back, trying to pull her with him; but his foot was off the bed, and he fell backward. He never reached the floor.

The darkness flowed from Alice around him, and in complete silence he seemed to fall for hours. Although he couldn't see or hear her, he tried to cling onto his sister's hands. Terror made him let go for an instant. He reached desperately into the emptiness, but his fingers closed upon nothing. "Alice!" he yelled. Her muffled response sounded miles and miles away.

The next thing he knew he lay in the hall outside his mother's room. The entire doorway into the room bulged with the pulsating void. It radiated dread. He scrambled up and bolted. Behind him a door slammed.

Into the stair hall, and down the stairs; but they were slick as oil. He lost his footing and tumbled, tucking his head. He struck something soft and squelchy, turned painfully over.

Inches away, Devonee stared straight through him into infinity. He yelped and scrambled away on the wet stairs. His knee hurt, his elbows, but Tazewell hardly noticed the pain.

Devonee looked like a rag doll that had been stomped on.

He pulled himself up along the bannister, tugged his nightshirt down. It was blotched everywhere with blood, most of which belonged to Devonee. The stairs were drenched in it. He tried not to look at her but couldn't help himself.

Carefully, he stepped down and over her body. James, he had to find James.

The first-floor cross hall lay empty and as abandoned as a tomb. He hobbled back into the stair hall, circled past Devonee, then limped down for the kitchen.

James must be back by now. He would know what to do. He always knew what to do.

Halfway to the bottom, he froze. Priscilla was down there, talking. "Zenobia, *please* either go find Mary or let me go get her. I don't care what's up there. For God's sake, it's my daughter!"

Tazewell crouched down where he was.

He'd kept a close eye on Priscilla the whole journey south on the train, at the funeral. Even though James told him she wasn't responsible for swiping that charm from Mother's room, Tazewell could see that she suspected herself. Nobody else realized. They saw her grieving. She'd been so close to Mother, and maybe that was part of it. But that wasn't all. She *knew*.

On the train coming back, when she went to tousle his hair and he pulled away—well, he couldn't help it any more than he could help that he was hiding from her now. Alice and Elizabeth had chided him for his disrespect, but they didn't understand. Priscilla—she was so shaken, so guilty, that she took Mary and went and wept at the other end of the train car while his sisters berated him, insisting he apologize, until he finally got up and left. Everybody was mad at him of course.

When they'd arrived tonight, he had immediately sought out James, but James was gone and nobody would say where. They acted strange. Deborah and Sally, they'd traded looks. They were keeping something from him. James was always here, so something was wrong, something had happened. It couldn't be that he was dead, or they'd all have been crying. And he couldn't be *gone*. James wouldn't abandon him or Alice. He wouldn't.

With no one willing to tell him anything, he'd withdrawn from all of them, gone to his room. He meant to wait up until he heard James return, but then everything had gone quiet, and he'd dozed off too.

Priscilla sounded like herself, but he still didn't trust her, didn't trust that she wouldn't turn again into the thing that had come into his mother's room. Zenobia said something about this floor being the only protected one, and then Tall George muttered angrily. It sounded like he *wanted* to go upstairs, but Zenobia told him "No." Tazewell wondered how many of the slaves were in there. Maybe everybody else, but not James.

Where the stairs were located, if he stepped out into the central hall they would surely see him. So he reeled across the entryway and into the scullery on the north side, where the dishes on which they'd earlier eaten their cold supper were stacked to be washed. From there through one of the pantries, into the darker depths of the meat curing room.

He had been in there before—quite likely he was the only inhabitant of the President's House who had set foot in every single room. Even James probably hadn't investigated all of the third floor. Of course, part of the time Tazewell had been spying on Mel as she placed her charms in the rooms up there. He had a feeling she'd always known he was watching, but she never said anything. He'd liked Mel.

The meat room was hung with hams, and strings of sausages, some white with mold. He could make out the wide carving block table in the middle. The illumination that fell through the hall door delineated the small kegs for brining that lined the north wall—the hall lamps were lit as if everyone was awake, and he supposed maybe everyone was after what had happened upstairs.

He ducked under a row of hams and crept to the carving block table. All sorts of things he'd never seen before lay strewn across it: a large stone mortar and pestle, dried leaves, berries, a pile of ugly roots with curly tendrils dangling off them, an old black-frame candlelamp, and a circular arrangement of stubby candles. Off to one side lay a couple odd objects sort of like the magic charms Mel had placed around the house. He picked one of them up. It was fat, almost round, and small feathers dotted its middle; glass beads on strings hung off it and it had all sorts of designs stitched into it. There was thread, needles, and more beads on the table beside it. The charm seemed to throb in his hand, making him feel stronger. He worked his arm. His elbow didn't seem so stiff all of a sudden.

He took the charm with him.

On a tray beneath the cutting surface lay cleavers, knives, and assorted other butcher's tools. Tazewell selected a boning knife, small and narrow-bladed. If he got dragged near that horrible void again, he intended to kill it and get Alice back. Nobody else had any idea what they were dealing with, but he did. He had seen it that day in the East Room beneath the black shroud that his sister had pulled aside; seen its bear-like, rippling shape, its eyes like two furious red stars glaring down at her—and then at him—in the instant before it vanished. He still didn't understand what had made it go away except that he had been watching. Now it was here somewhere, and so was she.

As he stood there, Jasper and Elizabeth passed the doorway. Jasper called out, "Zenobia! We got Mary 'ere!"

Tazewell hurried to peer around the door. A table with a night candle on it stood right outside.

Zenobia and Priscilla came out of the mess room, Priscilla crying, "Oh, Mary, oh, my darling!" He saw Sally and Olive too. They helped Elizabeth. Marcellus looked on like he wanted to help but didn't know what to do with a pregnant woman.

Tazewell drew back among the hams. Everybody must be in the mess room.

He considered what he needed. Opened the candlelamp, selected one of the candle stubs, then leaned cautiously out of the doorway again and lit it from the night candle, placing it back inside the lamp. He slid the knife through the iron ring on the top of the lamp, so that he could carry it and the knife ahead of him and still hold the fat round charm.

Lots of people started talking, their voices echoing across the vaulted ceiling. Deborah and Olive ran past, down into the room where they all slept.

Then the brick hall fell quiet.

He looked out. No one reappeared. He gathered his courage and crept into the hall in his bloody nightshirt.

He'd only gone a little ways when four women came out of the East Room. Tazewell sprang into the furnace room before they saw him. He didn't dare close the door all the way or they would hear.

Two shadows flicked past; but instead of following Deborah and Olive back to the mess, Mariama and Ethel went into the kitchen opposite. Conversing, they lit the lamps and set to doing something. He hoped they were making more charms or sharpening knives. Still, he could not enter the hall again.

His only course seemed to be under the south portico and up the steps to the Blue Saloon. The thing hadn't brought Alice down here anyway. Was anyone at all even looking for her?

He edged around the furnace, which reminded him that the other doorman—the crabby one he didn't like—wasn't here either. Where were they?

Reaching the door, Tazewell had to set his lamp down to open it. Then he stepped into the warm night. Hands full with the charm, the knife, and the lamp, he couldn't grab hold to latch the door and so left it ajar.

He stood awhile in the portico's shadow, listening to the crickets' chirr. The whole house might have been asleep, except there was lamplight falling through the two windows of the mess room and across the lawn. He stole up to the nearest one and peered in. The scene was much as he had guessed: everybody was in the room, including Osbert Drummond, the third doorman. If *he* was here, then maybe James and Renehan were back. If they were, they must be upstairs. They would be searching for Alice.

Tazewell headed up the curved sweep of steps. At first he didn't see the dark shape amassing on the porch above him—not until the light in his lamp began to wane did he look up. The storm cloud tried to engulf him. He didn't wait to see its awful eyes, but threw himself away from its embrace. It parted like fog.

Yelling, Tazewell flew down the steps and back through the furnace room door. Inside, he pressed against it, holding it closed, praying.

So much for bravery: He'd had his knife and in his fright had failed to use it.

When nothing banged on the door, he turned and peered out.

The darkness beneath the portico looked normal, his lamp reflected in the glass panes. Somehow, the monster had been unable to touch him, even though he had walked right into it.

The charm. It had to be the charm.

He retreated—maybe he could sneak out through the hall. But as he approached the half-open door, women's voices approached, and Tazewell feared they would see his light through the opening. He ducked into the nearest coal room. The voices—Sally and Olive—passed by.

It looked like the fireman hadn't shoveled any coal out of here all winter. His light fell on something at the far end, and he gingerly stepped toward it, but the small chunks of coal were almost impossible to distinguish against the floor thick with coal dust. He hissed and flinched as they bit into his bare feet.

Nearer, he made out a board laid flat across two mounds of coal. Scraps of cloth and small bowls lay upon it. One bowl contained broken-up animal bones, another looked like dirt. Between them a few embroidery needles glimmered. Next to the board were heaped some flour bags, all coated with dust as if they had been lying there for months, and a coiled pile of rope.

He stooped to pass under the large duct that fed the Green Parlor and East Room. The ductwork rumbled, startling him. He waited, the knife and lamp raised defensively. The noise stopped. The furnace wasn't on, he knew that. An odd notion occurred to him, and he held up the fat charm, touched it to the duct.

The duct flexed and shook. From inside it came clattering and a scrabbling sound.

"Alice?" he said, trying both to call out to his sister and not be heard in the kitchen. He said it again, a little louder.

Her answer was muffled, but clearly his name, so distant she could have been calling from the attic. He started to call again, but coal dust was sprinkling down from the duct as he inhaled. He began to cough, hard enough that he bent over, placing one hand against the duct to steady himself.

Something inside it chittered ferociously and slammed wildly back and forth hard enough to shake the metal as it thumped away, straight on through the wall into the laundry room.

"Tazewell, help!" came the distant cry.

He imagined the thing, *hidden inside*, had hold of her and was dragging her with it. Everyone was looking for the creature, and he had found it. It terrified him, but the charm had protected him. It would protect them both. He was going to get Alice back.

He took his knife and lamp, and the length of rope, and hopped through the coal again. The coal room had its own small door onto the hall, left over from the days before there had been a furnace.

At the door he pressed his head to the wood. Nothing seemed to stir on the other side of it, and cautiously he opened it and looked out. Across the way, the Gullah slave Ethel stood staring straight at him, her eyes as wide as if he were a ghost.

Before she could do anything, Tazewell shot across the hall into the east stairwell.

Alice—he had to save Alice.

Forty-Six

James Hambleton Christian

The center of the crossroads sprouted a huge ebony pole and crosspiece. At least that was how it looked from up the hill—tall as the mast of a ship buried somewhere deep beneath the ragged gray and purple landscape.

How I'd arrived here, I couldn't say. Whatever had pulled me through the mirror had let go.

Distant buildings was like those of Washington, but long after the city had died. Everything was colored wrong: the ruins all black, the sky above as copper as a cooking pot. Instead of a moon, there was a woman curled upon herself like a sleeping cat—a perfect circle except for the fall of her white hair, which nearly touched the ground as if she hung just above it. She drifted behind me, drawing the copper of the sky with her, and it grew darker down the hill.

I descended, expecting I don't know what, until I had almost come up to the crossroads, where I realized that what I'd seen to be a pole was a giant figure, skinny as a mantis, its arms held straight out at the sides, legs stuck in the ground like a single post. Its head could hardly be seen at first, hanging down as if asleep. My foot scraped the roadbed, and it raised up enough to look down upon me: two eyes blue as sky in a near-featureless face topped by two horns.

I knew, as if her voice whispered inside my head, that I was staring at one of Mel's *lwa*. Legba, the one who guarded doorways and crossroads.

He had a prick on him about five foot long and stiff as a hickory branch. I thought if he had a tail he would be pointing in all four directions at once.

His voice rolled down to me. "You a solitary traveler?" Before I could respond, something coiled and glided around the pillar of his legs—an enormous rainbow-striped serpent as thick in body as me. The snake slid up his torso and then slung itself over his right arm. Its head drooped down to my level, tilted back and forth as if trying to take my measure, but all the while staring at me coldly with golden eyes. Its tongue snicked out and in.

The snake settled itself as something poppled across the pillar of Legba's thighs. They seemed now less solid, more like a skinny doorway to someplace, and I beheld a figure striding toward me from a long ways off. It wore a tailcoat like I usually did in the President's House. I looked down, took stock of myself to find that I was now dressed the same as him.

When I looked up, he stood right in front of me.

His face was bare of skin, a skull, but more supple than bone, for it could grin and frown around the cigar he was puffing. He wore a tall top hat with a half-broken feather in the band. Him, I also knew. Mel and Abias had referenced him.

Samedi, the lord of the dead.

"And resurrection," he said, as if he heard my thoughts. To Legba above, he said, "He'm not alone. Mambo Mary with him. She arrived awhile back, you know." He leered at me. "You like the taste of her plenty, hey?" His tongue wiggled obscenely. "Miss her somethin' terrible."

"And those children," hissed the snake, "who aren't even him's own."

"Blood-tied," said a black rooster that walked out from behind Legba. Samedi picked up the bird and it transformed into a tall, round-hipped woman as white as the moon woman, but with pure black hair.

"Brigitte," he said soulfully. They could have been twins, opposites in every respect, except that Brigitte had a cross with a circle in its center burned like a slave-brand into her forehead. She reached up and slapped at Legba's prick as if it interfered with her view of the sky.

"Shortly, he's in his grave." Then to me she added, "They'll give you a cross for your many kindnesses. That's your sign for now. When the time comes, be sure and make 'em give one to your friend. He's *my* blood, you know."

I stared blankly at her, having no idea what she meant.

"But which road do we send him down?" the snake asked.

Legba waved his right hand. "Go down that one and he'll find death at the end."

Samedi laughed. "They all got death at the end." He walked up to me. "Most people can't tell the difference between they dead or alive, so death look the same as life. They only don't know it. Would that be you?"

Was that me—alive and dead? I understood the question then.

Mel and I had guarded ourselves so hard to escape the inevitable pain of one of us being sold off that we'd hobbled ourselves instead of living full while we could. We'd taken what little we could in the dark, denied everything in the light. Watching Tyler's disposition, we'd been split apart by something else, but split all the same.

Nothing was ever safe, and nothing was forever. We should have grabbed every moment, dark and light. Had the *lwa* let me see her, that's what I would have told her then.

Samedi waited for my answer, but he was already grinning like he knew it. I suppose he'd heard everything I thought.

"That used to be me," I told him.

"Hee-hee-hee." He clapped his hands and puffed smoke. "Pass him along!"

"World's not set right," hissed the rainbow snake.

Legba replied, "Never to be set right, and not by him nor us. He'm already died to fix what can be fixed. *Pass him on.*"

Samedi took the cigar from his teeth and blew smoke at me, so thick this time that it closed me in a fog. Something slapped my back twice, then slapped the backs of my thighs. It stung, but more, it shook me alert as if making the heart I no longer had beat faster. I was pushed through the smoke.

"Nothing in his life became him like leaving it," whispered Samedi.

I said, "I know that line."

"'Course you do." It was Brigitte, her voice receding. The moon woman was sinking. "Almost he saved you at the last."

"Who?"

"My blood. Martin."

I stumbled to a stop.

I was standing in a reddish dull darkness. On a table to my right, a lamp gave off just the barest glow from a wick turned to its lowest. Heavy curtains covered the windows. A daybed stood beside me, a chair right in front of me next to the lamp. A lifeless body slumped over the armrest.

Ettryne's room. I had arrived in the heart of his lair, and for one hopeful moment I imagined the body in front of me was his.

Forty-Seven

Lord Ettryne stood outside and watched the people gathered in one room on the kitchen level. He didn't see Priscilla, however. Perhaps she *had* taken her own life. It would explain the silence of her. One of the slave women was bawling about something and some of the others were patting her shoulders and bent over, talking to her.

There was no point in trying to enter here. He had already been jolted with some sort of charge at the east door. Protections were still in place on the kitchen level, put there by the first one—the one he'd had killed. There was nothing new in it, but it wasn't worth expending the energy.

He went up the steps of the south portico and entered through the Blue Saloon, meeting no challenge at that door. The room, in which he had listened to so many pompous, arrogant, and benighted fools pontificate, lay silent and dark; only the skunky residuum of cigars evidenced its more familiar state. Charles Dickens had compared this seedy house to a London men's club, and on that point the softhearted novelist and he agreed—this country's elite were little better than animals.

In the dark he moved sinuously around the furnishings so as not to make a sound. At the hall door he listened, but there was nothing to hear. They hadn't set a trap for him—there was no trap a third-rate *mamaisi* could set that mattered.

He stepped out into the cross hall. A few burning candles along its length attested to there still being people about somewhere; otherwise, there wasn't a trace of occupation. They were all cowering down below where that woman had created actual protections keeping him out. She'd known her business, that one. Without her they were merely fearful creatures in whose terror he delighted. Hiding like a pack of runaways in a cellar.

"The rest of the house belongs to me," he softly proclaimed.

Ettryne crossed the mat-covered floor to the east stairs and went up. In the stairwell on the private floor, he paused to push his senses through the spaces above. Again, he was alone.

At the top he crossed to the room that he had imbued as a parallel to his own. He had done so to capture Harrison. It was sheer blind luck that they had installed Tyler's wife in the very same room.

The body lying on the floor there surprised him. That slave, Christian, who had been in his room, and in the wagon with the girl and Renehan. It appeared the slave had managed to drag himself back here. He still wore dirty slave togs, obviously hadn't lived long enough to change into his uniform. His arm had some sort of blood-soaked makeshift tourniquet on it. That wound wouldn't have killed him. Probably if Ettryne turned him over, there would be a worse one, something suffered defending the girl and her magic. Or maybe the *baka* had killed the slave here before the mirror. He really should find out the situation.

The mirror reflected him darkly. Then the glass blazed to life, and in the center of it a vortex swirled, answering his call.

The darkness gathered into a shape like an elongated shadow. Its red eyes glared at him. It hated him now almost as much as it had Harrison. Without its other half, the counterpart was near-deranged with bloodlust. It wanted to be reunited and released into death, and he wasn't about to tell it this could never happen now because of a cunning blasted doorman. He would end their bargain swiftly when the time came. Once he had all the children.

The *baka* filled the frame of the mirror but did not emerge. He could feel its suspicious probing as it sought an explanation for why it couldn't deliver its captive to his room, why it could only slide now from mirror to mirror in this house.

"There's been trouble," he told it. "The one called Renehan destroyed some things. When the time comes, I'll retrieve your body from the duct and reunite you myself. In the meantime, work within the confines of this place. What do you have for me?"

Like oily tar, the *baka* came out of the mirror and flowed to the bed where Letitia Tyler had died, engulfing it. It hung suspended a moment, then swept back into the mirror. Upon the bed lay the body of Alice Tyler, insensate but not dead. That finishing blow belonged to Ettryne.

"I want the complete set. All of them. Drive them from the cellar somehow. We'll hold them in this room until his return. Tyler has to watch his children die. And if you find Priscilla, dead or alive, bring her as well."

The *baka* questioned that he didn't know her fate.

"As I said, there was trouble. I lost my connection to her at the same time as you lost yours to your halfling."

The darkness roiled.

"We're so close to it," Ettryne assured the creature. "Bring me the others and kill anything in your way. We end this tonight, and you gain your release." The blackness dwindled into the glass.

Ettryne leaned over the comatose Alice.

"Time's almost up, child. You're about to be as dead as your slave here—you and your family line come to an end, just as mine has because of your strutting, stupid, *expectorating* nation."

—»»»— ««««—

Tall George, armed with the leg from a broken table, was insisting for the fifth time that he wanted to go upstairs in search of Tazewell and Alice. Sally and Deborah were trying to calm Olive, who had earlier noticed something dark and wet dripping in the stairwell across the hall and as a result had gone up far enough that she'd found Devonee's body. She'd stopped wailing, but now she rocked her body and chanted over and over, "Oh sweet Jesus." At the far end of the table, Elizabeth Tyler clutched her belly and looked on as if unable to comprehend anything she saw.

Zenobia was just about to explain again to George that if he went up alone, he would end up exactly like Devonee, when the furnace ductwork rumbled overhead. Everyone turned to listen. The noise was distant, like a gathering storm.

Priscilla, who had come back in from the hall and placed Mary, obliviously burbling, in the chair beside her, said, "Surely the furnace is off."

Cyrus, beside Tall George, replied, "Yes, Miss Priscilla, it is. Be like warmin' the sun, lightin' that coal this time of year."

Then they were all talking on top of each other, save for Osbert Drummond, who stood directionless in the corner. Zenobia continued to stare overhead at the heat duct as if waiting for the sound to recur.

Ethel had gone to get some water for Olive, and she suddenly burst in, causing Olive to jump where she sat and the others to fall silent again.

Ethel said, "Dat chil' Tazewell jis' run up'um stairs tuh da first flo', skeered me tuh de't."

"Tazewell's here?" Priscilla's wide eyes filled with tears. "We have to find him!"

"'E come out'uh the coal rum," Ethel tried to explain.

"It's in the furnace duct," Zenobia said in awe, as everything fell into place for her. "In the East Room. That's where Tazewell's gone—to git Alice." She whipped about, faced Cyrus. "Come with me."

He looked at her as if she was crazy. "You tole George it ain't safe."

"It ain't. But I got five charms left. I put Abias' charms in the parlors, not the *tebo* nor the *bokor* can git in there like they can't git in *here*."

"I'm coming too." Priscilla stood.

"No," Zenobia said. "Miss Priscilla, you gotta look after your child, and Miss Elizabeth."

Priscilla's voice broke. "But I'm to *blame*," she sobbed.

Zenobia put a hand on her wrist. "No, you're not. Was never you. Was *always* him."

"Let me come, *please*. Elizabeth, you'll look after Mary. You're both safe down here."

Elizabeth nodded slowly, agreeing. She got up to sit next to Mary.

There was no argument to be made. Zenobia said, "All right. Cyrus?"

"No," Marcellus objected. He wrested the table leg from George. "I'm not letting you out of my sight."

Drummond stepped up behind him. "Don't try to stop me neither," he warned them all. "I'm comin' with you." He and Marcellus nodded, both inflexible.

"If that's how it's to be." Zenobia pushed them ahead of her. To the others in the mess, she called back, "Don't let nothing and nobody talk any of you into goin' upstairs after us. No matter *what*. Cyrus, don't you let 'em."

Then she charged across the hall and into the stairwell.

Forty-Eight

James Hambleton Christian

I reached for the lamp on the table in Ettryne's room and tried to turn up the wick. My hand passed straight through it, although the wick spit for a second like I could affect the flame but not touch anything solid.

Helpless, I stood there in the dimness, trying to figure out how I was going to do anything at all, much less anything respecting the *lwa*. I mulled over what Brigitte had said about how I should honor Renehan with a cross, and how the cross was my sign. *My sign.*

This room was covered in signs and all belonging to Ettryne—arcane letters and symbols he'd written everywhere. I drifted over to the nearest wall, behind the chair, pressed my finger to one of the mirrors, and drew a cross about the same proportions as Legba at the crossroads.

To my surprise, the mirror blazed to life, brighter than a candle. I repeated the gesture on other mirrors around it and they all glowed too, as if catching a sunrise. I turned back to the chair.

The body hanging out of it wasn't Ettryne. It was Martin Renehan, gray and waxen in death. The little three-shot Pepperbox pistol he liked dangled from his blood-drenched hand. One cylinder was still loaded. I followed the direction of his outstretched arm and floated over to the shattered dome, and the squat leather monster lying there, near split in half, a splinter of the dome sticking up from its head, the feathers broken along its back. One of the horrible red eyes had burst. The vessel of the demon was like a body—that's what Zenobia had said, and what Mel had tried to express. Martin Renehan must have figured to destroy the demon by destroying the body. Had it worked? Where was Ettryne then? Maybe gone to finish the job himself.

"How do I proceed? What am I supposed to do?" I called to the *lwa*, but they didn't manifest. Apparently, I was to figure it all out by myself.

I glanced around me at all the dozens and dozens of mirrors reflecting the room, expecting to see I don't know what—a scene of someplace, the way Ettryne had used them to see into the house. Save for the ones I'd lit, all I saw was bits of the room thrown back at me.

Except for one.

Among all the others, I didn't notice it at first—it was so small and unassuming, hung in the middle of the east wall, and about the size and shape of Miss Letitia's slate. The frame was cheap. The mirror looked like any other, except that its surface had turned green-black like a mirror out of antiquity. It threw back nothing.

As I crossed in front of it, the air around me seemed to thicken, until each step was like walking on the bottom of the ocean, and as cold as that too. The air froze.

I pointed through the strange pressure to paint my cross upon it, when a great blue spark jumped from it the way a smaller spark had jumped from Devonee before.

For an instant I was touching the heart of him. Glimpses of him drove through me like the exploded shards that had attacked us the last time I'd been here.

There was Ettryne answering the door of his room to Miss Priscilla—her eyes as blank as paper; Ettryne with her, naked on that daybed; then with others, women I'd ushered into a dozen levées, served drinks to, all of them here, insensibly naked and used on that bed, an army filing through one after the other, until the moment Renehan burst in and shot him, and even then he didn't die, he gloated over his plans and his split monster, not caring because he knew he was about to kill Martin—all of this poured into me till I was drowning in revulsion of him, but I did not interrupt the images.

Time and again Lord Ettryne came and stood before this tiny mirror; time and again, he went away burning like the ones I'd lit up. Martin had shot him point-blank and he hadn't died.

He hadn't died because his heart was right here.

I tried to pick up something to smash the mirror, but I couldn't interfere with anything in the room, couldn't touch it, same as the lamp.

I looked back at Martin's body. How I'd envied him his ability to act against villains, our enemies, anyone at all, when I couldn't, didn't dare for fear of the consequences.

He's my blood, you know.

Brigitte's blood. It might be her blood, but it had pumped out of him now. It covered his shirt, coated his hand, and dripped from the pistol. He'd sacrificed himself, same as I had with the potion. Here we were, twinned again… An odd idea occurred to me.

I went over to the chair. I started to sit, thinking none of this could work. Mel had possessed Mrs. Dickens, but Mrs. Dickens had been alive.

I don't know what that could have felt like to Mel's spirit. This was like wrapping myself in the skin of a dead fish, clammy and close and awful. Like I'd wrapped myself inside Death's bones and his maggoty fish-belly slickness.

Of Martin there remained only the dimmest glow. He was a fire a hundred miles farther down that road I'd stood on with Samedi. Closing myself up in him was me squeezing that glow, crushing the final bit of flame into me. It was a defilement and I prayed for his forgiveness.

But I stared hard at his hand, my hand; and slowly the fingers, our fingers, closed around the butt of the pistol. The glimmer of Martin Renehan was laughing, because he'd gone through this once already. I felt his strength flow into that arm. Together we raised the pistol, heavy as a 12-pounder ball. Aimed and steadied it. Together we cocked the hammer and pulled the final trigger. The Pepperbox jumped hard enough that it spun away and across the floor.

The ball struck the black mirror. Pitted it. Hit, flattened, and bounced off. We had failed!

But then the first tiny crack appeared. It spread, and another split it, and another. The surface, like sand, began to pour off. The pit became a hole. The hole ruptured.

A black wind roared through the room. It buffeted and tugged at me and yet nothing else was moving. I rose up, pulled from the body of Martin Renehan, dead as I'd found him, his spark exhausted.

All the other mirrors went dark.

The howling one sucked me straight into the devil's heart.

Forty-Nine

Holding a fat funeral candle, Tazewell Tyler leaned into the circular hole of the furnace vent. It had taken the fireplace poker to pry off the cast-iron grille beside the hearth, and some of the plaster had come with it, leaving broken, exposed lath where the hole had been cut.

The duct was so black with coal dust that it might have led straight down into the bowels of the Earth. He knew that wasn't the case—that it hugged the ceiling of the laundry room only a couple feet below.

"Alice?" he called into the hole. Softly, as though she was wedged deep in the ductwork or even the furnace itself, her voice answered with his name. Exactly as he'd thought, she'd been hidden in the duct.

He tied the rope around his waist, and the other end of it to the grille he'd prised loose. It was bigger than the hole, and he figured it wouldn't fall in after him, but to be safe he looped the rope once around the nearest andiron too. The room, the whole house, seemed absolutely silent, but he worried that the thing might still be roaming the halls. Then Alice's voice floated up out of the vent again: "Tazewell, help me."

He held the candle stub down inside the wall, but there was no sign of her. Wax pattered into the darkness.

He couldn't wait. If the creature had left her there, then he had to get her out before it came back. He would slide down, tie the rope to his sister, and then pull himself along it to get out. Then he would pull her out after him.

Tazewell turned and wriggled his legs into the hole, lowering himself until he was balanced folded at the waist. He could clamp the knife in his teeth and hold the candle in one hand, the charm in the other. And that was what he did, hanging on finally by just one hand, the charm pressed in his fingers against the East Room wall. Gathering his courage, he let go and slid; but the charm snagged on the exposed lath and tore from his tenuous grip to dangle out of reach above him.

The dust kicked up and swirled thickly in the confined space. Tazewell started to cough. The knife fell from his mouth, and he grabbed the handle before it could slide under and stab him. Then he rolled onto his back, his nightshirt smeared black with coal dust. As he'd known, the duct wasn't steep, and he lay almost horizontally in the tube, while he tugged the rope in until it went taut. He could only hope Alice was near enough that it would reach.

He spat out the dust. The duct flexed and thundered underneath him. They must have heard him all the way to the furnace, if not the dining room.

He gripped the knife and thrust the candle toward his feet, and called out, "Alice?"

No answer this time. Then something came scrabbling closer. It emerged out of the darkness—a fat, clawed doll, smeared wetly with creosote. The clacking noise it made was some kind of necklace. Its awful eyes were as red as pustules of blood.

Seeing him in the light of the candle, it rose up, triumphant. "Tazewell," it said in Alice's voice, revealing needle-sharp teeth in its stitched mouth. "Here I am."

It lunged.

He kicked with his heels, pushing himself backward toward the opening. His feet slipped and slid. To get out he would have to drop everything, knife and candle, turn his back on the creature and pull himself up the rope. He didn't dare.

The creature raked his ankle, and he screamed, yanked the leg back, and at the same time stabbed the doll with the boning knife. The leathery thing pulled back from the blade, but not as if hurt. An oily fluid leaked from the rip. If anything, the doll looked only more furious than before. It leaped at him again.

"Tazewell, Tazewell, Tazewell," it repeated, teasing him with Alice's voice.

He swiped the knife back and forth to keep it at bay. "Help!" he cried, and banged his fist against the duct, tossing wax everywhere, nearly guttering the candle.

"Tazewell!" It was Priscilla above him.

"Down here! Get me out!"

"Grab the rope," Zenobia told someone. Then, "What's this here? Oh, Lord, the charm!"

The demon latched onto Tazewell's foot, cutting him, and he kicked wildly to throw it off, banging his knee. The doll spun and tumbled along the tube. Immediately it got up and charged at him again.

Zenobia yelled, "Tazewell, here, grab this!" The round charm bounced and rolled down to him, coming to rest at his neck. He could feel it against his ear, but the only way he could grab it was to drop either the knife or the candle. He whipped and stabbed with the knife to drive the creature off. Then quickly, as the rope jerked, he dropped it and grabbed the fat charm.

The demon sprang upon him, jaws wide to rip out his throat. Tazewell jammed the charm at it, and the demon sank its teeth into the stiff greasy material.

It shook violently then, tearing itself and the charm away. It flipped over and over, screeching like a thousand crows. Its claws frantically shredded the cloth.

Abruptly pulled upward, Tazewell dropped the candle. It rolled toward the receding demon, and just before the flame went out, the leathery body burst, spraying fluid that sizzled and flared like hot oil in the duct.

Arms reached under Tazewell's and lifted him through the hole.

"Tazewell, honey, you almost got yourself killed." Zenobia set him down. He'd barely touched the floor before Priscilla clutched him to her. He stared past her at Marcellus, who finally let go of the rope. Behind him was the doorman, Drummond, holding what looked like a table leg in his hand.

"Alice wasn't there," Tazewell told them, his face scrunched up. "I was tricked."

"Mebbe," Zenobia said. "But you done for the *tebo*." She nodded at the oily smoke rising out of the vent. It smelled like rotten meat.

Priscilla asked, "Where is she then if she's not down there? We have to find her!"

"I don't know." Tazewell shook his head.

"I think I do," Zenobia said. "It's kept mostly to two places—this room and Miss Letitia's room. It passed back and forth through the mirror there."

"Where's James, Zenobia?" Priscilla asked.

She shook her head. "No time. We gotta find Alice fast, before him that made that creature finds *us*."

>>> ‹‹‹

Lord Ettryne felt the release of the *baka*. He couldn't understand how they had found it, much less slain it, but it meant they weren't hiding on their protected floor any longer and he could get at them.

He emerged from the room where Alice lay only to be met by the sound of people coming up the east stairs right to him. He stopped and considered if he should hide somewhere, but finally decided this would be more amusing. They didn't yet know he was in the house. The whole of Tenskatawa was gone now, but inadvertently he'd done the job asked of him: bringing the people right to Ettryne.

He posed in the middle of the hall, leaning on his walking stick, as though he'd been awaiting them all night, which in a sense he had.

The girl who shouldn't have had any power over him led them, followed by two men, Priscilla, and a filthy, coal-smeared Tazewell. The boy must have climbed into the vent and bested the *baka*. Seeing him, they stopped dead in the hall.

Ettryne grinned: They hadn't known he was here. Of course they hadn't. Still, he had to give them points for getting this far. They would be getting no farther.

He tried once more to take possession of Priscilla, but it was as if she wasn't there. Whatever they had done, he hadn't the time to undo it. Really, he didn't care. Let her watch helplessly while the children were torn asunder.

He shifted his focus to the tall young Negro beside her. "You," he said, "go bring me Elizabeth Tyler, and we'll put an end to all this."

Without hesitation, Marcellus turned about, his eyes frantic, and walked away down the stairs.

"Use the charms," Priscilla urged Zenobia.

She shook her head. "They all in the parlors."

Ettryne clucked his tongue. "All out of magic, witch? Oh dear." He flicked his left hand dismissively. Zenobia hurled back as if whalloped. She hit the wall and slid down. "You'd do well to stay there, girl. I only want these two. Same goes for you, doorman. This is not your battle."

Unheeding, Drummond stepped forward. He held the table leg up. With his other hand he drew from his belt the Colt Paterson. "Is now," he said, and pulled the trigger.

Ettryne flicked his left hand as if snatching at a fly. He took one step back but otherwise showed no effect. Still smiling, he held out his hand. A bullet fell from the palm. "Please," he invited, "feel free to waste all your shots if you so desire."

Drummond growled and charged him, the table leg raised to smash his skull.

Priscilla yelled, "Osbert, no!"

Lord Ettryne calmly, swiftly unsheathed his rapier and let Drummond run onto it. They both crashed against the wall, Ettryne blocking the table leg's descent with the blackthorn stick. He began to push Drummond away from him.

Drummond grunted and pawed helplessly at his murderer. With almost no effort, Ettryne knocked the table leg from his grip.

"Exactly as I did for your little brother." Ettryne sneered. He shoved Drummond away.

The doorman dropped to the floor, dead.

Ettryne took a deep breath. He wiped the blade along Drummond's coat and slid it back into the walking stick. "Another minute and we shall all join Alice in there." He whipped the stick in the direction of the room behind him.

Tazewell turned to flee, but Ettryne pointed the stick at him and Tazewell stopped, paralyzed. "No, no, no. No one's leaving." He addressed Zenobia where she lay against the doorjamb. "What did you do, girl, to this one"—he swatted ineffectually at Priscilla—"that I cannot take hold of her now?"

On unsteady legs, Zenobia got to her feet again. "Not my magic," she replied. "I cain't say."

Ettryne's expression darkened. "Well, whose magic would it be then?" When she failed to answer, he started toward her—two steps and then he abruptly clutched his chest. "God *damn*," he said, his face squeezed tight with pain.

When he drew his hand away, the white kid glove was wet and red. The wound from Renehan's pistol was leaking blood.

"This isn't—isn't possible. Who?" He looked from Priscilla to Zenobia. "Who's in my room?" He drew the blade again. "Who's left? What do you think you're *doing*?"

Behind him, Osbert Drummond suddenly sat up. His face remained vacant, but it turned toward Ettryne with an odd, almost clockwork motion so strange that Priscilla gasped. Ettryne turned about. He took two horrified steps back, the blade held at the ready. "You're dead."

Drummond rose all the way up, and teetered one step, then another, as if learning to walk. Ettryne backed up again. Now Drummond stood between him and the room where Alice lay. They faced each other for a moment that seemed to stretch on and on. Then Drummond charged.

Ettryne ran to the doorway of the west stair hall and turned about. He'd drawn his blade again, and drove it into Drummond all the way to the hilt. He might as well have stabbed a locomotive. Drummond slammed into him hard enough to lift him off his feet and propel him into the stairwell. The two of them crashed through the enormous fanlight window in the west wall and plunged to the promenade roof a story below. Ettryne managed at least to land on top.

He lay awhile dazed, coughed and felt ribs shift, broken. Drawing a breath was like swallowing hot coals. He had forgotten what pain could be like.

Drummond shivered a moment, then shoved him aside and sat up again. He was clearly dead, moving by some remote guidance. Ettryne knew the look well: A dozen women had wandered the rooms of this very house with that expression, under his control.

"Who are you?" he groaned.

Drummond stumbled to his feet. Something inside him popped but didn't seem to inconvenience him. He grabbed Ettryne by the lapels. Lifted him up.

It was agony—his ribs snapping—and he screamed hard as he hung in the air.

"Christian," said Drummond, his voice raspy, barely working. He carried Ettryne over to the edge. "James. Hambleton. Christian." He let go.

Lord Ettryne dropped straight onto the cover of the old disused well.

The boards split and gave way beneath him, but he grabbed onto the lip of the well and hung there.

Every breath was tearing new holes inside him. He tried to haul himself up, but the mechanical left hand separated from his wrist, and he dangled from his right hand alone.

Below him in the wet darkness, something with the voice of a rattlesnake's tail whispered his name. He dared a glance down. In the red mist of pain, Tenskatawa leered up at him. Hands like huge bear claws reached up and tore him from his hold.

>>> ⫷

By the time everyone came out the west door, only the gloved left hand remained dangling there. Priscilla kicked it into the well.

On the promenade roof of the colonnade, Tall George stood up from the body of Osbert Drummond to tell them all, "This man is for sure dead."

Fifty

James Hambleton Christian

We watched Ettryne vanish into the well, Drummond and I, but as he did, my tether to the doorman's body broke loose. He collapsed, fell down upon the colonnade roof, and I was drawn away into darkness. For hours or days or years, it was impossible to say because it was blank, a sleep with no dreams.

Then I woke to find myself standing over a grave upon a hillside, surrounded by a strange and lifeless version of Washington that looked as if it had been dressed for the funeral of everyone. The familiar buildings everywhere seemed carved from cinders. Down the misty avenue the Treasury, the Capitol, even the Indian Queen were somehow all visible to me, their windows so dark I felt I was looking through them as if they was all just empty façades. It was how it had looked past that crossroad, beyond Legba and Samedi. The dead city.

The iron-colored sky made me think it must be 4 a.m. In awhile, a streak of dawn would cut open the eastern horizon.

I found that I was one among dozens of mourners around the grave, Devonee's I supposed, then wondered why I supposed it; of course it was the cemetery itself—wasn't the one where they buried whitefolk. Mel's grave was here, and Isaac's. I bowed my head and offered a prayer for Devonee, who'd always looked after my sister so well and had died defending her child.

The body hadn't arrived yet. The black earth was turned, the hole open. A stone cross with a circle stood at the head of it, but the name carved there was unreadable. I looked for some explanation from the other mourners. They stood stiff and silent—veiled, almost faceless statues. No matter how I strained, I couldn't make them out. And now that I thought on it, why in the Sam Hill were we conducting a secret funeral in the hours before dawn? But my thoughts seemed to go sliding past me and I couldn't hang onto the question.

Someone called my name.

I turned to find Martin Renehan standing among the mourners beside me. He was dressed all formally, clean-shaved, his hair combed better than usual. There were copper coins where his eyes ought to have been.

"Martin," I said, "why are you like this?"

He threw his arms around me. "You did it, James. Ya finished him where no one else could."

"Finished him." I was sure I must know what that meant.

"Do you not realize it?" he asked. "You and Osbert together."

Now, that sounded right somehow. I looked past his shoulder for Osbert. Behind him I saw Isaac staring down at the grave, hair gone all white. He slowly met my eyes with his sad and grim expression. Gave me a nod, and I nodded in reply.

Renehan drew back into the line of mourners beside Isaac, and as he returned to facing the grave, his features blurred, same as the others.

I was standing among the dead. Renehan had been dead in a chair—I'd seen him. And Isaac was drowned. All dead, and I was one of them.

Once I acknowledged that, I began to identify others—field slaves, some of whom had died way back at Tidewater, Colonel Christian's plantation, when Letitia and I were small. There she was, twelve and running barefoot in and out among them, laughing. I almost reached to her across the grave, to take her hand like when we was just two children, not mistress and slave, but she darted behind a woman with ample hips. I looked up and there, Lord, stood my mother. I had not imagined that she might be dead. She smiled after Letitia and carried that smile to me when she looked my way, as young as the last time I'd seen her, the day I went off with Judge Christian to William and Mary.

A slim hand took and tugged me gently around.

Mel. She glowed like a candle. Smiling at me in that loose way as if to say, "James, you foolish man," and how many times had I seen that look, and how much had I missed it.

I drew her to me and held her as if I could squeeze us both into one body, one soul, which was all I wanted. "I so love you, Mel. I don't ever want to be apart from you again. Understand? Not one single day."

She pushed me back a little, drew my face down with her cool golden fingers, and stared up into my eyes. "You know I'm going to be waitin' for you, just like this, long as it takes."

"Waiting? Martin," I called, "what does she mean, waiting?"

He faced me again, but set upon the fine tailcoat it was the skull of Samedi, grinning around his cigar. "Hee-hee," he cackled. "Seems it ain't your time, son. Pass him along!"

The windows in all the buildings around us suddenly blazed like Ettryne's mirrors. It burnt away the darkness and all the people too.

"Mel!" I tried to grab her fingers but they were air. I shouted her name again. It came out a ragged and hoarse croak. Dirt fell in my mouth, and I choked and spluttered.

In a panic I wrestled to sit up.

Sparks danced in my vision like out of a chimney. I spat and wiped at my mouth, gasped deep. Rubbed my watering eyes.

It was dark still, but this time there were two lanterns, one at my side and another one above. Beside me, Zenobia knelt, keeping a hand on my back.

"Noooo," I moaned. I wanted to shove her away but my arms wouldn't work. "Don't bring me back, I was with her, God damn you. I was *with* her."

Zenobia's face caved in to weeping, and I stopped cursing her though I stayed furious, breathing hard.

I was sitting up in a pine coffin in a hole about three-foot deep. Above me and Zenobia, Marcellus stood holding the other lantern and a shovel. Cyrus sat on the ground beside him, looking amazed.

"I'm sorry, James." Zenobia sniffled, wiped at her nose. "I couldn't not have come for you. You wasn't dead or alive, couldn't be left like that."

I remembered Abias saying as much, making a big point of telling us that nobody could be left in that halfway place. The *lwa* would start feeding off you.

"How long?" I asked.

"Two weeks since you was buried all official. Tyler seen to it."

"Tyler?"

Instead of answering, she tugged on my arms. They tingled now, like I'd slept on them. "Let's git you outten here, an' cover it back up." She stood. Marcellus offered his hand to her like they were going to do a reel, as Cyrus slid down into the box with me.

"Here we go now," he said. He grabbed hold of me by the shirtfront and yanked me toward him, then caught me under the arms. My legs were tingling and wobbly, but Cyrus wasn't about to let go of me. He held me while I worked my legs and found the strength to stand. Then he pushed and Marcellus, having put down lantern and shovel, grabbed my hands and pulled me from the grave.

I crinkled my nose. I smelled like wet dirt, but was dressed in my fine butler clothes. Marcellus said, "Rained a bit this week." It was warm and humid, and looked nothing like the dead Washington of the *lwa*. Lights glowed off in the distance.

My cross was wood, not the stone one I'd seen. Maybe that one was Martin's. His sign.

Around me stood the other graves I knew. Mel's. Isaac's. And Devonee's now, beside my own, newly dug and covered, I suppose, at the same time as mine.

Cyrus dropped the lid on the box, then took up the shovel and began filling in the hole.

I turned to Zenobia. "Alice? The children—they all right, are they?"

"They's fine," said Zenobia. "Tazewell, he killed the *tebo*. We found Alice in her mama's bed, just beside you. She got no recollection of nothing after being woke up in the night."

Brave Tazewell. I would tell him so when I saw him next.

Zenobia smiled at something. "You was in Drummond, weren't you? That was you, took him down."

"Took him down." I nodded slowly, though the memory seemed to be leaving me, a dream drifting off on some dark tide.

She told me the Tylers, father and son, had returned a day later to find dead bodies, two missing doormen, smashed windows and well, and a house filled with people who'd been scared out of their wits. Miss Elizabeth tried to tell her father and brother what had really happened, but they stopped her, certain that she was pulling their legs. She tried again, but they would have none of it.

Miss Priscilla knew better and refused to say anything. Robert would not have listened if she'd tried. There was no point.

She, the other children, Jasper, and the slaves made a pact, settled upon the story of a drunken mob that had ransacked the house, knowing Tyler to be away. Drummond had died doing his duty and the other two, Renehan and Garvine, had given chase but were presumed dead, too, as they had not returned. When Renehan's body was found in Lord Ettryne's smashed rooms a day later, the Tylers concluded that the mob had been the revenge of the condescending British aristocrat, who'd fled the city. Renehan and his brother were laid to rest elsewhere with honors. Devonee and I were buried with no fanfare at all.

Mayor Seaton was called upon to find three new doormen: It was all too clear their presence was necessary for the safety of the president.

"Mr. Tyler had returned with papers," Zenobia added, "selling you to William Christian, Miss Letitia's nephew down in Richmond. He's made arrangements to sell off *all* the slaves what belonged to her. Deborah's already gone, bought by some rich man 'cross the river."

I'd been right, but there was no comfort in it. "What am I supposed to do then, if he's just going to sell me when I turn up?"

Cyrus stopped filling in my grave. He and Marcellus looked at each other. Cyrus chortled. Marcellus said, "You dead, James. You can't reappear. Says it right on this here cross. 1842."

"Cain't be sold neither," said Cyrus. "Not unless you're fool enough to go *announcing* your miraculous resurrection to Mr. John Tyler."

Grinning, Marcellus added, "We would not recommend that there course of action."

I couldn't believe how they found this amusing, like the night we three had sat on the portico steps, and it got my back up. "Well, what course of action then would you two *fine* gentlemen recommend?"

They both looked to Zenobia. "I spoke to your friend Bibb," she said, "at the Indian Queen? Told him of your…unusual circumstances. He thinks he kin secure you a position there. You gon' need a different name. 'Leastways, for awhile."

I shook my head. "Tyler and Webster could both turn up at the Indian Queen any time. Have before."

"Look, it ain't where you gonna end up, James, just where you gonna begin."

"Begin what? Hiding out?"

Cyrus said, "He don't understand."

"Man," said Marcellus, "you're *free*."

Zenobia added, "No one's got a bounty on your head. Ain't no one looking for you, and there's four thousand folks in this city what'll take you in, help you."

"Help you git *away*," Cyrus emphasized. "You tole him and me. You educated like *they* is. Smarter'n most of 'em. You'll git away."

"You laughed at me when I said it." It was like we were teasing each other now.

He shrugged his big shoulders. "Yeah, a little. Don't mean you weren't right." He and Marcellus traded another look as if to make sure they agreed on that. "Got a new life, James Christian. Man, you gotta take it."

I stared out over dark Washington. Down along Pennsylvania Avenue, a lamplighter was in the process of dousing the pole lights. One winked out as I watched.

Off behind the Capitol was the faintest glow of dawn. Save for these three, everyone I knew believed me dead already.

I stood at another crossroads. Behind me was everything I'd known, and everything lost to me now. That way was closed. I could take the short road to Mel, but she would never forgive me if I did that. She'd said she would wait.

The way ahead was some new beginning I couldn't yet put a shape to.

I dusted off my sleeves, straightened my coat, looked resolutely at the three of them who had rescued me. Samedi had asked was I one of those people who couldn't tell being dead from being alive. I knew the answer now for sure.

I was going to live.

Acknowledgments

The author would like to acknowledge the enormous assistance he got from two books in particular. First, *John Tyler: The Accidental President*, by Edward P. Crapol, which revealed everything from the "doormen," the first incarnation of the Secret Service, to the remarkable appearance of one James Hambleton Christian in Philadelphia years later, where chronicler William Still of the Vigilance Committee took down his brief biography. Otherwise, no one would know he'd ever existed. Second, *The White House*, by William Seale, which proved extremely informative regarding the shocking state of the house in 1841.

About the Author

GREGORY FROST is a writer across the spectrum of fantasy, horror, and SF. His most recent work is the RHYMER Trilogy, published by Baen Books. The first, RHYMER is set in 12th century Scotland and introduces the character if Thomas the Rhymer out of Scots balladry. Its sequel, RHYMER: HOODE, takes place a century later in England. Of it, author Rick Wilber says, "Intricately plotted and peopled with fantastic characters... Frost's Rhymer: Hoode occupies a fresh space in the legend of Robin Hood of Sherwood Forest. Very highly recommended." The third volume is due out in July 2025. Frost's previous fantasy novel, SHADOWBRIDGE, was an ALA Best Fantasy Novel cited for "a fine eye for the telling detail."

His collection BEYOND HERE BE MONSTERS, from Fairwood Press, is in bookstores now. A previous story collection, THE

GIRLFRIENDS OF DORIAN GRAY & OTHER STORIES, is available in ebook format from Book View Café online. Frost has been a finalist for Best Novel or Short Story for the World Fantasy, Bram Stoker, Nebula, Hugo, James Tiptree, International Horror Guild & Theodore Sturgeon Awards; he won an Asimov Readers Award in 2015 for a collaborative story with Michael Swanwick. He taught Fiction Writing at Swarthmore College for 18 years. Find him online at gregoryfrost.com, and at Bluesky at @GregFrost.bsky.social.